Frances Sargent Osgood
Complete Short Stories

EDITED BY
MAEVE BARGER

#FRANCESOSGOODSTORIES

Other Bottletree Anthologies

Best Poems of Frances Sargent Osgood Annotated
Leo Tolstoy's 20 Greatest Short Stories Annotated
Leo Tolstoy's 5 Greatest Novellas Annotated
Edgar Allan Poe Annotated Entire Stories and Poems

I revel in my right divine, I glory in caprice!

"Caprice"
February 1846
Graham's Magazine
FRANCES SARGENT OSGOOD

Had Greece known thee, there would have been
A change in classic lore;
The Muses would have counted *ten*—
The Graces had been *four*.

"Kate Carol to Mary S.,"
May 1847
The Columbian Magazine
FRANCES SARGENT OSGOOD

CONTENTS

Contents

Frances Osgood
Poetry in Prose

Currer, Ellis, Acton Bell, George Eliot, and A.M. Barnard were nineteenth century male pen names employed by female authors who did not want their literary works immediately discounted due to their gender. The Brontë sisters, Mary Ann Evans, and Louisa May Alcott, as they are better known, held a common belief that they were capable of meeting, if not surpassing the literary standard set by the male authors in the Victorian Age. When it came to breaking down these stereotypes, few women were as bold as Frances Osgood in the literary field for defining the role of an independent woman. She catered to the strengths of a female writer by bringing feminine qualities to the forefront to be romanticized, rather than shying away from or allowing them to be concealed by the less controversial male image.

Although Frances Osgood utilized pennames herself, such as Violet Vane and Kate Carol, she never allowed them to imply that a man had written her work. She desired the mystery that often surrounded pennames, without forcing them to conceal her own femininity.

It was this femininity that she echoed through nearly all of her works. It attracted a large audience of single women in the nineteenth century, causing her to be one of the most popular female writers of her time. She provided these women with the romanticized literature they craved. Even though some have criticized her works for being overly sentimental when it came the "flowery" nature of her some of works, such as in the seemingly fairy tale-like ending to one of her short stories, "Mabel," or the perfectionist beginning of "Carry Carlisle," or "The Last Tournament;" Frances Osgood used sentimentality as a means of expressing herself in the way she knew best. At the same time she appealed to women who shared her common sentiments and fantasized ideals.

Given her writing style in the Romantic Age she was quickly able to attract regular readers. This gave Frances

Osgood's literary works a frequent place in many literary magazines including *Graham's Magazine.* Given her commercial success she was able to be admired for her feminine contributions to literature and to the early literary business world as well. By creating poems and short stories that went to the very heart of relationships, she was able to build a loyal following. She was able to efficiently write stories and poems, providing her with a monetary return that could support her family without complete dependence on her husband.

With literary magazines paying upwards of ten dollars a page, Frances Osgood received over one hundred dollars a month given the combination of works she was able to write and have published, exceeding the incomes of many popular, male authors of the day including Henry Wadsworth Longfellow, Washington Irving, and Edgar Allan Poe. The later received a mere fifteen dollars for his most famous poem, "The Raven." This financial success by a female writer represented a rare economic independence that was not often gained, without first establishing one's self under a male penname.

Rather than allowing herself to be financially dependent on her husband, Samuel Osgood, a portrait painter of upper-class society, she sought to contribute her own revenue to the household. This was during a time where many women would have simply assumed the role as "housewife," or at least financial dependency on their husband. Frances Osgood's decision to not fear making a larger profit than her husband would serve her well in future years when Samuel Osgood eventually left her and her two children for the California Gold Rush in 1849, forcing her household to be almost entirely dependent upon her care and her literary revenue while she was battling tuberculosis.

Unlike most authors, Frances Osgood's personality was impossible to separate from her artform. She seemed to desire the romantic fantasies and dramatic events she so often wrote about and had her characters live through. Parallels can be clearly noted between some of her characters, such as Florence Errington lacking the love she desired or the flirtatious romance of Ida Grey. Her female characters often traveled from city to city, which mirrored the life of Frances Osgood.

She described her transient life in "Glimpses of a Soul." "But I must confess to, now and then, a feeling, I cannot say of home-sickness—for I, wanderer that I am, have no home . . .."[1] This statement stemmed from her bouncing from hotel to hotel throughout her adult life, rather than finding permanent residence in a home. It is possible that since she lacked a permanent refuge, she attempted to find one in the stability of her writing and her characters' lives.

This is illustrated not only through her dedication to her work and her adherence to the romanticism of the day but to her public flirting with Edgar Allan Poe. Frances Osgood seemed to enjoy the nature of the situation that not only allowed her to emulate the characters in her work, but resulted in her receiving positive literary reviews from Poe. This attests to her business savvy when it comes to gaining recognition in the eyes of the public and current or future readers. Poe was considered by many, including Frances Osgood, to be one of the harshest literary critics of the nineteenth century. He commented, "For the past five or six years the name of Frances S. Osgood has been a household word with the readers of our magazines; and perhaps no one of their contributors has been so universally popular. She has written for these works quite as much prose as poetry – but then the prose has been poetry itself."[2]

In his remark on Frances Osgood's success and fame, Poe touched upon a defining characteristic of her writing, being her repeated use of poetry throughout her works. Many of her short stories are laced with poetry; whether it is because it was the medium she felt most comfortable with or partly to increase story length, and therefore profits as well. Regardless, Frances Osgood took it upon herself to blend poem and prose whenever presented with the opportunity.

Frances Osgood left other unique marks on literature, too. She appears to have coined the popular phrases "shoot the man in the moon" and "puff piece." Frances

---

[1] "Glimpses of a Soul," Frances S. Osgood, *Graham's Magazine*, February 1847, vol. 30, no. 2, p. 90.

[2] "Literary Criticism," Edgar Allan Poe, *Godey's Lady's Book*, March 1846, vol. 32, no. 3, p. 134

Osgood also wrote in a stream of consciousness style to address current topics that was unique. She also became the first author to address her own pseudonyms in the first person, further immersing herself in her own stories by intertwining herself as a character. Frances Osgood's tendency to address her readers directly, as well as scattering common French terms and phrases in her short stories, serves as a further means of highlighting her individualistic style.

With Frances Osgood's understated feminist influence, unique style and her full-hearted dedication to her craft, it is a wonder that a complete collection of her short stories has not been published much sooner. One hundred and sixty nine years after her death, Frances Osgood deserves her place in history, not just in relation to female literature, but history in its entirety.

Romance of Real Life in New England[1]

THE SIMPLE facts which are the foundation of the following tale (forming in themselves a wild romance of most intense and powerful interest) can gain nothing from the pen of their narrator by either alteration or embellishment. None, therefore, has been attempted. The heroine of the story is personally known to the writer, and neither in the description of her character, nor in that of the two heroes, has there been any attempt at exaggeration. In a beautiful village towards the northern part of Vermont, dwelt, in the year 1822, a being wild, lovely, and romantic as the scenery which had surrounded her from childhood. At the time my story commences she was just sixteen—an only daughter—of course a petted one—an heiress, and a belle. Young, rich, and beautiful—indulged and flattered as she was—she yet remained unspoiled,—a very child in her simplicity, her guileless and confiding truth.

Yet there was at times a dash of wild thoughtlessness in her manner—a glimpse of wayward willful petulance, that made the prudent tremble for her safety. SHE never trembled: she was all joy, and hope, and confiding tenderness. You should have seen her then in her unclouded days: perhaps in the summer twilight among her flowers, in her simple, white, childish dress, her little straw bonnet garlanded with a natural and fragrant wreath, and shading her deep blue eyes, and her dimpled hands filled with roses not more blooming than herself;—or in the autumn in the depths of the gorgeous woodlands—crowned like some sylvan queen with a chaplet of oak-leaves, whose brilliant hues of green and crimson showed so richly on that hair of golden brown, arranged and braided with a classic elegance of which she herself was unconscious;—or, lovelier still, in one of those fierce and glorious snow-storms, which all our mountain-

---

[1] "Romance of Real Life in New England," Frances S. Osgood, *The Court Magazine and La Belle Assemblée*, May 1836, vol. VIII, no. 5, pp. 189-196

girls so revel in-tripping light and free as the feathery flakes around her, right against the wind—her crimson cloak and hood blown backwards, and revealing the pretty, graceful form, the lovely, laughing face—whilst her fair curls float in the morning light, and glitter with the feathery sparkles which are constantly falling and melting among them;—every instant deepens the warm glow of her cheek and lips—the rich wild lustre of her eyes to intenser bloom and brilliance—till she seems the very spirit of the sunshine and the snow. Alas! those frost-pearls smiling and dying in that wavy wealth of hair are but an emblem of her own youthful joys—as fair as fleeting.

One afternoon towards the end of July, Mariel Harris (such was her name) stood leaning on the rails of the pretty bridge that spanned the village stream, in earnest converse with her friend Kate Campbell. The sun was setting, and through the dark and distant foliage a gleam like molten gold betrayed the beautiful Connecticut. Calm and hushed it seemed—that noble river—as if conscious of the unearthly loveliness that lay dying on its bosom, and awed to stillness by the thought. On the right was seen Ascutney, a picturesque and somewhat lofty mountain, bearing, like a king, his gorgeous crown, the farewell gift of day. The weather had been sultry; the girls hailed the fresh mountain-breeze as a blessing, and as it blew the light hair over Mariel's eyes, and swayed to and fro the rustic bonnet which she had hung upon her arm, the reflection of her youthful form made a very pretty picture in the stream. For a while she seemed intently gazing on the water, but her thoughts were far away. At last, with a tone and look unusually pensive, she spoke:

"It will never do, Catharine; I cannot, cannot love them—nay, I will not. In the first place there is Nicodemus Stickney: he is well enough, but I can't abide his name. How it would sound—Mrs. Nicodemus Stickney.—Just think:—and Obadiah Tibbetts, too!—why will people have such awful names? As for Jonathan Frost—that is not so bad, because I *could* say John 'before folks.' But then, Kate, to tell you the truth"—and here Mariel spoke in a whisper, and looked very serious, "to tell you the plain truth, I am in love already. You needn't laugh—I am, certainly: now don't you tell for the world—will you? Well, then, you shall hear all about it. When I was a little girl, about so high," and she lowered her pretty hand as she spoke, "I staid a fortnight with Aunt Chase in Lebanon. Aunt sent me to school to have me out of the way, for I was a real little torment *then.—Ah!* you smile at the emphasis—thank you! Well, among the boys who went to the same school, was one whom I shall never forget— never! He was three years older than I—his name was Edward Atherton. Isn't it a beautiful name? Once when my aunt didn't send for me, he offered to lead me home, and after that, while I stayed, he always did. As we tripped along hand in hand through the wood which led to aunt's house, Edward would gather whole handfuls of violets and fill my little white apron with them: I believe that is the reason why I have always loved violets better than any other flower. One afternoon he led me by what he called a prettier way home—at all events it was a great deal longer, and the sun was setting when we came to a little crazy bridge, or rather plank, seldom crossed by the villagers, for there was a better one farther up the stream. Edward went first to try its safety, and then held out his hand for me. I know not why it was, but I grew dizzy at the first step—faint with terror, I tried to reach his hand—my foot slipped, and I fell. I knew nothing more till I found myself in his arms on the bank. The moment I opened my eyes the poor fellow burst into tears; and I remember as if it were but yesterday throwing my little arms around his neck, looking up in his face with a soothing smile, and whispering, 'Don't you cry, Eddy! I won't be drowned any more!' It was dark ere I reached home. My aunt, angry at my delay, and still more at my dripping dress, made me tell her all, and comforted me with the assurance that Edward Atherton was a naughty boy, that I was a trial, and that she should certainly send me home the next day. To go home—to leave Edward and without even bidding him good by, seemed a misfortune too cruel to be thought of; but I was obliged to submit, though all the way back, and for a week after, I cried for Eddy Atherton to play with me! I have never seen him since; but even now, whenever the thought of marriage enters my head, that remembered face is sure to come between me and whatever I chance to be looking at;—oh it is so beautiful! you would love it too if you could see it—such dear dark eyes, and such splendid hair, and such a kind sweet smile, and then such *a name!*

Edward   Atherton—Nicodemus   Stickney!   Edward Atherton—Obadiah Tibbetts!—ha, ha, ha!" and her clear, bird-like laugh rang sweetly over the water, and was re-echoed by the opposite rocks, as if even their rugged nature (like those of old when Orpheus sang) were softened to music by the sound. But again her tones changed to deeper sadness than before.

"I shall never marry, Kate. I feel tonight a presentiment of evil, and I'm sure there is no greater evil than that of being an old maid, like Miss Priscilla Primrose for instance—unloving and unloved. No, I shall never marry: my fate will be like—like this pebble, Catharine. You shall see now when I throw it—it will make a little stir at first, and the waters will smile and circle around it for awhile—then it will sink to rise no more, and they will close over it calm as ever and reckless of its fate." As she spoke, she threw it into the stream: at that instant as the pebble touched the wave, a small stone thrown from a neighboring thicket struck it, and they sank together. There was a slight rustling in the wood, and a stranger appeared. As he approached he gazed earnestly at Mariel, who, overcome by some sudden and powerful emotion, and covered with blushes, grasped her companion's arm convulsively, and exclaimed as soon as he had passed,

"It is he, Kate! as I live it is he himself! Edward Atherton. I should know those eyes among a million, and he did not know me! Oh! let us go home, for I am tired to death!"

That evening, as she stood before her glass preparing for a party to be given in the neighborhood, her heart fluttered with the thought that he too might go, and her hands trembled amid the soft braid which she was arranging with unusual care. "But he will not know me," she sighed, and her blue eyes filled with tears. As she entered her friend's drawing-room, modestly arrayed in a simple graceful dress of white muslin, meeting at the throat (for with a taste peculiar to herself Mariel, though so beautifully formed, always wore a high dress), with her sun-brown hair braided behind, and falling low in front in a cluster of curls on either side of her face, her cheek glowing with excitement, and her rich lips parted with eager hope, many a rustic admirer, and many a female friend (for Mariel was a general favorite) hastened to welcome her, and whispered that she had never looked so lovely. Edward Atherton was there; and after an eagerly-sought introduction, remained all the evening by her side as if spell-bound by some irresistible charm; and yet, although every now and then he would fix his dark eyes earnestly upon the face of the blushing but delighted girl—though she met them whenever she dared to raise her own, and *felt* them when hers were averted, still there was a strange and dreamy unconsciousness in their gaze, intense as it was, which showed a wandering mind. Was it (her young heart beat quicker at the thought)—could it be, that touched by some resemblance, he was recalling the playmate of his boyhood? And ere the pretty, childish smile, awakened by the fancy, had faded from her dimpled cheek.

Atherton looked again—he started—

"It is very strange!—forgive me, Miss Harris," he continued, "you looked just then so like a little girl I once knew, that I could not conceal my surprise."

Tears, blushes, smiles, were all on the wing in poor Mariel's heart, and ready, whenever she would let them, to spring into her face; but with a powerful effort she succeeded in quelling her emotion, and said in low tones,

"May I ask her name?"

"Her name?–oh! her name was Mariel."

"And was that all? Had she no other?" said Mariel archly.

"Upon my word until this moment I never even thought of her having any other! Every one called her Mariel, and that alone was so pretty a name that I for one was quite satisfied with it. Now I think of it, it might have been Chase, for she lived with an aunt of that name; but I only knew her a fortnight!" and here our hero heaved a very deep sigh, which Mariel caught and treasured in her "heart of hearts," as the miser hides his store to feast upon in secret. Wishing, with her usual love of romance, to delay for the present a denouement, and fearful of betraying her feelings, she now rose to depart, and returned home with a heart full of new and undefinable emotions. Sweet dreams, unutterably sweet, were with her through the night, and the sigh which Edward had breathed to her memory floated like music through them all. The next afternoon, instead of calling for Catharine as she was wont—she sauntered out alone to her favorite path through the woods. There, seated on a moss-grown rock, and unconsciously gathering the violets which clustered around her, she was startled by the voice of Atherton, who had approached unheeded. He seated himself by her side, and entered into conversation.

"Are you fond of violets, Miss Harris?"

"The violet is my favorite flower," she answered, repressing her playful smile.

"It was hers, too," he murmured.

"Whose?"

"Oh Mariel's."

There was a pause. For a moment she could not speak—she could hardly breathe. At last, she said, with a voice that *would* falter, in spite of her struggles to command it, "Do you stay long in W—, Ed—Mr. Atherton?"

"No! shall leave to-morrow for Lebanon. I am going there to try and recover some lost property of mine. It was stolen many years ago by the little girl I spoke of."

"What, was your Mariel a thief?"

"Oh, yes! a desperate one. I dare say she has robbed many others since; but the truth is, Miss Harris, I am sadly afraid that all you mountain-nymphs are given to that sin, and it is only fear of a similar robbery that hurries me away from W—."

"Thank you, Mr. Atherton! But what was this terrible loss? Some trifle, after all, I dare say."

"Allow me to thank *you,* Miss Harris. The trifle was—my heart!"

"And is it for the thief, or the heart, you are so anxious?"

"Oh, if I once obtain the thief, I shall be sure of the heart, you know; but I fear that both are lost for ever. I have been for the last week a wanderer, asking for Mariel wherever I went; and many a fair girl have I found of that name, but not *my* Mariel yet. I have often reminded myself of the lover in the old song,

> 'Shepherds, tell me have you seen
> My Mariel pass this way?'

But you must be weary of this subject."

"Oh, no! no! I could listen for ever!" she exclaimed, with all the artless *naiveté* peculiar to her character; "do tell me more of this desperate little thief, as you are pleased to call her."

"You are very kind; but I have little more to tell." And again he sighed. "An accident occurred the last time I saw her, which I believe was the cause of her sudden departure from Lebanon. I had imprudently led her to a bridge, the planks of which were decayed and very loose. She became frightened in crossing it, and ere I could reach the dear little hand held out to me for protection, her foot slipped, the plank tottered, and she fell. I plunged into the stream, bore her to the bank, and hung over her in speechless agony; for she had fainted, and I thought her dead. Imagine my feelings when the dear child opened her eyes, and looked up smiling in *my* face I burst into tears, and I shall never forget the sweet caressing tenderness of her manner, as, throwing her arms around me, she said—"

Mariel laid her hand suddenly on his arm. "Shall I tell you what she said?" She raised her eyes to his, and the artless smile of childhood played on her lips as she spoke. "'Don't you cry, Eddy! I won't be drowned any more!'"

"Good heavens! Is it—can it be? Her smile—her very tone!" And he caught her hand, and pressed it passionately to his lips. "How strange that I did not know you, dear, dear Mariel! *May* I call you so? Oh, I am half wild with happiness!"

We will not pursue the scene. Suffice it to say that ere Mariel reached her home, she had plighted her maiden troth to Edward Atherton, and referred him to her mother, a widow, for her consent to their union. This was readily granted, when strict inquiry had satisfied the good lady of his unblemished character, his prosperous circumstances, and his persevering industry in business. He was a merchant of Boston, where, after another week of happiness with his Mariel, he was to return to make some preparations prior to their marriage in the autumn.

Swiftly, too swiftly they fled, those sunny hours, for they fled never to return. Never again will those young hearts know the unshadowed joy which filled them then They are doomed till their last throb to fear, remorse, mistrust, and untold sorrow! But I will not anticipate.

The moment of separation was at hand; and Mariel, overcome by the same strange and shadowy presentiment of evil which she had owned in her conversation with Catharine on the bridge, clung in a passion of uncontrollable grief to her lover's arm, and besought him not to leave her. Surprised, flattered, and almost unmanned by the violence of her sorrow, he kissed away her tears, and soothed her with assurances of his speedy return.

"In one month, dearest, we shall meet again; and then, if you only love me then as you do now, how happy we shall be!"

"Oh, Edward! Have I not loved you from childhood, and can I change now? You know I cannot!" Such were her last words, for she could not say, "Farewell!" After a long and silent embrace, they parted.

A few days afterwards she received an invitation to visit a friend at a little village about thirty miles distant. Her mother, observing her low spirits, persuaded her to accept it, and accordingly the following day she was on her way to W—, still depressed by the strange presentiment of sorrow, whose shadow in her young heart seemed to grow larger and darker every hour.

At sunset she reached the home of her friend, who, as the servant said, had gone to walk with her husband, but would soon be back. While awaiting their return, she seated herself at a piano-forte, and began to sing, with much feeling, in a sweet, tremulous voice, of more pathos than power, some verses which had constantly haunted her fancy during her melancholy journey:—

> I never shall be happy, never—
>   "A shadowy sense of coming ill"
> Floats o'er this trembling heart for ever,
>   And clouds its all of sunshine still.
> A strange wild doubt—a dread—a dream
>   That Love's sweet ties too soon will sever,
> Darkens o'er hopes that brightest seem—
>   I never shall be happy—never!

She had scarcely finished, when a deep manly voice close beside her caught up the air and repeated the last line. The tones were low and rich, and strangely sweet, and Mariel felt their power with a thrill of fearful pleasure. Rising from her seat, she met a pair of wild black eyes, whose ardent gaze almost overwhelmed her with confusion.

"My dearest Mariel," said Mrs. Walter, who now came forward with her husband, "how kind you were to come to me; but before I tell you how delighted I am, let me introduce to you this impatient youth, Mr. Gerald Seaton—Miss Harris, Mr. Seaton. I hope you will be very good friends."

A smile of peculiar meaning played around his mouth as he bowed to Mariel, and answered, "That depends entirely upon Miss Harris; to see her is to be *her* friend. But is it possible, Mrs. Walter, that this is the being whose irresistible gaiety you described as her greatest charm? Can this pensive lady, who, it seems, is 'never to be happy, never!' be the Miss Harris of whose wildness and vivacity I have heard so much?"

A gleam of returning playfulness illumined Mariel's eyes, as with a low courtesy she replied,

"I am very sorry that I have lost all my charms, Mr. Seaton, and regret your evident disappointment; but it will teach you not to trust a report from another time."

"Lost them!" he exclaimed. "I was just about to entreat you, in pity's name, to resume your vivacity, for I defy it to be more resistless than your sorrow."

He had seated himself by her side on a sofa, and spoke in a low tone. There was a singular fascination in his manner. Mariel felt confused, yet pleased, she knew not why; and when at a late hour she retired to her room, after an evening of earnest devotion on his part and of thoughtless levity on hers—for her spirits were raised unconsciously by flattery so new to her—she recollected with surprise and self reproach that she had not once thought of Edward since her introduction to Seaton.

"But then he knows I am engaged, so he cannot, of course, mean anything by his attentions." And with this poor consolation she sought her pillow.

"Dear Edward!" she murmured, as she yielded to approaching sleep, but even with the sound the eloquent eyes of Gerald Seaton were before her. "Dear, *dear* Edward!" she said again, more earnestly, as if there were a spell in that name to charm away all evil spirits; and she sank to rest and dreamed that Edward, returning unexpectedly, surprised Gerald at her feet.

Reader, ere I pursue my story, I must reluctantly confess that besides the thoughtlessness of which I have spoken, there was another failing in the character of my heroine—a want of firmness, a weak and yielding softness of disposition, which, whilst it won the love of all around her, proved to herself a source of unspeakable sorrow.

Gerald Seaton, who was a daily visitor at Mrs. Walter's, became by almost imperceptible degrees the constant companion of Mariel in all her walks and rides. Possessed of brilliant talents, graceful ease of manner, and most insinuating address, he soon won upon the unsuspecting girl to confide to him, as to a brother, the story of her childish love. She knew not then, what she discovered when too late, that she was trusting to a libertine and a gambler—that her seeming friend, Mr. Walter, a brother gamester, was his partner in a plot laid long before, of which she was to be the victim. Aware of her fortune, which was considerable, they had agreed, if she accepted Mrs. W.'s invitation, that Seaton should exert all his arts to induce her to violate her engagements with Edward, and, by marrying her before her return to her mother, obtain possession of her property. This, from Mrs. Walter's account of her volatile and childish thoughtlessness, they deemed an easy task. They saw not through that almost infantile vivacity of word, and look, and action, the exhaustless wealth of feeling, unknown even to herself, which lay in latent power beneath. Day by day the hitherto guileless Mariel became more deeply entangled in the snare—hour by hour the bewildering voice of her tempter lured her more widely from the path of prudence and integrity. Edward Atherton had never flattered her; his affection was too elevated and sincere; and wholly unaccustomed, from her retired life, to the almost chivalric devotion with which the elegant Seaton seemed to regard her, the incense which he offered stole with beguiling sweetness to her heart, and enervated it to his purpose. She now began to listen with trembling pleasure to his passionate protestations of love, still striving to lull her fears with the thought, "He knows my engagement— my devotion to Edward; besides, I am going home in a few days, and shall probably never see him again."

The evening preceding the appointed day of departure had arrived. Her friends had earnestly entreated her longer stay, but, haunted once more by her former presentiments, fearing she knew not what, and yearning for repose to which her heart had long been a stranger, she was for once resolved. As she sat on that evening absorbed in painful thought, she did not at first perceive that Mr. and Mrs. Walter had left her alone with Seaton; and when she did, unconscious of the lateness of the hour, and thinking they would soon return, she still remained in conversation with him.

He grew more fervent than ever in his avowal of devoted love. He threw himself at her feet, declared that he could not, would not, live without her—conjured her, if she valued his peace, his life, to bless him with her hand before she returned home, and wound up the whole with a solemn vow that he would not survive her refusal for a moment. Alarmed by the increasing violence of his manner, she flew to the door—it was locked. She screamed. He told her it was in vain—that her friends approved his love, and had gone out purposely to give him an opportunity of declaring it. Then with wild and apparently uncontrollable passion he threw his arm around her, and swore that she should not leave the room till she either promised to be his the next day, or beheld him dead at her feet. Terrified out of all self-possession by his wildness, maddened by the thought that she was wholly in the power of a being so desperate, she hastily gave the required promise. He released her, and she hurried to her room, where she passed a sleepless night, a prey to the bitterest anguish and remorse.

Early the next morning she sought Mrs. Walter, confided to her all her feelings, and besought her advice, her assistance, and her protection home, for she was resolved not to abide by a promise so forced from her.

Her friend laughed at her fears, extolled the person and accomplishments of Seaton, but finally promised to return with her. They were soon equipped and seated in the carriage which was to convey them to W—, when, to Mariel's great alarm, Mr. Walter and Seaton also joined them. They drove very rapidly till they reached a small retired village, and stopped at the house of a justice of the peace. Half suspecting their purpose, Mariel asked why they did not drive to an inn. They no longer attempted to conceal from her that they expected the performance of her promise, and that they should consider her guilty of perjury if she violated it. With the timidity natural to a young and inexperienced girl, dreading to create a disturbance in the public street of a place where she had neither friends nor acquaintance, and thinking she might yet retract, she weakly suffered herself to be led into the presence of Mr. M—, with whom arrangements had already been made for the ceremony. It commenced immediately, and exhausted by her previous agitation, overwhelmed by a sense of utter helplessness, her pale lips moved unconsciously in the responses dictated to her by the compassionate justice, who saw in her agony only the confusion natural to her situation, and therefore hurried the ceremony. Hardly was it concluded when she fainted in the arms of Mrs. Walter. The usual restoratives were successfully applied, and she was conveyed again to the carriage. There Seaton bade her a tender farewell, telling her he must return to settle his affairs and prepare for her reception, and in three days he would join her in W—, claim her as his wife, and take her home with him. She was too weak to answer, though she could have blessed him for the reprieve.

Arrived at home, where Mr. and Mrs. Walter took their leave, she threw herself into her mother's arms, told her all, and entreated her to save her from Seaton, whom she now regarded with fear and abhorrence. Mrs. Harris, filled with grief and astonishment, knew not what to advise. Edward was expected daily; how should she meet him whom she had so injured The very next morning, as she leaned, pale and weak with suffering, against the casement, a stage stopped at the gate, and Atherton, springing from it with a lover's impatience, and glancing towards the window a smile of rapturous recognition, stood the next instant by her side. She had turned to meet him, but her strength failed, and sinking into a chair, she burst into tears and covered her face with her hands. He tried to draw them gently away.

She shrank from him, and shuddered; but the next moment, touched by his look of wonder and reproach, she laid her head on his shoulder, and told in broken accents her tale of treachery and sorrow. Poor Edward listened in mute astonishment, a prey by turns to anger and despair; but when he looked on the pale and almost heart-broken being before him—when he saw by her pale cheek and the mournful hopelessness of her expression how deep and sincere was her repentance and her suffering—when he heard her faltering voice wildly entreating his protection from the hated Seaton—pity for her wrongs prevailed, and drawing her to his generous and nearly bursting heart, he solemnly swore to save her from the power of one whose desperate character he too well knew. But he could effect his purpose only by an immediate marriage, and an effort to prove the former one invalid. This he thought could easily be done, and this, with the impetuous ardor of inexperienced youth (he was but nineteen), he urged her to consent to. The thoughtless girl, wholly ignorant of the world, and seeing no other chance of escape from what seemed to her a life of misery and dishonor, madly agreed to the proposal; and before sunset on the following day she was far from her home, the bride of her early love. She had fled without her mother's knowledge, for, with an instinctive consciousness of error which yet she would not acknowledge to herself, she felt that her parent would never consent to so wild a step.

What was the rage and astonishment of Seaton, when, stopping at an inn on his way to W—, he read in the same weekly paper—nay, in the very paragraph which announced *his* union with his victim—the marriage of Mariel Harris to Edward Atherton! Ere he laid aside the paper, he swore a fearful oath of vengeance, and well has he kept that oath. He commenced a lawsuit against them, which is still, I believe, undecided; and ever since, with the fearful malice of a fiend, he has tracked the steps of the devoted pair. From one place of refuge to another they have been driven by his murderous threats, for he openly avows his purpose of securing the person of Mariel, and sacrificing the life of Atherton to his revenge. But it was not until some weeks after her second marriage that the erring Mariel began to realize the full effects of the dangerous step she had taken.

She had accompanied her husband to Boston, where they had engaged lodgings; and while waiting one evening his return, she fancied she heard his step upon the stairs. With the welcoming smile of love upon her lips, she sprang to meet him at the door, and found herself in the arms of the dreaded Seaton. Conscious of his powers of fascination, he fancied he had only to exert his wonted eloquence to effect his purpose; and leading her gently to a seat, he urged her to fly with him, telling her he freely forgave her desertion, knowing that her heart was still his, and that her too gentle nature must have been wrought upon by the artful persuasions of his rival. She was nearly senseless with terror, yet she shrank from his lightest touch, and with all the firmness she could command, bade him instantly leave her. But when she saw him unmoved by her evident agony, in momentary dread of her husband's return, she threw herself on her knees at his feet, and entreated him in mercy to go. Her hands were clasped, her eyes were raised imploringly to his, when the door suddenly opened, and Atherton stood before them, the picture of astonishment and indignation. Seaton sprang from his seat with the fury of a demon, and snatching a pistol from his bosom, snapped it at the motionless intruder. Fortunately it was unloaded. Enraged at the failure—

"By Heaven" he exclaimed, "I'll be revenged!" and ere his rival could recover from his momentary stupefaction sufficiently to oppose his escape, he was gone.

Mariel had heard the fearful click of the deadly weapon; and, with a woman's instinct, rushed forward to shield her husband from danger. For the first time, she found her caresses not returned; for the first time the eyes of him she loved were averted, and the voice cold and strange which had been the music of her life. From that hour the frank and fearless brow of Edward Atherton was ever and anon clouded with doubt and gloom. He still loved his young wife fondly, fervently—he pitied her misery, he wept tears of anguish over her blighted bloom. But he felt that he could never again confide in the strength of her affection for himself. He saw in her uplifted eyes, when kneeling at the feet of Seaton, the glance of an humbled and self-reproaching spirit. It was too imploring, too meek for conscious rectitude. He felt that an injured woman, secure in innocence and truth, would never thus have humbled herself to one so low; and that fatal moment revealed to him what poor Mariel herself had never dreamed of, that the love of years had been shaken for a time by the fascinating arts of a stranger and a libertine; and if once shaken, why not again? Alas! he knew not then the change which a bitter and terrible experience had wrought in her suffering heart. Her former careless gaiety had given place to a meek and touching resignation, which rendered her far more worthy of his love than she had been in the brightest hours of girlhood. Her devotion to him was ardent and unbounded. She felt to its fullest extent the generous sacrifice he had made to her; and her lonely and retired life—for few would visit "the wife of two husbands," as she was called—only served to concentrate all her thoughts and feelings more exclusively in the one object of her love.

But the suspense and suffering she endured was hourly undermining her delicate constitution. Her constant dread of Seaton, the displeasure of her mother, the desertion of her friends, and her consciousness that Edward felt their neglect even more bitterly than herself, gradually wrought upon her nerves with almost fatal power. A brain sever was the result, during the paroxysms of which the name of Seaton was often on her lips, and always coupled with some expression of fear or abhorrence. Of Edward, too, she raved, unconscious that her burning hand was fondly clasped in his, and moistened with his tears. She would conjure him by all her love, which she avowed had never failed, even in the wildest hour of temptation, to save her from her enemy. At last the gentle and never-ceasing cares of Atherton effected a partial restoration; and when in the first moments of recovered consciousness she raised her blue eyes, filled with tears of gratitude and love, to his, he felt once more that she was all his own.

Since then they have been wanderers, not only in their own but in foreign countries, seeking in vain a balm for wounded peace. With Atherton nothing has prospered since his rash marriage. Nearly all his little property has been lost in improvident speculations, and Mariel's still awaits the decision of the law. The lives of both are embittered by their dread lest that decision should separate them for ever. Gerald Seaton still pursues his victim from place to place, and is only baffled in his design by the vigilance of her husband and her few remaining friends.

"Do you remember, dear Catharine," she said, in a late melancholy letter to her early confidant, "do you remember my sad presentiments on the little bridge of W—? Do you remember the omen? The stone which Edward tossed to the reckless waves struck my poor little pebble, and they sank together, and the waters closed again and smiled above them in undisturbed tranquility. How fearfully prophetic of our fate! But, alas! it was not the prophecy or the omen; it was my own idle coquetry, my foolish vanity, that wrought our ruin. Farewell, dear Catharine, we shall never meet again in this sad world, for I feel that I am wasting away, slowly, perhaps, but surely. When I am gone, I know there are two faithful beings— Edward, dear Edward, and yourself—who will weep over my early grave, and pity and forgive the errors of the unhappy Mariel."

The Crumpled Rose Leaf[1]

THE CARRIAGE was at the door, ready to convey us to a ball given by the Duke of D—, in honor of our recent nuptials. Ellen was still in her dressing-room. I had left her there completing her toilet, and while awaiting her appearance, I half-buried myself amid the luxurious cushions of an ottoman, and reveled in sweet dreams of the past and blessed anticipations for the future. I had been three weeks a husband, the happiest of the happy. My bride was young, lovely, loving, and beloved—my fortune ample—my health and spirits excellent—and my friends many and pleasant. But there was one crumpled rose-leaf in the Sybarite's blooming bed, and even my reverie was not all of joy. In order to explain the little incident which had slightly ruffled my composure, it will be necessary to recall a previous period in my history.

Among the numerous aspirants to the fair hand of Ellen Fitzroy, there was none whose attractions I had so much cause to dread, as those of my friend—the handsome and fascinating Lord Henry de Lisle. He was gay, good-humored, and thoughtless, and though evidently sincere in his devotion to the beautiful girl, possessed an elastic temperament which would be sure to rebound from disappointment. I, on the contrary, had staked my all upon the issue; and whilst my friend, with the light-hearted carelessness peculiar to his character, allowed me to profit by many an opportunity which he might have improved to his own advantage, I was jealously fearful of his slightest advance in her favor. As for Ellen, she was all gentleness and sweetness to both; and to a casual observer, there was not a perceptible shade of difference in her manner towards Lord Henry and myself. But I, who watched her with a lover's solicitude, detected much that was invisible to others, whether favorable to my

---

[1] "The Crumpled Rose Leaf," Frances S. Osgood, *The Court Magazine and La Belle Assemblée*, September 1836, vol. IX, pp. 126-129

wishes or otherwise, for my life I could not determine. I saw the soft blush spring to that youthful cheek at my approach, as if a rose—the rose of love—were just born in her heart! but whenever I dared to breathe of passion and of hope, though her sweet mouth smiled as bewitchingly as ever, her eyes, downcast or averted, were sure to fill with tears; and she would often turn abruptly from me, as if my presence were painful, and, linking her arm with a sister's freedom in that of my friend, suffer him to lead her unresistingly away. One evening—it was the eve of her birth-day, which was to be celebrated by a ball on the ensuing night—none were present save her sisters, Lord Henry, and myself. The young ladies were gaily discussing their dresses for the occasion, and Ellen, turning playfully towards us, asked if she should wear diamonds or pearls.

"Oh! diamonds in that beautiful dark hair, by all means," exclaimed Lord Henry.

"Pearls and blue eyes," said I, in a low tone.

For an instant those eyes were raised to mine, and, though immediately withdrawn, there was something in their eloquent glance, which made my heart throb with emotions of hope and rapture, such as I had never before experienced. The sisters meanwhile were unanimous in their condemnation of my taste and in approval of Lord Henry's; and then, with arch looks and meaning tones, wondered "which Ellen would wear *now*."

Ellen blushed and smiled, but did not speak; and I, unable to command the feelings which that thrilling look had raised, hastily took my leave.

The visions of that night decided my fate; for I dreamed of leading the sweet girl to the altar: and early the next morning, after purchasing a pearl chain of rare beauty, I enclosed and sent it in a letter, containing an ardent avowal of affection, and requesting, that if there were the slightest hope of reciprocity, its pledge might be her wearing my gift on her birth night. The day passed in a fever and ague of hope and fear, and in the evening, at a most unceremoniously early hour, I drove to Lady Fitzroy's. I was the first arrival: but was soon joined in the drawing-room by Lord Henry, and, in a few minutes after, by the sisters of Ellen. The youngest, a gay, thoughtless thing, who was wild with delight at being allowed to appear for the first time at a ball, exclaimed, the moment she saw us—

"Ah, you may both wear the willow now. Ellen will have nothing to do with either: she has lent her diamond-chain to Georgiana, and given me her pearls. To the last, *particularly,*" she continued, with an emphasis playfully malicious, "she declares she has conceived a sudden and *unconquerable* aversion."

As she finished speaking, the handle of the door moved, as if a tremulous and hesitating hand were upon it—it turned—the door half-opened—there was a moment's pause—and Ellen, with a faltering step, and an air of timidity wholly at variance with her usual graceful self-possession, slowly entered the room. As I sprang forward to lead her to a seat, the color mounted to her temples; but my heart was chilled; for I looked in vain for a glimpse of my morning's gift, from the rich braids of deep brown hair to the curved and snowy throat—it was not there! And I was just about to murmur a reproach for her cruelty, when the trembling of her hand upon my arm attracted my attention towards it. What was my emotion, when I perceived the faint light of those beautiful pearls struggling through the folds of a full gauze sleeve, which draped her delicate wrist! The dear girl, unwilling that any but the eye of love should detect her choice, had converted the chain into a bracelet. I could hardly refrain from raising it to my lips; but a strong effort at self-command proved successful, and I had my reward, when, towards the close of the evening, I contrived to detain her alone in the conservatory, and won from her faltering lips a timid confession that my attachment was returned. And now for the ruffled rose-leaf!

We had passed the few weeks immediately succeeding our marriage in happy retirement at a country seat, and had returned to town the day previous to that with which my story commences.

As this was to tie Ellen's first appearance as a bride, I felt a little lover-like anxiety that she should wear my birth-day gift—the pearl chain, the associations with which were, I doubted not, as pleasant and dear to her memory as to mine. But "the crumpled rose-leaf."

I had slightly hinted my wish before I left her, as I said, in her dressing-room;—and while I lingered at the door in fond admiration of her excelling loveliness, she turned smiling towards me, and, raising a diamond band to her brow, said in a playfully positive tone—"I think I shall wear this to-night. I don't like pearls very well."

It was the recollection of this, that, in spite of her sportive manner, had disturbed my repose.

Although Lord Henry had been among the first and warmest in his congratulations upon my engagement, I had not yet forgotten the uneasiness his attentions to Ellen had created, and the sight of the diamonds forcibly recalled my former fears.

Gradually yielding to my jealous meditations, I lay, with half-shut eyes, absorbed in dreamy reverie. One by one, however, all darker and colder feelings melted away, as I thought of her exquisite grace and beauty, the bewitching sweetness of her disposition, and, more than all, her affectionate devotion to me. As I became more drowsy, these thoughts grew more and more indistinct, and at length I was conscious only of a vague sensation of luxury and happiness, when the voice of Ellen roused me from my trance. In a few moments I found myself in the splendidly lighted apartments of the Duke of D—. I was not aware that Ellen had left my arm, until I caught a glimpse, through the crowd, of her elegant form, encircled by the audacious arm of Lord Henry de Lisle, and floating, like a dream of light, through the mazes of the waltz! Strange to say, until that moment I had quite forgotten my jealous fears about her choice of ornaments; I had not even noticed her dress. What then was my surprise and anger, when at every turn of the dance the glare of *diamonds* broke upon my view, flashing like stars through her luxuriant hair! There was a sort of triumph in their blaze, that I knew not how to look. There was triumph, too, in her own beaming smile; and worse—oh! worse than all—there was joy, exultation, defiance, in the bold black eyes of Lord Henry, as he met my look of astonishment and rage. I thought I had never seen her look unlovely until then. She had never waltzed before with any one but me. At last an opening in the crowd revealed her whole figure to my view. Her graceful head, her soft and exquisitely molded neck, her arms, her very waist, were all wreathed and radiant with the richest and most beautiful brilliants! She moved literally in an atmosphere of splendor. But where could the thoughtless creature have obtained them? Could they have been the secret gift of Lord Henry? There was distraction in the thought. Her dress, too! When I left her at her toilet, she was arrayed, at my request, in the bridal satin, whose pure and snowy hue seemed peculiarly appropriate to that ethereal refinement of beauty for which she was remarkable. Now, for the first time, I observed, that over this she wore a light robe of rose-coloured gauze, the wavy folds of which floated around her, as she moved, like the blushing mist of morn around a star! Animated by the wild, voluptuous music, the increasing rapidity of the dance, and the concentrated gaze of the brilliant crowd around, the color deepened in her delicate cheek, the light of her rich blue eyes became every instant more intensely radiant, and a smile of ecstasy played round her eager and half-parted lips! All eyes were upon her—a murmur of admiration arose—and, maddened by the scene, the sounds, and utterly unable to control my feelings, I rushed wildly from the room. I had been only a few minutes in the open air, in the beautiful grounds adjoining the house, when the sound of coming footsteps interrupted my bitter reflections.

I know not why, but my heart instinctively told me to whom those footsteps belonged, and, with a sort of desperate calmness, I silently waited their approach. On they came, nearer and nearer. Her light robe brushed me as she passed—I felt her very breath upon my cheek—I heard the low whisper of De Lisle. "My own sweet Ellen!" he murmured. I raised my arm to dash the traitor to the earth; but a hand, a voice arrested me. It was a fairy touch, a magic tone, for they broke the fearful spell for ever. And was it all a dream? A dimpled arm was round my neck, a fragrant mouth was breathing close to my cheek, and sweet blue eyes looked smiling into mine.

"Will you never awake, dear George?" said a soft, imploring voice. I rubbed my eyes, and looked wildly around. Yes! I was still upon the ottoman, in our dimly-lighted drawing-room. And there was my own blessed Ellen, bending tenderly over, and looking lovelier than ever in her modest bridal dress, with her dark hair smoothly parted on her brow, and her only ornament the simple chain of pearls wound lightly round her head. Love's "crumpled leaf" was smooth again. And as I seated myself beside her in the carriage, I made a solemn, though silent vow, that *jealousy*, at least, should never more ruffle its soft and holy bloom.

A Day in New England[1]

IT WAS a lovely September afternoon, when my friend and self stepped on board the elegant steamer, General Lincoln, which was to convey us to Hingham, a small and picturesque village on the coast of Massachusetts. We were glad to leave Boston, for, though summer had gone by, her warm breath and sunny smile still lingered in the air, and anyone who has been so unfortunate as to pass that season in a city, can tell how their bland and balmy purity, which is such a blessing amid the woods and fields, is lost amid the harsh glare of a brick wall, and the crowd of a public street. We found the deck alive with children—the pupils of a free school, who, accompanied by their teachers and a band of music, were going to pass a holiday, as a holy hour, in the country.

It was a glorious day—the clear, rich sun smiled at his own bright face in the waters. The children laughed and sung, and chased each other in their glee, as if their very hearts were just let out of school—and the wanton sea breeze, frolic as themselves, tossed their free wild curls into the golden fight, and played with the roses on their dimpled cheeks, till the wavy hair grew bright, and the warm face rosier still.

The rainbow gleamed in the foam like a girdle of gems by our side—the waves leaped up like living things, all redolent of light and joy—and many a gaily painted boat did we pass, and many a majestic ship, with its curved sails changing from grey to gold as shade or shine prevailed. At length the band suddenly struck up a popular air. The broad white deck was cleared for the quadrille; the sets were quickly formed; and the children, smiling and blushing, bounded lightly through the mazes of the dance. Altogether it was quite delightful; and, impelled by the same impulse of admiration, we both drew our pencils from our pockets to commemorate the scene—

---

[1] "A Day in New England," Frances S. Osgood, *The Court Magazine and La Belle Assemblée,* November 1836, vol. IX, no. 5, pp. 179-182

my friend, by a drawing in his sketch-book; and I, by some verses in a blank page of a volume of *Bums*. As I raised my head to think of a simile for the sweet season of childhood, my eye was attracted by a fairylike boat, with a single sail, dancing merrily over the waves, as if it possessed a human spirit to rejoice in the beauty of the day. The following lines, suggested by the sight, may not be inappropriate here:

> How swift o'er the waters it dashes!
> The spray-jewels spring to its prow.
> The sunny foam over it flashes.
> And Heaven looks soft on it now.
>
> With its balmy breath wooingly pressing.
> The zephyr has curved the light sail,
> And the bark in that playful caressing,
> Goes gracefully on with the gale.
>
> A cloud o'er the far away billow,
> So down-like and delicate rose.
> So soft, it would seem a lit pillow
> To cradle a seraph's repose!
>
> Yet we know not what darkness and danger
> It bears in that bosom of light,
> The smile of the beautiful stranger
> May change to a frown ere the night.
>
> Ah! thus, in Life's rapturous morning
> We float with the breeze and the beam:
> The shadows of destiny scorning.
> We see but the sun-lighted stream.

The beautiful islands which are scattered over the harbor of Boston, render this sail one of the pleasantest in the world. There are two, on which forts were erected in war-time, Fort Strong and Fort Independence. But the most interesting one of the present day is Thompson's Island, on which is an excellent asylum for indigent boys, called the Farm School. The island contains one hundred and sixty acres of land, all of which is in a high state of cultivation. Most of the work in the extensive gardens is performed between school-hours by the pupils, now numbering just one hundred. The younger boys have small garden-lots assigned to them, which they are allowed to call their own, and in which they of course feel a lively interest. The school-house is erected on a prominent part of the island, and commands a rich and varied prospect.

Another object worthy of notice is a monument, called Nix's Mate, raised many years ago to commemorate the murder of a mate, perpetrated on the spot, by a captain of that name. It formerly occupied the center of an island, which has since been washed away, and the restless waves now lash in vain the lone and lasting memorial of guilt. It is built of granite, and there is something grand in its desolate appearance, as it stands unmoved and stern, in sunshine and in storm, amid the ever-heaving sea!

Among the many objects of interest, along the shore of the main land, is seen the still unfinished monument on Bunker Hill, erected in memory of the unfortunate—I should say, the fortunate—men who fell there at the commencement of the Revolutionary War. It has been many years in progress by subscription, and, as a sarcastic friend of mine lately observed, it is to go a few thousand dollars' worth higher this year. It is to be of solid granite, in the shape of a pyramid.

Hingham is of late becoming a fashionable resort from the city. It is the oldest town in New England excepting Plymouth, which is within a few miles' distance of it. Our purpose in going thither was to visit an invalid friend, who, with her mother and sisters, was boarding at a cottage in a lonely and romantic part of the village, called Rocky Nook. Our walk from the boat was delightful, through most luxuriant woods, whose foliage had been suddenly changed, by the magic wreath and smile of autumn, till it glowed like a living rainbow. The house was situated on a gentle eminence, and, as we approached, a bright face vanished from the window, and the next moment my friend was flying down the hill to welcome us. How perfectly lovely she looked at that moment! Her white morning dress simple and graceful as herself—her pale brown hair wreathed with wild flowers, and drooping in long curls on her cheek—the tremulous glow of returning health—the fair Madonna forehead, full of purity and intellect—every feature of that face so delicately beautiful—the whole contour of the small, elegant head, and curving throat so entirely classical:—Raffaele, could he have seen, would have made her his model, and given new grace to the canvas. Behind her, in swift pursuit, came her youngest sister, the pet of the family—a little rosy rogue, three years of age, with wild disordered curls, that absolutely gleamed with light and looked like a net for sunbeams. She was a strange bright child, at times so full of fun and frolic, and at others so thoughtful and demure.

"If all who are born must die," she said to her mother one day, "I wish God would *unborn* me, for I don't want to die." At another time, after some one had told her that it was God who clothed the sky with clouds, she seemed for a few moments absorbed in thought, and then exclaimed—"Mamma! is God the mantua-maker of the sky?"

At the door we were met by the rest of the family, and ushered into a small parlor, most tastefully adorned with natural flowers. After partaking of a delicious repast, consisting of new milk, eggs, bread and butter, pies, honey, and a cake made of Indian meal, called by the good housewives of New England "journey-cake," we adjourned for the evening to the spacious barn, where, by the brilliant moonlight, the children amused themselves with the swing, and the rest of the party with singing and conversation. Our number was soon increased by the arrival of some village friends. But the evening air grew cool, and we were about to return to the house, when some one proposed a dance.

"Ah, but we have no instrument," said another.

Hardly had she finished speaking, ere an inspiring waltz was heard from some invisible flute! It was surely in the air! Was Prospero alive? Had Ariel come again? And the low melodious laugh, which followed our exclamations of wonder, and which sounded directly over our heads, did not lessen the delusion. But the pleasant tune went on; and so enlivening were the notes, that several sprang from their seats, and joined in the graceful dance, while others searched in vain for the enchanter. At last a slight rustle betrayed its hiding place. "The loft! the loft!" they cried.

There was a sudden rush towards the ladder leading to the hay-loft, and several gentlemen ascended. Then there was a playful struggle, renewed laughter, and they reappeared at the head of the bidder, dragging forward our Ariel with his flute in his hand—a romantic youth, who loved solitude, and often sought it in the cool and quiet loft. At our request, he continued his music, and a merry country dance ended the amusements of the day.

Early the next morning seats were arranged in the large hay-cart for a trip to Mantasket beach, about three miles distant, and seven miles in length. All the most romantic of the party, among whom was myself, were eager for a scat in this rather rickety vehicle; the rest were contented with the more rational carry-all. I did not envy those in the latter, for they were not half so gay as we. A poet, a painter, a lawyer, and an editor, were our attendant beaux, and many a *jeu-d'esprit* and many a lovely sentiment was ours, as jolt-ti-ti-jolt we rattled over the rough and rocky road; talking, laughing, and occasionally joining in the chorus of the beautiful airs which poured in sweet succession from the lips of a dark-eyed, rose-lipped girl, who seemed to sing because she could not help it, she was so happy. A glorious creature she was, all genius and enthusiasm, with a soul as fall of fire as her eyes, and a voice so rich, and sweet, and wild! I never heard any one sing with such pathos and expression. She was a wit withal. I will give a single instance of her quickness at repartee. She had long been tormented by the importunate attentions of a certain oddity, whose devotion was the more provoking, as she could never discover whether he was in jest or earnest. The youth affected great originality in his remarks, and once at a party, offering her his arm, he asked—

"Will you vibrate, Miss L.?"

"I have no objection."

"And to what favored quarter of the apartment would your vibrations tend?"

"Wherever yours do not."

He was silenced for a moment, but soon renewed the attack. "Well, and how do you flourish now-a-days?"

"I leave all flourishes to you, Mr. W."

"You look fatigued."

"I am weary of this stupid world."

"Can you give me a definition of stupidity?"

"Yes."

"And what is it?"

"Mr. W—."

There, was a stare of surprise, and another pause.

"Miss L., will you favor me with a new idea?"

"I think I saw a primer on the table; suppose you should look there for one."

But to return to the hay-cart. Our poet was another original. He had a deal of sly humor, which no muscles but his own could resist: and his conversation was a constant flow of playful wit, or most exalted sentiment. In feature, he resembled a portrait I have seen of Dr. Johnson; and I believe under that demure and almost stupid expression he concealed nearly as much strength of thought and ready play of humor. I never could quite understand him. He was either the most sincere and simple and unsophisticated, or the most artful, of human beings; but of this I am quite sure, that he always acted according to his own notions of right and wrong, without caring for or paying any regard to the opinions of the world.

Once when visiting the city of Charlestown, in South Carolina, a lady invited him to sit in her pew the following Sunday. She went to church, expecting to meet him there; but prayers commenced, and he had not yet made his appearance. Happening, however, to turn her head, while kneeling with the rest of the congregation, she saw to her dismay her new acquaintance walking gravely up the aisle, with his great clumsy country-made shoes in his hand, and his large feet clothed in hose of coarse blue woolen yarn! Reader, the lady did not scream! Was not her self-command worthy of an Indian chief? Another of the party contributed much to our gaiety, a younger sister of my friend, about seventeen years of age, whose childish artlessness was a constant source of amusement to her family. She always acted from impulse; but they were the prettiest impulses in the world: for she was a sweet affectionate creature, with a warm heart, a bright face, and a voice like an Eolian harp. She loved a country life, and when allowed to visit Hingham, was always wild with joy. She used to say, she did hope Heaven was "all country." Her mind, which was naturally rich, would have been a paradise with proper cultivation; it was neglected, and the weeds half choked the flowers; but with all its faults, it was still a garden of Eden to her lover, for he seemed to glory in it. She was full of a lovely and glowing enthusiasm, which no experience seemed likely to subdue. I remember once, in attempting to describe a picture of a lake by moonlight, she at once conveyed an idea of its peculiar loveliness to my mind, by exclaiming:

"Oh! it was so thrillingly beautiful, that as soon as I saw it I began to whisper!"

We were almost sorry when the beach appeared, our drive had been so pleasant. But we were soon quite as happily engaged in gathering shells and watching the distant sails. We here noticed a very beautiful phenomenon, which I have since been told is a common one. We saw the shadow of a ship inverted in the clouds. There was something so unearthly in the delicate softness of the outline, that you might have dreamed an angel, looking down from Heaven, had seen the winged wanderer of the sea, and, charmed with its majestic beauty, had drawn its likeness there. It reminded me of an idea, which I think I have heard a Swedenborgian express, that the things of earth will have their likeness in Heaven, only softer and purer and more beautiful. I have read somewhere of a man, who, standing on the summit of the Pic du Midi, saw a monstrous figure in the clouds imitating his movements, which proved to be his own shadow; and I thought how ludicrous at first must have seemed to him the sight of a giant returning his bow from the sky, as if the man in the moon had made his appearance in good earnest at last.

After a lunch, which we had brought with us and spread upon a large flat rock, taking our wine from the snow-white hollow shells with which the place abounds, we amused ourselves with scribbling on the beach, and many a sweet and many a silly verse did the restless waves erase. Two only of these impromptu effusions still linger in my memory. Some one had written the name of a favorite bard in the sand, and another, indignant at the sacrilege, inscribed the following beneath it:

What!—write the Poet's name in sand!
A name that rings throughout our land,
Linked with bewildering music, such
As tremble to a seraph's touch!

See, the next wave, in reckless play,
Will wash the hallowed word away.
Oh, rather let it live, impressed
In yonder granite's changeless breast.
Nay, even that to time must yield
Where, then, may we that word engrave?
Oh! be our hearts its shrine, its shield!
'Twill there defy Oblivion's wave!

The other was composed on seeing a child at play with the waves:

They come! they come! the laughing waves
And each thy pathway lightly laves.
And at thine eager feet flings down
His crown of foam—his dazzling crown!
But thou dost gaze in sad amaze,
And wonder where the gems have fled,
That seemed to wreathe with starry rays.
Before he came, his shining head.
Ah, thus the hours of after life,
To thee, are all with glory rife;
And thus thou'lt sigh, as now dismayed,
To see that treacherous glory fade.

We returned in time to see the sun set from the summit of Turkey Hill, a somewhat lofty eminence near the house, commanding a prospect of great beauty and variety. No language can describe the glowing splendor of the scene, as we reached the highest point of the hill. The rich woods—the calm and verdant vale—the winding, gleaming stream—the distant heights—the heaving sea—and, fairer than them all, the graceful drapery of the landscape, the gorgeous ever-changing clouds, paling gradually from the glowing gold and purple to the violet and rose! I never felt so much the want of words in describing scenery as when viewing one of those magnificent sunsets, which are, I believe, peculiar to New England.

In the evening, we were invited to a ball at the hotel, where the beaux and belles of the village were all assembled before eight o'clock, and where on a floor, elastic as Hope, as my friend poetically observed, we tripped it merrily till midnight, and then walked home through the woods by the light of the full harvest-moon!

"Ah!" said Miss L., as we reached the door of the cottage, "it seems, sometimes, as if I could hear old Time himself sighing as he goes by to leave such scenes behind."

Florence Howard[1]

CHAPTER I.

IT WAS a brilliant morning in the April of 1838. A warm west wind stole in through an open window overlooking the Regent's Park, and waving aside a profusion of soft brown curls, revealed the beautiful countenance of Florence Howard, alone and deeply absorbed in thought, with her fair hands folded before her, and her dark blue eyes veiled by the long and all but curling lashes, which even when raised so shadowed and subdued the laughing fire beneath. A small desk of exquisite workmanship occupied a table before her, and on it was a sheet of paper half filled with her own peculiarly delicate and graceful handwriting. The last sentence was unfinished, and ran as follows:

"But you wrong him, dear sister, you do indeed. He is noble and generous as yourself, I could not love him else, and I am convinced that were I even now suddenly dispossessed of that fortune which you so unjustly accuse him of coveting, he would only the more urgently press the suit so long, and, I might say, so unreasonably denied. But I will hesitate no longer: this evening we are to meet at the Duke of B.'s long talked of *fête,* and my destiny shall then be decided; and yet I tremble when I think."

It was here that poor Florence had broken abruptly off, and well might she tremble as she thought. Young, gay, and brilliantly beautiful, the possessor of immense wealth, the belle of the season, she was surrounded by a crowd of flatterers from whom her fancy, which she mistook for her heart, had singled out the most elegant and accomplished, but at the same time the most unprincipled of them all.

Lord William Fitzherbert having wasted at the gaming-table, and other haunts of dissipation, the bulk of a noble fortune, had hailed with avidity the debut of a new "spec."—as he termed it. Young, inexperienced, and

---

[1] "Florence Howard," Frances S. Osgood, *The Court Magazine and Belle Assemblée,* April 1839, vol. XIV, pp. 378-382

almost unprotected as was the orphan, Florence Howard, from the evening of her first appearance in the fashionable world he had devoted himself assiduously to her pleasure, and fascinated by his genius, and touched by his preference of herself to all others, Florence believed herself in love, and though reluctant, from a little girlish spirit of coquetry, and perhaps from a slight but unconfessed presentiment of evil to acknowledge her affection, she had long resolved in her own mind that Fitzherbert alone should win the hand so many sought in vain.

But let us return to the small and richly-furnished room in which we left her. There she still sits in the same graceful attitude, half reclining on the luxurious sofa, while a crimson reflection from the sunlit drapery of the windows plays alternately now on her delicate cheek, and now on the soft folds of her white morning dress. But, hark! a light vehicle dashes rapidly up to the door and stops—an impatient knock is heard, the small hands of Florence Howard are clasped in sudden joy, a smile of delight flashes up into her lifted eyes, blushes and dimples spring simultaneously to her cheek, and her lovely lips are parted in happy expectation. The door opens; Lord William Fitzherbert is announced, and the proud and wayward girl recovering instantly her self-possession, receives him as calmly and demurely as if he had not been the sole object of her thoughts for the last half hour. "But, my dear Miss Howard," said his lordship, after some conversation upon indifferent subjects, "you surely will not keep me longer in suspense; you know that I have staked my happiness, my life upon your reply; will you not bless me now with that one little monosyllable which would be such music from those lips?"

Florence averted her head, and her sweet voice faltered as she replied, "We shall meet this evening, and then."

"And then, dearest, loveliest! you will say, 'yes.'"

The lady turned her dark eyes full upon him, while a smile of sportive scorn lightened through the still lingering tears "Are you quite sure, my lord, that I shall not say 'no?'"

"Nay, lady, I spoke not in confidence, but in hope; but I will not press you farther. I trust to your promise for this eve. And now may I use that fairy pen of yours to scribble a note, which in my haste to see you I had forgotten? It will be too late for the post if I delay it longer."

"Certainly, my lord, but just shut your eyes, if you please, while you place that half-finished letter in the desk."

Lord W. did as he was bid, and hastily writing his *billet*, pressed upon it a delicate sheet of silver paper which lay before him, sealed it with Florence's pet seal, and rose to go. She raised her eyes from the book which she had taken up, and bade him "good bye" with a look so full of trust and happiness, that his own involuntarily sank beneath it, and he hastened away lest she should observe his confusion.

As he closed the door the enthusiastic girl caught up the silver paper which his hand had pressed, and exclaiming, "It is hallowed by that touch, I will keep it for ever," was about to place it in a secret drawer of the desk, when her own name traced lightly upon it arrested her eye. She had turned the paper, and nearly the whole impression of Lord William's *billet* was visible in faint characters through the transparent tissue.

The pulse of Florence beat high at the sight. "He has been writing of his love to some confidential friend. Perhaps he has been praising me," and her young heart thrilled, her pure cheek glowed with the thought. "Oh, how sweet, how delicious it would be to read his praises of myself! But of course that is out of the question. I have no right even to look at the paper again," and resolutely closing her eyes against a temptation to which her keen and delicate sense of honor would not permit her to yield, she hastily folded her treasure and placed it in the drawer. At that moment a sweet eager voice was heard on the landing, and her cousin, Charles Leslie, a beautiful boy between five and six years of age, bounded into the room, and sprang with the loving confidence of childhood to her knee, exclaiming as he did so:—"here I am at last, dear Florry; I have been so good all the morning, and mamma said, I might come to you as a reward. And, oh! I have such a secret to tell, but do not ask me what it is, for I said I wouldn't tell Florry. Wouldn't you give anything to know? Oh! what a pretty seal!" And quite forgetting his secret and his question, the restless boy only suffered his fair cousin to part the bright curls from his brow, and print one kiss upon his laughing eyes, and then escaped from her embrace and climbed the sofa to her desk.

Florence again took up her book, and was soon absorbed either in its contents or in those of her own heart Nearly half an hour had thus elapsed, when she was suddenly roused by the voice of little Charlie, who had seated himself with mock dignity in an arm-chair opposite, and with as much pomposity of tone as his soft little voice could assume, was lisping out the contents of the identical silver paper, which she had thought so safely concealed. "Oh, stop, Charlie, stop!" she exclaimed, as the first strange words met her ear, and she hid her glowing face in her hands; but Master Charlie was too much absorbed in his self-assumed importance to heed her entreaty, and the bewildered girl, half stupefied with wonder, indignation, and grief, and unable either to move or speak again, sat a spellbound listener to the following interesting epistle.

"Yes, mia cara, carissima! the prize is mine at last. Florence Howard, the haughty and beautiful Florence, has at length deigned to smile upon my suit. I am to have her decided answer tonight, and I cannot doubt its purport. Even now, as I looked up (I am writing at her house), I caught her rich eyes fixed upon me with an expression of interest and admiration which I could not mistake, and when caught, the bashful and blushing confusion with which she hurriedly resumed her book only confirmed my hopes. Yes, my adored Victorine!—I repeat, the golden prize is mine. With her immense fortune I shall more than repair the ruin of my own. I shall insist upon an early day for the wedding, and as soon as the tedious ceremony is concluded, can you doubt where love will lead me, where, but to the feet of her who alone possesses my heart. Till then, *ma belle adieu*! Your devoted,

"FITZHERBERT."

CHAPTER II.

The palace-like mansion of the munificent Duke of B., was gorgeously illuminated, and gay and brilliant was the assembly in the superb suite of rooms thrown open for the *fête*. But among that throng there was one whose countenance was irradiated with a smile of triumphant success that eclipsed the light in every other; that one was Lord William Fitzherbert, and all who noticed him acknowledged that his wit and conversational talent had never been so happily displayed as on that evening. It was in the midst of a laugh, excited by a more than usually brilliant repartee, that his attention was attracted to a slight bustle at the principal entrance. The crowd parted before it. All eyes were turned towards the spot, and an irrepressible murmur of admiration ran round the assembly as Florence Howard, looking more bewitchingly beautiful than ever, entered the room with a party of distinguished friends. She had discarded for that evening the simple and girlish style of dress in which she was wont to appear. Her rich glossy hair was braided and wreathed with jewels. Her graceful form arrayed in a sweeping robe of velvet, and she looked, moved, spoke with a queen-like grace and dignity which she had never before assumed. There was a fire, too, in those proud blue eyes, a curve in the Hebe-lip, a haughty carriage of the graceful head, which awed into unwonted silence the crowd of admirers who had been eagerly awaiting her appearance.

That night not one among them dared to address the youthful beauty, radiant as she looked, with the honeyed words of flattery or love.

The truth is, the discovery of the morning had wrought a revolution as powerful as it was sudden, not only in the demeanor but in the mind and heart of Florence. It had changed her from a child, a thoughtless, joyous, confiding child, to a proud and self-relying woman. It had opened her eyes to the dangers of her situation, to the mercenary views of many who courted her smiles, and she sighed as she thought, "Is there one who could love me for myself alone?" Yes, memory whispered her of one, the playmate of her early days; one, who in after years had devoted himself to her when she was left a lonely orphan, without the slightest prospect of that wealth which had since been bequeathed to her by a distant and almost forgotten relation. Her cousin, Wallace Leslie had, at that time, three years previous to the date at which my story commences, received an offer from government of a distinguished and lucrative appointment in a foreign land; but listening rather to the voice of affection than to that of ambition, he had thrown himself at the feet of his lovely and beloved Florence, and besought her to share with him his small but secure competence at home, declaring that she was more than the world or the world's wealth to him, and that all the brilliant prospects which he might be enabled to realize without her, were not worth a thought in comparison with the blessing of her love. But Florence, young as she was—and she was then barely sixteen, and unprotected too—was too considerately generous to indulge his youthful passion at the expense of his worldly prosperity. She felt too that she loved him only as a brother, and such love, fond as it was, would be but a poor return for the ardent attachment of her cousin to herself. With a firm, but grateful and affectionate refusal, she bade him farewell; and convinced by her manner that it would be useless to renew his suit, he immediately left England and proceeded to his appointment in India. And now let us return to the *fête*. "I did not dream she could queen it so bravely," said Fitzherbert to himself, while he gazed at a distance upon his expected victim. "And all this splendor is for my sake," he continued exultingly, "ah! *ma petite* Victorine, you have a more dangerous rival than your vain heart imagines. Faith, I was never so struck with her beauty before. But she is expecting me; I won't seem too much in a hurry, though; it will turn that pretty head of her's if it be not already turned. "And so thinking, he sauntered towards the place where Florence stood, surrounded by the most *distingué* men of the assemblage.

With the air of one who is conscious of a superior claim, Fitzherbert made his way through the throng to her side, and bending his head whispered a word in her ear. The lady had seemed till that moment wholly unconscious of his approach and presence, but when he spoke she turned suddenly towards him, her blue eyes flashing with scorn and indignation, and said, "My lord, you spoke in so unwarrantably low a tone, that I did not fully understand the purport of your observation; oblige me by repeating it."

Lord William's face was pale with rage, but forcing a laugh, he replied, "I merely requested, fair lady, your decision with regard to the invitation I gave you this morning."

"You shall have it, my lord. The duke's page has been seeking you with a *billet* from me, and here in good time he comes."

A lovely, dark-eyed Spanish boy, in a rich suit of amber velvet embroidered with gold, glided lightly through the throng, and presented to Lord William, on a magnificent salver, a little rose-colored and rose-scented note.

"Love's proper hue!" exclaimed Fitzherbert with revived hope, as he turned it to break the seal, but the device caught his eye, and he paused to examine it. It was a lifeless Cupid in the coils of a serpent, with the motto, "Falsehood is fatal to love."

"You had better read it when alone, my lord," said the low, but laughing voice of his intended victim. But Lord William had already torn open the envelope and unfolded the note within. It was the unfortunate sheet of silver paper, and as he glanced his eye over it, he saw at once that his villainy was betrayed.

"It cannot fail to meet your approbation, my lord, since it is only a reflection of your own honorable aspirations," muttered Florence again, as he crushed the fatal proof of guilt in his hand. The disappointed suitor made no reply, but biting his handsome lip with ill-concealed vexation, he bowed stiffly to Miss Howard and hastily left the circle.

Every one near them had noticed the lady's undisguised contempt and its effect upon her admirer; but there was no time now for comment, for the crowd again parted to admit the venerable Duke of B., who now approached, leaning on the arm of a young and interesting stranger. An eager whisper went round; "it is young Leslie, just returned from India, recalled, they say, for some higher office at home. Handsome fellow, by Jove!"

Meanwhile the wondering Florence, without waiting for the duke's formal introduction of his friend, held out both her hands to him and exclaimed, while her whole face beamed with blushing recognition and dimpled with delight, "Wallace Leslie, my dear cousin, how glad I am to see you!"

"Florence! Miss Howard! Can I believe my eyes? How little did I dream, when his grace said he must introduce me to the star of the season, that I should see in that star my own sweet cousin."

CHAPTER III.

"Yes! you have guessed it, Florry. Wallace was my secret," said our little pet Charles, a few days subsequent to the *fête*. "And now, since it was I who prevented your marrying that wicked Lord William, mayn't I be bridesman when you do wed, cousin?"

"Yes, Charles, I may safely promise that, for I shall never marry," replied Florence, with a demure shake of the head and a most novel-like sigh.

"Won't you, though?" said the roguish boy, sportively shaking his dark curls in imitation, and mimicking her plaintive tone; "but you will remember your promise if you do?"

"Certainly, Charles."

"And you will let little Georgy be bridesmaid?"

"Little Georgy, indeed! She is just your age, you rogue."

"Oh, yes, they call us twins, but somehow I always feel bigger than she."

"I dare say you do, little self-importance," said his cousin, patting his rosy cheek.

"But promise, Florry, promise."

"Well, there I do promise, torment; and now be done pulling my hair out of curl, and let me read in peace."

The entrance of a third person interrupted the playful struggle which ensued. Florence rose to receive him with her bright hair disordered, and her eyes yet laughing from the frolic: and she wondered what her heart could mean by fluttering as it did, when Wallace Leslie seated himself by her side. She was very much provoked too with her fair cheek for blushing, just because he happened to take her hand in his, and ask her if she remembered the happy hours of childhood, when they were always together. But when she looked again at the singularly graceful and intellectual head which was bending over that captive hand, and caught another glimpse by stealth of those superb black eyes, whose fire was just then subdued by the most intense and touching tenderness, she began to think it was not so very strange after all; and then she blushed still more, and tried to withdraw her hand, but the saucy youth retained it nevertheless, and bye and bye Florry quite forgot that it was there.

CHAPTER IV.

One pleasant morning in the following autumn, a fair bridal train swept up the central aisle of St George's church and paused before the altar. The bride was young, lovely, and graceful, richly but simply and modestly arrayed, with a veil of costly material floating to her feet, and her fair hair bound with pearls. Her drooping lashes were wet with tears, but a willful little dimple laughed up now and then through the blushes that dyed her cheek, and her rich voice did not falter as it breathed the solemn vow which bound her to the noble-looking youth at her side.

Two children, a boy and girl, evidently twins, and both exquisitely beautiful, followed with timid self-possession the steps of the bridal pair. The venerable Duke of B. gave the lady away, and many distinguished people of both sexes were assembled to witness the ceremony.

CHAPTER V.

The clock had just struck two. Lord William Fitzherbert was still yawning over his coffee and the *Morning Post,* when a short paragraph in the latter fixed his eye and arrested his yawn. "On Wednesday morning, by special license, at St George's church, the Hon. Wallace Leslie, to Florence, only daughter of the late General Howard."

In a sudden fit of passion his lordship struck his forehead with his clenched hand, threw the paper into the fire, dashed the delicate cup of Sevre china at the head of his astonished valet, glanced at half a dozen "long-drawn" bills which lay upon the breakfast table before him, and ordered, in a voice of thunder, post horses for Dover.

The Doom,[1]
A Tale of the French Revolution

IN A retired hamlet, towards the northern part of France, lived at the time of the Revolution, but as yet undisturbed by its horrors, Leon Duhesme, and his sister, Leonor—orphans and twins. Lonely, beautiful, and idolizing each other, they resembled two blossoms on the self-same stem, as like, as lovely; the zephyr, that fanned the soft bloom of the one, the other would be sure to feel, and if the storm should come, alas! the blight must fall on both! So striking was the similarity that, only by their difference of dress, were they known apart.

The hazel eyes of Leon's were like his sister's as if their luminous beauty emanated from the same un-shadowed soul. Glossy as silk on either head, waved the brown and curling hair. Soft and clear, but dark, was the dimpled cheek of Leonor, and Leon's was the same, while the rich glow, that quivered there, with the slightest emotion, sudden and beautiful as the rosy heat-lightening of summer, when it plays through the sunset cloud, seemed but a reflection of the changeful hue of his.

Often, while yet a child, the wild and graceful Leonor would playfully don her brother's cap and frock and mimic sword, and march demurely through the village street, pursing her pretty, roguish lip, to hide its smile, while her down-cast eye gleamed archly through the shadowing lash; and while the puzzled villagers accosted her as— "Leon"—she would clap her little hands exultingly, and laugh in innocent delight.

Leonor loved her gentle brother so fervently, that in after years, this resemblance was still the pride and joy of her heart, and when, as he emerged from childhood, the flowing tresses of the boy were sacrificed to the fashion of the times, she begged, with tears in her earnest eyes that,

---

[1] "The Doom," Frances S. Osgood, *The Ladies' Companion,* August 1840, vol. XIII, no. 4, pp. 188-192

hers too might be cut, lest the change should lessen their likeness to each other. Her request was laughed at as a babyish whim; but the spirited, and then, with his soft child was resolved and would not be thwarted. With lips pressing firmly together, and his slight and fragile frame nerved to unwonted strength, by his beautiful resolve, he turned, with a steady step, towards the appointed place of meeting. The girl stood, for a moment, motionless, and then slowly followed her brother. contour to the utmost advantage,—heightening at the same time, that piquant and beaming openness of expression, which was the peculiar charm of her countenance.

But while in external feature, the likeness was perfect, in the characters of the orphan-twins, there was a striking dissimilarity. Both were high-hearted, gentle, and each devoted to the other. But the love of Leon resembled the soft, caressing tenderness of a girl, to whom love is life. He was, a timid boy, of a thoughtful and dreamy nature, over shrinking from contact with strangers, and happy only in the society of his worshiped sister.

The laughing Leonor, on the contrary was the fearless child of impulse; ardent, impetuous and often uncontrollable, always in search of excitement, and finding it, where a colder soul might seek in vain: yet wild and wayward, as she was, her affection for Leon amounted to idolatry: full of romantic daring herself, she cherished his more yielding spirit, with the protecting fondness of a mother. It was an intense and beautiful feeling, to which all others were rendered subservient. This peculiar difference was often perceptible in outward expression. A word or look of unkindness, from another, and the tears of wounded feeling would steal from the drooping lashes of the sensitive boy, while Leonor's lip was curling, with eloquent scorn, and her eyes filling with the fire of an indignant spirit.

The orphans had reached their sixteenth year, when the peaceful inhabitants of — were one day alarmed by the intelligence, that a recruiting sergeant, with a file of soldiers, was within an hour's march of the village. The excitement was universal. The fond mother gazed on her boy, and clasped her hands in agony, at the fearful image, which rose to her mind. She saw those little and youthful limbs—trampled in the dust by the iron hoof of battle; the fair, soft locks were stained and dim, the laughing eyes were closed, in the sunless sleep of death! The maiden wept in the arms of her betrothed, and the young and timid wife clung wildly to her husband, trembling with terror as she heard the faint beat of a distant drum!

The crisis came at last. Every man, able to bear arms, was summoned to the sergeant's presence, there to decide, by lot, his future destiny. For the first time in her life the cheek of Leonor was blanched with fear. It was Leon's turn to play the hero then. He had never before dreamed of a separation from his sister, and now, the very thought was agony; but, for her sake, he struggled with his emotion.

"Even if I should draw the fatal lot, dear Leonor," he said, "I shall not be far from you, for, they say the General's army is encamped with two days' march of the village. I shall often obtain leave of absence, and I must not shrink from danger, love!"

He clasped her to his heart, and then, with his soft lips pressing firmly together, and his slight and fragile frame nerved to unwonted strength, by his beautiful resolve, he turned, with a steady step, towards the appointed place of meeting. The girl stood, for a moment, motionless, and then slowly followed her brother.

She reached the scene, just as Leon was opening the paper he had drawn. She marked the scarcely visible start; the dark eye drooped, the clear, brown cheek flushed and paled again, the lip quivered and was calm, and Leonor knew that hope was vain!

Among the foremost in the group, was a noble-looking youth of frank and fearless mien, who opened his paper with an eagerness, which showed that fear was stranger to his soul. This was Victor St. Cloud—the pride and boast of the village. Many a bright eye glanced eagerly at his approach, for his bold bearing and manly beauty won the admiration of all; and many a pretty lip was seen to pout with vexation at the rumor of his engagement to the young and timid Louise de l' Orme;—Louise! the orphan—the friendless and destitute! whose sad, blue eyes were seldom listed, save in prayer, and to whose soft, cloudless cheek, the rose of beauty and of joy was unknown, 'till it woke to life beneath the hallowed kiss of love!

"What a strange taste he has!" exclaimed the village belle, as she shook the dark curls from her glowing face, and gazed with a smile in her mirror, "Louise is a mere statue—so pale and cold and still! I am sure she cannot love him; she has not feeling enough!"

But let us return to Victor. He opened the paper; an exulting smile illumined his countenance, as he glanced at the contents, and he uttered an involuntary exclamation of joy. It was echoed by a piercing shriek from one among the group of women, who were awaiting the decision at a little distance, and a fair, young girl rushed wildly forward, and fell fainting at his feet! The glad smile instantly gave place to an expression of mournful tenderness; his black eyes filled with tears, and raising the lifeless Louise gently in his arms, he bore her from the scene.

The stars, that smiled that night through the untroubled heavens, serene and lovely as angelic eyes, looked down on many a scene of sorrow; for the little troop was to march, at sunrise, the next day. In one of the lowliest huts of the village dwelt a widow with her only son. The woman was infirm and poor. She looked to the unwearied exertions of the affectionate boy as their sole means of support. He was all the world to her; her life, her hope, her joy! would see her desolate and comfortless; for he too had drawn the fatal lot. They were seated together beside the low window of their room, and the youth held her thin, weak hand, fast locked in his. Silent they sat— the silence of despair; for, to them, there was no hope, not a glimpse, not the slightest chance of relief! The mother's dim eyes gazed mournfully on the face, which, for seventeen years, had been as sunshine in her darkened home.

"I shall never, never see it more!" she murmured; and closing her eyes, with a slight shudder, she leaned her head against the high back of her chair, and remained for a few moments, motionless and mute. Gradually the shadow of despair passed away from that pale face, and was succeeded by an expression of still and beautiful serenity. She rose feebly from her seat. "Let us pray! my child!" she said, "It will comfort us both!"

They knelt together, before a rude picture of the Virgin, and the young man bowed his head reverently, while his mother breathed a prayer for his safety and return.

As she rose from the performance of this pious duty, a tap was heard at the door, and a youthful stranger hastily entered the hut. He was enveloped in a cloak and cap, the dark and drooping plumes of which, effectually, shaded his face from observation. His mission was soon told. He had come to offer himself as a substitute for the widow's son.

"You," he said, turning to the latter, "must surely be loath to leave your only parent, alone and destitute: she would die if you were gone. I, alas! have none to mourn for me!—and my only hope of happiness is in what I now propose: let me go in your stead."

It will readily be imagined how thankfully the widow and her son assented to this welcome proposition. The former wept tears of joy at the unlooked for reprieve, and blessed the stranger youth, with all the fervor of a grateful heart. But he turned from their eager acknowledgments, and rapidly retraced his steps 'till he reached a lonely cottage, which he entered, and proceeding to an inner chamber, hastily closed the door.

He tossed the cap impatiently from his head, and a profusion of long, light hair fell glistening in the moonlight. A delicate hand emerged from the dark folds of the cloak, and tremblingly unfastened its clasp: as it dropped from the shoulders, a white dress and girlish form were suddenly revealed, and Louise de l' Orme, for it was she, threw herself on her lowly bed, and burying her face in her hands wept long and bitterly. She was aroused by a low voice at the open window.

"Louise!" it said, "my own Louise! I have come to bid you good bye!"

A slight smile arched the sweet lip of the maiden, as she rose and went to the casement. She laid her pale, cold cheek tenderly on the arm of her lover, listened to his passionate farewell, and received in silence his parting kiss and blessing.

"He is gone!" she murmured, as he turned reluctantly away, "and now for my preparations for the morrow:— dear, dear Victor! and can he think I would part with him thus? he does not know Louise."

Long before sunrise, the sleepless Leonor rose from her pillow, and hastily dressing went to her brother's apartment. She knocked; no answer was returned, and softly opening the door, she stole, with a noiseless step, to his bedside. How beautiful is the slumber of the innocent and young! His head was pillowed on his arm, while its brown curls, moist with the balmy dews of sleep, clung in graceful disorder to the fair and blue-veined temples. A tear was on his glowing cheek; but a smile, lovely as the light, and full of angelic tenderness, played round the gently-parted lips. With a gaze of unutterable affection, Leonor leaned over the slumbering boy, and kissed away the tear. Then kneeling by his side, she prayed for a few moments, silently, but with fervor, for that beloved being, from whom she was so soon to part, perhaps for ever. She rose relieved, awoke the sleeper, and left him to complete her preparations for his departure.

The moment of separation arrived. It was one of agony to both; but it was soon over, for there was no time for delay. A lingering kiss—a scarcely audible farewell—another last embrace! and Leonor was left alone with her sorrow, while her brother hastened to his already assembled comrades.

One alone was missing. It was the widow's son. His name was called, but no one answered the summons. It was repeated.

"His substitute is here!" replied a low, sweet voice; and a youth unknown to all, with downcast eyes and faltering step, suddenly took his station in the ranks. The tremulous tones were scarcely audible, yet Victor St. Cloud startled at the sound, and turned, with a bewildered gaze, towards the speaker. Those gentle accents strangely harmonized with the dear image, in the contemplation of which, he had just been absorbed; but the raven curl, the rosy cheek, and military attire of the young recruit were discord to the music, and the lover resumed his reverie. He saw again his own Louise, as she lay, motionless, in his last embrace: again her delicate eyelids closed beneath his kiss, the silken lashes drooped on her pale, soft cheek, and her fair hair, floated like a veil around the slight and youthful form! As the vision melted away, a sad, but indefinable foreboding stole suddenly to his heart. Once again—*but* once was that beautiful image to be realized, and then to fade forever in darkness as in death! But Victor saw not this, and he struggled, with manly resolution, against his unwonted presentiments of evil. They were soon forgotten in the novel excitement of a soldier's life.

The little troop commenced its march towards the frontiers, where Dumourier, the Republican General, with his brave Carmagnoles, was steadily opposing the progress of the Prussians and the French Royalists, under the Duke of Brunswick. Two days after they joined the main army, an engagement, near Valmy, took place between the hostile forces. In that contest, short and undecisive, as it was, the youthful Leon, though he fought with instinctive courage, experienced all the horror and disgust, with which a first scene of bloodshed must ever inspire a mind like his, naturally gentle, refined and sensitive, and hitherto devoted to peaceful and intellectual pursuits.

One fatal incident, in particular, impressed him with an abhorrence of the fearful trade of war, which not all his after efforts could control.

Towards the close of the battle, he found himself near Victor St. Cloud, the gay and gallant Victor, who had fought like an inspired hero through the day. He was, at that moment, engaged in a single and desperate combat, with a Prussian of athletic frame, who, by some accident, had disarmed, and brought him to the ground. Undaunted by his own defenseless condition and the raised and threatening sword of his powerful foe, who haughtily bade him surrender, Victor sprang to his feet; but ere he could close with his enemy, a youth, whose constant presence at his side, during the day, had before surprised him, suddenly rushed between him and the Prussian, and received, in his breast, the sword intended for Victor, sank at his feet, with the red life-stream gushing fast from the wound.

It was the same mysterious and beautiful being, who had appeared so suddenly among the ranks, on the morning of their march; and who, since then, had won the love and interest of all, by his patience, sweetness, and almost unearthly loveliness of feature and expression. Astonished at the young stranger's unaccountable devotion to himself, and maddened by the fatal result, St. Cloud sprang forward to avenge him. His fury lent him a supernatural strength; he wrenched the sword, yet warm with the blood of that innocent victim, from the hand of the foe, and laid him lifeless at his feet,—then, raising in his arms, with mournful solitude, the seemingly breathless form of the boy, he hastened from the field.

"Victor!" murmured a faint, sweet voice, he stopped abruptly. It was like the voice of Louise, yet surely it issued from the pale lips, that rested on his shoulders. "Victor!" it whispered again! Sickening with a sudden and vague, but dreadful apprehension, he sank on one knee to the ground, resting the stranger's head upon the other. "Dear Victor!" He could bear no more!

He wildly dashed off the military cap, that shaded the pale features of the youth, with it fell that dark hair, which had so effectually disguised those features, and the fair tresses of Louise de l' Orme floated like light to the ground! Speechless with agony and horror, the lover bent over the devoted girl, who now lay motionless in his arms; and long and wildly did he gaze upon the face, beautiful even in death! Once, only once, the white lids moved, the soft, blue eyes looked up to his, with a dim smile of touching and mournful tenderness; then they closed forever! Victor knew that she was dead!

For some moments he did not move; he scarcely breathed; by degrees, his face grew calm, almost rigid in its expression; his lips slowly and sternly compressed, as if closing over some desperate mental resolve. Whatever this determination may have been, he sealed it with a long, long kiss upon the forehead of his lost Louise, and rising calmly, transferred her to the arms of Leon, who had been a deeply interested witness of the scene. Victor did not speak; but as he resigned his precious burden, he pointed to the battle-field, with a wild and meaning smile, and dashed once more into the thickest of the fray.

It was night. The soldiers slumbered in their tents. The battle was over; but its dreadful sounds and sights still haunted the fevered imagination of Leon. If he closed his eyes to sleep, the wan face of the murdered Louise rose before them, and he was fain to re-open and fix them on some real and less awful object, in order to displace the unearthly vision; but he could not dispel the fearful images, which crowded upon his mind, and gradually, as his memory brooded, with an intense and uncontrollable power, over the scenes he had witnessed, as they became, more and more, terribly distinct, more painfully minute, his brain grew wild, his senses wavered, and starting from the ground, he glided out of the tent, unconscious of any definite purpose, save a vague and desperate resolution to fly from the spot; whither he knew not, cared not. On he sped, as if pursued by demon, his light step unheard, his flitting form unheeded, by the drowsy sentinel. As he passed the bodies of the slain, lying ghastly in the moonlight, the sight only served to redouble his speed, and he flew like a spirit, winged with fear, instinctively taking the road, by which he had marched, with his comrades, a few days before. We will leave the poor, crazed boy in his flight, and return to his sister.

On the afternoon of the sixth day succeeding the departure of Leon, from the village, as Leonor stood at the door of their cottage, absorbed in mournful thoughts of the absent one, her wandering glance was suddenly arrested by the figure of a soldier, running swiftly towards her. Long before he reached her, she recognized her brother, and with a cry of pleasure and surprise, hastened to meet him. Panting, breathless, almost fainting, he sank into her outstretched arms, and there the strength, which had seemed, until then, to have been upborne by some supernatural agency, suddenly failed; he was utterly exhausted from fatigue and want of food, and it was with much difficulty, that he was enabled, by his sister's assistance to reach the cottage.

Leonor was alarmed by the extreme paleness of his face, his wild, haggard expression, and still more, by his incoherent and extravagant demonstrations of rapture at being once more with her, who was his all on earth. Gradually, however, she soothed him into calmness, and persuaded him to account for his unexpected return. He told her, shuddering with renewed horror, as he did so, of the sad and agonizing scenes, which he had been compelled to see and share, and of their overwhelming effect on his excited imagination. He had fled from the tent, he said, in a state bordering upon frenzy, and as he passed the dead bodies, that strewed the battle-field, a wild fancy took possession of his heated brain; they seemed to rise up and pursue him as he flew, with their white faces and blood-stained garments, gleaming strangely in the moonlight! From that horrible moment, all consciousness had forsaken him, and he knew nothing more till he found himself in the arms of his beloved sister.

Leonor listened and wept with affectionate sympathy; but the sufferer needed food and sleep; the former was soon supplied, and after bathing his fevered brow and soothing him with her gentle caresses, she persuaded him to retire for the night. Restless, herself, she wandered from room to room, and at last, unable to control her anxiety, stole to her brother's apartment. He slept; alas! how different now his slumber from that, which she had watched over on the morning of his departure! Then he lay, blooming and beautiful, in the rosy rest of health and youth and innocence. Now, weak and worn with physical and mental exhaustion, the glow had left his cheek, the sunny smile his lips! His eyes were half unclosed, as if his rest were troubled with unwholesome dreams. His lips quivered with a convulsive effort to speak; "Ah! save me, save me, Leonor!" he cried.

"Yes, yes! I will save thee, dearest!" said the pitying girl, fondly believing that the voice he loved would soothe him even in sleep. She was right. His head sank back upon the pillow, his eyes closed, his slumber gradually grew deeper and more tranquil. Leonor bent over him, for a while, then turned to leave the room. The moon shone unclouded, and as she passed the open window, she was startled by the appearance of several men, who were evidently approaching the cottage. She caught the gleam of armor and her heart misgave her. "They are soldiers, they have come for Leon," she said to herself.

Alas! it was too true, and ere they reached the gate, she had heard enough to confirm her wildest fears. From their conversation she learned, that as soon as the fugitive was missed from the camp, they had been sent in pursuit. The words, which followed, struck on her senses with the force of a thunder-bolt.

"Poor boy!" said one, "he will pay dearly for his desertion! shot probably—some I know have been guillotined. It is a hard fate for one so young and gentle!"

"Bah!" replied another in a brutal tone, "I have no pity to waste on cowards."

With wonderful presence of mind, Leonor repressed the shriek, which had nearly burst from her lips. She withdrew hastily from the casement. She gazed around in wild despair. Was there no means of escape for the fair and innocent being, who lay before her, unconscious of his danger! Suddenly a ray of moonlight fell upon his uniform, lying in a chair by the bedside; as suddenly flashed a wild thought through the mind of that heroic girl! With a trembling hand she grasped the clothes, gave a last, fond look at the slumberer, and hurried from the room. She hastened to equip herself in the military garb; but ere she had completed her disguise, she heard an impatient knock at the door of the cottage, and the next moment, the sound of a heavy tramp in the room below. Dreading lest the noise had awakened Leon, she finished her task, and stole once more, with a throbbing heart to the open door of his chamber. He still slept calmly. She descended and stood before the soldiers.

"Is it I you seek?" she said.

"Ah, ha! my bird! Have we caught you at last!" The rough soldier seized her arm, as he spoke, as if fearful she would again escape.

"You may well call him a bird," said his comrade, gazing, compassionately, on the delicate frame of the pretended boy, "for his voice is as sweet as a nightingale's. But let us be off, we have no time to lose."

And Leonor, rejoicing in the success of her stratagem, suffered herself to be led unhesitatingly away.

The morning sun rose brightly over the tents of Dumourier's army; but it smiled on a scene of still and awful solemnity. In an open space without the camp, a file of soldiers were drawn up in a line. They were armed with muskets, and remained motionless and grave as if awaiting their own doom of death. Facing them, and about ten yards distant, was a youth bare-headed and disarmed. The reader will readily recognize the victim. It was Leonor Duhesme. Firm in her heroic self-devotion, and exalted above all fear, by lofty and generous enthusiasm, she stood, like a beautiful statue, with a face as pale as death, while her rich dark eyes, flashing with excitement, were fixed, in a steady unswerving gaze on the weapons of the band before her, loaded as she deemed with her doom; But it was not so to be.

Several officers, deeply interested by the youth, beauty and innocence of the prisoner, had petitioned for a reprieve in his favor, and Dumourier, himself, was so touched by his unresisting, yet fearless submission to the sentence, that he was easily prevailed upon to remit it. Some punishment, however, was deemed necessary, as a warning, and it was accordingly decided, that he should remain ignorant of his pardon until the last moment. In order, that he might realize, in imagination, at least, all the horrors of his doom, by hearing the discharge, which he believed would seal it, the muskets of the soldiers were loaded with blank cartridges. In the midst of the death-like silence, which prevailed for a few moments before the signal to fire was made, a faint voice, as of one exhausted, came from afar and a pale and panting figure was seen speeding, as if for life towards the spot. The next instant, the word of command was given! The soldiers levelled their muskets, fired, and Leonor stood unharmed and wondering at her safety!

Alas! the fatal report had reached another's ear less able to endure it. Leon had heard it, the gentle and tender Leon, for the toil-worn stranger was he! Already enfeebled by illness, anxiety and fatigue, the sound struck to his heart, with a blow, as sure and deadly in its effect, as if it had been itself the winged bullet of destruction! He staggered and fell to the ground! They raised him—he was dead.

Pictures from a Painter's Life[1]

IT WAS a balmy morning in the month of June. The school-bell in the little village of F—, Maine, was ringing its last warning peal, and a troop of rustic children were gathered at the porch. As the tall, gaunt master stalked through the throng, that divided hurriedly to make way for him, the frown deepened on a brow habitually stern; for he missed the fair face of one, who was too often a truant from his power. And where is he? The river-beach, about a mile distant from the school, is smiling in the light of the morning sun, and there, basking in its beams, on the warm and sparkling sand, sits a beautiful boy of seven years old.

A profusion of golden hair waves back from the fair, transparent temples, and reveals a face glowing with health and joy. His red lips are slightly parted, his blue eyes raised, and gazing with more than childish ecstasy on the changes of the light clouds, as they float in the blue air above him. In his dimpled hand he holds a slip of elderberry, with which he has been tracing figures in the sand. A ship—a hut—a tree—rudely sketched indeed, but still with a fidelity to nature, wonderful in one so young. And now he resumes his occupation with an earnestness, that proves his whole heart is in his play. We will not interrupt him; we will not tell him that the innocent and lovely little hand, which now yields him, with its skill, so pure a pleasure, is destined, to-morrow, to the torture of a ferule. We will leave him to his present enjoyment, and perhaps we may meet him again.

A large, grated apartment in the common jail at Charleston, South Carolina, is filled with prisoners. One of them is a fair, slight boy of ten years, in the graceful garb of a sailor. His cheek is pale by privation and early suffering; but in his eye, the fire and energy and truth of a high and dauntless spirit, are still unquenched. He is

---

[1] "Pictures from a Painter's Life, Frances S. Osgood, *The Ladies' Companion,* January 1841, vol. XIV, no. 1, pp. 149-150

mounted on a barrel, and has sketched, with a bit of charcoal, the image of a spread eagle, beneath which he is now scrawling—"Liberty and Independence for ever!" At the sight of this motto—strange enough on a prison-wall— a shout arises from the spectators, and the youth turns his head and smiles. It is he!—the truant of the village school. But the scene changes. He is standing at the prison door. A lovely child, the jailor's daughter, is beside him. Her dark eyes filled with tears, are raised imploringly to his. She holds towards him the keys of the jail, while she intreats him to escape ere her father's return. With a smile of mingled pride and gratitude, he replies—"No, Mary, I should involve you in disgrace, if I did, and I would rather brave again the tyranny of the cruel captain, than so repay your kindness; but fear not, dear, I shall again escape from that hated ship, and will be more cautious than before, you may be sure."

On the summit of the Caraccas mountains, stands, with bare and bleeding feet, a youthful pilgrim. There is a faint flush on his cheek, which is yet soft and fair with the innocence of childhood, and his wild, sad eyes kindle with involuntary rapture as he gazes at the scene below him. Slung over his shoulder, on a staff, is a little knapsack, containing all his worldly possessions. It is the runaway sailor boy. He has seen but little more than ten years of actual life, but his heart, in that time, has lived *an age* of misfortune and grief and endurance. He is alone in the wide, wide world—poor—wretched—friendless. Does he weep? No! He has no tears left for himself—he has shed them all on the far off grave of his parents, and his keen blue eyes are tearless, but dark with unspeakable woe. He has walked, barefoot, nearly an hundred miles, in the course of eight days—sometimes sleeping on the ground, and once or twice, sheltered in the hut of some hospitable Indian or Spaniard, whose heart his tender youth—his patient, suffering, angel-smile have melted to compassion. He is now faint with hunger and fatigue. Does his young spirit fail him? No! There is a desperate pride and power within, that will not let him yield. He almost glories in his forlorn destiny, strange and sad as it is for one so young! He lifts his resolute brow to heaven with a trust that no danger or grief can subdue, and goes calmly on his way. A traveler meets him, and touched by his beauty and desolate appearance, offers him money. The boy's heart swells within him;—with a proud smile he thanks him, and refuses. No! with all his woes, he is still independent, thank God! He has still half a real—six cents—in his pocket, and shall he, who, since the age of eight years, has earned his own livelihood—shall he receive the bounty of a stranger? He passes on with a firmer step, forgetting his weariness in his pride. He hopes to find at La Guyra, an American ship, in which he can be allowed to work his passage home—to his mother's grave! and he strains his eyes to discover, through the mist, the starry flag of his native land. But suddenly his steps are arrested—he forgets all—his grief, his hope, his pride, his poverty—in the wondrous beauty of the scene beneath him. I will describe it in his own words, written, years afterwards, to a friend.

"A storm had been gradually brewing over the ruins of Caraccas, which lay at the foot of the mountain. The huge dense clouds gathered and rolled along the valley, 'till the place where I stood seemed but an island in mid-ocean. The birds flew wildly about. The creeping things hastened to their holes in the earth—the moan of the winds was hushed, and an awful silence spread over the rocky eminence. But the mist beneath, with its continual and ever-lovely changes in color and in shape, who would have dreamed, that the fierce tempest was brooding in the bosom of so much beauty? Yet so it was. Even the sun-born rainbows, smiling with their soft bloom through the shifting and darkening vapors—even they—evanescent and exquisitely beautiful as they were, seemed but bridges raised for the demon spirits of the storm to pass from cloud to cloud, directing as they went, the dread thunderbolt on its errand of destruction. The lurid fire shone even in the sunlight, and striking a little below the pinnacle, on which I stood, hurled from its bed a massive rock, which, in descending the steep and rugged side, forced every thing before it, while hill to hill re-echoed the fearful sound long after it had reached the valley below. A more sublimely beautiful, yet terrific scene, could hardly be imagined; my soul swelled within me, and I was half frantic with delight, as I stood above the clouds and the storm, in the sunshine, and alone! It was a strange balm to my wounded and desolate heart, to feel that what to others of my fellow beings wore a gloomy and threatening aspect, to *me,* assumed a glory brilliant and gorgeous beyond description. But alas! the vision faded! the clouds were borne away upon the western wind, and I resumed my journey down the side of the mountain."

Gentle reader, let the author's wand—namely, his pen—transport you for a moment to a scene in London. One of the royal family is receiving, in his gorgeous saloon, the élite of English society. The Ducal palace is brilliantly illuminated. At the moment we raise the veil, the noble host courteously addresses a guest, in whom he seems particularly interested. It is a young, self-taught, American artist, whose pencil, employed for some of the noblest and loveliest in the land, has gained him a celebrity, which his genius and his inexhaustible energy richly deserve. A slight but elegant frame, evidently spirit-worn—a pale, intellectual face—eyes beaming with the beauty of an ardent soul—a forehead singularly fair and pure—a well-formed head, slightly, and rather proudly thrown back—a calm and graceful address. Can this be the poor and wretched sailor-boy, who stood, twelve years ago, with his little knapsack, alone, on the heights of Caraccas? Look at the white throat, the curved lip, with its sweet, yet half-disdainful smile; it is the same! He is happy now. Sought and caressed by the noble, the fair and the wise; loving and beloved by one, to whom his smile is dearer than the light of heaven. Is he quite happy? His restless ambition is still unsatisfied. He is nothing if he be not first; and he must still toil for preeminence.

Reader! do you care to know his present whereabout? More than twenty years have rolled by, since he was a happy truant from the village-school. But they have not chilled his heart, or weakened his spirit, or subdued his enthusiastic love of his profession. He has returned to his native land, prosperity and fame attending his steps, and his rooms are daily thronged with the lovely and gifted, of one of the principal cities in the union.

The Waltz and the Wager[1]

CHAPTER I.

"WE ARE quite ready, papa," said Georgiana Melton, as she entered her father's library, with her sister Caroline. "Do let us go this very minute—I am so impatient!"

"I see you are, my love, and therefore you will be good enough to sit quietly down, 'till I have finished my paper."

Georgiana bit her beautiful lips, and threw herself on a sofa opposite a large mirror, while Caroline smilingly stopped to caress an Italian greyhound, which had sprung from the hearth when she entered.

While the three are thus occupied—Georgy with herself, Carry with her dog, and their fond father ever and anon feeding his paternal vanity, by a shy peep over the edges of his paper, we, my dear reader, will, with your permission, take the same liberty, with the sincere, but scarcely reasonable hope, that you may experience as much pleasure in the survey, as did Sir Richard Melton.

No wonder the frown gradually cleared away from the polished brow of Georgiana! No wonder her superb, hazel eyes are so proudly lighted up, as she gazes a the reflection, in the mirror, of her brilliant and aristocratic beauty. She cannot be more than nineteen years of age; yet there is perfect majesty in her mien, and in the noble contour of her form and feature, as she lies with her small head thrown haughtily back, her white throat curved, and her fair round arms folded gracefully before her. Her dress is of rich white satin, fitting closely to her beautiful bust, and reaching nearly to the throat, where it is terminated by a row of swan's down. The satin falls, which drape her dimpled elbow, are trimmed in the same chaste and simple manner: but look! As she moves, the sudden flash of diamonds from amid the rich softness of the down betrays, that simplicity alone cannot satisfy the regal taste

---

[1] "The Waltz and the Wager," Frances S. Osgood, *The Ladies' Companion*, April 1841, vol. XIV, no. 4, pp. 254-256

of the wearer. She is evidently fond of those "stars of the darkling mine."

They girdle her waist; they are wreathed on her snowy arm; they gleam like chain lightening amid the braids of the dark brown hair, which is parted smoothly from her white veined temples, and plaited behind. Her head is exquisitely formed, her forehead is fair and broad, her eyes are eloquent with the beauty of a proud and generous soul. The bloom on her cheek is the richest hue of health and youth and hope, and the expression of her arched and glowing mouth is inimitably spirited, yet sweet as a newborn rose. Altogether, Georgiana Melton is about as radiant a creature as ever thought fit to illumine this sad, cold world of ours. And now for the fairy Caroline. Poor Carry! by the side of her brilliant and stately sister she is like the lily of the valley in the shade of magnificent magnolia. Her form—what there is of it—is pretty and light; but her hands and feet are so small, that people wonder what they are good for. Nevertheless, she is very lovely, and very graceful, and though her timid beauty, overspread as it is, by the more striking charms of Georgiana, is seldom noticed, yet the extreme delicacy of her complexion—the profusion of her silken ringlets, that fall in a shower of light on her shoulders—her dimpled cheek, rosy mouth, and melting blue eyes, looking so bewitchingly bashful beneath those drooping lashes—all these, combined with an air of the most perfect child-like innocence and purity, may well render the little petted Carry, what a friend of mine emphatically called her, "a charm!" She too, is dressed in white; but her dress is muslin, of the simplest fashion, and wholly unadorned. Carry is just sixteen and just "coming out".

But see! They are preparing to go. Sir George is putting down his paper, Georgiana is wrapping a magnificent shawl around her queenly form, and Carry is tying her cloak. They pass through a line of liveried servants—they enter the carriage—they are gone to an evening party at Lady C—'s. Let us go too, dear reader. We have no invitation it is true—*n' importe*—Lady C— is, by far, too luxuriously indolent to trouble her graceful head about us. She will only raise, in languid wonder, her large, soft, dreamy eyes, and be glad of an excuse to arch still more her already beautifully curved eyebrows. So then, here we

are, and just in time to hear the announcement of Sir
George and the Misses Melton, and to see the eager gaze of
admiration which follows the first appearance, this
season, of the beautiful heiress, Georgiana. "Remember,
love, no waltzing!" whispered Sir George, as he led them
forward. "Remember, love, no waltzing!" was echoed in a
low, playful tone, on the other side, and, turning,
Georgiana met the dark and earnest eyes of her betrothed
lover, Vincent Lorraine. She had deemed him far distant,
and could not wholly repress the smile and blush of
delighted surprise, that stole to her cheek at the sound.
But she averted her face to conceal them, for she was
provoked at his presumption, as she haughtily deemed it,
in daring thus to dictate to her. "He knows," she said to
herself, "that I have never waltzed, even with him; indeed,
he never presumed to ask it; but he shall learn that his
commands are not to be my law; and papa, too! what
could induce them both to force me into an alternative so
very disagreeable? not that I see any great harm in
waltzing, except that a man's arm round one's waist must
be a bore."

During these very reasonable cogitations of his docile
daughter, Sir George led the ladies to a sofa, and left them
in charge of Lorraine. "I could never," said the latter to
Carry, as he took his seat beside them, wholly
unconscious of the wayward mood into which Georgiana
had wrought herself, "I am sure I could never respect a
woman who would submit to the familiarity necessary in
that voluptuous dance."

"Miss Melton," said the young and graceful Duke of B—
—, bowing low to Georgiana, "I hardly dare ask the honor
of your hand for the next waltz." Georgiana smiled
encouragingly. "Will you indeed be so gracious?" offering
his arm. Georgiana rose and accepted it. The Duke looked
surprised and vexed, while Caroline raised her eyes
imploringly to her sister's face.

"*Georgy!*" she whispered, "you *will* not waltz after what
papa and Vincent have said?"

"Papa and Mr. Lorraine do not know me!" and she cast
a glance of playful, but slightly scornful defiance at her
lover. She was rather startled, and very much provoked at
the look he gave her in return. It haunted her through the
waltz, and though she had never looked so brilliantly

beautiful, and never danced with such bewitching grace, the smile on her lip was a falsehood, for her heart was ill at ease.

We must now explain the evident disappointment betrayed by the Duke of B—, when Georgiana accepted his proposal to waltz. On his way to the mansion of Lady C—, with a band of gay companions, he had rashly laid a wager of considerable amount, that only one unmarried woman in the room would refuse to waltz with him, and that to that woman, whoever she might be, he would propose before the end of the season. Georgiana Melton was in his mind's or rather his heart's eye, when he made the bet. A passionate admirer of beauty in all its forms, he had borne her radiant image away from many a festive scene, and worshipped it in solitude and silence.

He had heard, with a species of exultation, a few evenings previous, her dignified refusal to waltz with the most distinguished individual in the room and he had thought how well the ducal coronet would grace a brow so noble and so pure. Gay, profuse, and seemingly thoughtless as he was, he had nursed in secret a noble refinement of soul, which rendered him fastidious, even in trifles, and he could not forgive Miss Melton her evident eagerness to join in a dance he disapproved, although her favored partner was himself. He was vexed with her for failing to reach the standard of perfection he had raised in his own mind, and when the dance was done, he turned away with a sigh, that told of blighted hope.

Georgiana mistook that sigh for one of love; for she had often marked his earnest gaze of admiration, and, in spite of her long cherished affection for Lorraine, her young heart fluttered at the thought of the brilliant conquest she had made.

As the Duke left her, her cousin approached. Her eyes fell beneath his, and her very temples flushed with the agitation of her heart. He seemed about to speak as he took her trembling hand; but suddenly letting it fall again, without a word, he hurried by and left the room. Georgiana smiled as her fancy pictured an interesting reconciliation, which she intended should take place in her boudoir, the next morning, at farthest.

CHAPTER II.

"I have lost my wager," whispered the young Duke to his friend, Lord N—, "and what is worse, I have lost the loveliest woman in England,"

"Pardon me, my friend," said Lord N—. "You have lost neither your bet nor your bride."

"How! Have I not waltzed with every unmarried woman in the room? (Thank Heaven there are not many!) and is not Miss Melton the star of the season?"

"Do you see that delicate creature at her side?" replied his friend.

"Who can see any thing where *she* is, but herself? Ha! but she *is* beautiful! who is she? do you know her? I hope she don't waltz. I dread to ask her, lest those sweet lips should simper "yes." I shall detest that word in future." And ere Lord N— could reply, the Duke was requesting from Georgiana an introduction to her sister.

Caroline's eyelids drooped, and a soft blush warmed her delicate cheek, when he hesitatingly requested her to join the waltzers. He almost trembled for her answer. It was simply, "No, your grace!" and the young nobleman thought he had never heard a voice so thrillingly sweet before. "Will you not indeed?" he involuntarily exclaimed. "I am so happy to hear it."

Caroline opened her blue eyes wide with wonder, and Georgiana grew stately; but they soon forgot the seeming rudeness of the remark, in the delight which his eloquent conversation inspired, and the generous heart of our heroine exulted at the impression which her "fairy pet," (as she fondly called her sister,) had evidently made.

"I am sure you have bewitched him, sweet!" said Miss Melton to Caroline, the next day, while talking over the ball, "and what a charming little Duchess you will be!" she continued, fondly twining her jeweled fingers in the ringlets of her sister, as the latter closed her tell-tale eyes on her shoulder. "But haste! That was Vincent's knock—I am sure it was!" and she stooped and kissed Carry's fair brow, to conceal the emotion which glowed in her eloquent face.

"What an enchanting picture!" exclaimed the Duke of G—, as he entered the room at the moment.

Georgiana started in disappointment, and Caroline in blushing delight, at the voice. And where was Vincent Lorraine?

The servant answered her heart's unuttered question, by handing her a letter, with which, making a scarcely audible excuse, she hurried from the room.

CHAPTER III.

One bright afternoon in September, about four years subsequent to the date of the incidents related in the preceding chapter, a luxurious boudoir in Belgrave Square, was occupied by two ladies, both young, and one almost child-like in her appearance. The form of the latter was of fairy-like proportions, with the roundness and grace of a Hebe. She might have personated that goddess in face as well as figure; for her deep blue eyes were full of joy and love; her mouth had the fresh and dewy red of a ripe, but unplucked cherry—her cheek was bright with tender bloom, and countless curls of a rich, golden hue, clustered softly round its dimpled beauty, and enhanced the bewitching sweetness of its expression. Young as she was, she was evidently a mother, for a lovely, sportive infant lay in her arms, and a miniature of herself, a tiny girl, between two and three years of age, stood at the knee of the other lady, turning over the gilded leaves of an annual.

It would be difficult to describe the singular beauty of the face, which was bent towards the child; the large hazel eyes were filled with a wild and passionate melancholy. The cheek was perfectly colorless, yet so transparent, that any unusual emotion would instantly reveal itself there, illumining that spiritual paleness with a brilliant glow, momentary indeed, but exquisitely delicate. The hair was glossy, and intensely black, lying in rich masses on either side of the face, and braided loosely behind. The eyelashes were long, of the same jettish hue, contrasting strangely with the tintless purity of her complexion. The grace and majesty of her form were finely developed by her rich but simple dress. It was a black velvet, sweeping in ample folds below her feet, and wholly without ornament, excepting a frill o black lace at the throat. She was seated in a deep crimson chair, over the arm of which, hung a super Indian shawl, bright with the gorgeous colors of the eastern loom.

"Oh! isn't that a pretty picture, aunt?" exclaimed the little prattler at her knee, and the lady stooped still lower, until her pale cheek touched the round and rosy one of the child.

The door opened, and two young men entered the room, one of them saying, as he did so, "I have brought you an old friend, Caroline, whom I am sure you will be happy to see, and you also, Georgiana."

While the youthful Duchess sprang eagerly forward to welcome the stranger, the dark-haired lady languidly raised her eyes; but they fell again instantly, and the color mounted to her brow, when she met the earnest and admiring gaze of the Duke's companion.

"Miss Melton," said the deep and musical voice of Vincent Lorraine, while his lip quivered with emotion, "this is indeed a happiness I did not dare to hope; but after a four years' absence from all I love best upon earth, you will not surely refuse to welcome me home again."

Georgiana threw back her stately head; but she could not repress the glowing smile of joy, which lighted up her beautiful face, as she replied, "*My* welcome can be of but little importance to Mr. Lorraine; but it is freely given, nevertheless." And she frankly held out her hand.

"I wish you success, most heartily, my dear fellow!" said the Duke, as he and Lorraine were riding through Hyde Park a few days afterwards, "but I must candidly tell you that you have but little chance with 'the statue,' as she is called, by all her male acquaintances. She has refused all who ever overcame their awe of her, sufficiently to propose, and seems determined to keep herself to herself, with all her beauty of mind and person. To tell you the truth, I was quite astonished at her condescending to shake hands with you the other day. It is a liberty which no one else would presume to take with her. In truth, she has odd ideas about some things, which I cannot account for. In my opinion, she is over-fastidious, if a woman can be so. No, no, though she is the light of *our* household, she will never grace another, I fear; I should say, I *hope*, for what would Carry and the children—what should I do without her? With the exception of my own little wife, she is the purest minded, and most disinterested woman I ever knew."

The reader may account, although the Duke could not, for the smile which grew brighter and brighter on the countenance of Lorraine during the foregoing speech, and for the exulting tone in which, at its close, he exclaimed, "She is mine if there be truth in woman!"

"What *can* you mean, and where are you going, Lorraine?"

But the youth was out of sight ere the sentence was finished, and the wondering Duke pursued his way alone.

"Will you never, never forbid me to waltz again?" asked Georgiana, playfully, as her restored lover implored her consent to their immediate union.

"Never, never, my precious!"

"And will you never run away again for four long years at a time, truant?"

"Death only shall part us, my own!"

"And I may waltz when I choose?"

"Yes, love!"

"And with whom I choose?"

"Yes, yes, yes!"

"There, then!" (and she gave him her hand,) "this day twelvemonth, it is yours for ever."

Poor Lorraine pleaded, but in vain, for an earlier day.

"No! dear Vincent," said Georgiana, seriously, "if you are going to repent a *second* time, I choose it should be before our marriage; it would be rather inconvenient afterwards."

"What has animated our statue?" asked her sister, entering at the moment. "I have not seen such a smile, nor such a blush on her face these four years."

May Evelyn[1]

BEAUTIFUL, BEWITCHING May! How shall I describe her? As the fanciful village-poet, her devoted adorer, declared;—"The pencil that would paint her charms should be made of sunbeams and dipped in the dewy heart of a fresh moss-rose." Whether this same bundle of beams and fragrant rose-dew would have done full justice to her eloquent loveliness, I cannot pretend to say—having never attempted the use of any brush less earthly than are made of hog's bristles, nor any color more refined than a preparation from cochineal. Her eyes were "blue as Heaven," the heaven of midsummer—when its warm, intense and glorious hue seems deepening as you gaze, and laughing in the joyous light of day.

Her hair, I could never guess its true color; it was always floating in such exquisite disorder over her happy face and round white shoulders—now glistening, glowing in the sunshine, like wreaths of glossy gold, and now, in shadow, bathing her graceful neck with soft brown waves, that looked like silken floss, changing forever and lovely in each change. Blushes and dimples played hide and seek on her face. Her lip—her rich sweet lip was slightly curved—just enough to show that there was pride as well as love in her heart. She was, indeed, a spirited creature. Her form was of fairy molding, but perfect though "petite!" and her motions graceful as those of the Alpine chamois.

Reader, if I have failed in my attempt to convey to you an image of youthful grace, beauty and sweetness, I pray you repair my deficiency from the stores of your own lively imagination, and fancy our dear May Evelyn the loveliest girl in the universe.

And now for her history. Her father, of an ancient and noble family, had married, in early life, a beautiful but extravagant woman, who died a few years after their union, leaving him with two lovely children and an all but exhausted fortune. On her death he retired from the gay

---

[1] May Evelyn, Frances S. Osgood, *Graham's Magazine*, March 1842, vol. XX, no. 3, pp. 145-149

world, and settled with his infant treasures in Wales, and there, husbanding his scanty means, he contrived to live in comfort if not in luxury. There, too, brooding over the changes of human life—the fallacy of human foresight, and the fickleness of human friendship, he became "a sadder and a wiser man." His two beautiful children, Lionel and May, were the idols of his heart, and well did they repay his love.

May's first serious trouble arose from hearing her father express one day his desire to purchase for Lionel a commission in the army. The boy was high-spirited and intelligent, and had cherished from childhood an ardent desire for military life; but there was no possibility of raising sufficient money for the purpose, without sacrificing many of their daily comforts.

At this time May was just sixteen; but there was in her face a childlike purity and innocence, which, combined with her playful simplicity of manner, made her appear even younger than she was. She hated study, except in the volume of nature; there indeed she was an apt and willing pupil. Birds and streams and flowers were her favorite books; but though little versed in the lore of her father's well-stored library—she had undoubted genius, and whenever she did apply herself, could learn with wonderful rapidity.

The only science, however, in which she was a proficient, was music:—for this she had an excellent ear and, when a mere child, ere her father's removal to Wales, had been under the tuition of a celebrated master. Her voice was rich, sweet and powerful, and her execution on the guitar, piano and harp, was at once brilliant and expressive. She had, also, a pretty talent for versifying, and often composed music for words, which, if not remarkable for power or polish, were certainly bewitching when sung by their youthful authoress.

During most of the day, on the morning of which Mr. Evelyn first mentioned his wishes with regard to Lionel, the sunny face of our heroine was clouded with sorrowful thought; but towards evening, as her father sat alone in his library, the door suddenly opened, and May, bounding in, her eyes beaming with enthusiasm, exclaimed—"Papa! papa! I have just thought—I know what I'll do!—I'll be a governess." Her father gazed at her in astonishment.

"A governess, May! What can have put such an idea into your head? Why should you be a governess!"

"Oh! for Lionel, you know. I can soon earn enough to buy his commission."

"And it is this then, my child," said Mr. Evelyn, tenderly, "that has so repressed your usual spirits!" But while he spoke seriously, he could scarcely repress a smile at the thought of the wild, childlike being before him, transformed into a staid, dignified teacher.

During the six weeks following, the devoted girl deprived herself of all her usual outdoor amusements, and, with wonderful energy applied, under her father's guidance, to study. At the end of that time, she laughingly declared that she knew a little of everything; but still her passion for birds and flowers was far greater than for books.

Ere the six weeks had well expired, she heard from some young friends, who were on a visit to Wales, from London, that the earl of — was in want of a governess for his four children. She begged them, on their return, to mention her. This they did, and with youthful exaggeration extolled her talents to the skies.

The Earl understanding that she was the accomplished and amiable daughter of an aged naval officer, saw, in his mind's eye, a learned lady of a certain age, who would, perhaps, prove a mother in kindness and usefulness to his orphan children, and gladly acceded to the desire of his young friends, that he should make trial of her.

The poor things were not aware what a little ignoramus they were recommending; for the youthful Lionel, who, sometimes took a peep into the library, and stared in surprise at the various apparatus for study, had boasted all over the village in which they resided, that his sister knew everything under the sun, and had mentioned, in corroboration of this sweeping declaration, that she was always poring over French, Spanish, Greek or Latin books. This, her enthusiastic young friends, who, by the way, had only known her a fortnight, took care to make the most of—and the result was, that May was considered, by the Earl, as a most fitting instructress for his children, and dreaded by them as a prim and severe restraint upon their hitherto unchecked amusements.

CHAPTER II.

It was the morning of the day on which the dreaded governess was expected, Julia, Elizabeth, Georgiana and William—the first 15, the second 10, the third 8, and the fourth 7 years of age, were at play in the garden of the Earl's country seat. They had heard awful things of governesses from some of their young companions, and the younger children had been whispering to each other their dread of the expected tyrant.

They had, however, resumed their gambols, and forgotten the matter, with that charming versatility which makes them so interesting, when their nurse appeared with the news that the governess had arrived, and was waiting to be introduced to her young charge in the school-room. A sudden change was observable on the countenances of all. It was amusing to watch the expression on each of those young faces. Julia—the pensive and graceful Julia sighed, and bent her soft eyes sadly on the ground, as she instantly turned her steps towards the house. The little willful and spirited Willie began to strut manfully backward and forward, declaring that the others might do as they liked, but that he would not go near the ugly old woman. Georgy pouted—and Lizzie burst into tears. At the sound of weeping, Julia turned back—soothed and cheered them all by turns— kissed away the tears of one sister—smoothed the other's frowning brow with her soft and loving hand, and laughed at Willie till he was fain to join in the laugh in spite of himself. She then desired them to follow her to the school-room—which they did—clinging to her dress, however, as if they expected to see a monster in the shape of a governess; but as they reached the flight of steps which led from the lawn to the house, their courage failed, and, leaving Julia to ascend alone, they suddenly and simultaneously turned to escape, and hurrying away, concealed themselves in the garden, where they soon resumed their sports.

In the meantime Julia had ascended the steps and stood gazing in silent astonishment through the glass door opening into the school-room. The object of her dread was there—but not as she had pictured her—a prim, severe old-maid. A girl apparently younger than herself, with a sweet glowing face, shaded by a profusion of lovely hair,— her straw bonnet flung on the floor, and her simple white dress looking anything but old-maidish—was stooping to caress their favorite dog, Carlo, while the pet-parrot sat perched on her shoulder, mingling his gorgeous plumage with her light brown curls, and crying with all his might, "old-maid governess! old-maid governess!" As our heroine raised her head, wondering at the strange salutation, (which, by the way, master Willie had been maliciously teaching him for some time previous,) her eyes encountered those of the smiling Julia, who, equally surprised and delighted at the scene, already saw, in Miss Evelyn, a friend after her own heart, such an one as she had long ardently desired.

At this critical moment, the good old nurse entered from the lawn, and seeing the mutual embarrassment of the parties, said simply to May—This is your oldest pupil, madam." At the words "madam" and "pupil," both May and Julia tried hard to repress the smiles which would peep through their eyes and lips—in vain. The dimples on the cheek of the youthful governess grew deeper and deeper—Julia's dark eyes flashed through their drooping fringes more and more brightly, and, at length, the smothered merriment burst irresistibly forth. No sooner had the latter's eye caught the arch glance and her ear the musical laugh of May, than she sprang forward to clasp her readily extended hand, exclaiming, "I am sure you will be my friend!"

"That I will," said May, "if you won't call me 'old-maid governess' again."

"Old-maid governess, old-maid governess," screamed the parrot from his cage.

May began to look grave, and Julia, blushing with vexation, led her gently to the cage, outside of the door, and pointed to the bird in silence. "How stupid I was!" exclaimed May; "I quite forgot the parrot when I saw that beautiful dog. I do so love dogs—don't you?"

"Yes! but I love you better," said Julia, affectionately, throwing her arm around her new friend's neck, and sealing her avowal with a kiss.

At this moment, Willie was seen peeping and stealing slyly round the shrubbery—his roguish face subdued to as demure a look as it could possibly assume. For a moment he stared at the pair in amazement, and then clapping his hands, he shouted,

"Georgy! Lizzie! Georgy! come and see Julia kissing the governess!"

"Oh! you lovely boy!" exclaimed May—bounding down the steps, "I must have a kiss!" and away she flew after the little rosy rogue—he laughing so heartily as to impede his progress, till at last helpless, from very glee, he fell into her arms, and allowed her to kiss him half a dozen times before he remembered that she was the teacher so dreaded by them all. When he did recollect, he looked up half incredulously in her face.

"You are not old!" said he,—"no, nor yet prim, nor cross. I don't think you are so very ugly either, and maybe you don't know much after all. I say, governess, if you please, ma'am, can you spin a top?"

"No!" said May.

"Hurrah! I thought so—hurrah, Georgy! she don't know so much as I do now—hurrah! hurrah! I'll stand by her for one!" and, tossing his hat in the air, he sprang into the lap of May, who had sank into a low rustic seat, quite exhausted from her exercise—her cheeks glowing—her hair in disorder, and her lips parted with smiling delight.

By this time the two little girls, who had been peeping a long while, ventured, followed by Julia, to approach;—Georgiana leading, or rather dragging the shy but lovely little Lizzie in one hand, and holding in the other a freshly gathered rose-bud, which she timidly presented to our heroine, as if to bribe her not to be harsh with them. May stooped to kiss the intelligent face whose dark and eloquent eyes looked so pleadingly into hers; while Julia, who stood behind her, stole the rose from her hand. "Let me wreathe it in your hair," she said.

At that moment, while she was yet engaged in her graceful task, the Earl suddenly appeared before them. It must be remembered that he had seen, from his library window, the before-mentioned chase, and rather curious to know who the beautiful visitor could be, (not having been apprised of Miss Evelyn's arrival,) he had followed them to the spot on which they were now assembled—May on the seat, parting the dark curls from Lizzie's bashful and downcast brow; Willie on her knee; Georgy gazing up in her face, and Julia placing the rose-bud in her hair. All started at the sudden appearance of the Earl. Willie sprang to his arms, and little Lizzie, afraid of every new comer, laid her curly head on the knee of her newly found friend, and turned up her bright eyes inquiringly to her father's face.

"Do not let me disturb your play, my children," said the Earl. "I only come to remind you, that your governess will soon be here, and that you must welcome her with respect and attention. But, Julia, you must introduce me to this merry young friend of yours, who runs as if her heart were in her feet;" and so saying, he playfully patted the drooping head of the blushing and embarrassed girl, who, all this while, had been striving to hide her fears and her confusion by pretending to be deeply occupied in twisting Lizzie's silken ringlets round her little taper finger. The moment she had heard Willie exclaim, "papa!" all her former dread of that awful personage returned, and, with it, for the first time, a full sense of her own inefficiency to perform the task she had undertaken. His voice so deep and yet so sweet and playful, banished half her dread, but only increased her confusion.

Julia, however, came instantly to her relief, with a tact and delicacy uncommon in one so young—saying simply and seriously, "This is our governess, papa. Miss Evelyn, this is our dear papa."

The Earl started back,—tried to repress his smiles, bowed low to conceal them, and then taking her hand respectfully in his, bade her welcome to the castle.

The word "governess" had acted like a spell upon May's faculties; it restored her to a sense of the dignity of her situation, and rising instantly and drawing her beautiful form to its full height, she received and returned the compliments of the Earl with a graceful dignity and self-possession, that astonished him, as much as it awed the poor children. And when, in his courteous reply, he begged her pardon for his mistake, in a tone at once gentle and deferential, she found courage, for the first time, to raise her eyes. It was no stern, old, pompous nobleman, such as her fears had portrayed, who stood before her, but an elegant man, in the prime of life, with a noble figure and singularly handsome face, full of genius and feeling.

His dark eyes were bent upon her with a gaze of mingled curiosity and admiration; but, as they met hers, he recollected himself, and wishing her and his children good morning, and resigning Willie, as if it were a thing of course, to her arms, (a circumstance, by the way, which he could not help smiling at half an hour afterwards,) he passed on and left them.

And now came innumerable questions from all but the silent Georgy, who contented herself with nestling close to the side of our heroine as they wandered through the grounds—and gazing with her large soft eyes into her face, now dimpled with the light of mirth, now softening into tenderness, and now shadowed by a passing thought of "papa, and Lionel, and home."

"And oh!" said Lizzie, "you won't take away my doll and make me study all the time, will you?"

"No, indeed, darling! I would much rather help you dress your doll."

"And I may spin my top all day if I like—may I not?" asked Willie.

"Yes, if papa is willing."

"Oh! but papa told us to obey all your commands."

"Commands," thought May, "oh, dear, I shall never do for a governess!"

The day passed on in sport. Our heroine's duties were to commence on the next; but she would not allow her fears for the morrow to interfere with her present delight. In the meantime, the Earl, amid his important duties, was haunted all day by one bewitching image;—a fair sweet face glanced brightly up from every book he opened, from every paper to which he referred; and, in his dreams that night, he led to the altar a second bride, more lovely, more beloved than the first.

CHAPTER III.

Early the next morning, as May sat teaching Willie to read, with a demure face, through which the rebel dimples would peep in spite of her assumed dignity; while Julia, with a look equally demure, was bending over an Italian book; Georgy drawing, and Lizzie hemming a wee bit 'kerchief for her doll—the Earl entered the school-room from the lawn.

Unseen, he paused at the open door to contemplate the lovely *tableaux* within;—the governess in her pretty girlish morning dress, with her long ringlets shadowing half her face and neck, as she bent over the boy, pointing out to him the word;—Willie by her side—one hand holding the book, the other his top, kicking the chair impatiently—first with one foot, then with the other, and looking round every minute to see what his sisters were doing;—Georgy smiling as she drew; Lizzie sitting upright in her little chair, with a doll almost as large as herself on her lap, ever and anon trying the 'kerchief round its neck to see the effect; and the simple, modest Julia, looking even older than May, with her dark hair smoothly parted—raising at times her eyes with looks of loving sympathy to those of the youthful teacher.

It was indeed a sunny scene; but the silence was broken by the voice of Georgy requesting assistance in her drawing. The young governess rose, and taking her offered pencil, retouched the sketch in a few places, at the same time giving the child directions how to finish it. Suddenly the pencil trembled in her hand,—the sweet low voice stopped—went on——faltered—ceased again, and May burst into tears! The Earl had stolen behind them to watch the progress of the drawing. May had felt, rather than heard, his approach,—and confused by his presence, half suspecting her own deficiency in the art, yet afraid to discontinue her directions at once, her face suffused with blushes, she tried in vain to proceed. Little Lizzie saw her tears, and springing from her seat, climbed a chair to caress her, exclaiming, "Don't cry! papa won't hurt you! Papa loves you dearly—don't you, papa?"

Here was a situation! It was now the Earl's turn to color; but the artless and innocent May, who had as yet known only a father's and a brother's love, did not dream of any other in the present case; on the contrary, she was soothed by the affectionate assurances of the child, and, smiling through her tears, looked up confidingly in the Earl's face. Charmed with the childlike sweetness of her expression he could not resist taking her hand, with almost paternal tenderness, in his, while May, reassured by the gentleness of his manner, ventured to acknowledge her own ignorance, and to request his assistance in the sketch before them. This, to the delight of all, he willingly consented to give, and when, at two o'clock, the nurse came to take the children to dinner, she found May seated alone at the table, intent on a newly commenced drawing—the Earl leaning over her chair and instructing her in its progress—Julia singing "Love's Young Dream," and the three children gone no one knew where.

The next day, and the next, the Earl was still to be found in the school-room, sometimes spinning Willie's top, sometimes reading an Italian author aloud to his daughter and her governess—often sharing the book with the latter, and oftener still, blending his rich and manly voice with hers as she sang to the harp or piano. One day a visitor asked Willie how he liked his new governess? "Oh!" said the boy, "*papa* is governess now. May is only our sister, and we are all so happy!"

Thus passed a year—Julia and May daily improving under their indulgent and unwearied teacher—and imparting in their turn instruction to the younger branches of the family. May had confided to Julia all her little history. She had written often to her father, and had received many letters in return. From one of them she learned, to her great joy and surprise, that Lionel had received his commission from some unknown friend. At the same time, her father advised her, as she had engaged for a year, to be contented until the expiration of it. "Contented!"

The last day of the year had arrived—May had lately been so happy that she had forgotten to think of being separated from the family she loved so much.

On the morning of the day, the Earl was in his library, Julia making tea, and May on a low ottoman at his feet, reading aloud the morning paper. Suddenly she paused, dropped the paper, and covered her face with her hands. The Earl, alarmed, bent tenderly over her, and Julia was by her side in a moment.

"What is it, dear May?" she said.

"Oh, the paper—look at the paper, Julia!"

The Earl caught it up—"Where—tell me where to look, May?"

"At the date—the date!"

"The date—it is the first of June—and what then?"

"Oh! did I not come the first of June and must I not go to-morrow? I am sure I shall never do for a governess!" and she hid her face on Julia's shoulder, and wept afresh.

The Earl raised her gently—"Perhaps not; but you will do for something else, sweet May!"

"For what?" she asked earnestly—half wondering whether he could mean housekeeper!

"Come into the garden with me, dear, dear May, and I will tell you," he whispered in her ear.

At once the whole truth flashed upon her heart.

"She loved—she was beloved!" She was no longer a child—that moment transformed her; and shrinking instantly from his embrace and blushing till her very temples glowed again—she said in a low and timid voice, "I think I had better go home to-morrow—perhaps to-day: my father will expect me."

"Julia," said the Earl, "run into the garden, love, and see to Willie—he is in mischief, I dare say." His daughter was out of sight in a moment. May stood shrinking and trembling, but unable to move. The Earl gazed, with a feeling bordering upon reverence, at the young girl, as she stood alone in her innocence. He drew slowly towards her—hesitated—again approached, and taking her hand with respectful tenderness, he said—"You know that I love you, May—how fondly—how fervently—time must show for language cannot:—will you—*say* you will be mine—with your father's consent, dear May—or say that I may hope!"

Her whole soul was in her eyes as she raised them slowly to his and dropped them instantly again beneath his ardent gaze. "But—papa!" she murmured.

"We will all go together, and ask 'papa,' dearest; and now for a turn in the garden. You will not refuse now, love?" And May Evelyn, blushing and smiling, took his offered arm, wondering what "dear papa and Lionel" would say to all this.

It was a lovely evening in the early part of June, that, while Mr. Evelyn sat dozing in his arm chair and dreaming of his absent children, a light form stole over the threshold, and when he awoke, his gray hair was mingled with the glistening locks of his own beautiful and beloved May—his head resting on her shoulder, and her kiss warm upon his cheek!

"My Lord," said May, demurely, as she entered, with her father, the drawing-room in which the Earl awaited them—"papa is very glad that I have given *satisfaction*;—he thinks your visit a proof of it—although he could hardly have expected so much from his little ignoramus, as he will persist in calling me."

"My dear sir," said the Earl, cordially pressing the offered hand of his host, "she has given so much satisfaction, that I wish, with your consent, to retain her as governess for life, not for my children, but myself."

The reader has already foreseen the conclusion. Mr. Evelyn's consent was obtained;—Lionel was sent for to be present at the wedding;—the ceremony was quietly performed in the little church of the village;—and for many succeeding seasons in London, the graceful and elegant wife of the Earl of — was "the observed of all observers," "the cynosure of neighboring eyes."

Waste Paper;
or
"Trifles Light as Air"[1]

"GOOD BYE, Vivian, don't fall in love till you see Miss Walton. God bless you, my dear boy!" And Vivian Russell shook his kind uncle warmly by the hand and sprung into the stage coach, which was waiting for him at the gate. "All right!" said the guard—the bluff coachman smacked his whip, and away they sped along the road to London.

They will not fly so fast, but that you and I, sweet reader, can overtake them when we list, though the swift steeds of Fancy must be harnessed for the purpose. So please you, then, we will follow them anon. In the meantime, sit you down by my side on this sunny bank, opposite the gate, where Vivian's uncle still stands and gazes after the fast receding vehicle, and I will tell you all I know about him. You had time to see, ere he took his seat in the coach, that he was a tall, nobly formed youth, possessing, in an eminent degree, what the French call, "*Un air distingué.*"

You could not but notice the thin silky intellectual looking curls, which waved on his classical head, (don't laugh at the word "intellectual!") Think a moment! Is there not expression even in hair? Does not thick, bushy, *stubby* hair, especially if it curl, give you an idea of dullness, sensuality and want of refinement? If it doesn't, my precious reader, take my word for it, you don't see with your "mind's eye," or at any rate, with my mind's eye. Did you observe his eyes? They are black, brilliant and expressive, full of that great rarity, in this whig and tory world, soul. His complexion is glowing and slightly brown by exposure. There is a dimple in his chin, his nose is just like that of the Apollo Belvidere, and his forehead, how shall I describe its beauty? broad, white, spiritual,

---

[1] "Waste Paper; or 'Trifles Light as Air,'" Frances S. Osgood, *Graham's Magazine*, September 1842, vol. XXI, no. 3, pp. 146-150

beaming with thought, I cannot do it justice. There is the least perceptible curl on his beautiful lip; but you cannot see it when he smiles; for his smile is tenderness itself. In his manly bearing too, there is, perhaps, a dash of aristocratic haughtiness, at first, but it soon wears away upon acquaintance. The difficulty is to become acquainted with him; I defy a dull or a vulgar person to do it.

The cheerful, healthy looking old gentleman, who is just turning front the gate towards that white house among the trees, is, as I told you, his uncle. Vivian's parents died during his childhood, and left him to this uncle's care. He has just returned from abroad, come of age,—taken possession of his paternal estates,—left the old gentleman to look after it, in his absence, and gone for the first time to pass a month or two amid the gaieties of the metropolis. And now let us after him with what speed we may.

See! there is my friend, Fancy; just in time! descending in her opal chariot, drawn by a score of peacocks, which fly or creep, as the wayward goddess wills. Her rainbow scarf flutters in the air, her wild blue eyes sparkle with excitement, as she beckons us towards her. Give me your hand, sweet reader! so, one bound, and we are safe by her side; and now we too are on our road to London, and our vehicle glances like a meteor through the air. Since then we are so comfortably on route, let me just explain my motive for having been, as some will think, unnecessarily minute in my description of our hero.

It was because I wished my young lady readers,—for whom this story is especially intended, to be interested in him, and I thought the surest way of making them so, was to let them trace, in his person as well as mind, a remarkable resemblance to some favored acquaintance of their own. Have I succeeded? Mary, Caroline, Julia, Isabel! Is he not the "perfect *image*" of—you know who? There— don't blush, dear! I won't tell. "*Revenons à nos moutons.*" Hey day! what have we here? A traveling chariot broken down in the road! Our friend Vivian bearing a lady in his arms towards the neighboring inn, which the stage coach has already reached! An old gentleman, probably her father, staring and hurrying after them as fast as the gout will let him, and the servants, postilions &e., busy in untackling the horses and righting the injured vehicle. We won't stop to inquire the cause of the accident. Fancy will tell us that at her leisure. Let us enter the inn.

CHAPTER II

"My dear Margaret, are you well enough to proceed?" said the old gentleman to his daughter.

"Oh! yes—papa!—quite well—" and she rose to tie her bonnet. "But papa!"—Margaret hesitated and blushed—"well, child! What now?" "Don't you think before we go, we should thank the young man, who so politely assisted me?"

"Fudge! we shall have time enough to thank him,—we must go in the same coach. I can't stay here all night to have the chariot repaired. Come, child!"

They took their seats in the coach; Vivian entered after them and found himself opposite the dark-eyed girl, who had been thrown from the chariot, fortunately without injury, and whom he had carried half fainting to the inn. By her side was her father, and by Vivian's side, a spruce and fidgety youth, a would-be exquisite, daintily arrayed as that peculiar race are wont to be.

The refreshed horses galloped steadily forward; the first mile-stone was passed; and poor Margaret's graceful neck really began to ache,—she had looked so long out of the opposite window, to avoid Vivian's earnest, though half furtive gaze. So she calmly drew from her pocket a suspicious looking twist of a *billet*, and, drooping her dark lashes, began gravely and assiduously to tear it into small bits, placing them carefully in a bag which hung upon her arm.

And now Vivian could indulge his passionate fondness for the beautiful to his heart's content; for the old gentleman was fast asleep, and Margaret only once raised her eyes, and, meeting his, dropped them again to her work, while a swift, bright blush stole up for a moment to her cheek, and left it pale as before. Her countenance was singularly beautiful. It was not dark, but there was a soft, mellow, sunny tone all over it, which, with her glossy, raven braids, rosy mouths, and long black lashes, produced a strangely rich effect. She wore a dark and very elegant traveling habit fitting closely to her beautiful bust;

while a bonnet of ruby velvet formed a striking contrast with her deep, bright eyes and almost colorless cheek.

As she continued her employment, drawing from her pocket and disposing of note after note, Vivian could not but watch and admire the wonderful play of expression on the lip, brow and cheek before him.

It seemed to him, that he could trace, on that ever changing and ever eloquent countenance, the shadow of each succeeding thought, as it passed from her mind. Its prevailing expression was that of endearing tenderness and sweetness; but ever and anon,—a sudden arching of the lovely lip, a starry gleam of dimples on the cheek, and a momentary flash of irrepressible merriment through the fringing lashes of the half raised hazel eyes, betrayed that mirth was making holiday in her heart. But why? And to whom was that sportive glance directed? Not to Vivian, alas! but to the stranger at his side; and though he had never seen the lady before—had not been introduced, and was ignorant even of her name, a pang of jealousy shot like an icicle through his heart, at the thought. But when he turned to look upon the object of the fair girl's evident enjoyment—he too smiled involuntarily. Nearly all the scraps of paper, that escaped from the slight fingers of Margaret, had alighted on the precious habiliments of the bean, who, when Vivian turned, was busily employed in brushing them off, with a look of solemn distress, that was irresistibly ludicrous. Alas for the dandy! His was an endless task. He had no sooner succeeded in disengaging the intruders from one part of his dress, than they flew to another, and at last dared to settle even in those shining and scented locks, which he had taken off his hat to display. This was too much. He put up both his hands. He shook himself. He tried to look up to his own hair! As a last resource, he contrived to raise his enormous mouth and blow upwards into his curls! Imagine, reader, that long and stupid face, in the awkward position I have described! The head 'bent, the almost white eyebrows elevated, the chin depressed, the under lip protruded and the lugubrious looking youth puffing with all his might! It was all in vain, and growing desperate, the hapless dandy meekly leaned towards Vivian, and said—"May I trouble *you*, sir?" Our hero returned his imploring look with one of petrifying *hauteur*.——"Did you address yourself to me, sir?"

"Yes, sir!—I—I—would you be so good, sir, as to—to—"

"Well,—sir?"

"In short, sir, will you have the goodness to release my hair from the white favors, with which the young lady opposite has been so kind as to honor me."

Vivian bowed low and replied with equal solemnity, "Sir, I beg to inform you, that I have never been so thoroughly initiated into the mysteries of a barber's vocation, as to do justice to your hyacinthine ringlets." So saying, the haughty youth turned once more to gaze at his lovely *vis-à-vis*.

She was looking very demure, pursing her pretty mouth, and quietly bending her dark eyes upon the paper, which, she took care, should no longer annoy her fellow traveler. Vivian gazed at her with mingled surprise and admiration. What could be the meaning of her strange occupation? He would not condescend to feel inquisitive; yet he could not help fancying it was some clandestine correspondence, which she was ashamed to have known, but with which she could not bear to part altogether. When once this idea had taken possession of his mind, he could not dismiss it, and he was just working himself up into a most unreasonable fit of anger with his unconscious and unoffending companion, when, to his dismay, the coach stopped at the Saracen, Head in London, and he was obliged to bid the lady a reluctant good-morning, without a hope of ever seeing her again.

The truth is, he was desperately in love for the first time in his life, and a thousand times did he lament his carelessness, in not having endeavored to discover her name and residence in town. All the information he could gather from her conversation with her father was, that they were hurrying home from the country in expectation of a visit from a friend.

The first fortnight after his arrival was spent in vain inquiries among his friends about the fair engrosser of his thoughts. As he was ignorant of her name, he could of course obtain no information with regard to her.

One morning, at breakfast, he received a letter from his uncle; but before I apprise my reader of its contents, I must state a fact which has hitherto been forgotten, namely, that one object of our hero's journey had been to fulfill an engagement, which his uncle had made for him, to pass a few weeks in the neighborhood of London, at Walton Hall, the residence of an old friend of his father's, whom he had never seen. He had half promised his uncle that he would give but three days to the novelties of the metropolis, previous to the promised visit. The following is an extract from the old gentleman's letter.

"My dear boy, I have just received a letter from my old friend Walton, in which he expresses his surprise that you have not yet made your appearance at Walton Hall. I am anxious and disappointed at this, for I have been fancying you already deeply in love with my pet Maggie, and indeed I dreamed last night that I saw you together," etc., etc.

One of Vivian's virtues was decision, and another was energy. Without the latter, the first would be almost valueless. Ere two hours had elapsed, he was seated in the drawing-room at Walton Hall, awaiting the appearance of its owner. He recalled, with some misgivings, the contents of his uncle's letter. "He has set his heart upon my marriage with Miss Walton, and I have set mine upon this bewitching unknown. My poor, kind uncle! I regret his disappointment. I dare say Miss Margaret is a very nice, well-behaved young person, but my affections are irrevocably devoted to another, and it can never be!" Just as he came to this sublime conclusion, he heard a far off voice, the very first tone of which he could not help loving, it was so sweet, so rich, and seemed so fresh from the heart. It was warbling snatches of a simple ballad, one only sentence of which he could distinctly hear; but that sentence he never forgot—

One only she loved, and forever!
    She wore an invisible chain
That Pride wildly struggled to sever;
    And daily more deep grew the pain!
    "Ah, vain," she would sigh, "each endeavor!"
    And Echo still answered "in vain!"

And as the voice sang, it came nearer and nearer, and did not cease till the singer, a beautiful girl, tripping gaily into the room, beheld and, blushing deeply, curtsied to our hero. Could he believe his eyes? "It is—it is—"

"Miss Walton," said the lady, finishing the sentence for him, and recovering instantly her self-possession.

"You wish to see my father? I will send him to you immediately;" and she glided from the room, leaving poor Vivian in doubt whether he were dreaming or awake. If awake, then were the half-dreaded Miss Walton and the lovely unknown of the stagecoach one and the same person! And he had wasted a whole precious fortnight, that he might have passed in her society! Well, he would make the most of his present visit at any rate; and so thinking, he made his best to bow to Mr. Walton, who now entered, and who, most cordially shaking hands with him, welcomed him to Walton Hall, as the son of his oldest and dearest friend.

"When you sent up your card," continued he, "I little thought that I should find in Vivian Russell the youth who so kindly assisted my daughter when our chariot was overturned. I regret that we did not know you then; but we must make up for lost time. Your uncle promised me a long visit from you, and I trust you have come to fulfill the promise." After a short conversation, Vivian agreed to return in time for breakfast the next day, and remain for several weeks.

CHAPTER III.

"Down, Vivian, down!" exclaimed Margaret Walton, as she entered the breakfast room, from the lawn, and gracefully welcomed Mr. Vivian Russell to the Hall. The dog had been named and presented to her father, by our hero's uncle, a short time before; and Vivian thought he had never known the music of his own name, till now, when pronounced by that sweet and playful voice. Margaret seemed to him lovelier than ever, in her plain white robe, her color heightened by exercise, and a few wild flowers, carelessly wound into the soft braids of her hair.

"Papa is a late riser, Mr. Russell, and we must wait breakfast for him; but he will soon be down now—" as she spoke, she seated herself, and began, with an arch, sidelong glance at Vivian, who could not repress a smile—

yes! actually began, to tear in pieces another of those tormenting little notes!

"Hum!" said Vivian to himself, "the clandestine correspondence goes swimmingly on, it seems. I will think of her no more."

"Think of her no more!" He thought of nothing else all that day and the next and the next; and each day with a more fervent and impassioned devotion! She was so mild, yet so noble!—so tenderly beautiful! he half worshiped her already. And yet those papers. He detested deceit from his soul. Falsehood, equivocation, deception of any kind, from a child he had been too proud to stoop to them; and here he was, irretrievably in love with one who had evidently something wrong to conceal.

One day, the servant brought her a note—"From Sir George Elwyn, Miss."

A smile dimpled her cheek as she read, and then it shared the fate of many that had gone before it, and the bits were preserved as usual in the little basket by her side. "This then," thought Vivian, "is the secret! This Sir George, confound him! is the lover—the beloved!"

And for three whole days after this wise conclusion did our hero sulk in silent misery; and for three whole days did the wondering Margaret weep, when alone, for his waywardness, and, when in his presence, laugh more gaily than ever, or curl her sweet lip, in maiden pride, at his moody replies to her attempts at conversation.

The third day was the sabbath, and as they walked home from church, a fine-looking young man passed on horseback, and bowed, with an air of "empressement," to Miss Walton and her father. "He's a confounded handsome fellow! don't you think so, Vivian?" said Mr. Walton.

"Who, sir?" said Vivian with an abstracted air.

"The young man, who just passed, Sir George Elwyn. He is to dine with us, to-day."

Vivian started at the name and gazed earnestly at Margaret, who, of course, blushed as was her wont. That blush decided him.

"I was right!" he exclaimed internally, and making a hurried excuse to leave them, he hastened by a shorter path to the house—wrote a note, in which, disclaiming dissimulation, he only begged his kind host to forgive his abrupt departure from the Hall, left it on his dressing-table, mounted his horse, and galloped back to town, thinking himself the most miserable fellow in existence.

CHAPTER IV.

"What the deuce!" exclaimed Mr. Walton, as he read the farewell *billet* of our hero—"Margaret,"—and he suddenly looked enlightened on the subject—"I hope *you* are not the cause of this!"

"*I*, sir! I the cause?" replied the conscious girl, with a very demure look of surprise—"What have *I* done?"

Her father could not well say *what* she had done, so he said nothing; but he looked annoyed and sorry, and he found fault with the dinner.

That night Vivian Russell had a strange, and, as he thought, a very provoking dream. He thought he was toiling over brake and brier, in pursuit of Margaret's paper basket, which hovered like a "will o' the wisp" before him, and enticed him into all sorts of dangers, up hill and down, through hog and stream, till at last, when, on the top of a high mountain, he thought it just within his grasp, an angel-face gleamed for a moment from a low cloud close by, and a white arm, reaching out, snatched the treasure from his outstretched hand, and vanished with it from his sight!

For a week afterwards, our hero, wretched and restless, tried hard to forget the maiden and her folly, as he chose to term it; but her image would not leave him. Sleeping or waking, he saw her destroying, to conceal yet preserve, the *billet-doux* of the happy and handsome Sir George Elwyn.

"What a shameful waste of time!" he exclaimed one day in a sudden fit of virtuous indignation. "To be sure, she does a great deal else: She writes, reads, draws, sews for the poor, &c., &c.; but then many a moment, which might be more profitably employed, is squandered in this preposterous occupation, which she really seems to make a business of."

"What a shameful waste of time!" whispered conscience in return. "To be sure you ride, lounge, sleep, eat, &c. &c., but then many a moment, which might be more profitably employed, is squandered in these preposterous reveries, which you really seem to make a business of."

In one of his daily rides, Vivian felt himself irresistibly impelled towards the Hall, and after wandering for sometime within sight of the house, in the vain hope of catching a glimpse of its fair inhabitant, he strolled without any definite object into the village.

As he approached a low cottage, he saw a form, which he could not mistake, entering the door, followed by a footman. The door closed after them; but the window was open, and Vivian glanced in. It *was* Margaret! She was in the act of taking a pillow from the hand of her attendant. "See!" she said to the poor woman of the cottage, who was lying on a bed, looking very ill, "I have brought you another pillow. I hope it will ease your poor shoulders; it is softer than the last, for I tore the papers, with which it is stuffed, much finer;" and tenderly raising the invalid, she placed the pillow beneath her.

"The papers, with which it is stuffed! and this, then, is their destination! and Sir George's note is in the old woman's pillow! And I called it a waste of time!"

Vivian was half wild with joy and surprise. He staid to hear no more, but flew rather than walked back to the Hall, and contrived to make his peace with Mr. Walton, and accept an invitation for dinner, before the unconscious Margaret had returned from her errand of benevolence. As he saw her approach from the window, he hurried out to meet her, his face glowing with the joyous excitement of his discovery, and, hastily drawing her arm through his, exclaimed,—"I am so happy! It is all right! I was quite mistaken; I'm so happy!"

When she first recognized him, Margaret's beautiful features lighted up, for a moment, with irrepressible joy; but the glow faded as she recalled the discourteous manner of his departure, and though she did not withdraw the arm he had taken, she received his protestations of happiness at their meeting, with a quiet dignity and reserve, which amply punished our impetuous lover for his fault. But though she would not deign to inquire in what he was mistaken, by degrees the reserve wore off beneath the genial and irresistible influence of Vivian's frank and joyous demeanor, and for the rest of the day she allowed herself to be as happy as her heart bade her.

As our hero sat by her work-table after tea, a sudden thought came into his head. "I will see if my writing will share the fate of others," said he to himself. And scribbling, upon some paper, the verse he had heard her sing on his first visit—beginning with, "One only I love and forever," be cut it into small pieces and placed it on the table before her, at the same time laughingly pointing to the fatal basket. Margaret began to join the pieces, succeeded in the first line, colored, smiled as she read, and making a playful feint of putting them in the basket, threw them at last, with would-be carelessness,' into a book, which lay open on the table.

Vivian's heart beat high! and higher still, when, gently taking his pencil from his hand, she wrote on a card, and cut to pieces, the following lines, which after much puzzling he placed correctly together. "I sincerely congratulate the 'one only.' He or she, whichever it may be, will be happy certainly in the *invariable* devotion you display."

Vivian bit his lip at the word "invariable;" for he remembered his fit of ill-humor. But he did not despair, he wrote again, as follows,—

Nay! If this heart's devotion changes,
    'Tis only as the needle turns,
With trembling truth, howe'er it ranges,
    To where the pole-star beams and burns:
Star of my life! howe'er I flee,
    So Fate has linked *my* love to thee!

Margaret seemed to become suddenly sensible that this at least was a clandestine correspondence; for blushing again more deeply than before, she rose and left the room, with the paper still in her hand. She did not return that evening, and our hero began to fear that his half playful, half in earnest declaration had offended her. They met at breakfast, however, and save a slight additional shade of reserve, her manner was the same as usual.

Vivian knew not what to think. He pined to be relieved, but he would not, without further encouragement, hazard another and more formal declaration.

Awaking from his reverie, he found himself alone in the breakfast-room, turning, unconsciously, the key of

Margaret's work-box. Suddenly a little secret door sprung open at his accidental touch, and there, on a tiny shelf, lay a paper with "Vivian," written on the outside, in a delicate female hand! Bewildered with love and hope, he opened it ere he thought of the dishonor of so doing, and found—(yes! it was no dream and he was the happiest of the happy!)—the very bits of paper, which he had laid before her the night previous, and which she had thrown so carelessly into a book! Forgetting, in his passionate delight, the impropriety, the indelicacy of allowing her to know that her secret was betrayed, he hurriedly penciled on a card—"Dearest Margaret; by a blessed accident, I have discovered the secret shelf—its contents are a token to me that you have rightly construed my earnest devotion of word and manner. Dare I imagine it also a token that you approve that devotion? Tell me, sweet Margaret, say but one word, but let that word he 'yes,' and I am yours only and forever, Vivian."

He placed it on the shelf, hastily closed the little door, and left the-house; after meeting Mr. Walton on the stairs, and promising to call the next day.

CHAPTER. V.

Vivian was punctual to his appointment; but Miss Walton received him with a cold and quiet dignity, for which he could not account. Her cheek was flushed, and she looked as if she had been weeping bitterly. She was slowly tearing a note. As soon as she had finished, she touched the spring of the secret door, and, taking from the shelf the unfortunate card, deliberately tore it into atoms, and placed the bits in the basket. Vivian gazed upon her in mingled astonishment and despair.

"Won't they hurt the poor woman's head?" asked he, attempting to smile.

"Not so much as they have hurt my heart," replied Margaret in a low tone, and rising as she spoke, she was gone before he had time to reply. He resolved to ask an explanation, and simply writing, "How have I offended you?"—he again used the secret shelf as a repository for his thoughts.

The next day he called again. The box was still on the table, but the little door, the shelf, the note, had vanished, and only a hollow space disfigured our heroine's beautiful India work-box. It seemed she was determined to have no secret correspondence, either with him or any one else. Vivian thought himself alone, and, leaning his head on the box, sighed deeply. His sigh was echoed, and, looking up, he caught Margaret's eyes bent mournfully upon him—blushing she turned away. He sprung up, caught her hand, drew her gently to the sofa, and pointing to the box, looked imploringly, but silently, in her face.

"Oh!" she said, in a faltering voice, "how could you so humble me in my own eyes, as to let me know that you had discovered the only secret I ever had in my life?"

A sudden light flashed upon Vivian's mind!

"Was that it, dearest Margaret? It was wrong, it was indelicate; but I did not think of it then, I was so happy, and Heaven knows I have suffered enough for my fault! Forgive me! you *will* forgive me?"

"I have already forgiven you, Vivian."

"But that is not enough; you must do more than forgive, you must love me, dear one!" he murmured, drawing her tenderly towards him.

"Must I?" said Margaret playfully; "Well, then, if I must, I must! I have always been a pattern of obedience—have I not, papa?" and Mr. Walton entering, as she spoke, the happy but embarrassed girl escaped from Vivian's ardent thanks, and flew to her chamber, to recall his every look and tone, and to live over again in fancy the joy of that delightful interview.

An hour afterwards, he joined her in her walk, and gave her the whole history of his love, his suspiciousness and his jealousy.

"And so, Mr. Vivian Russell," said the lady, when he had concluded, "those harmless atoms of paper have been the cause of all this misunderstanding and estrangement. Truly, indeed, said the bard that,

> "*Trifles light as air*
> Are, to the jealous, confirmation strong
> As proofs of holy writ."

Truth[1]

"This above all—to thine own self be true!
And it must follow, as the night the day,
Thou canst not then be false to any man."

CHAPTER I.

A Mother's Influence.

"MOTHER! MOTHER!" exclaimed a sweet, eager voice, and the speaker, a child of thirteen years burst into the room, where Mrs. Carlton sat at work, "don't you think there is to be a prize given on exhibition day for the best composition! And I mean to try for it—sha'nt I?"

She was a little, harum-scarum looking imp! I suppose she had run all the way home from school, for her straw bonnet hung on her neck instead of her head, and a profusion of soft dark hair was streaming in such disorder about her glowing face, that you could not tell if she were pretty or not; but you could see a pair of brilliant, gray or blue or black eyes—they certainly changed their color with every new emotion; but I think they were really gray—full of laughter, and love beaming through the truant tresses, and all eloquent with the beauty of a fresh, warm soul. This change in the child's eyes is no freak of a foolish fancy; for every one noticed it; and her school-crony, Kate Sumner, used to declare, that when Harriet was angry they were black; gray when she was thoughtful; violet when sad; and when happy and loving, they changed to the tenderest blue.

Mrs. Carlton drew the little girl toward her, and smoothed back the rebellious curls, at the same time exclaiming, with a long drawn sigh, "My *dear* Harriet! how you *do* look!"

---

[1] "Truth," Frances S. Osgood, *Graham's Magazine*, December 1842, vol. XXI, no. 6, pp. 316-319

"Oh, mother! it's not the least matter how *I* look! If I were only a beauty, now, like Angelina Burton, I would keep my hair as smooth as–as *any* thing; but I wouldn't rub my cheeks though, as she does always, just before she goes into a room where there's company—would *you*, mother?"

The mother gazed at her child's expressive face, as she spoke, with its irregular, yet lovely features, the strange, bright eyes, the changing cheek, the full and sweet, but spirited mouth, and said to herself, "Whatever you may think, my darling, I would not change your simple, innocent, childlike unconsciousness, for all Angelina's beauty, spoiled as it is by vanity and affectation."

"But, mother, do give me a subject for composition, for I want to write it now, this minute!"

"Harriet," said Mrs. Carlton quietly, "go and brush your hair, change your shoes, and mend that rent in your dress as neatly as you can."

Harriet half pouted; but she met her mother's tranquil eye; the pout changed to a good-humored smile, and kissing her affectionately, she bounded off to do her bidding.

While she is gone, you would like—would you not, dear reader?—to ask a few questions about her. I can guess what they are, and will answer them, to the best of my knowledge.

Mrs. Carlton is a widow, with a moderate fortune, and a handsome house in Tremont street, Boston. She has been a star in fashionable life, but since the loss of her husband, whom she tenderly loved, she has retired from the gay world, and devoted herself to her child—a wild, frank, happy, generous and impetuous creature, with half a dozen glaring faults, and one rare virtue which nobly redeemed them all. That virtue, patient reader, you must find out for yourself. Perhaps you will catch a glimpse of it in

CHAPTER II.

Aunt Eloise.

Harriet was busy with her composition, when her aunt, who was on a visit to Mrs. Carlton, entered the room. Aunt Eloise was a weak minded and weak hearted lady of a very uncertain age—unhappily gifted with more sensibility than sense. She really had a deal of feeling—for herself—and an almost inexhaustible shower of tears, varied occasionally by hysterics and fainting-fits, whenever any pressing exigency in the fate of her friends demanded self-possession, energy, or immediate assistance. If, too, there happened, as there will sometimes, in all households, to be an urgent necessity for instant exertion by any member of the family, such as sewing, watching with an invalid, shopping with a country cousin, poor Aunt Eloise was invariably and most unfortunately seized with a sudden toothache, headache, pain in the side, strange feelings, dreadful nervousness, or some trouble of the kind, which quite precluded the propriety of asking her aid.

Every morning at breakfast Aunt Eloise edified the family with a wonderful dream, which the break-fast-bell had interrupted, and every evening she grew sentimental over the reminiscences which the twilight hour awakened. It was then that innumerable shades of former admirers arose. Some doubted if they had ever been *more* than shades; but Aunt Eloise certainly knew best about that, and who had a right to deny, that Mr. Smith had knelt to her for pity; that Colonel Green had vowed eternal adoration; and that Lawyer Lynx had laid his heart, his hand, and his fees, which were not quite a fortune, at her feet?

Aunt Eloise had been—at least she hinted so—a beauty and a blue, in her day; and, to maintain both characters, she rouged, wore false ringlets, and scribbled love-verses, which she had a bad habit of leaving, by accident, between the leaves of books in every frequented room of the house.

She thought and avowed herself extravagantly fond of her niece, during her early childhood, and imagined that she displayed a graceful enthusiasm in exclaiming, every now and then, in her presence, and in that of others, "Oh! you angel child! I do think she is the sweetest creature! Come here and kiss me, you beauty!" &c. &c. But no one ever saw Aunt Eloise taking care of the child, attending to its little wants, or doing any thing for its benefit. The only tangible proof of her affection for her niece, was in the shape of bonbons and candy, which she was in the habit of bringing home from her frequent walks in Tremont street. Harriet regularly handed these forbidden luxuries to her mother, and Mrs. Carlton as regularly threw them in the fire.

"Isn't it a pity to waste such nice things, mother? Why not give them to some poor child in the street?" asked the little girl one day, as she watched, with longing eyes, a paper full of the tempting poison, which her mother was quietly emptying into the grate.

Mrs. Carlton did not disdain to reason with her child—.

"That would be *worse* than wasted, dear. It would be cruel to give to another what I refuse to you on account of its unwholesomeness."

But Harriet had now been for a long time out of the spinster's books—as the saying is—and this misfortune occurred as follows—

One morning, when she was about six years old, the child came into her mother's room from her aunt's, where she had been alternately pelted, scolded, and teased, till she was weary, and, seating herself in a corner, remained for some time absorbed in thought. She had been reading to her mother that morning, and one sentence, of which she had asked an explanation, had made a deep impression upon her. It was this—"God sends us trials and troubles to strengthen and purify our hearts." She now sat in her corner, without speaking or stirring, until her mother's voice startled her from her reverie.

"Of what are you now thinking, Harriet?"

"Mother, did God send Aunt Eloise to strengthen and purify my heart?"

"What do you mean, my child?"

"Why, the book says he sends trials for that, and she is the greatest trial *I* have, you know."

The indignant maiden was just entering the room as this dialogue began, and hearing her own name, she had stopped, unseen, to listen. Speechless with rage, she returned to her chamber, and was never heard to call Harriet an angel child again.

But we have wasted more words on the fair Eloise's follies than they deserve. Let us return to Harriet's all-important composition.

The maiden-lady, selfish and indolent as she was, took it into her head sometimes to be exceedingly inquisitive; and officious too, particularly where she thought her literary talents could come into play. She walked up to Harriet and looked over her shoulder.

"What's this, hey? oh! a story! That's right, Harriet, I am glad to see you taking to literary pursuits. Come, child! give me the pen and I will improve that sentence for you."

"Thank you, aunt! but I don't want it improved."

"Not want it improved! There's vanity!"

"Indeed, aunt, I am not vain about it, and I would like you to help me, if it were not to be shown as mine. It wouldn't be fair, you know, to pass off another's as my own. I am writing for a prize."

"For a prize! So much the more reason that you should be assisted. There, dear, run away to your play and I will write it all for you. You'll be sure to win the prize."

With every word thus uttered, Harriet's eyes had grown larger and darker, and at the close, she turned them, full of astonishment, from her aunt's face to her mother's. Reassured by the expression of the latter, she replied,

"But, Aunt Eloise, that would be a falsehood, you know."

"A falsehood, miss!" cried the maiden, sharply, "It is a very common thing, I assure you!"

"But not the less false for being common, Eloise," said Mrs. Carlton; "pray let Harriet have her own way about it. It would be far better to lose the prize, than to gain it thus dishonestly."

Aunt Eloise, as usual, secretly determined to have *her* own way; but she said no more then, and Harriet pursued her employment without further interruption.

CHAPTER III.

The Prize.

The exhibition day had arrived. Harriet had finished her story several days before, and read it to her mother. It was a simple, graceful, childlike effusion, with less of pretension and ornament, and more of spirit and originality than the compositions of most children of the same age contain.

Mrs. Carlton seemed much pleased; but Aunt Eloise had criticized it without mercy. At the same time she was observed to smile frequently with a cunning, sly, triumphant expression, peculiar to herself—an expression which she always wore when she had a secret, and secrets she had, in abundance—a new one almost every day— trivial, petty secrets, which no one cared about but herself; but which *she* guarded as jealously as if they had been apples of gold.

The exhibition day had arrived.

"Goodbye, mother; goodbye, aunty," said Harriet, glancing for a moment into the breakfast-room.

She was looking very pretty in a simple, tasteful dress, made for the occasion. She held the story in her hand, neatly enclosed in an envelope, and her eyes were full of hope—the cloudless hope of childhood.

"Don't be surprised, Harriet," said her aunt, "at any thing that may happen to-day. Only be thankful if the prize is yours, that's all."

"If Kate Sumner don't win it, I do *hope* I shall!" replied the eager child, and away she tripped to school.

At twelve o'clock Mrs. Carlton and her sister took their seats among the audience, in the exhibition room. The usual exercises were completed, and it only remained for the compositions to be read aloud by the teacher.

The first was a sentimental essay upon Friendship. Mr. Wentworth, the teacher, looked first surprised, then amused, then vexed as he read, while a gaily and fashionably dressed lady, who occupied a conspicuous place in the assembly, was observed to toss her head and fan herself with a very complacent air, while she met, with a nod, the conscious eyes of a fair and beautiful, but haughty looking girl of fifteen seated among the pupils.

"By Angelina Burton," said the teacher, as he concluded, and laying it aside without further comment, he took up the next—"Lines to a Favorite Tree," by Catherine Sumner."

It was short and simple, and ran as follows—

> Thy leaves' lightest murmur,
>   Oh! beautiful tree!
> Each bend of thy branches,
>   The stately, the free,
> Each wild, wavy whisper,
>   Is music to me.
>
> I gaze thro' thy labyrinth,
>   Golden and green,
> Where the light loves to linger,
>   In glory serene,
> Far up, till yon heaven-blue
>   Trembles between.
>
> I shut out the city,
>   Its sight and its sound,
> And away, far away,
>   For the forest I'm bound,
> For the noble old forest,
>   Which ages have crowned!
>
> I lean on its moss banks,
>   I stoop o'er its rills,
> I see, thro' its vistas.
>   The vapor-wreathed hills,
> And my soul with a gush
>   Of wild happiness fills:
>
> I pine for the freshness,
>   The freedom, the health,
> Which Nature can give me—
>   My soul's dearest wealth
> Is wasted in cities;
>   Where only, by stealth,

> The mountain-born breezes
>   Can fitfully play,
> Where we steal but a glimpse
>   Of this glorious day,
> And but by the calendar,
>   Learn it is May.
>
> But away with repining,
>   I'll study, from thee,
> A lesson of patience,
>   Oh! noble, old tree!
> Mid dark walls imprisoned,
>   Thou droop'st not like me;
>
> But strivest forever,
>   Still up, strong and brave,
> 'Till in Heaven's pure sunshine,
>   Thy free branches wave!
> Oh! thus may *I* meet it,
>   No longer a slave!

The next was a story, and Harriet Carlton's eyes and cheeks changed color as she listened. It was the same, yet not the same! The incidents were hers, the sentiment more novel-like, and many a flowery and highly wrought sentence had been introduced, which she had never heard before.

She sat speechless with wonder, indignation, and dismay, and though several other inferior compositions were read, she was so absorbed in reverie, that she heard no more until she was startled by Mr. Wentworth's voice calling her by name. She looked up. In his hand was the prize—a richly chased, golden pencil-case, suspended to a chain of the same material. The sound, the sight recalled her bewildered faculties, and ere she reached the desk, she had formed a resolution, which, however, it required all her native strength of soul to put in practice.

"Miss Carlton, the prize is yours!" and the teacher leaned forward to throw the chain around her neck. The child drew back—

"No, sir," she said in a low, but firm and distinct voice, looking up bravely in his face, "I did not write the story you have read."

"Not write it!" exclaimed Mr. Wentworth, "Why, then, does it bear your name? Am I to understand, Miss Carlton, that you have asked another's assistance in your composition, and that you now repent the deception?"

Poor Harriet! this was too much! Her dark eyes first flashed, and then filled with tears; her lip trembled with emotion, and she paused a moment, as if disdaining a reply to this unmerited charge.

A slight and sneering laugh from the beauty aroused her, and she answered, respectfully but firmly, "The story, I did write, was in that envelop yesterday. Some one has changed it without my knowledge. It was not so good as that you have read; so I must not take the prize."

There was a murmur of applause through the assembly, and the teacher bent upon the blushing girl a look of approval, which amply repaid her for all the embarrassment she had suffered.

Aunt Eloise took advantage of the momentary excitement to steal unobserved from the room. Harriet took her seat, and Miss Angelina Burton was next called up. The portly matron leaned smilingly forward; and the graceful, little beauty, already affecting the airs of a fine lady, sauntered up to the desk and languidly reached out her hand for the prize.

"I cannot say much for your taste in selection, Miss Burton. I do not admire your author's sentiments. The next time you wish to make an extract, you must allow me to choose for you. There are better things than this, even in the trashy magazine from which you have copied it."

And with this severe, but justly merited reproof of the imposition that had been practiced, he handed the young lady, not the prize, which she expected, but the MS. essay on Friendship, which she had copied, word for word, from an old magazine.

The portly lady turned very red, and the beauty, bursting into tears of anger and mortification, returned to her seat discomfited.

"Miss Catherine Sumner," resumed the teacher, with a benign smile, to a plain, yet noble-looking girl, who came forward as he spoke, "I believe there can be no mistake about *your* little effusion. I feel great pleasure in presenting you the reward, due, not only to your mental cultivation, but to the goodness of your heart. What! do *you*, too, hesitate?"

"Will you be kind enough, sir," said the generous Kate, taking a paper from her pocket, "to read Harriet's story before you decide. I asked her for a copy several days ago, and here it is."

"You shall read it to the audience yourself, my dear; I am sure they will listen patiently to so kind a pleader in her friend's behalf."

The listeners looked pleased and eager to hear the story; and Kate Sumner, with a modest self-possession, which well became her, and with her fine eyes lighting up as she read, did full justice to the pretty and touching story, of which Harriet had been so cruelly robbed.

"It is well worth reading," said Mr. Wentworth, when she had finished; "your friend has won the prize, my dear young lady; and, as she owes it to your generosity, you shall have the pleasure of bestowing it, yourself."

Kate's face glowed with emotion as she hung the chain around Harriet's neck; and Harriet could not restrain her tears, while she whispered,

"I will take it, *not* as a prize, but as a gift from *you*, dear Kate!"

"And now, Miss Sumner," said Mr. Wentworth, in conclusion, "let me beg your acceptance of these volumes, as a token of your teacher's respect and esteem," and presenting her a beautifully bound edition of Milton's works, he bowed his *adieu* to the retiring audience.

.   .   .   .

"Will you lend me your prize-pencil this morning, Harriet?" said Mrs. Carlton the next day. She was dressed for a walk, and Harriet wondered why she should want the pencil to take out with her; but she immediately unclasped the chain from her neck, and handed it to her mother without asking any questions.

She was rewarded at dinner by finding it lying at the side of her plate, with the single word, **"Truth"** engraved upon its seal.

The Coquette;
or
the Game of Life[1]

THE BRILLIANTLY lighted saloon in which Mrs. Clifford's company were assembled was suddenly darkened. At the same moment the curtain rose, and displayed to expectant eyes the first "*tableaux vivant.*" It was strikingly beautiful. A dark, fierce looking slave-dealer stood behind a Persian girl, from whose graceful form and face he had just withdrawn the veil, thereby revealing to the gaze of a voluptuous looking Turk, seated on a pile of cushions, so rare a galaxy of charms, that not only his eyes, but those of all the spectators, were riveted upon her. The shrinking timidity of her attitude, as she stood with her drooping hands locked languidly and meekly before her, was exquisitely graceful—her downcast eyes were "darkly, deeply blue," "and auburn waves of gemmed and braided hair" fell glistening over her rounded form, in its becoming vest of scarlet cashmere, and reached nearly to the feet, which peeped out beneath the full white satin pantaloons, in slippers gorgeous with jewels and embroidery.

For a moment the lovely vision glittered, and was gone—and seen no more until the closing *tableaux*, which represented Retzch's thrilling picture, called "The Game of Life." A youth with Satan playing at chess—his stake, a soul! The guardian spirit of the latter is seen at his side, with half averted face, gazing in mingled sorrow and compassion on the game, which he has almost lost. And in that white robed angel, the beautiful form and features of the Persian girl again appeared, so touchingly lovely, so pure and spiritual, that the gazers held their breath in rapture.

"Tell me—tell me her name!" exclaimed a young artist, as the curtain fell.

---

[1] "The Coquette; or the Game of Life," Frances S. Osgood, *Graham's Magazine*, January 1843, vol. XXII, no. 1, pp. 24-28

"It is Lilian Clifford, the daughter of our hostess," was the answer.

"But where is Fanny?" said another.

"Oh! she is nursing her little brother, I suppose. He is an invalid, you know, and she is devoted to him. But we shall see her by and by, for her mother insists upon her appearing at the ball, though she could not persuade her to take part in the *tableaux*. But hark. I hear the band—let us join the dancers."

A fancy ball followed the *tableaux*, and as the artist stood near the door, watching for the entrance of the angel, a young and blooming girl, in the ancient dress of a French marquise, glided by him, and with a low and playful courtesy to Mrs. Clifford, took her station by her side, whence she was immediately led to the dance by the Lucifer of the *tableaux*. Could it be Lilian?

The transformation was so complete, that he could hardly believe his eyes. The beautiful hair powdered—drawn back from the brow, and raised to an enormous height—tiny black patches here and there setting of her exquisite complexion—the dark still brocade looped up over white satin—the monstrous fan—the dainty French lisped out at intervals of the quadrille—the stately, graceful minuet motions—all, all was perfect!

"What a study!" murmured the fascinated artist, who, by the way, looked very picturesque himself, as he stood leaning against a pillar, in a Spanish costume, worthy of Murillo.

"My guardian angel!" whispered the youth who had been Lucifer's antagonist in the *tableaux*, and who now appeared in the garb of a sailor, "will you not dance the next quadrille with me? I need your protection more than ever, amid the temptations of such a scene as this."

"*Je toujours veille sur toi!*" replied the lady, with an eloquent smile, and a bow of assent. Lucifer scowled malignantly, and muttered in the sailor's ear—

"Julian Delaney, you will lose the game!"

The young man's eyes flashed fire as he answered, "You are a skillful player, Burton, but I, for one, defy your arts!"

A slight sneer was the reply, but Delaney passed on without deigning farther notice of his rival. At the same time, a modest looking, dark-eyed girl, in the simple dress of a quaker, approached, and whispered—

"Lilly, dear, I wish you could come to the nursery for a moment, after this dance; Willie wants to see your dress."

"Nonsense, Fanny, I can't leave till the ball is over. Willie must wait—"

"But he will be asleep then, Lilly!"

"Well, well, I can't help it if he is!" and with a bewitching smile, and the grace of a Hebe, she turned her partner in the dance. Fanny sighed, and the artist sighed too, and soon after begged an introduction, not to the coquettish marquise, but to the timid quaker girl.

"Who is that noble-looking being with my sister?" suddenly exclaimed Lilian Clifford to a friend, struck for the first time, by his manly form, and dark, but beautifully chiseled face, lighted up by a pair of brilliant Byron eyes, and a mouth full of expression.

"That? Why, Frank Russell, the artist, to be sure. Don't you know—he has just returned from Italy. What do you think of him?"

"Think of him?" He looks like a *man*—and that is more than you can say of any one else in the room. Look at that attitude! and then his voice!—hark! did you ever listen to such tones—so rich—so deep? I should like to hear him read poetry—and his manner, too—there is a calm and gentle dignity about it, which makes one involuntarily look up to him as to a superior being. I must go and speak to Fanny."

And tripping up to her sister, she tapped her cheek with her fan, exclaiming, "A penny for your thought, Fanny. How abstracted you look!"

"A thousand guineas for the thought, Miss Clifford," said Russell, in a low tone, and with an earnest gallantry, which well became his chivalrous beauty and bearing.

"Tell him you will give your thought for his," whispered Lilian, playfully, "for he too was in a reverie."

"Nay, I would give an age's thought of mine, for one moment's of yours, and rejoice in the exchange," murmured Russell, with a smile, still bending his dark eyes upon Fanny's drooping lids.

"Come, Fanny, you shall tell it now," continued her sister.

"I cannot—don't ask me, Lilian," faltered Fanny, while a deep blush stole into her pure, pale cheek.

"Well, at least have the sense to introduce me to your new beau—can't you?" whispered Lilian, pettishly.

The introduction took place, and the graceful coquette tried all her sportive and beguiling wiles, without any apparent effect upon the heart of the handsome stranger.

While thus engaged, Delaney claimed her hand for the dance.

"Oh! Julian—you will excuse me, I know, and dance with Fanny this time, for dear little Willie has sent for me. I will be back soon. Mr. Russell, may I trouble you for your arm through this crowd?"

"That's right, dear Lily, I am so glad," cried Fanny, her sweet face beaming with joy, at her sister's supposed kindness to the little invalid.

"You are Willie's guardian angel, too, then, Lilian," said Delaney, with a look of admiring affection.

The artist sighed again—but gave his arm to the lady, and accompanied her to the foot of the stairs. On their way she contrived to tell a dozen different people where she was going.

"Wait for me here a few moments. Mr. Russell shall hate to enter the room alone," and she glided up the stairs, and vanished from his gaze, like a dream of light.

The artist leant against the balusters, and lost himself in thought—how long he knew not; but he was awakened by a low melodious laugh at his side, and starting, he found the soft hand of Lilian Clifford on his arm, and her lovely eyes raised smilingly to his.

"Is it your pleasure, noble don, that we re-enter the saloon? I have had my arm in yours for some three minutes, patiently awaiting your movements."

Russell colored, as he asked her forgiveness, and unable to resist the witchery of her every word and look, abandoned himself to her influence during the rest of the evening.

CHAPTER II.

Luxurious as a lady's boudoir, was the studio in which Frank Russell was seated, three weeks after the ball at

Mrs. Clifford's. Lounges, ottomans, damask drapery, mirrors, paintings, statues and books, were all arranged with a graceful and careless elegance, which told of the artist throughout—while he himself, in his rich crimson tunic, his dark hair waving beneath an embroidered velvet cap, completed the beauty of the picture.

Before him, on his easel, was the half-length of a girl in a Spanish costume. She was looking over her shoulder, with an arch smile—the tip of a superb fan, which she held, was pressed to her dimpled chin, and a black lace mantilla, thrown back on her head, fell over her snowy shoulder, to her waist; while clusters of soft dark hair mingled their golden glow with its shade, and softened the brilliant beauty of a face radiant with youth, love, and happiness,

"My own, my precious Lilian," murmured the artist, as he gazed at his own exquisite creation, "I am sure she loves me—just so she looked last night, when I begged her to grant me an interview this evening. She guessed my purpose, and her whole soul was in her eyes, as she looked her reply. But I must touch that arm once more—it is hardly round enough yet."

He passed behind a marble pedestal, on which was a statue of Love, to a table, where lay his palette and brushes. Ere he reappeared, a party of ladies and gentlemen entered the room.

"Lilian Clifford, it is you to perfection!" exclaimed one of the former.

"Is it a likeness of the laughing elf?"

"A likeness! No! by heaven—'tis she herself!" exclaimed a gentleman of the party, and then the cold, sneering voice of Burton, the *tableaux* Lucifer, was heard—

"But where is your artist lover, Miss Clifford? We thought to find him at his devotions, before your portrait. Report declares the sittings to be not 'like angel visits,' but most unreasonably prolonged."

Frank waited to hear her indignant reply to this impertinence. How was he confounded by what followed.

"Nay, Burton, report can hardly accuse me of so preposterous a purpose, as that of encouraging a nameless artist."

"It accuses you of encouraging a nameless poet, as well."

"You refer to Julian Delaney. Be assured, sir, that they themselves know me better."

The statue fell with a crash at her feet, and the artist confronted her with folded arms, and flashing eyes.

"Thank God, madam, I *do* know you, ere it is too late!" and bowing haughtily, he left the room.

Lilian turned pale, but forced a laugh, and began to criticize the pictures.

Fanny Clifford sat alone that evening by the fireside, when Mr. Russell was announced. "I have come to thank you for your kindness during my sojourn here, my dear Miss Clifford, and to bid you 'goodbye.'" Fanny started, but by a brave effort restrained her emotion, and said, in a low tone—

"Are you to be long absent?"

"Only a year or two!"

Only a year or two! Fortunately for Fanny, at that moment the door opened, and Lilian, attired for a ball, and radiant in beauty, entered. She colored, when she saw her lover—her eyes filled with tears, and springing forward, she caught his hands.

"Frank! dear Frank! forgive me!"

"Lilian Clifford, you little know the heart your lightness has lost you. Farewell!"

"As you please, sir!"

With a light laugh, she drew up her graceful figure, and walking with the step of a queen, a fairy queen, to the glass, adjusted a gem in her hair, as calmly as if nothing had happened to ruffle or to grieve her.

He turned again to her sister. He took her hand—it trembled violently in his—he gazed on her blushing and downcast face, and wondered that he had never seen its beauty before. Pure, soft and spiritual, with an exquisite delicacy and transparency of complexion, and an expression ever varying with her varying emotions, Fanny's face was not one to strike the beholder at first sight, but it grew upon his heart, and once seen in all its beauty, lighted up by the full warmth of her lofty and generous soul, it left an impression which was never afterwards effaced. Fanny *lived* in the truest sense of the word. Her heart was in all she did, and said, and looked, and a great heart it was—but alas! how little appreciated by those around her.

Well! Frank departed, and Lilian, as he closed the door, threw herself into her sister's arms, and poured out her sorrow and repentance. And Fanny soothed her with her loving voice, and half forgot her own deeper grief, in pity for her sister's.

CHAPTER III.

Three years passed, and again was the artist, no longer a nameless one, seated in his studio, in Bond Street, New York; and again stood Fanny and Lilian Clifford by his side. They were in mourning for the little brother, mentioned in the commencement of my story, and Fanny was paler and sadder than of yore; but Lilian was gay, and brilliant, and beautiful as ever.

"Mr. Russell," she said, with her sweet, persuasive smile, "I will have a look at this picture turned to the wall."

Russell colored, as he sprang forward to prevent her. It was too late—she had turned it and revealed a striking likeness of her sister, in the quaker dress which she had worn at the fancy ball!

For one instant, Fanny's eyes met the thrilling gaze of Frank's. The next, the lashes fell, but they were wet with tears, as she turned away, touched to the soul by this proof of his remembrance. And Lilian, after gazing at both, with a proud curl of her beautiful lip, exclaimed—

"Oh! I see it all now—excuse me, good people—I would be the last to interrupt so interesting a *tête-à-tête*. Good morning."

And ere Fanny could move to detain her, she was gone. They were alone, and Russell turned to the trembling and bewildered girl at his side with a look of mingled reverence and affection.

"Fanny, you see there a proof that I have treasured your image in my heart—would to Heaven I might wear the original there. Speak, dearest, will you—can you be mine?"

Fanny's eye and cheek grew luminous, with the rapture of that moment. But the light, the glow died away, as suddenly as it came. She thought of Lilian, and though she blamed her coquetry and folly, she pitied her disappointment. With one glorious effort she repressed her tears—the sighs, that struggled for liberty, and replied in a low, but clear voice,

"Mr. Russell, I can never be your wife!"

Struck by her calm, decided tone, he stood for a moment gazing at her in despair; but that gaze called to her cheek a blush so speaking, that hope revived, and with all the glowing eloquence of which he was master, he besought her to retract her resolution. Overcome by his passionate entreaties, Fanny could only falter, half unconsciously, in reply—

"But Lilian—"

"Lilian has wronged me—but that light dream is over. Do not, oh! do not disappoint me in one far dearer and holier love."

Poor Fanny! it was a moment of strange trial, but her heart was strong. She raised her clear, sad eyes to his, and again replied—

"Russell, I can never be your wife!"

He dropped her hand. With a slow but unfaltering step she passed from the room—reached home—locked herself into her chamber, and for once giving way to the full tide of her emotions, wept for hours unceasingly. Her tears relieved her, and after a fervent prayer to Heaven for strength, she was able to resume her occupations, with a subdued and self-approving heart.

"Mr. Russell, you have grown very stupid of late, do read me something," said Lilian, one evening, as they sat with a few friends in the library.

"And what?" said Frank.

"Oh! there is a new, fresh, uncut volume of poems by Tennyson on the table. Isn't that delightful?"

"But I shall want a paper knife."

"That you shall have, and keep it, too, as a reward for your trouble,—and oh! congratulate me! I have just had an idea!—while you are cutting the leaves, I will scribble it down. Lend me your pencil, Frank!" And ere he had divided half a dozen leaves, she had traced in fairy characters the following lines:

Ah! had I power, I'd charm my gift
    To be a magic treasure;
For it should never part a page
    That should not give you pleasure!

Rolling the paper in as small a compass as possible, she screwed it into the top of the pencil-case and returned it to him with a grace so bewitching, that his old dream began to disturb him again.

He hurriedly turned over the leaves of the book and smiled half in bitterness, as a few lines caught his glance and told upon his heart. Fixing his eyes earnestly upon Lilian's face, he said in a deep meaning tone, "I have found a poem which I think you will appreciate. Shall I read it?" The poem was that strangely moving one, called "Clara Vere de Vere," and his low, rich, manly, but melancholy voice thrilled to her very soul as he proceeded.

The second verse commences as follows:

Lady Clara Vere de Vere,
    I know you proud to bear your name;
Your pride is yet no mate for mine,
    Too proud to care from whence I came.

These lines, and those which follow, called the fire into Lilian's eyes and cheeks; but she tossed back her graceful head with a proud and careless smile.

Lady Clara Vere de Vere,
    Some meeker pupil you must find;
For were you queen of all that is,
    I could not stoop to such a mind.

But when he came to the words—

Not thrice your branching line have flown
    Since I beheld young Lawrence dead.

Oh! your sweet eyes, your low replies,
    A great enchantress you may be;
But there was that across his throat
    Which you had hardly cared to see.

Poor Lilian struggled for a moment as if suffocating, and then fell at his feet insensible.

Fanny sprung forward to raise her, exclaiming, "Oh, Frank! why did you read that verse? You surely could not have heard—"

"What—what—Fanny?" he cried, as he hung over the lovely, lifeless form of her whom he now felt to be dearer to him than ever.

Too soon, he heard the truth! Too soon? *Too late* for his revived affection. Julian Delaney, who, as the reader already knows, was passionately devoted to Lilian, had been, during Frank's last visit in Italy, alternately petted and scorned as the attentions of his rich rival Burton had varied from cold to warm; until at length the growing empressement of the latter's manner had decided her to dismiss, at once and forever, the unfortunate and interesting victim of her coquetry. That very day his lifeless body was borne home to a widowed mother,

> "And there was that across his throat
> Which Lilian had not cared to see!"

The same paper which announced this tragic event, also announced the elopement of the Lucifer of my tale, with the wife of his most intimate friend. Lilian recovered from her fainting fit to find her artist lover bending over her with a gaze in which his whole soul spoke to hers; but the instant he met her eye he turned away, determined never again to betray his feelings to her scorn. Still he visited the house from time to time, and was often allured to the very verge of a declaration by her bewildering beauty and the childlike, pleading, playful sweetness of her manner.

One day he took up a book, in a blank page of which she had been scribbling some lines. When she saw him turn to them, she sprung up with a bright blush, and sportively placed her little hand over the words. Unable to resist the temptation, he pressed his lips to it involuntarily.

She immediately withdrew it, but leaned over his shoulder as he read—

> My bark is on a dangerous sea,
>   A wintry sky above it,
> And no one minds the helm for me,
>   And no one seems to love it.
> Oh! would that in a kinder world,
>   Ere storms its frail mast shiver,
> Oh! would to God its sails were furl'd
>   Forever and forever!

Touched by the sad sentiment, he looked up in her face. Her eyes, filled with tears, were bent upon him, and her hand trembled as he took it. "Are the verses yours, Lilian?"

"Oh, Frank! I should not have let you read them!"

He was thrown off his guard. "They *are* yours, then? And I—may not I 'mind the helm?' Dear Lilian! say that I may."

She hid her eyes upon his shoulder. Her soft hair touched his face. He laid his cheek to hers—their destiny was sealed. The next moment she raised that beautiful face, bathed in blushes and smiles, and clasping her hands with a sweet, low, ringing laugh, exclaimed in the words of one of our finest poets—

> "Now, helmsman, for a hundred lives,
>   Oh! Steer the bark aright!"

He caught her to his heart.

Ah Frank! You little know what a frail, light thing you have undertaken to guide. Be happy while you may.

CHAPTER IV.

A twelvemonth after the wedding—a charming cottage in Brookline—Lilian, Frank and Fanny in the former's boudoir. A beautiful instant lying on the rich cushions of the couch. There is a light cloud on the noble brow of the artist;—he has been looking over a milliner's bill! His young wife looks listless and weary.

"Will you lend me your pencil, Frank?" said Fanny. He handed it to her; there was no lead in it. She unscrewed the top—and out fell the little roll of paper, placed there long ago by Lilian.

"May I read it, Frank?"

"Certainly, dear."

She read it—started—changed color; but without farther sign of emotion, quietly returned it to the pencil-case. Lilian looked imploringly at her, and Fanny rose to leave the room. Frank saw it all.

"Stay, Fanny; did *you* compose those lines?" Fanny was silent—she trembled like a leaf. Russell continued, "I saw in your scrap-book, the other day, signed by your name, a copy of some verses which Lilian gave me on the day of our engagement. Here they are. Are they yours or hers?" Fanny shrunk back; but he insisted, and she took the paper—read the first line—

"My bark is on a dangerous sea,"

and burst into tears. He stood before her pale, but resolute.

"Speak, Fanny, I implore you, *are* they yours?" She hesitated; but she could not lie. She looked at Lilian and flew to her side.

"Oh, Frank! she is sainting; come to her quick!"

"Let her come to *herself*, she has deceived me.
Let her *forgive* herself, if she can!"

The sternness of his tone aroused her.

She rose, and tottering toward him, threw herself in tears at his feet. "Oh, Frank! do not look at me so! They *are* Fanny's lines; but it was to win your love that I deceived you! Will you see your Lilian suffer and not forgive her?"

Who could resist those eyes—those sweet, imploring tones—that almost angel loveliness. Frank could not. She was forgiven, and the game of life went on.

CHAPTER V.

"Lilian, is not that the ring Burton was showing you the other day? I am astonished you should have kept it so long. It was imprudent, dear, very."

"I shall see him to-morrow, and will return it then, dear Frank. There, now, smile again—do, there's a darling."

The next evening the ring had disappeared, and Frank smiled approvingly as he took her hand in his. "I could not bear to touch this dear little hand yesterday, Lilian, but I love it now."

"Oh! because Burton's ring is gone. He was glad to have it back, for he thought it lost."

Six weeks afterward, Frank found the ring in a box, where she had requested him to look for a missing bracelet. Inside the ring was an inscription—"My heart goes with it, Lilian." It was a gift, then! not a loan as she had declared! His heart grew chill with the thought. He looked at her and murmured, "So lovely, yet so light and false!"

She was half dressed for a ball, and oh! how exquisitely beautiful she looked! She was braiding her rich brown hair, and those slight, snowy, jeweled fingers glanced down the luxuriant tresses with the speed and light of a snow-flake gleaming in the sun. She turned toward him; the truth flashed upon her. She remembered the ring, and pale with fear, she staggered to his side. He looked up, without a word, placed the ring in her hand and left the room. The ring was returned to the giver; but not to Lilian, who returned the love and confidence of her husband.

She had never been strong, and from that day she faded. Frank watched over her with Fanny tenderly and truly; but she felt his trust was gone. In a few months he followed her to her untimely grave. For years he wandered mourning and alone. At length, he renewed to Fanny the offer of his hand and heart. Firm, but sad was her reply.

"Dear Frank, I can never be your wife; but I will be a mother to your precious child."

"Take her, then, and teach her to love me, as none have ever loved me yet." And Fanny hushed the beating heart that still worshiped the very shadow of that noble form, and devoted her life, with all a mother's tenderness, to the child of her lost and lamented Lilian.

Dora's Reward;
or
the "Ruse de Guerre"[1]

CHAPTER I.

"HEAR me, but for one moment, Imogen," exclaimed the youthful sculptor, as the lady of his love turned coldly away from his impassioned gaze.

"Nay, Mr. Stanley, hear me and answer me! What have I ever done to authorize this presumption? Let me tell you, sir, Imogen Howard would sooner die than stoop to be the bride of an obscure and unknown artist like yourself. Release my hand!"

And it *was* released, ere the words had passed her lips, and George Stanley stood before her with folded arms and a face pale with suppressed emotion.

She was a queenly creature. Her brow, with its regal beauty, would have graced the fairest coronet of England's court; but her proud lip blanched and her dark eye quailed beneath the stern and reproachful gaze of him whose love her coquetry had so cruelly betrayed.

At length, a smile of quiet and lofty scorn broke gradually over his fine face, and, turning calmly away, he left her without a word; he left her, in her luxurious and elegant home, to seek, with an aching heart, the lowly lodgings of poverty; but he left her to a grief more deep and more enduring than his own.

As the door closed, the haughty girl threw herself, in wild abandonment to the most passionate sorrow, on the rich velvet cushions of the sofa, from which she had risen to address him; and there, to that wo which her own pride—the petty pride of wealth and station—has caused, we too will leave her, as he left, and give the reader a

---

[1] "Dora's Reward; or the 'Ruse de Guerre,'" Frances S. Osgood, *Graham's Magazine*, June 1843, vol. XXII, no. 6, pp. 357-362

slight sketch of our hero, his character, his situation and his prospects.

He was poor and proud; of humble origin, but noble in person and in mind. High-spirited, witty, with, at times, a dashing, daring recklessness, which involved him in many an embarrassment; he had still a lofty sense of honor, which no difficulty had yet impaired.

His face, though not beautiful, was strikingly interesting. His hair, intensely black, was flung, in wild glossy masses, from his broad and spiritual forehead, and a pair of flashing eyes, of the same singularly deep hue, expressed every passing emotion of his soul. His mouth was almost femininely sweet, his form tall and finely proportioned.

A sculptor, by profession, he had displayed remarkable genius in the few graceful groups which adorned his studio; but though visitors, impelled some by taste and some by curiosity, crowded his room, his sitters were few and far between; for it generally happened that those who best appreciated the beauty of his works were, like himself, poor and dependent upon their own talents for a livelihood.

That a prophet has seldom honor in his own country is a proverb too generally true, and George Stanley began to despair of realizing the glorious dreams of fame and fortune which boyish ambition had formed.

At the time my story commences, he had just completed, in marble, a full length of Imogen Howard—the only daughter of one of the wealthiest merchant princes of Boston, the city in which the scene of my story is laid. She was represented as the fabled Atalanta, at the commencement of the chase, just springing forward in flight, her lips slightly parted, her hair and garments fluttering in the air, her dart in her hand, and her graceful head half turned for a parting glance at her lover. The design had all the spirit and beauty with which the original was so singularly gifted; and Stanley hardly knew with which he was most in love, his own exquisite creation or the lovely model which nature had molded so perfectly before him.

Charmed by her beauty, her wit, and playful blandishment of manner, the youthful sculptor, at every meeting with his fair subject, had become more and more passionately attached to her; and, at length, forgetting the difference of station, had rashly, and perhaps prematurely, declared his love, during the interview with which my story commences.

CHAPTER II.

George Stanley entered his humble studio, threw his hat and cloak desperately upon a chair, and, seating himself by a table, buried his face in his hands. He had not noticed, as he entered, a young girl sitting, with a book in her hand, in a retired corner of the room, who seemed to be awaiting his approach. She rose, as he came in, but, seeing his evident emotion, hesitated to address him. We will not lose so favorable an opportunity to describe her, as she stands there with her little hands clasped in sympathizing sorrow, and her blue eyes fast filling with tears. She is apparently about fourteen years of age, small, slight, but exquisitely formed, with a delicate, child-like face, whose chief beauty is its expression of angelic innocence and purity, enhanced perhaps by the soft spiritual-looking hair of palest brown, which falls not in curls, but in graceful waves upon her neck.

Her dress is a simple robe of white, lightly confined at the waist with a ribbon of the same hue. Beside her is a nearly finished statue of little Nell seated upon the church-yard stone. The child is doubtless the original of the beautiful design; for the dress, the form, the face are hers; but see! with a light though faltering step she crosses the room and lays, with timid tenderness, her soft pure hand upon the flushed forehead of the sculptor. He feels—he knows—he loves the touch; but, though inexpressibly soothed and comforted, as by a fairy spell, he does not at once look up, the influence is too sweet to be thus disturbed, and so he remains perfectly still, while she smooths his hair with her caressing fingers, and presses her innocent cheek upon his brow. At last, weary of the silence, she insinuates her tiny hand into his, and then he starts and presses it fondly to his lips, unable longer to resist her childish tenderness. Blushing, with a new and strange emotion, she hastily withdraws it.

"I came to sit, Mr. Stanley."

"Dora! you are a blessed child!"

"But—I came to sit."

"Why do you tremble so? You are fatigued! Take this chair, dear Dora, and I will be ready for you in a moment. There! now clasp your hands before you, and droop your head a little. That's right! don't move—it is perfect! Dear, sweet, lovely little Dora!—Nell I mean!"

"Oh! why did you change the name? It makes me so happy to have you praise me, and yet I know not why, but the tears always come into my eyes when you speak so, and I cannot help sighing as if I were sad, but I am not— only too happy to smile."

"Darling, precious little Nell!—Dora, I mean!"

The child's low and musical laugh rang out like the warble of a bird, or peal of fairy bells.

"There, Dora, you may rest now, and I will read you those verses I spoke of, written for little Nell's statue, by a friend of mine.

Dear Nell! thou didst not sit alone,
    Although the eye could trace
Naught breathing, near the church-yard stone,
    Beside thine own sweet face.

Thou dost not sit alone, dear Nell,
    And well the sculptor knew,
While 'neath his high art's wondrous spell,
    Thy form's soft graces grew,

That, when on earth, the True, the Pure,
    Doth linger, wheresoever,
An angel-presence waits on it,
    Its guard and guide forever.

An angel-presence fills his room,
    Although the eye may trace
No holier object through the gloom,
    Than thine own tender face.

We *feel* the wave of viewless wings,
    And the soul hears a tone—
A strange, sweet voice, that softly sings,
    Beside that church-yard stone!

And now, dear Dora, I must bid you good-bye. I am going away for a long time."

"Oh! how long?" asked the child, looking up sorrowfully, imploringly in his face, "for a whole week?"

"For years, perhaps!"

Dora did not speak; she moved hastily away, tied on her little coarse straw bonnet, pinned her faded shawl over a heart heaving with unspeakable anguish—turned again toward him a face white almost as the marble one of the Ariadne beside her, pressed his hand lightly, almost coldly, to her lips, and was gone!

The paragraph containing the news of George Stanley's departure for England was read at the same hour, the next evening, by both Imogen Howard and Dora Sullivan; the one in her gorgeous saloon, dazzlingly arrayed for a ball, and awaiting her carriage; the other in her little bed-room, preparing for the night's repose. The haughty heiress, bravely repressing a shriek of surprise and despair, threw down the *Transcript*, exclaiming, "How stupid these papers are growing!—there never is anything worth reading in them!"

The innocent and loving child, after bathing it with tears, knelt in her night robe by her humble bed, and prayed meekly and fervently to her Father in Heaven, that he would protect and bless her friend, and keep her good till his return.

CHAPTER III.

A year passed by. Nothing was heard of young Stanley, and few had cared to hear; for all the world—that is all the fashionable world of Boston—was crowding to the richly furnished rooms of a dashing, whiskered, moustached, fierce-looking corsair of a sculptor—fresh from his native Italy—a miracle of genius—a young, elegant, interesting, *distingue* being, whom all the ladies petted, and all the gentlemen patronized.

"He is so saucy and so accomplished! His hair curls divinely, and he plays the guitar '*a raviment*;' and he sings '*Eccoridente!*' with such impassioned feeling! His broken English, too, is perfectly bewitching. Oh! Imogen! you must go and see him!" exclaimed Miss Angelina Seraphina Elliot to her friend, as they sat one evening in the elegant boudoir of the latter.

"But you know I hate artists!" replied Imogen, languidly.

"Yes—common artists; but this is a *rara avis*! Every one is sitting to him, though his charges are enormous. They say his fortune was immense before he came, and that all he makes here is bestowed in charity. Come! tie on your new *'François premier,'* and that little white plush hat, and go with me directly."

"Yes," said Imogen, bitterly, and half aloud, "they grant to this impudent foreigner's moustache and broken English, what they denied to poor Stanley's lofty genius and purity of character. *Him* they allowed to linger on in neglect and poverty, for the very reason that he *was* poor, and really needed their assistance! Well, Angy, I want a walk, and we might as well go there as any where; so just touch that bell at your side and I will tell Florine to bring my hat, &e., here."

A slight flush crossed the dark brow of Signor Julio di Cajolerini, as Imogen Howard entered his saloon; but he bowed low, and with Italian grace, to her courteous address, and then rivetted his black eyes, with a gaze of mysterious meaning, upon her beautiful face, till she was fain to turn away from them, blushing and embarrassed. What was there in those eyes that so moved the haughty girl? There were few who could daunt her from her graceful and high-bred self-possession; yet this bold Italian had, with a single look, abashed her.

She felt annoyed, provoked, yet charmed, she knew not why; and again and again her brilliant hazel eyes met those of the handsome stranger, and again and again they fell beneath his gaze.

At length he spoke. Imogen had moved away to examine an exquisite statue of Psyche; but, at the sound of that voice, deep and sweet, lingering on the rich musical syllables of his own native Italian, she turned hastily round! Once more she caught his eye. "Let us go!" she said to her companion, and with a cold, proud bow, met by the sculptor with one equally haughty, she turned to leave the room.

"But, Imogen!" said her friend aloud, "you know your father wishes you to sit to the signor, and you have made no arrangements about it." Again the young lady turned toward him. He was looking provokingly *nonchalant*, leaning, in a careless and graceful attitude, against a superb Apollo, with his splendid purple robe *orientale* embroidered in silver folded around his stately form. He bent his head slightly, as Imogen addressed him.

"At what hour, sir, can you attend me at my father's house, to make arrangements for a sitting?"

"Pardon me, *mia bella signora*! my time is so occupied that I shall unfortunately be obliged to forego the honor you design me."

Imogen's dark eyes flashed an unutterable reply, but she did not speak; and, with another cold and slight bow, they parted.

CHAPTER IV.

In a low room, at the north end of the city, was seated a girl of sixteen. She held in her hand a small embroidery frame, in which she had half finished, for a screen, a wreath of delicate roses, and forget-me-nots. Upon this work depended her livelihood. She had promised it should be completed the next day.

> "But though her eye dwelt on her knee,
>   In vain her fingers strove;
> And, though her needle pierced the silk,
>   No flower Tarifa wove!"

Her young head was bent, and her light and beautiful hair, as it fell over the frame, half veiled her drooping eyes. Her cheek was slightly flushed with the love-dream at her heart, and she sang, in a low, sweet, sighing voice, as follows:

> "There are tones that will haunt us, though lonely
>   Our way be o'er mountain and sea—
> There are looks that will pass from us, only
>   When memory ceases to be."

A light, quick knock at the door is unheard by the dreaming girl. It opens, and a stately stranger approaches. It is the Italian sculptor! What does he here with those mysterious eyes of his, and that bright, beguiling smile?

Beware, little dreamer! Shut up, in that pure and loving heart, the image of the absent one, and let not *his* displace it!

"Pardon me, Miss Sullivan, for intruding thus abruptly upon you. I should not have presumed to do so without this letter of introduction from our mutual friend, Mr. Stanley."

The dainty color burned and faded in the delicate cheek of the girl, as she reached her hand eagerly out for the letter, and as quickly withdrew it, abashed beneath the earnest and admiring gaze of the stranger.

"Will you not take the letter?" said he, smiling.

She did take it, but held it unconsciously in her hand, with her head bent earnestly forward, her eyes downcast, her very heart waiting to hear that voice again.

Signor Julio di Cajolerini! are you a serpent, that you thus strangely charm each bird that flutters in your path?

"Will you not *read* the letter, Miss Sullivan?"

"Oh, yes! certainly! I beg your pardon. What did you say?"

And she gazed upon him, with a bewildered look in her child-like eyes, till he repeated the question.

She opened the letter, it ran as follows:

"My dear Miss Sullivan, allow me to introduce to you my most intimate friend, Signor Julio di Cajolerini. He wants a living model for the statue of the Roman Virginia, and I have ventured to name you as one who will suit him exactly, and who needs the liberal price he will pay. I hope your devotion to your invalid mother has long ere this met its reward in her recovered health. Remember me kindly to her, and believe me always and truly your friend,
"GEORGE STANLEY."

Utterly unconscious of the Italian's presence, Dora had perused this simple letter half-a-dozen times ere he ventured, or indeed wished to interrupt her. It was sufficient happiness for him to watch her changing face as she read. "The flitting blush," the playful smile, the half-stifled sigh, the touching eloquence and grace of her whole expression and attitude were a study worthy of Praxiteles; and the signor, entranced and almost breathless with delight, at length closed his eyes over the sweet picture, as if to shut it up forever in his soul.

"May I hope for the honor of a sitting from you at your earliest convenience?" said he, after a long pause.

Dora started, and remained for a few moments in silent thought. She hesitated, because she felt a natural reluctance to sit to a stranger. Stanley had been her friend from childhood, and with him the case was different; but she could hardly reconcile herself to the idea of going, alone and unprotected, to the studio of the signor. Then she thought of her poor and invalid mother, for whom she could thus earn many little delicacies necessary to her recovery.

"Yes, sir," she said at last, "at any hour you will name, I shall be happy to attend you."

"At ten o'clock to-morrow, then, if you please, Miss Sullivan. Good morning," and, bowing with an impressive and respectful air, he took his leave.

CHAPTER V.

The heiress stood that evening longer than usual at her mirror. She was dressed for a ball, at which she expected to meet the lion of the day, Signor Julio di Cajolerini.

Her dress—a delicate rose-colored crape, looped with azaleas over white satin—was cut low at the bosom, too low for taste and maiden delicacy, though the fair neck, which rose above, was soft and beautiful as that of the fabled Cytherea. Her dark hair, parted in front in luxuriant masses, was braided at the back of her head, and confined by a net of the rarest pearls. Her zone and bracelets were composed of the same precious ornaments. In her hand she held a rare bouquet, and a superb Indian fan, glittering with gems, hung upon her round and snowy arm.

She was looking very lovely. There was a brilliant glow upon her cheek, and the sportive dimples played round her beautiful mouth, like sunshine round a rose! But the servant announces her carriage; and, with one parting gaze at the mirror, she allows Florine to tie on her little white satin cloak, and vanishes.

Poor Florine! and you are to sit up for her! What will you do with yourself? She has left you some work, but you will delay that until to-morrow; I know you will by the expression of that willful little mouth of yours. Can you read, Florine? Oh yes! for you have already a splendid annual in your hand, and have opened into the middle of a love story. Poor child! How you wish you were the heroine, do you not? with all her trials and sufferings, rather than the slave of an heiress' caprice!

The hours roll on. Twelve o'clock! Florine has finished the story, and read all the poetry in the book, and now she sings. Hark! it is a love-song! Ah! Florine! you have a lover, then! No wonder you like poetry.

Yes! I will go away with thee,
Beloved, o'er the bounding sea;
I care not where my lot may lie,
So it be 'neath affection's eye;
I care not what my home may be—
A hut were heaven, if shar'd with thee!

Whate'er the shore our feet shall press,
Thy beaming simile that shore will bless;
Whate'er the cares our way that thrall,
Thy look of love will lighten all;
And, dark or bright the prospect be,
I will not shrink—I go with thee!

The hours roll on. One o'clock! Florine yawns. "Oh dear!" she sighs to herself, "I am so tired of singing and reading! What shall I do? I know, I'll try on all her caps and capes!" And forthwith she goes to a bureau and decks herself out—parading before the full length mirror and mimicking, or rather caricaturing her young mistress' airs and graces with ludicrous fidelity. "She won't be home these two hours yet! I might just as well see how I look in the new French pelisse and hat."

She had hardly arranged these to her satisfaction, ere a carriage stopped at the door. "It is she—so early!—how provoking!" The cloak and hat were restored to their respective boxes, and the little artful French maid, to all appearance sound asleep upon the sofa, when Imogen entered the room.

"Florine, take my cloak!—unclasp these pearls! and leave me!" The girl started, rubbed her eyes, and did as she was bidden. Imogen was alone.

The belle—the heiress—"the evening star," as her attendant beaux had entitled her? How different now from the gay and brilliant girl who had stood there three hours before, exulting in her beauty and her pride! Her hands were locked languidly before her—her dark disordered locks streaming loosely over her pale face and beautiful form—her drooping lashes wet with tears that mocked the curl of her haughty lip! The glow of joy was gone, and her flowers had lost their freshness and their bloom

"Oh! Stanley!" she murmured, "I have deserved this— the cool indifference with which this princely stranger meets me is but a just retribution for my disdain of your love, and yet it is only his strange resemblance to you that *causes* this foolish infatuation—I will never see him again! The coxcomb—he would not even accept my flowers!" and she flung her bouquet, with passionate violence, on the floor. As it fell, a little folded paper which had been lying perdu amid its leaves, dropped from it at her feet. With a beating heart and blushing cheek, she snatched it up and read the following lines:

Do you weed your *garden* gaily,
   Training flowers with loving care!
Why not weed your *heart*, too, daily?
   Why not train the blossoms there?

Scorn and o are weeds, false lady!
   Oh if thou dost care to make
"Sunshine in a place that's shady,"
   Pluck them out, for love's sweet sake!

"Saucy and presuming! like all he says and does," exclaimed the disappointed girl; and, tearing it into shreds, she flung herself, without undressing, on the bed and wept herself to sleep.

CHAPTER VI.

"Dear Dora, say, at least, that you will try to love me!" exclaimed the young signor, and he sought, with respectful tenderness, to take her hand in his; but Dora gravely withdrew it, and replied, with a faltering voice and tearful eyes,

"Sir! you have been generous to me thus far; be so now, or I can never come to you again! I love you—as a friend—as a brother, if you will; but not as I love—another! Oh what am I saying? I did not mean to tell you this; but you are so kind, so gentle, that I feel as if I *must* confide in you. Do not betray me! You will not?"

She covered her blushing face with her hands, and stood trembling before him.

"Nay! dearest, I love you too well to betray you; but let me claim a brother's privilege, since you have yourself bestowed that precious name, and tell me—is it my friend you love? Stanley told me, long ago, that he had cherished your image as the dearest treasure of his soul."

The color spread to her very temples, and her slight, girlish frame quivered like an aspen-leaf, but she could not speak.

"You need not answer me, Dora, I see it all; but he was poor and humble, and had little hope of ever being able to marry, while I have wealth and station! Dora, think of your poor mother!"

The young girl withdrew her hands and looked up calmly, almost proudly in his face. "My mother loves me, sir. She would sooner die than see her child degrade herself by marrying for mere wealth and station, unsanctified by love."

She turned coldly away.

"Dora, my precious, noble Dora! Look at me, dear, and love me!"

That voice! it was surely *his*! She glanced timidly round. Yes! George Stanley himself was there! The moustache, the whiskers, the artificial color, the curls, all, all had vanished; and there he stood, his dark face lighted up with exulting joy, his arms outstretched to receive her! Dora sprung with a faint cry, to his heart.

CHAPTER VII.

"Two scraps of news this morning, *ma belle*, one of which, I am sure, will interest you! What will you give to hear them?"

"Nothing, Angy, for nothing interests me now."

"Well, since you will give nothing, will you promise to accompany me wherever I may choose to go this morning, if I will tell you the most important one?"

"Yes."

"Well, then, your friend, Signor Julio di Cajolerini—the genius, the marvel, the lion, the meteor has vanished—no one knows why, when, where or how!"

> He came—he has gone! We have met!
> To meet, perhaps, never again!

"Thank Heaven! if it be true; but I can hardly believe it. Angy, there is something unaccountable, almost supernatural, in that man's influence over me."

"So I thought, for I could never comprehend it, though all the girls were bewitched with him. But come! you have promised to go with me."

"Well, just let me finish this touching letter of Willis'; it is his last from under a bridge, and is exquisitely beautiful. Come here and read it with me! There! is not that an appeal that none but he could write!—oh dear, your hand is just where I am reading, there, now I can see—beautiful! beautiful! oh Angy!—no wonder the tears are in your eyes. Well, we will go now."

The elegant walking-dress was donned with care, and the two lovely girls met many an admiring gaze, as they tripped from Beacon into Tremont street.

At one of the handsome marble buildings in the latter, they paused and ascended the stairs.

"Where are you taking me, Angy? Another poor artist to be patronized?"

Angy made no reply, but smilingly ushered her friend into a splendid suite of rooms, furnished with Eastern luxuriousness, and adorned with exquisite specimens of art in painting and sculpture. Vases of various graceful shapes were crowned with the rarest exotics of the season;

books, magnificently bound, lay scattered on tables of the richest mosaic. Crimson drapery, superb in texture and in hue, shaded the windows, and musical instruments of different kinds completed the *"tout ensemble."* But the gem of this charming assemblage was a newly finished statue in marble of the daughter of Virginius, as described in Macauley's noble "Lays of Ancient Rome."

"Just as thro' one cloudless chink in a black stormy sky,
Shines on the dewy morning star, a fair young girl came by
With her small tablets in her hand, and her satchel on her arm,
Home she went bounding from the school, nor dream'd of shame or harm."

A young man came forward to receive them, exclaiming, as he did so, "Miss Howard, Miss Elliott I am most happy to see you. Pray be seated." It was George Stanley. Imogen's early dream of love stole warmly back to her heart. He was a far different being now from the poor, obscure, desponding youth she had known two years before. She bent her dark eyes tenderly upon him. His returned her gaze with a smile of peculiar meaning, which struck like an icicle to her heart. Where had she met that smile before? Confused by his look, she took up a guitar which lay by her side and struck a few notes to cover her embarrassment.

"Though you do not understand Italian, Mr. Stanley, perhaps you would like to hear a little song I have just composed. The words and the music are both mine, and Angy thinks them pretty."

He smiled again. "I shall be most happy to hear it, Miss Howard."

And Imogen sang, with a faltering but impassioned voice, the following simple song:

Io amava,
　Sempr'io amo!
Io sperava,
　Speranza andú!

Oime! l'amore,
  D'ai sperme, tire
La tutta splendore
  Chi l'illumina

Pero desolato
  Non egli morra!
Coustante è piato,
  N'el onetra resta!

Ah! Io sperava,
  Speranza andú!
Ma io amava,
  Sempr'io amo!

"You have improved, Miss Howard; you sing with much more *feeling* than you once did. Will you allow me to give you an *impromptu* English translation of your graceful song!

"I thought you did not read Italian" she said, in a tone of surprise and dismay. He took the guitar from her hands and sang in a low but rich voice, and with much expression,

I loved I love always!
I hoped Hope has fled!
Ah, Jove drew from hope
All the glory it shed!

Yet, alone, it is breathing,
Through good and through ill;
Ah! I hoped Hope has fled!
But I loved, and love still!

The agitated girl looked hurriedly round. Her friend was absorbed in admiration of the statue of Virginia. Imogen approached the sculptor. "George! dear George," she murmured, "do you indeed still care for me?" Before she could reply, a sweet, eager voice, as of echo, repeated afar off, "George, dear George." The next instant the rich folds of a curtain at the farther end of the room were parted, and a fair, young and happy face glanced out for a moment and vanished!

Stanley sprung up, disappeared behind the drapery, and instantly returned, leading in his blushing and beautiful Dora, in a rich but modest bridal dress.

"My wife, Miss Howard!"

Imogen bore it bravely. She saluted the bride with a calm but courteous kindness; held out her hand to Stanley and congratulated him, though the tears were in her eyes as she did so, gave them a card for her next soiree, and turned to leave the room, with a cheek somewhat paler and a statelier step than usual.

Stanley was touched; he hurried forward to detain her. "Imogen—Miss Howard! I have something to show you." He drew her into an adjoining room. "I have wronged you, dear Imogen; I did not give you credit for the feeling, the spirit, the strength of character which you displayed but now; I can only expiate my fault by making to you a confession which but one other has drawn from me. Betray me if you will, but forgive me for the sake of my early devotion and disappointment!"

He passed into a recess, and re-appeared in a few moments in the gaudy robe, whiskers, rouge and moustache of Signor Julio di Cajolerini! Imogen gazed at him for a moment in mute amazement, and then burst into a fit of uncontrollable laughter, in which she was soon joined by Dora and Angeline, who were drawn thither by the sound.

"Yes, Miss Elliott, your fashionable friends gladly, nay eagerly, accorded to the rich and dashing foreigner what the poor native artist, with the same genius and less pretension, needed so much more and looked for in vain— patronage, sympathy, attention. Impelled, partly by my natural inclination for a frolic, partly by pride and perhaps revenge for the undeserved neglect which I had experienced, at the instigation of a young and wealthy Englishman, whom I met on board the ship and who lent me money for the purpose, I adopted the disguise and the plan of which you have seen the result. That I sincerely repent the imposition, you will be convinced from this voluntary confession. My end is answered, and I will no longer owe to imposture what ought to have been freely accorded to genius alone. All the money, all the property, which I have gained in this unworthy manner, shall be disposed of as I intended from the first, in charity. I have saved, from my former honorable earnings, more than sufficient to enable us to reach England, and, when there, my friend has promised me sufficient employment for a livelihood. Rich or poor, my Dora will love me; will you not, dear one?"

"Oh a thousand times better *poor*, my husband, than with riches thus falsely obtained."

He laid his hand affectionately on her head, and Dora placed her own upon it to retain it there.

"And now let me repeat to both of you, betray me if you will, but forgive me!"

"My dear Mr. Stanley!" exclaimed Imogen, smiling through her tears, "I will keep your secret and so shall Angy, upon one condition."

"Name it, *mia cara signora!*"

"It is that you shall let me sit for a bust, which I have promised Angeline for a birth-day gift, and that you will allow me to become the purchaser of that lovely little Nell which I see in the corner there."

"I cannot sell my little Nell, for my little Dora is the original of it; but I shall be most happy to fulfill your first condition. Have you any other to make?"

"Yes, one more; teach your sweet wife to love me, as I already love her, and I am content."

She had hardly finished speaking ere Dora's dainty little hand was in hers, and Dora's soft and plaintive voice murmuring in her ear. Readers we must guess what she said, for she spoke so low that none but Imogen could hear.

Pride and Penitence[1]

Love took up the glass of life, and turned it in his glowing hands;
Every moment lightly shaken ran itself in golden sands;
Love took up the harp of life,—and smote on all its chords with might;
Emote the chord of self, that trembling passed in music out of sight.
TENNYSON.

CHAPTER I.

From that, dark eye—the lightnings fly,
As from a cloud its glory
And on her cheek, doth feeling speak
Its own impassioned story!

SHE WAS the wildest child I ever saw. Nobody could manage her, not even her mother, whom she almost idolized. Proud, high-spirited, with a temper which nothing but tenderness could control, and beautiful withal as a half-blown rose,—a stark, but clear glowing beauty, which, ever and anon suddenly lighting up from within, startled the beholder with its brilliancy, like an illumined and richly colored transparency.

At boarding-school, she was at once the pride and torment of her teachers,—learning her lessons with inconceivable rapidity,—and forgetting them almost as quickly,—dashing off a composition glowing with wit and girlish enthusiasm, in a shorter time than the sedate Mrs. Wilton employed to read it, and occupying all her leisure moments, which were many, in keeping the rest of the school in an uproar of mirth or mischief.

One of her girlish freaks, when she was about thirteen years of age, had nearly led to at least a temporary dismissal from the school. A lovely, and affectionate little girl, younger than herself was in disgrace, and the other pupils were forbidden to speak to her during the day. She was sitting alone and disconsolate in the schoolroom, with

---

[1] "Pride and Penitence," Frances S. Osgood, *Ladies' National Magazine*, September 1843, vol. IV, no. 3, pp. 73-78

a pet kitten in her lap,—her only companion—when Juliet Clyde, our heroine, suddenly bounded through the low open window, and seated herself by her side. With all her fearlessness she did not quite like openly to disobey the teacher's commands, for she knew a dismissal would be the consequence, and that would grieve her mother; so—instead of speaking to little Lucy, she contented her with addressing her kitten, in terms of the most tender endearment, evidently intended to reach and to soothe the sorrowing heart of her companion.

"You dear, sweet little pet!—you darling beauty! I love you so very much—and I am sorry you are so lonely here, but you shant be alone any more, for I've left them all on the play-ground to come and stay with you and talk to you. I have such a pretty story to you, little Kitty, all about the fairies! Should you like to hear about the fairies, little Kitty?"

Juliet's voice was always sweet—even in anger—but now it assumed the most winning, *petting*, loving tone imaginable—and though "little Kitty" only purred in reply— little *Lucy's* eyes began to glisten with mingled tears and smiles. So the pretty and youthful comforter laying her arm fondly over the kitten, that it might touch Lucy's which was also caressing it, told the following story:—

THE LAST FAIRY.

Once there was a little girl, and her name was Mary, and she was a sweet, good little girl. She looked like Lucy Grey. Do you know Lucy Grey, Kitty? Well, Mary had just darling, deep-blue eyes, and just such soft, wavy hair, and just such cunning, pretty playful ways.

One evening at sunset Mary was leaning all alone, and half asleep on a fresh bank of moss in the woods. She gazed dreamily up through the dark trees, and she felt very happy, for the blue sky looked down upon her with a soft, soft smile, and the breeze whispered amid the many-colored leaves in musical, mysterious tones, and the pleasant tranquil flowers sighed out their happy love at her feet, and all things ministered to her, for her spirit was pure and true. Little Mary had heard so many charming fairy tales that she wanted very much to believe in fairies—

but as she had never seen one and her mamma never had either—she was afraid it was silly—but she still could not help now and then watching the key-holes, half hoping, half dreading to see a tiny, gauze-winged spirit fluttering through, and she would even fancy sometimes that she felt one in her thimble dancing on the tip of her little round finger, and she would peep into a shell for hours, pining to catch a glimpse of the little singing-sylph which she was almost sure was imprisoned there, for had she not distinctly heard it murmuring a sad, low, plaintive song, and its far-off home in the sea?

Now it so happened that close by her side as she lay half asleep in the woods grew a great Aloe tree, which the oldest man in the village where she lived had once seen bloom—but that was almost an hundred years ago. This old man had often told her that there were plenty of fairies in his time, and that once, just at sunrise, he had seen a whole troop of them tripping round that very tree when it was just shedding its wonderful blossoms. He had heard that daylight was fatal to the elfin race, and he had watched to see what effect the sunshine would have, for they had rashly prolonged their dance to a later hour than usual. Sure enough, at the very first gleam of light he heard a faint shout, or rather moan of dismay and sorrow from the troop, and they gradually faded from his view like stars at the dawn of day. They were never seen of hear of afterward.

Mary thought of all this as she lay at the foot of the tree and she said to herself—"If I had been there I would have told the dear, little fairies that the great, staring sun was coming up the hill, and that they must all run away quick before he saw them, and then he would not have killed them with that dazzling, burning eye of his!"

While she was thus *reverieing*—do you know what reverieing means, Kitty? It means soliloquising—that is, meditating—that is, thinking—well! while Mary was thinking thus, and still looking drowsily up at the tree, all at once one of the buds began slowly, very slowly to unfold, and to her wonder and delight she plainly saw a pair of luminous rose-colored wings fluttering softly up from the flower—and then—can it be?—yes!—it is—it must be a fairy!—a real fairy!—flying like a sunbeam personified to her feet, and there it stands gracefully poised upon one little dot of a foot which rested on a violet, gazing earnestly up in her face as if asking her how in the world she came there.

Mary was not the least frightened—good children seldom are. She held out her dimpled hand with a smile of invitation, and the cunning and beautiful creature sprang at once to her little finger, and said in a voice light and clear and delicate as the faintest tinkle of a music-box, but sad and wild as an Æolian harp—

"They are all gone but I—I am all alone now!—when the cruel and unexpected beam of daylight pierced them with its fatal heat I only escaped—for I had hidden in sport in a seed of the Aloe flower. But that destiny which doomed my sisters to death, doomed me to a fate as sad. It sealed the seed where I had rashly crept, and for nearly an hundred years; for not till then could the blossom bloom again, have I bided my time in darkness but in hope. Now once more I am free, but oh! how lonely! Will you take me, Mary, and let me live in your thimble or the top of your silver pencil-case. I will sing to you every night if you will. Hear now how sweetly I sing—

> Like the stars from the sky,
>   Like the dew from the rose,
> Like Love's latest sigh
>   Did their sweet life close,
> Exhaled as they flew,
>   And lamenting I moan,
> Oh! sisters of airs,
>   I'm alone, all alone!

There was a fairy impromptu, Mary. But will you let me come? I shant trouble you much—I shall only want a fresh rose-leaf every day for a bed—and a tender smile or a tear of love for my breakfast, dinner and supper—for love is a spirit's food—but you must let me come out at night, for then the flowers and stars will expect me. Will you, Mary?"

"Yes! You precious, lovely, little darling, indeed I will!—I will take you home and introduce you to some other pet fairies I have that live in my beautiful rose-colored shells—I call them sylphs of the shells. They have never shown themselves to me, though they treat me to a bit of music sometimes—but I am sure they will let *you* creep in and play with them. Come, let me see if you can sit comfortable in here," and so she unscrewed her pencil-case, and the fairy had settled nicely in when alas!—something unforeseen happened—a great disappointment. Poor Mary awoke!—and found it was all a dream. Shouldn't you like to have such a dream, little Kitty.

Our heroine was so intent upon amusing little Lucy, that she never once raised her eyes, and did not dream that she was watched—that a young cadet, on a visit to his aunt, Mrs. Wilton, happened to be crossing the lawn when he saw her light form in the act of springing through the window, and that irresistibly attracted by the grace and spirit of the action, he had followed her and stood concealed by the jessamine that shaded the lattice, a smiling witness to her little stratagem, and an enchanted listener to the fairy romance.

But yet another and less indulgent auditor had been in the adjoining room, the door of which was partially open, and after enjoying the story, had hastened to Mrs. Wilton with the tale of Juliet's disobedience. It was Margaret Mansfield, the informant against poor little Lucy; and one, who, for her envious and peevish disposition, and her mean habit of tattling, was disliked by all, and treated with lofty contempt by our impetuous and independent heroine.

CHAPTER II.

When the pupils assembled to their afternoon exercises, Mrs. Wilton, looking calmly round upon them, said in a quiet tone—"Has any one disobeyed my commands as to conversing with Lucy Grey?" Juliet had not anticipated the question; but she scorned both falsehood and concealment, and she instantly rose from her seat,

"*I* have, Mrs. Wilton—I could not bear to see her suffering unjustly, and I did all I could to comfort her."

Margaret smiled maliciously, and Lucy burst into tears. Mrs. Wilton resumed,

"You know, I presume, the consequences of disobedience, Miss Clyde?"

"Oh, Mrs. Wilton!" said Lucy sobbing, "do not punish her! She did not *quite* disobey you—she talked to my little kitten, and never said a word to *me*."

Miss Mansfield sneered and muttered rudely—"a nice way to come off, indeed! Another of Lucy Grey's white lies, I suppose."

Juliet turned with flashing eyes toward her—"Lucy has told the simple truth, Miss Mansfield: it would be well if you would take a lesson from her."

"Be silent, young ladies!" said Mrs. Wilton, sternly. "This, if it be a falsehood, is not the first that Lucy has been guilty of to-day. Miss Clyde I am astonished that you should be willing to take refuge in her weakness—that you should have talked to her kitten and not to her is a most improbable story."

Juliet's spirit was thoroughly roused by this unmerited charge, and with haughty indignation, she replied—"Mrs. Wilton, I wish for no refuge from the *truth*, but then—" she was interrupted by a little, pale and trembling girl, who stole from her desk to Mrs. Wilton's side, and with a half-frightened glance at Miss Mansfield, said in a faltering voice,

"I will tell you the whole truth if you will make Margaret promise not to beat me."

"What is all this?" asked Mrs. Wilton in amazement, drawing the child toward her. "Tell me the truth at once, my dear, nobody shall harm you for it."

"Well, it was Margaret who took the cherries this morning. I saw her; and then she went and put the stones in Lucy's desk, so as to make you think it was Lucy; and she said if I told she would beat me, and—and—." But at the word "beat" the poor little child began to cry, and she could not finish the sentence.

Miss Mansfield was pale with rage and shame; Lucy's tears fell faster than ever; and Juliet, springing toward her, with tears in her eyes, in defiance of all rule, threw her arms around her neck and kissed her a dozen times.

"I knew—I knew she was innocent!—I *said* she was—you would not believe me!" she exclaimed, turning reproachfully to Mrs. Wilton. "She has told the truth in both instances; but since you accuse me also of falsehood, I presume I may be allowed to retire, to prepare for my return home by the evening coach." So saying with a rather stately, but still respectful bow, she quietly left the room.

The young cadet was with his aunt when Juliet approached to take a final farewell. He heard it with surprise, and he could not refrain from asking, as the latter turned to the window to hide her emotion, what was the cause of this sudden departure. In a few hurried words Mrs. Wilton related the affair, and expressed her regret at being obliged to part with her favorite.

"Is that all, my dear aunt?" exclaimed George Wilton, startling Miss Clyde by his eager and delighted tone—"I am glad to have it in my power to clear up the mystery. I fortunately witnessed this young lady's generous efforts to soothe and amuse little *Kitty*." Juliet could hardly help echoing his laugh, as he uttered the last word with an arch glance at her tearful, blushing face; and then he told the whole story, with the exception of the rather indecorous bound through the window, which, though he remembered it years afterward, he at that moment most unaccountably chose to forget.

It is hardly necessary to any that Lucy and her wild, but warm-hearted friend were, at his intercession, fully restored to favor, and that Miss Mansfield was immediately dismissed.

CHAPTER III.

Juliet never forgot the looks, the tones, the graceful beauty of the youthful stranger, although a few hours after that one short interview he left for West Point, and she saw him no more while at school.

But when at seventeen she made her debut, a belle and an heiress at the first ball of the season Lieutenant George Wilton was her favored attendant through the evening. As for him he was perfectly charmed with her beauty, her wit, her wild and brilliant gaiety, and after a month of devoted gallantry on his part, and of graceful, but somewhat tyrannical coquetry on hers, their engagement was announced to the fashionable world of Philadelphia, where they resided.

And now came to him "the tug of war;" for how to manage the wayward, whimsical, saucy, loving, bewitching, and imperious beauty to whom he had rashly bound himself, was a question that would have puzzled a more profound philosopher than our friend, Lieut. George Wilton, U.S.A.

Scarcely a day passed that they did not quarrel take an eternal farewell of each other, separate, meet again, and become, for the next twenty-four hours, more tenderly attached than ever.

One evening the lover accidentally overheard a bold and dashing young foreigner propose driving Miss Juliet to Laurel Hill the next afternoon. Her reply was so low that it escaped him, but he *thought* it sounded like an assent, and he was wretched and restless until the gentleman took his departure. He then approached her, and said in a serious, but affectionate tone,

"Juliet, is it possible that I heard aright? Can you really have engaged to drive with that young man?"

Coloring with surprise and anger at his suspecting her of such levity, Juliet threw back her graceful head, but deigned no farther reply.

"It is true, then," said he in a hasty tone of vexation.

"And what, sir, if it be true! I have yet to learn that *you* have any right to control my movements."

"I pretend to no right, Miss Clyde. I can only say that if you do take the drive proposed you will forfeit not only my love, but my respect."

"Do you threaten, sir?" exclaimed the willful girl with a quivering lip, and tears of passion in her beautiful eyes, "then hear me! I do intend to take the drive; and your respect is of as little importance to me as your love. Leave me! I would be alone!"

"Good God! has it come to this!" cried the incensed and unhappy lover, as striking his clenched hand upon his forehead, he rushed from the house. He paused on the threshold a moment, and gentler feelings came over him— "I was very hasty! Perhaps she is sorry!—I will try her once more!" he said to himself, and with that impetuosity which marked his quick but generous temperament, he ran up the stairs and entered the room he had left.

Juliet had buried her face among the cushions and was sobbing as if her heart would break; softened still more by her grief, he sprang to her side, and drawing her tenderly toward him, waited for some expression of regret for her unkindness. A moment before the wayward girl would have given worlds to recall him and implore his forgiveness; but now that he was here again, as she though, in her power, her pride and love of empire resumed at once their sway. Withdrawing herself with assumed coldness from his embrace, she gazed at him a moment in cool and lofty astonishment, and then, without farther notice of his presence, indolently lay back on the sofa, and began a careless song.

> "Love comes and goes
> Like a spell—"

"Juliet, listen to me—I implore thee."

> "How no one knows,
> Nor can tell!'

"Heartless! unfeeling! *Will* you hear me?"

> "Love should be true
> As the star—"

"You will not! You will regret this when it is—"

> "Seen in the blue
> Sky afar!"

"Farewell, then, and forever!"

> "Now here—now there
> Like the lay
> Of harps in the air,
> Well a day!"

He heard her exquisite voice warbling these last words as he again descended the stairs, and he said to himself— "No—she never loved me! I will see her no more!"

Juliet cried herself to sleep that night, and awoke the next morning with a dull weight on her heart, and an undefined impression that something terrible had occurred. However as the hours rolled on she recovered in some degree her spirits in the hope of a reconciling interview with her lover. She had made up her mind to be gentle and good and forgiving, and to tell him voluntarily that she had not once dreamed of accepting the foreigner's invitation, until he himself had wounded her by supposing that she had consented to it, and that even now nothing would tempt her to go. But the day passed and he came not: he never came again!—months and years rolled on, and Juliet only heard of her lover twice—once as performing feats of valor against the Mexicans, and again as suffering from wounds and hardships in a hospital at New Orleans. She was dying with the untold pang at her heart, when this last news reached her—a burst of uncontrollable anguish followed its recital, and then, suddenly, a new hope, a new life appeared to animate her; the color returned to her cheek, and her strength was rapidly restored.

CHAPTER IV.

One day as she was sitting in the midst of preparations for a journey and writing a letter—the door of her chamber suddenly opened, and a beautiful girl, tripping in with the lightness and grace of a sylph, threw her arms about the neck of the astonished Juliet, and gave her a loving kiss.

"You do not know me, dear Juliet!" she exclaimed after a moment's pause, in a sweet, plaintive, childish voice, which struck a chord of memory in the heart of her listener; "and I should hardly have known you had not your mother directed me to your room. But look at me well and guess!" And parting from her lovely face the soft, light tresses that clustered around it, she bent her blue eyes upon our heroine with a smile of enchanting tenderness.

"Can it be Lucy Grey?"

"Ah! do you recognize at last your little pet at school! Well, then let me sit at your feet, as in old times, and tell me of this weary illness, which has paled your cheek and dimmed your eye, yet left you even lovelier than before. Do you know that it is five long years since I bade you good-bye in Mrs. Wilton's porch?"

"Nay, Lucy, I cannot overshadow this sweet meeting with my too well deserved misfortunes. Let us rather talk of yourself, and of the conquests you have made since you left school, with those violet eyes and that darling, little dimple. I have heard of you often, and always as the 'star of the festive hall.'"

We will drop the veil, or rather close the chapter over Lucy's blushes, as she shook her bright curls, and laughingly disclaimed the charge.

CHAPTER V.

In a crowded hospital at New Orleans lay an officer almost at the point of death. A young woman sat at his bedside. She was dressed in the coarse and unbecoming garb of a sister of charity; but the hand, with which she soothed and soothed and cooled his fevered brow, was soft and delicate as the down of a snow-white swan-and even the heavy folds of her garments could not wholly conceal the grace and elegance of her almost girlish form. Day after day she tended the half-delirious sufferer with a modest fortitude and unassuming tenderness, which won the respect and admiration of all around her. Thanks to her unremitting care, he soon became convalescent, and then she would have withdrawn to other invalids in the establishment; but the young officer had learned to know and love the hand that so gently ministered to his wants, and the old the physician advised her to humor him for the present.

"You have never told me your name," said George Wilton, one morning to his youthful nurse. Our reader has anticipated that the invalid officer was he. A light flush burned and faded in the usually pale and transparent cheek of the girl, and bending her head to conceal it, she replied in a hardly audible voice—

"Sister Magdalen is the name my superior has given me."

"Well, then, Sister Magdalen, do you know that your voice and your hand and your eyes, whenever I catch a glimpse of them, remind me of one whom I loved, and still love devotedly? Why do you tremble so! Are you ill? You are weary with watching!—No? Well, then, let me still talk of my Juliet, for I think of her all the time; but she was not like you in one respect, for she wronged me cruelly, and *you* have been an angel of mercy! Good God! what does this mean! You are weeping! sobbing!—by heaven!—throw off that hood—that coif! It is—it is—my own, my precious Juliet!—but oh! how changed!—and I—I have done this!"

He fell back insensible. While applying the usual restoratives, Juliet bitterly reproached herself for her want of self-control, and resolved that she would leave him for other duties immediately. On his recovery she told him this gently but firmly. He tried a thousand passionate and earnest arguments to induce her to change her resolution; to give up her present employment, and to return home as his wife.

For an instant her woman's heart heaved beneath the serge that covered it. The next she tranquilly replied,

"I did not adopt this sacred garb for the mere selfish purpose of restoring to myself a lover. When I entered upon the duties of my office, it was with a calm resolve to continue in them while my health would permit. I feel that it will not be long, and I do not regret my choice. I am but a wreck, dear George, of my former self, and should only be a burden to you; but I thank God that sickness and sorrow, and the stern task which I have imposed upon myself are doing his work, are chastening and subduing the proud and willful spirit, to which we both owe our misfortunes. Henceforth, dear friend, let our love be that of brother and sister. *You* will, ere long, find a bride more worthy in every way of your affection and your pride than the poor and feeble Sister Magdalen." She laid her hand lightly and tenderly upon his brow—she breathed a blessing and a prayer—he looked up—she was gone!

CHAPTER VI.

Three years had elapsed after the interview related in our last chapter. In the library of a house in Walnut street, Philadelphia, were seated a gentleman in a military undress and his wife—a young and lovely woman, whose simple and becoming morning-cap of embroidered muslin, confined, without concealing the fair, soft hair, which shaded her youthful cheek. It was the depth of winter; a cheerful fire was burning in the grate, and a pretty child of four months old lay on the rich rug at her feet, glancing alternately from the blaze to its mother's face, which was bent toward it with an expression of unutterable love. The father was gazing delighted at the graceful picture, when the door opened, and a servant announced "Sister Magdalen!" With exclamations of surprise and joy, both wife and husband hastened forward to welcome and seat her by the fire. Lucy, for it was our old friend, Lucy Grey, who had now become the beloved, and therefore happy wife of Juliet's former lover, Lucy Wilton gently removed the hood of the almost exhausted stranger, and seating herself, as in their school-days, at her feet, looked up with childish fondness in her face. It was fearfully altered, but oh! how lovely still! A faint smile of angelic purity and tenderness played in the large, clear, dark eyes, and the pale, but perfectly transparent check was luminous with that seen through the vivid hues of health.

"I have come," she said, in a scarcely audible voice, "to see and rejoice in your happiness, before I die. Place your sweet babe in my arms, dear Lucy; for I am too weak to lift it." Lucy's tears fell fast amid the light, soft curls of the infant as she placed it on the knee of her dying friend, and George knelt down by her side with a feeling of affectionate reverence. Once more was that frail hand laid in blessing upon his head; but ere the benediction was concluded, the hand dropped lifeless at her side; the pale lips moved inaudibly, and the pious prayer, began on earth, was finished at the mercy seat of Heaven.

Grace Melvyn;
or
Which is the Bluestocking?[1]

CHAPTER I.

"'NO MORE of that, an thou lovest me, Hal,'" replied Charles Elliott to his friend Curtis, as they stood together at Mrs. Richmond's *soirée*; "anything but a learned lady—anything but a *blue-stocking!* Bah! the very name gives me the blues, already. Besides, in these times, a man wants a wife that can condescend to see to household matters now and then, and I never knew a blue-stocking that could do that."

"But you know your aunt's last words were, 'Be sure you obtain an introduction to that little genius, Miss Melvyn.' The old lady has set her heart upon the match, and, at any rate, there can be no harm in becoming acquainted with her."

"Yes, there can. I wouldn't know her on any account. I can see her now 'in my mind's eye'—frowsy, yellow hair, braided, curled, bewitched with an endeavor to look romantic—sky-blue eyes, upraised to heaven—red nose—thin, sharp mouth—scraggy form—unhealthy complexion—clumsy, slipshod feet—croaking voice—bold expression—dowdy dress—bah! I will never marry a blue-stocking. What are you laughing at?"

"Mr. Elliott," said a gentle voice at his elbow, "come with me, and be presented to my friend Miss Melvyn. I promised your aunt you should become acquainted with her."

There was a pause.

"Do you not hear me, Mr. Elliott?" And the young lady looked surprised at receiving no answer. But Mr. Elliott's silence was soon explained. His eyes and mind were

---

[1] "Grace Melvyn; or Which is the Bluestocking?," Frances S. Osgood, *Graham's Magazine*, August 1843, vol. XXIV, no. 2, pp. 93-97

riveted on a young, and brilliantly beautiful girl, about seventeen years of age, who was tripping gaily down the contra-dance, as if her soul were in her feet, little as they were. She was almost, not quite, a brunette, with a pair of melting, black eyes, shaded by long and glossy lashes—a bewitching mouth, daintily curved and richly colored—a cheek glowing warmly with feeling and animation—soft hair, bright and black as jet, plainly parted on her smooth, graceful brow, and twisted, with simple taste, behind— delicately formed and exquisitely dressed; she was, indeed, a being formed to enchant a less susceptible heart than that which Mr. Charles Elliott now felt to be beating faster than ever it had before.

"Ah! my dear Miss Richmond," he exclaimed, as, startled from his trance by the tap of her fan upon his arm, he turned toward her, "I beg your pardon—I did not see you. Tell me, who is that beautiful creature in white! there, dancing with that officer? Will you introduce me to her?"

"Yes, if you will let me introduce you to Miss Melvyn."

"What! to blue-stocking!"

"Those who know of her accomplishments only by report have given her that name, I understand, but I am sure you will forget it when you know her. Come!"

"Well, then, I will do penance for my sins, with the hope of reward for my virtues. You promise me an introduction to the beauty, too?"

"Yes—come!"

The beauty was now seated, and by her side was a lady, almost the very counterpart of Elliott's ideal of a blue-stocking. Miss Richmond led him toward her.

"Miss Melvyn, allow me to present my friend, Mr. Elliott." The stiffest of bows were exchanged.

"Miss Grace Melvyn, Mr. Elliott." And the beauty smiled, and bent her graceful head.

Elliott drew a chair, and, seating himself near them, commenced a conversation. Miss Melvyn was cold, dull and taciturn, but her sister, Grace, was all sweetness and vivacity, though with a certain arch and mischievous expression about her rosy mouth and radiant eyes, which he puzzled his brain in vain to account for, not having noticed that Miss Richmond had whispered a few words in her ear, as he turned for the chair; probably a brief summary of the conversation she had overheard between the two young men. Meanwhile, her frank and gay simplicity of word and manner, her child-like *naiveté*, and the soft, enchanting grace with which she spoke, looked and moved, completed the fascination of our hero; and, ere the hour of parting arrived, he had fairly—no! not quite fairly—lost his very *loseable* heart.

CHAPTER II.

"Where can the child be!" exclaimed the widow Melvyn, glancing through the open window, as she took her seat at the tea-table, with her oldest daughter and Mr. Elliott, who had now become a frequent and welcome visitor at her house.

"Oh! here she comes, as usual," she continued, "with a little ragamuffin in one hand, and a basket of flowers in the other," and, as she finished, Grace showed her earnest, glowing face at the window. "Mamma! Mr. Elliott! please give me that loaf of bread from the table, and a bit of that nice cheese, too! (It was a country tea-table, reader.) This poor child has had nothing to eat since morning! Thank you! that will do. I can put them in the basket." And, throwing the flowers hastily in upon a table that stood near, she placed in the basket the bread and cheese, and, giving them to the boy, bade him haste home to his mother, and tell her she would see her the next day.

After tea, Charles watched her as she bent over a beautiful vase, arranging in it the flowers she had brought, and he said, to himself, "She loves flowers better than books—I am glad of that. Anything but a blue-stocking! I hope she hasn't studied Botany."

"*Have* you studied Botany, Grace?" said he, approaching her. Grace stopped her ears with a playful shake of the head.

"Now don't! You know how I hate hard words. You know I had to look out 'Idiosyncrasy' in the dictionary the other day, when you wouldn't tell me its meaning, and now you are going to frighten me out of my love for these dear little rosebuds by telling me their order and class. Just as if I could enjoy them any the more by knowing that they were of the class Tetro—how is it?–Tetro-dynamia, or the order Poly-gynia! oh! it positively hurts my mouth to say it. Only be quiet, and you shall have the sweetest I can find—there! isn't that a darling?" And placing in his hand a half-blown rose, with one laughing glance at her mother and sister, she continued her graceful employment so demurely as to set them both laughing.

"I almost wish you *could* read German," said Charles, as he turned over the pages of a volume of Schiller, for then you could enjoy, with me, this glorious poem to the Ideal."

"What a pity, now! isn't it?" replied Grace, drooping her head and turning up her dark eyes to his, with an expression half plaintive, half comical, and altogether bewitching. "But read it, by all means, for I like the *sound* of the German."

And Elliott read, half sighing, as he did so, that the lovely, but simple, little Grace could not share in his delight. As he came to the lines which have been translated as follows—

And but for one short spring-day breathing,
Bloomed Love—the beautiful—no more!

He looked up, involuntarily, and caught those dark, deep eyes bent full upon him, and filling fast with tears. She turned away in blushing embarrassment, and Charles began to think he must have a very expressive voice and face, since they alone could have so moved "the child," as her mother called her.

CHAPTER III.

"Though she looks so bewitchingly simple,
There is mischief in every dimple."

To HENRY CURTIS, Esq.

Roxbury, Monday Morning.
"She is mine! I have won her!" Congratulate me, my dear fellow! She has consented to be mine, and she is

the veriest little ignoramus in the world! She hardly ever reads—she never uses hard words—she never punctuates her notes (that's rather *too* bad though)—she talks delicious nonsense, with now and then a flash of real genius, which startles, but delights me—she is afraid of sensible people, (so she says, and yet, come to think of it, she never shows much awe of *me*, I must ask her what she means by that.) She is a capital housekeeper—she can sew like a professed seamstress, and sing like a St. Cecilia. If she only understood Italian, now! Her voice would make it more than music. She dances divinely, and, to crown the whole, she loves Charlie Elliott with all her heart and soul! But here she comes—and she insists upon reading my letter, too—she always will have her own way—I must break her of that. It seems to amuse her mightily, this letter! She is laughing and clapping her little hands, in a perfect ecstasy of delight. My aunt still insists, in her long epistles, upon my want of taste in preferring her to her accomplished, intellectual, talented sister—the genius, the learned lady, the *blue-stocking*—bah! Here she is again! If she could only understand Schiller's 'The Witch!' I must finish another time; she has made me forget all I was going to say.

Monday Evening.

Oh! Harry! how completely I have been misled, bewitched, deceived, duped, humbugged! She is a blue-stocking—the blue-stocking, after all! confound her!—bless her, I mean: Yes! "darkly, deeply, beautifully blue." Good heavens! Harry, would you believe it? the little rogue can read Latin, Greek, French, Spanish, Italian, German—and, for all I know, Choctaw and Cherokee, too—as well as I can, almost!

This morning, after laughing, as I told you, at my letter, she suddenly grew very serious. The tears came into her beautiful, earnest eyes; she took my hand in both hers and said, "Charles, I have deceived you. I never realized till now how wrong it was. I did it only in sport, not dreaming that we should ever be so foolish as to fall in love with each other. But I cannot continue the deception. Come with me into the library." I followed her, dreading I knew not what; but half expecting an introduction to some country clown, to whom she had been betrothed in childhood, and whom she was virtually and sublimely determined never to desert!

Had even this fear been realized, I could hardly have been more astounded than I was to see her take from the shelves a volume of Sophocles, and, opening to the *Prometheus*, read, with a faltering voice and blushing cheek, but with just and graceful emphasis, a portion of that glorious work! Perfectly transported with wonder and delight, I caught her in my arms and stopped her sweet mouth with kisses. "Should you like to read Schiller's 'Ideal,' again?" said she, when I released her, trying to look demure, but smiling in spite of herself. She took from the table, and handed to me, a MS. translation of the verses signed "Grace!" It was charming. I was dumb with astonishment.

"And now, will you have a French song, or shall we discuss a law question?—perhaps you would prefer hearing the *Iliad* in the original, or a page or two of Danté's *Inferno*, or a bit of philosophy from Seneca— anything you choose—I am quite at your service, sir." And she dropped a low courtesy, with a grace so enchanting and a smile so exquisitely saucy, that I was more fascinated than ever.

Then she seated herself at a harp. "If you will be very good, and never call me a 'blue-stocking' again, I will sing you a Spanish song, of my own composition, Charles." And she warbled, with deep and serious feelings, a brief song, of which, as you do not understand the language, I will give you an English version:

My heart is like the trembling flower;
   It shrinks, it folds its leaflets warm,
When dark the clouds of coldness lower,
   Or evil eyes portend the storm.

But when love's holy sunshine gleams,
   From eyes that seem a heaven to mine,
It wakes, it blooms from tearful dreams,
   And turns to win the light divine.

At the close of the song, she approached the sofa, where I sat entranced with her beauty, her feeling, her genius, and, seating herself on a low stool, she laid her head on my knee, looked up in my face, and said, in a low and solemn tone, "Good-bye, Charles!"

"Grace what do you mean?"

I mean good-bye, Charles! You know, you 'will never marry a blue-stocking.' You 'wouldn't even know one, on any account.' 'Croaking voice—bold expression—dowdy dress—bah! What are you laughing at?'" Harry, did you tell her that?

"Grace—my angel, Grace forgive me!"

"Forgive me, Charles, and I will try to forget all I know, just as fast as I can, and, in future, learn only to love!" The darling!—her own dear heart taught her that long ago.

It seems, Harry, the little gipsy has had a passion for study from infancy, and, as her worthy mother did not choose she should neglect her other duties for it, she has been in the habit for years of rising an hour or two earlier than the rest of the family, in order to prosecute her favorite pursuits. She is almost entirely self-taught, and her mind is as original and brilliant as it is highly cultivated. No wonder my dear aunt wondered at my taste when I told her the *genius* of the family, which, of course, I set down poor Mary to be, was the last person I should choose for a wife. I know my letter has proved an unconscionably long one, but forgive me, and I won't write again these six months.

Yours, faithfully,
CHARLES ELLIOTT.

CHAPTER IV.

A year had elapsed ere Elliott wrote again, as follows:—

Providence, July 18.

Harry, you know what I have lost, within a few months, by my blind confidence in others—"a moderate fortune, and that fortune's friends!"—but you do not know what a treasure, beyond price, I have gained.

As soon as I had ascertained that my losses were irreparable, I went, with an aching heart, to Grace Melvyn, to take a last farewell. I might have written, but I could not leave her without one last look. She had not heard of my misfortunes, and I knew that if I betrayed to her the cause of my determination to dissolve our engagement, her generous nature would refuse compliance, and I could not bear the thought of her enduring the hardships and struggles of poverty on my account. I thought her pride, once roused, would support her in her disappointment. I was wrong, Harry, cruelly wrong. By a candid statement of facts, I should have spared, both to her and myself, all the heart-rending anguish we have endured.

She flew to me, when I entered, with her accustomed welcoming caress—

"Charlie, dear Charlie! what is the matter? How stern and cold you look—what have I done? Charles, speak to me, I implore you!"

"Grace, I have come to release you from your engagement, and to bid you—farewell."

She looked at me for a moment, as if doubting the evidence of her senses, and then drew haughtily back, with a flushed cheek and flashing eye.

"Grace!"

"Sir!"

"Will you not say farewell?"

Save that the lip slightly quivered, she stood motionless as a statue—a glorious statue—with her proud young head thrown lightly back, and the dark, drooping lashes wet with tears. I took her hand—with averted face and a cold, calm voice, I bade her farewell and left her. As I passed from the room, she murmured almost inaudibly, "Farewell, Charles, may God forgive and bless you!"

The following lines, which I composed in order to calm, in a degree, my excited feelings, will show you how much I suffered in thus dissembling to her, whom I loved far more than life.

THE PARTING.

I looked not, I sighed not, I dared not betray
The wild storm of feeling that strove to have way!
For I knew that each sign of the sorrow *I* felt,

Her heart to fresh pity and passion would melt,
And calm was my voice, and averted my eyes
As I parted from all I most tenderly prize.

I pined but one moment that form to enfold,
Yet the hand that touched hers like the marble was cold!
I heard her voice falter a timid farewell,
Nor trembled, though soft on my spirit it fell;
And she knew not, she dreamed not, the anguish of soul,
Which only my pity for her could control.

It is over, the loveliest dream of delight
That ever illumined a wanderer's night!
Yet one gleam of comfort will brighten my way,
Though mournful and desolate ever I stray—
It is this, that to her, to my idol, I spared
The pang that her love could have softened and shared!

I left Roxbury immediately, and came, by my aunt's invitation, to Providence. Here excitement of mind soon brought on a sever, which confined me to the house for several weeks. When I was convalescent, my friend D—, who had been constant in his inquiries and attentions during my illness, insisted upon driving me out to his country-seat, to pass a few days.

We arrived just at twilight. As it was a summer's evening, the lamps had not been lighted, and it was difficult to distinguish the half dozen people to whom I was introduced in the drawing-room. Among them were my friend's wife and sisters, and a fragile looking girl, whose name I did not distinctly hear. This lady was entreated to sing, and was led, with apparent reluctance, to the piano-forte by Mrs. D—. The first notes of her rich but tremulous voice startled and affected me strangely. The song was that lovely one of Moore's—"Thy Heart and Lute"—and her sweet tones were just trembling on the words—

"Though Love and Song may fail, alas!
To keep Life's clouds away,"

when suddenly lights were brought in, and revealed to my eager gaze—the pale, inspired countenance of Grace Melvyn! Spiritualized by suffering, it was more divinely beautiful than ever.

I hastily approached the instrument—she gazed upon me with an expression of tenderness indescribably touching, and then playing a short and plaintive prelude, began another song. The words went to my heart. I was sure they were her own; and that she had learned the cause of my apparently cruel conduct was evident from their tenor. They were as follows—

> You say you release me from every fond vow,
>   You think even now it were better we part,
> You bid me forget you, ah wrong me not so!
>   'T was not to your wealth, love, I plighted my heart!
>
> Ah, no! though misfortune o'ershadow your way,
>   Though riches and false friends together have fled,
> They leave you to one who will never betray!
>   It was not your fortune I promised to wed.
>
> Then say not forsake me! I die if I do
>   I part with all hope, if with you, love, I part:
> More dear in your sorrow, I worship but you;
>   'T was not to your riches I plighted my heart!

I bent over her in deep emotion. Fortunately the family were at the other end of the room, and our backs were toward them. She went on playing unconsciously, almost blinded by her tears, while I poured forth my love, my gratitude, my sorrow, my remorse; but her feelings overpowered her; gradually the notes grew wilder—weaker—ceased; and she fell back into my arms insensible!

While my friends were employing the usual remedies, I informed them, in a few hurried words, of the truth; and the next morning, thanks to their consideration, had a long and uninterrupted interview with Grace, in which, convinced of my unaltered devotion, she generously insisted upon sharing and lightening my lot "through good and ill," "for better and for worse."

We have been married a month. I have commenced the practice of law in Providence, with a fair prospect of emolument, and my noble and truehearted Grace is teaching music and the languages to a few young ladies, whose parents pay her a high price for her valuable instruction. After all, if I had taken a mere doll, instead of a learned lady, to wife, I should not have been as I am now, in a fair way to retrieve my shattered health and fortunes.

Fill your glass, Harry, with pure Croton—pure as her spirit—and drink a bumper to the Blue-Stocking!

CHAPTER V.

To Miss JULIA RICHMOND, Roxbury, Mass.

Providence, September 1st, 18–.

I promised you, dear Julia, that when I had been married two whole years, I would write and tell you if all those fond anticipations of happiness, which you were wicked enough to smile at, had been fully realized. Oh, Julia! my wildest and dearest dream could not equal the reality, "the sober certainty of waking bliss," which I now experience. Let me describe my home to you. You remember that beautiful little brown cottage, on the hill, with green blinds, built in the Elizabethan style of architecture, and surrounded by forest trees, which we both admired so much when we saw it, three years ago. You remember how you laughed as I exclaimed—"Ah! 'love in a cottage' like that could not well help being charming!" Little did I then dream that the charming cottage, with the charming love in it, would one day be mine! But it is, indeed! It was a wedding-gift to me from Charlie's generous aunt; and oh! it is so pleasant!

I am sitting in a little room—which Charlie calls "the Muse's *boudoir*"—it is adorned and enriched with books, pictures, flowers, birds, *bijouterie*, most of them bridal presents from my friends. The sun shines softly in through the muslin curtains. My baby, my darling Louise—I have named her for mother—it is a pretty name, isn't it? Louise Elliott, she is playing with the sunbeams on the richly colored carpet. Julia, I have no words to tell you how charming, how lovely she is!—"the softened image of her noble sire," with a slight dash of the mother's saucy expression about the mouth and eyes, and rather more than a dash of her vivacity in manner.

Charlie worships her, and well he may! plump, and white, and soft—as—swan's down, gay and graceful as a kitten, with a rosy, cherub mouth, and eyes divinely blue, dark-brown, glossy hair, curling naturally; it is gold now in the sun. Oh, Julia! let me stop one minute just to kiss the precious creature and tell her how much I love her, for the hundredth time this morning!—There! I have turned my back upon the pet, for I cannot write when she is before me; and now let me answer your questions of "How I pass my time," etc.

If I say that the description of one day will serve for the rest, you will call our life monotonous, and it is, in a degree; but, oh! such a soothing, pleasant, musical monotony, that it lulls my heart and does not weary it. Well, then, we will take yesterday. I rose at five, and after taking my cold bath, which you know I deem indispensable to health and comfort, I dressed myself and the baby, and at six gave her an airing in her little carriage, composing on the way a sonnet to her eyelid, beginning with,

> The baby on its mother's breast,
> A blossom on a wave,—etc.

Returned, resigned her to the maid, and mended stockings till half past seven—the breakfast hour. After breakfast, superintended household matters till nine; from nine till twelve, received and attended to my pupils; from twelve till two, busied myself in the kitchen and the nursery with my pets, flowers, birds and baby, then dressed for dinner and seated myself at the window with a book, to watch for Charlie's return; flew to the gate to meet him; entertained him at dinner with a rapturous account of all the pretty and winning things Louisa had said and done; after dinner read him my sonnet, sang to him, and then accompanied him to and left him at his office; made a few visits to poor and rich; called again for Charlie, and took a long, delicious sunset walk with him to Slate Rock, where Roger Williams landed, you know; returned, undressed the baby, washed her, and sang her to sleep; Charlie meanwhile enjoying the operation with all his heart and eyes.

Should you like to hear one of my impromptu nursery songs? The one I sang last night Charlie calls a free translation from the Greek of Euripides! Isn't he saucy? Thus it runs—

Good night, little Looy! Good night! go to bed!
Lay on the pillow that dear little head,
Sleep all night, still as a star!
Wake in the morning, and—

here Miss Louise invariably interrupts me with "kiss, mamma!" which she lisps out exultingly, proud of having learned the words from only once hearing me sing them. The evening is employed in reading, music, sewing, or visiting.

Are you weary of Louise and her mamma? Well, I have only one thing more to say, and that is, that Charlie is the best, the noblest, the kindest, the dearest, the handsomest husband that ever lived—except yours that is to be—and the harshest word he ever says to his willful little wife, be she ever so wild and naughty, is—"Blue-stocking!"

Lizzie Lincoln[1]

CHAPTER I.

Oh! I see the old and formal, fitted to thy petty part,
With a little board of maxims, preaching down a daughter's heart.
Tennyson.

FORM AND FEELING.

THEY WERE twin sisters, and so alike in form and feature that at a first glance you could not tell them apart; but you had only to watch them for five minutes to be quite sure that Lizzie was Lizzie and nobody else but her own sweet self, and that Priscilla was Priscilla—for in mind, in heart, in expression, they were as different as sunshine and moonlight, or a statue and painting, and with the same sort of difference too; both beautiful—but the one cold, calm, pale and still—the other glowing with life, full of spirit, genius and sensibility: Priscilla stately, formal, reserved, apathetic—Lizzie wild, loving, trustful, playful and frank; and as soon as you detected this difference in their natures, you would begin also to perceive that in person, too, they differed slightly: Lizzie had a fuller, richer lip, a deeper, darker eye, a cheek more warmly tinged, and ever changing with her changing mood, a lighter and more yielding form, a step of more aerial grace, a sunnier smile, a sweeter voice, a softer, yet a merrier laugh; even her hair had an expression about it that did not belong to Priscilla's; both were deep brown in hue; but Lizzie's had a natural wave that caught the light and changed with it to gold.

Everybody loved Lizzie and petted her; that is, everybody whose love was worth having. She was welcome and refreshing to their hearts as a sunbeam, or a flower, or a singing-bird, or a balmy breeze, or a shower at noon

---

[1] "Lizzie Lincoln," Frances S. Osgood, *Graham's Magazine,* October 1843, vol. XXIV, no. 4, pp. 184-187

in midsummer, and Lizzie loved her friends warmly and faithfully, without stopping to ask herself why. She did not blind herself to their faults, but she loved them faults and all. She was a rare, sweet child; yes! still a child at heart, though fifteen summers had somewhat subdued and softened her too impetuous temperament.

They lived with their mother—a widow of moderate means—in a picturesque village of England, and at the time my story commences were in hourly expectation of a visit from an uncle, by the father's side, supposed to be rich, and known to be cross, gouty and disagreeable.

"Elizabeth," said Mrs. Lincoln, seating herself at a window to watch for his arrival, "I must once more enjoin upon you, that policy, as well as duty; requires of us to humor your uncle in every whim, to agree with him in all things."

"But, mother!" said Lizzie, with a pleading look, "I never can act from policy, and as to pretending to agree with him when I don't, that would be an absolute impossibility to me. I will promise to do all that is right to please him."

"I do not choose to argue the matter, Miss. Remember that I insist upon obedience. I only wish you were as precise in other matters as you are in your absurd notions of right and wrong. You, my dear Priscilla, will, I am sure, obey me without a question."

"Certainly, mamma!," replied the demure young lady in a placid voice.

The tears sprung to Lizzy's lovely eyes; but she smiled them away, and going to the piano-forte, began to play and sing in a soft, soothing voice, *her mother's favorite song—*

"Though storms may gather o'er us,
The sun will smile again;
Though dark the way before us,
We 're led by Love's true chain.

"Though sadly heaves the bosom,
Joy always follows care;
There's many a summer blossom
In winter's tangled hair!"

Two young and distinguished-looking men, passing at the time, involuntarily glanced in through the open window, and as Lizzie raised her head at the rustling of the vine leaves, which they brushed in going by, she encountered from a pair of dark gray eyes a momentary glance of earnest admiration, which she never afterward forgot. For almost the first time in her life, Lizzie Lincoln fell into a deep reverie; but it was soon broken by the arrival of a carriage, from which alighted a bundle of shawls, flannel, ugliness, gout and grumbling, which was introduced by Mrs. Lincoln to her daughters as their invalid uncle.

Lizzie, before he entered, had silently placed the easiest chair, with a stool before it, in the pleasantest corner of the room; but she allowed her mother and sister to assist him into it without offering her aid.

"My dear sir," said Mrs. Lincoln, "you are looking ten years younger than when I last saw you, and so like my poor, dear husband!"—her husband by the way had been considered a remarkably handsome man—"Doesn't he, Priscilla? Doesn't he, Lizzie?"

"Very much," said Priscilla. And nothing said Lizzie; but walked quietly out of the room.

"That is a singular young person—that daughter of yours ma'am"—grumbled the old gentleman, "don't think she takes much pains to please her rich uncle."

"Oh! my dear sir, you must forgive her; she is timid to a fault. Is she not, Priscilla?"

"Yes, mamma," said echo.

And where did Lizzie go? My youthful readers, if you have not kind and warm hearts like hers, you will never guess; but I dare say you have, and that you would have done the same thing. She went straight to the spare chamber appropriated to her uncle, to see that everything was arranged for his comfort, then into the garden, whence she brought fresh flowers to adorn the room, then to her own little chamber, from which she took a Bible to lay on the table by his bed, and then into the kitchen to oversee the preparations for his supper.

Meanwhile, the two young men pursued their walk and their conversation.

"Yes, my dear Howard," said he who had attracted Lizzie's notice, "I tell you the simple truth; I am weary of my rank, my wealth, and the insufferable attentions which they bring upon me from ambitious daughters and manœuvering mammas. How delicious it would be to settle quietly down in this charming village with such a wife as that bright, beautiful, artless-looking girl whom we saw just now through the window! But I fear I shall never marry, for I shall always be haunted by the idea that my wealth is the object of attraction. Unless—Howard! I have it! Glorious!"—and, with his fine, manly face kindling and glowing with enthusiasm, the young earl passed on in earnest conversation with his friend. Perhaps he will reappear ere the close of the story; but in the mean time we must introduce our readers to a new chapter and a new schoolmaster.

CHAPTER II.

"Taming my wild heart to thy loving hand."

At twenty-two years of age Charles Welford came to the village of S———, poor and unknown, but his mild dignity of manner, his prepossessing appearance, his youthful and handsome countenance, gained him a host of friends, and the small number of pupils to which he had limited himself was soon made up. Mrs. Lincoln sent Lizzie and Priscilla to be perfected in French and Italian—and the former made wonderfully rapid progress—if not in the languages, at least in the affections of her teacher.

"Miss Lincoln," the master would say, endeavoring, but in vain, to look stern, "I shall be obliged to detain you after school hours, if you persist in talking and laughing;" and Lizzie would blush and maintain a demure composure for the next three minutes and a half—then he would hear the little gipsy buzzing away again, for the least sound of her sweet voice always attracted his notice, and calling her to him with a grave face, but inward delight, he would point silently to a little chair at his side.

Poor Lizzie, half pouting, half pleased, "with a smile on her lip, and a tear in her eye," would quietly obey. I rather think Lizzy liked the punishment upon the whole; for his dark eyes had talked to her soul a language more pleasant than French or Italian—and after looking earnestly up to them for a moment to discover if he were really offended—

reassured by the glance of affectionate interest which he returned to her inquiring gaze, she would study for hours by his side, happy, and tranquil, and silent, as a dove in its woodland nest.

Now and then, when she had been more than usually wild and uncontrollable, Mr. Welford would feel it his duty to detain her after the other pupils had left, in order to give her a serious lecture upon the lightness of her conduct; but the serious lecture generally ended in a long ramble through the woods, after flowers to assist their botanical studies. And during these rambles, they would confide to each other's sympathizing hearts their memories, their hopes, their tastes and preferences. Lizzie with all the simple, trustful tenderness of a child, and Charles with the frankness natural to a spirit still fresh, pure and untrammeled.

"Do you know, Mr. Welford," said Lizzie one day, "I would give a great deal that my uncle was poor?"

"Poor! Lizzie—what a strange wish! Why?"

"Oh, because—he is so ill, and cross, and unhappy that I pity him from my heart, and I would be so very, very kind to him if he were not rich; but as it is, mother *makes* me treat him coldly."

"How? I do not understand you. I thought she was all attention to him and wished you to be so too."

"Yes! that is the very reason I can't be. She keeps telling me he will leave us all his money if we indulge his whims and agree with him in his queer opinions—and so I make it a rule to be inattentive to him, except in his absence, and *then* I do all I can for his comfort; but that is not much. I should so like to soothe his pain, by reading to him, or singing, or caressing him. I am afraid he won't live long, and he seems to suffer a great deal at times—oh! don't you wish he were poor?"

Lizzie was right. Ill in mind and body, the unhappy old man was daily wasting away. Of all his relations, of all the world, Lizzie Lincoln was the only one he loved; and she alone of all apparently neglected him. Yes! in spite of her neglect, he loved her. He struggled against the preference, but in vain; he could not help it—she was so frank, so sweet, so frolicsome, and, above all, so like his favorite brother. Importuned, beset, followed, fawned upon for his wealth alone, he had become disgusted with life, and his naturally kind heart embittered by suspicion.

CHAPTER III.

Muffins and Mystification.

"Mrs. Lincoln, don't you prefer cold muffins to hot ones?" asked the uncle at breakfast one day, with a look of dogged determination that rather mystified his auditors. Mrs. Lincoln changed an involuntary wry face into an acquiescent one—if there was anything she preferred hot rather than cold it was a muffin—and replied, "Oh! decidedly, my dear sir! They are infinitely more palatable cold. I only ordered hot ones to please *you*. We will have some cold ones immediately. John, bring some cold muffins." A sardonic smile flickered on the old gentleman's furrowed face as he turned to Priscilla—

"And which do *you* prefer?"

Priscilla, as usual, glanced at her mother and then replied—

"Cold ones, sir, of course."

"Of course," he repeated sarcastically—"And you, Miss Lizzie?"

Lizzie looked up frankly in his face—"Uncle, *you know* I like hot ones best, and I think your taste a very singular one if you prefer them cold."

"Who said I preferred them cold? Not I. Come, Lizzie, we will share this nice one together, and here comes John with the cold for your mother and Priscilla. Hand them to your mistress, John. I am sorry, ladies, you have been eating hot muffins merely on *my* account." And he glanced at Lizzie so comically while her mother reluctantly helped herself to the unpalatable bread, that she could scarcely restrain a smile.

CHAPTER IV.

Death and Disappointment.

A few weeks after the conversation alluded to in the last chapter, the old man sent for the family to his bedside, which he had not left for several days, and with a half repressed chuckle of satisfaction, informed them that he had an important secret to reveal. Mrs. Lincoln bent eagerly over him, Priscilla seated herself with her usual quiet composure, and Lizzie half drew back.

"You have repeatedly told me, madam, that it was for my own sake, you valued me so highly—for my own superior qualities of mind and heart, for my striking resemblance to your deceased husband, not for my wealth—that wealth was nothing in the eyes of affection, etc. I thank you as you deserve for this assurance. I will not insult you by a moment's doubt of its sincerity." Mrs. Lincoln smiled benignly, and Lizzie turned impatiently to the window. "I have taken you at your word, and fully trusting to its truth, have made my will accordingly. It is in the hands of my solicitor. I have left the whole of my vast property, in specie and landed estate—with the exception of a trifling gift to one who is very dear to me—to a distant relative, the only one who has never troubled me with his company, his attentions, or his flattery, a poor apprentice at a dry-goods store in America."

Unable to conceal her disappointment and vexation, Mrs. Lincoln hurried from the room. Priscilla followed with a still statelier step than usual, and Lizzie, springing from the window, clasped her uncle's hand, exclaiming, "I am so glad! I am so glad! Now I can nurse you with pleasure, and love you as much as I choose!"

The old man was speechless at first with surprise and joy, at length he exclaimed—"Is it possible you really care for me?"

"Dear, dear uncle, were you not kind to my poor father in trouble? Did you not assist him with your purse and your influence? and do you think I can ever forget it?"

The invalid sunk back on his pillow with closed eyes, through which tears, the first he had shed for long years, stole over his withered cheeks, and murmuring, "Thank

God!" fell into a tranquil sleep, still holding Lizzie's hand fast locked in his. From that time until his death, which happened in a few days, she nursed him with the tenderness and attention of an affectionate daughter.

Mrs. Lincoln was agreeably surprised to find on the opening of the will, that the "trifling gift to one very dear to him," was no less than a sum of £2000, bequeathed to her daughter Elizabeth.

The latter generously, or as *she* said *justly*, shared this sum with her mother and sister, and affairs went on as before, excepting that somehow the rambles after flowers in the woods grew longer and more frequent.

"We are trying to find the little blue 'Forget-me-not,' which Mr. Welford is sure grows in these woods somewhere," said poor Lizzie, blushing and smiling, when one day a friend questioned her rather too closely upon the subject.

CHAPTER V.

Lizzie and a Lover.

Autumn had come, with its cheerful fires, its picnic *fêtes* and evening dances, and with it came to the village of S——, a young and wealthy nobleman, who fell desperately in love with Lizzie at a party, and one afternoon when she came into her mother's little parlor, looking particularly bewitching in her simple straw bonnet and graceful mantilla, and found him there alone, he suddenly offered her his hand and heart. But Lizzie laughed the matter off, by telling him she could not possibly stop to accept it, as she was in a great hurry to go into the woods, in search of a certain little blue flower called the "Forget-me not." Away she tripped, and when she returned an hour after sunset the youth had vanished, and the village "that had known him, knew him no more."

CHAPTER VI.

A Tableaux Vivant.

Trust me, cousin, all the current of my being sets to thee.
Tennyson.

A flood of warm golden light from the setting sun pained in through a vista of the woods, and lighted up a picture there well worthy of such an illumination.

A young and graceful girl was leaning against the trunk of a noble tree. Her straw bonnet lay on the mossy rock beside her. Her soft curls fell showering round her face as she bent over a flower which she held in her hand. It was the little blue "Forget-me-not," from whose mystic petals many a romantic village maid has learned her destiny.

Leaf after leaf the blushing girl pulled off, murmuring as she did so, in a low and trembling tone, half sportive, half in earnest, "He loves me—he loves me not—he loves me—he loves me not"—only one leaf remained—"He loves"—the flower was gently withdrawn, and the hand that held it pressed passionately to the lips of a noble looking youth who had stolen unperceived around the tree. "Let me speak for the last leaf, Lizzie," he whispered, "He loves thee more than life! Dear one, may he believe his love returned?" Lizzie smiled through her tears—he drew her to his heart!

For a moment the lingering sunshine rested softly on the fair tableaux, then passed and left it to the holier light of love.

CHAPTER VII.

"You remember Ellen, our hamlet's pride,
How meekly she blessed her humble lot,
When the stranger William had made her his bride,
And love was the light of their lowly cot!"

"Have you found the blue 'Forget-me-not' yet?" said the good old rector of S——, with a meaning smile, to a fair and white-robed maiden at his side, as they sat with others at the bridal feast about a year after the performance of the forest-*tableaux*. Lizzie Welford looked up in her husband's eyes, which were bent fondly upon her, and smiled, but did not reply.

Pleasant and comfortable, but simply furnished, was the cottage in which the schoolmaster and his beautiful and happy wife passed the first few months of their marriage. But Charles grew restless then, and he persuaded Lizzie—who never could resist his persuasions—to take a little journey with him.

In their own humble chaise, they traveled through the delightful and richly cultivated country, and Lizzie was enchanted with almost all she saw. There was but one drawback on her happiness; and that had always been her chief trouble from childhood—her sympathies were too powerful to allow her to behold poverty or misery in any shape without a pang of pity and an ardent wish to relieve it; and this her humble means would not always allow her to do. As she passed some beggars on the road, to whom she had thrown some silver, she turned to her husband with tears in her eyes and said—

"Oh, Charles! I never care for wealth for my own sake, but would it not be a divine happiness to possess the power of relieving others?"

Charles smiled, rather too gaily she thought, but he pressed her hand so tenderly that she could not chide him. At the close of the second day's journey, they came to a beautiful and extensive park, through the vistas of which, they could catch now and then a glimpse of a magnificent mansion. Lizzie thought it must be a palace. Her eyes flashed with delight, and then filled with tears. She was excited and nervous she knew not why. She had read of such places, but she had never seen one, and she begged Charles to stop the chaise for a few moments, that she might gaze her fill.

"We will drive through the park," said her husband, "I know the owner well."

She thought his voice trembled, and looking up in his face she saw that it was lighted up with a glow of lofty exultation, which so well became his refined and aristocratic beauty that she involuntarily raised his hand to her lips and kissed it fondly, yet with a vague fear for which she could not account.

They drove through the park to the principal entrance of the house; as they approached it was flung wide open! and from a train of liveried servants stepped forth an old man, who smiled an earnest welcome as he respectfully assisted Charles to alight. Lizzie was dumb with wonder.

"Come!" said her husband holding out his hand.

"Where are you taking me, Charles?"

"To my *home*! dear Lizzie," he exclaimed, pressing her fondly to his bosom, as he bore her half fainting into the library, where a pleasant fire was kindled.

"Welcome to my home—to the home of my fathers! my own, my precious wife!"

"And who then are you, my husband?" asked the bewildered and half frightened Lizzie, sinking on a sofa by his side.

"My dear Howard," said he laughing, to a young man who at this moment hastily entered the room, "before you welcome me, introduce me to my wife!"

"The Earl of E——, dear madam," said his friend, coming forward with a smile.

"The Earl of E——, sweet countess," echoed Charles, "think you that dear forehead will ache beneath this toy?" And taking from a casket a coronet of diamonds, he placed it on her head and kissed her tearful eyes. And what did the youthful countess do? Forgive her etiquette! Forgive her, Mr. Howard! She was weary—almost exhausted with excitement and fatigue—and closing her lashes, still wet with tears, upon her husband's shoulder, she murmured a blessing upon his name, and fell fast asleep, like a tired child, as she was!"

Courteous reader! if you have not already followed her example you may do so now—for my story is ended.

Daguerreotype Pictures Taken on New Year's Day[1]

IT WAS the first of January, 1843. A carriage drew up to the door of the Astor House, and into it stepped two young men—both well dressed, both handsome, but very different in feature, manner and style. The most striking in appearance of the two was a tall, dashing, manly looking fellow, with bold black eyes and hair of the same hue—a dark but brilliantly colored complexion, a Roman nose, and a mouth expressive of great resolution and energy of character.

The other, more modest, more unassuming in mien, was, perhaps on that very account, by far the most interesting of the two. His head and face were perfectly Grecian; a profusion of remarkably beautiful hair of a light brown, fine, soft and wavy, seemed to harmonize with the expression of his hazel eyes and his delicately chiseled mouth. His whole tone in look and demeanor was that of refinement, purity, moral and intellectual elevation.

After ordering the coachman to drive to Union Square, they commenced a conversation, of which the following is an abstract.

"Do you know, Fred," said the last mentioned of the two, "I have a sort of presentiment that my fate will be decided this day for life?"

"And do you know, Charlie, that I too have 'a sort of presentiment' of the very same kind? For I fully intend this day, if appearances warrant, to propose to the beautiful widow in Union Square."

"Beautiful! You are joking! Where can her beauty be?"

"In her diamonds, to be sure. They are a fortune in themselves, if real, and as I intend to have a pretty close survey of them today, I cannot be deceived on that point."

---

[1] "Daguerreotype Pictures Taken on New Year's Day," Frances S. Osgood, *Graham's Magazine*, November 1843, vol. XXIV, no. 5, pp. 255-257

"But you do not seriously mean to marry the woman! Why she is almost an idiot, and old enough to be your mother."

"So much the better for me, my dear fellow. The truth is, Vernon, my purse is getting low, and my bills are getting long, and if I don't fill the one and settle the other soon—why I shall be settled myself, that's all."

"But how can you possibly hope to succeed? Senseless as she is, she has a certain cunning, which will be sure to penetrate your motives."

"Let me alone for that—she thinks herself a beauty still, and lends as willing and confiding an ear to the voice of flattery as she did at sixteen. But once touch the string of vanity in such a woman's heart, and that of caution rings in vain. But once whisper your admiration of her eyes, and she forgets her diamonds."

"Well, Richmond, I cannot wish you success, for if you *do* succeed I shall pity both you and your victim, from my heart."

"Spare your pity, if you please, sir, and explain your presentiment."

"I intended to have done so; but I cannot now. You would only laugh at it in your present reckless mood."

As Richmond was about to reply, the carriage stopped at a door in Union Square. The friends were shown into a gaudily furnished drawing-room, where, on an orange-colored lounge, reclined the lady of the mansion—a little, sallow, withered, peevish-looking woman, who forced, not a smile, but a smirk, as they entered, and bade them, in a small, cracked voice, be seated.

Frederic Richmond drew a chair close to her sofa, while his friend, sauntering through the spacious room, surveyed its furniture and its occupant with a look of mingled pity and surprise. There was a vulgar and glaring ostentation in both, which was revolting to his taste. The ornaments of the room were rather showy than rich; but the lady's apparel was blazing with a profusion of the most brilliant diamonds. Her dress was a bright rose-colored silk, deepening by contrast the sallow tint of her skin. A smile of gratified vanity broke over her thin and wasted features, "like moonlight o'er a sepulchre," as she listened to the extravagant compliments of Richmond; but the glare of light from bracelet, brooch, *ferroniere* and necklace seemed so bitter a mockery of the ruin it illumined, that Vernon turned away with a sigh and hurried from the house.

He had waited but a few moments in the carriage, when his friend joined him with an exulting smile on his thin, disdainful lip.

"The diamonds are mine, Vernon!" he exclaimed as he seated himself, "and next week I shall want your services as brideman."

"You must choose some other, Frederic, it would be very painful to me to countenance so heartless a proceeding."

"As you will, sir, I shan't quarrel with you for your ridiculous fastidiousness; but let us talk of something else."

The next person to whom they made their bow was an authoress, who had published, under the signature of "Malvina," some very *Sapphoish* effusions, entitled "Lays of a Wounded Heart." Perhaps my readers never heard of it.

This lady was seated in an *attitude*, on a cerulean colored ottoman, with her light, very light blue eyes bent pensively on a book. Her dress—cold as was the day—was of white muslin, and her yellow hair hung in unnatural ringlets on her shoulders.

Though the gentlemen would not sit, and were evidently in haste to be gone, she insisted upon reading them an impromptu sonnet, which, she said, she had just composed, beginning with—

"Break, break my heart! for why shoulds't thou
Still linger on in misery?"

One would have thought that the voice must have been a sighing one to match those pleading attitudinizing eyes; but, unfortunately for the sentiment of the sonnet, it startled and astounded the hearers by its extraordinary gruffness; and they were constrained to come to the conclusion that it would require repeated blows to "break" a " heart" whence such a voice proceeded.

Richmond scribbled on a card, ere he took his leave, and handed to the lady, with a theatrical air, the following ridiculous and *bathetic* couplet.

"Request no more so sweet a heart to break!
Entreat it not to for thy Frederic's sake!"

"She looked down to blush, and she looked up to sigh," and kissed her lily hand to him in graceful gratitude as he bowed out of the room.

CHAPTER II.

Like a gem in a beautiful casket, or rather like a lovely portrait in a fitting frame, sat the young and graceful Mrs. L. in her reception-room, receiving with blushes and smiles the compliments of the day from a circle of fashionable admirers. Her hair, black and brilliant as jet, confined beneath a net of gold—her small but exquisitely molded form arrayed in a changeable silk of a pale golden hue—a delicately wrought French cape, rivaled in whiteness by the beautiful neck it veiled—the tiniest and prettiest foot imaginable peeping from the full robe, and resting on an embroidered cushion. It was indeed a charming picture, and the two friends would gladly have passed more than the fashionable minute in gazing and admiring, had not their engagements called them elsewhere.

Their next visit was to the fashionable and beautiful Mrs. M. and her two accomplished daughters, Virginia and Grace.

Distinguished in society by their loveliness, elegance and refinement, blessed with every luxury except the best and dearest of all—the riches of the heart—these three lovely beings are victims to a restless passion for excitement, which nothing seems to allay, and their lives are passed in a succession of frivolous amusements, frittering away, from hour to hour, heart, mind and soul, until they have almost forgotten that such things are!

"With a desperate attempt to escape from the ennui of an unfurnished and unsatisfied mind;" they hurry from rout to ball, until in the din, the loud world music of fashion and gayety, "the still, small voice of that inward spirit which is to inherit the immortal ages" is stifled and unheard.

As the two heroes of my story entered the splendid apartments, a graceful *tableaux* caught—it was intended to catch—their eyes. The still beautiful Mrs. M. in a highly tasteful cap, and a dress of crimson velvet, was seated on a sofa, and at her feet, on a low stool, her youngest daughter, Virginia. A cloud of amber curls veiled her soft cheek and snowy shoulder as she leaned her head against her mother's knee, with her dark blue eyes half closed, and a faint, sweet, dreamy smile flitting about her rosy mouth. While her sister, Grace, in an attitude which at once recalled her name, stood bending over a classic vase of flowers, with her dark and braided hair, pale cheek and soft yet brilliant black eyes presenting a striking contrast to her fairylike sister.

A silk dress of the palest rose-color fitted closely to her beautiful form, and was terminated at the throat by a small embroidered collar of linen cambric. She was listening with downcast eyes to the ardent compliments of a handsome young Spaniard who stood by her, and was just about handing him a half-blown rose, when, seeing Vernon enter, with a well-managed start of affected surprise and pleasure, in the true spirit of coquetry, she let it fall at her feet.

Ere the Spaniard noticed the apparent accident, Richmond had sprung forward, raised the flower to his lips and hid it in his bosom, and quick as lightning the graceful girl had drawn another from the vase and placed it in the hand of the young foreigner, whose dark eyes flashed with delight as he received it. A low, musical, but somewhat affectedly prolonged laugh from Virginia betrayed her knowledge of the *ruse*, which none had seen but herself.

"My dear Virginia," whispered her careful but unconscious mother, after the gentlemen had departed, "don't laugh *too* often, unless there is something to laugh at. It sounds affected. The laugh is very sweet, my love, but you must not waste its sweetness. Neither of the gentlemen just gone is a desirable match, you know. And, Grace, I must beg of you not to disarrange another bouquet for the sake of a person so utterly insignificant as this Don Juan Jose del Hernandez.

CHAPTER III.

It was eight o'clock on the evening of the same day. The ladies' drawing-room at the Astor was brilliantly lighted, and Charles Vernon, fatigued with the social duties of the day, threw himself on a sofa beside a very beautiful woman, who welcomed him with her sweetest smile, exclaiming—

"I have left but one visit unpaid, and that must remain so, for I am weary, stupid, flat and unprofitable. I have exhausted all spirit, wit and sentiment, and have but one idea left, and that is—"

"What?" said the lady, tapping her foot impatiently.

"That I would rather be here than anywhere else in the universe."

"But how can you presume to be here after the acknowledgment you have just made, that you have brought neither wit, spirit, nor sentiment to amuse me with?"

"For that very reason did I come—knowing that the magic of your presence would restore them if anything could."

"And whose is the name on your list that you treat with such neglect?"

"It is a pretty one; but I never saw the original. I was introduced to her on board a steamboat, by her father, last summer; but she had a thick, green veil over her face—I always had a blue horror of green veils—her form, however, was beautiful; and on the strength of that I promised her father to call upon them."

"And what is the name?"

"Amy Arnold."

"Amy Arnold! She is one of my pets! Go this moment and fulfill your promise! You will not regret it."

"But I am so tired."

"Go!"

"But I am so happy here."

"Go!"

"Well, then, since you will be so cruel, I must quote my friend Miss Squeers, of Dotheboy's Hall – "Artful and designing 'Tilda! I leave you.'"

The lady laughed, and the gentleman, with a sublime shake of the head, departed.

CHAPTER IV.

It was a pleasant scene upon which young Vernon intruded about an hour afterward. A large, old-fashioned parlor lighted by a blazing fire, Amy Arnold, blindfolded, in the midst of a dozen little boys and girls, pursuing them with outstretched arms, her dark hair braided smoothly on her brow, her beautiful lips parted with the excitement of the chase, and her form seen to advantage in a rich silk of silver gray, plainly but very gracefully made. The merry shouts of the children had prevented her hearing the door open, and one roguish little urchin had pushed the intruder almost into her arms, ere she was aware of his presence. She laid her soft hand eagerly, but gently, on his shoulder, exclaiming, "Ah, papa! is it you I have caught? I am so glad! Untie the blinder for me, do! for I am really tired," and she bent her beautiful head before him.

Taken by surprise, poor Vernon could only obey without a word; but in his confusion he fumbled so long at the knot that she put up her own hand to assist him. She started as she met his touch—it was not the rough clasp of Capt. Arnold that she felt. The blinder fell! and she raised to our hero's face a pair of soft, gray eyes—Vernon thought them the loveliest he had ever seen—and there they stood for a full minute gazing on each other. She with the color deepening in her fair young cheek, and a look full of wonder, dismay and confusion—and he with an expression of mingled embarrassment and admiration.

Fortunately at that moment Capt. Arnold himself came in, and greeted his young friend with a cordial welcome to his house. While the little frolicsome Harry, who had caused all the trouble, sprung to his father's knee, and relating the *contretemps* with infinite glee, set them all laughing together, so that case was at once restored. And when, at eleven o'clock, Vernon rose to take his leave he could not help blessing in his heart the fair lady on the sofa in the Astor House drawing-room, who had insisted so imperiously upon his leaving her three hours before.

CHAPTER V.

"My dear!" said Mr. Frederic Richmond, in his softest voice, three weeks after his wedding with the widow, "You have never shown me your splendid set of diamonds since the happy day on which you promised to be mine."

"My set of diamonds! What do you mean, Mr. Richmond," replied the lady in a sharp tone, which grated rather harshly upon his musical ear.

"Don't trifle with my feelings, love. I mean the set you were last New-Year's day."

"Oh, yes! You can see THEM *any* day at Marquand's—I hired them for the occasion!"

"The deuce you did! And how the devil am I to settle with my creditors, I should like to know?"

"Don't swear, Mr. Richmond, it wears upon my nerves."

"Hang your nerves, madam!" and the disappointed fortune-hunter, striking his clenched hand upon his forehead, hurried from the room, and soon after from the country.

"I told you, you would never regret it," said the fair belle of the Astor, as she stood, a week ago, with Charles Vernon and his beautiful Amy—no longer Amy Arnold—in the library of an elegant mansion on the banks of the Hudson—and Amy lifted her dark eyes fondly to his face and whispered with a sportive smile,

"*Do* you regret it, Charles?"

The Wife[1]

> "All precious things, discovered late,
>   To those that seek them issue forth;
> For Love, in sequel, works with Fate,
>   And draws the veil from hidden worth."

CHAPTER I.

COLD AND white as the bridal blossoms in her hair was the youthful cheek, which a glow of love and pride should have kindled into color—for Harriet Percy, though about to become the bride of one of the most admired and distinguished men in the country, was too well convinced of his indifference to be happy in the prospect. She knew that with him it was a marriage of expediency. That he was poor—that he required means to further his ambitious views, and that, though uniformly kind and respectful in his manner when they met, he had scarcely bestowed a thought upon her mind, heart or person, during the three weeks which intervened between their introduction to each other and this their bridal morning.

For years before that introduction, even from childhood, she had worshiped his lofty genius, and admired at a distance his noble form. He was the idol of her every dream—her hero—her ideal! His haughty bearing, his coldly intellectual expression, which would have repelled a less ardent and romantic heart, had for her an inexpressible charm. And when, at a party given by a mutual, match-making friend, during the first season of her entrance into society, he had been introduced to her, she was so agitated and confused by her various emotions, that she could only blush and reply in monosyllables to his polite attempts at conversation.

Poor Harriet was angry and mortified at herself; and utterly unsuspicious, in her own guileless truth, of any

---

[1] "The Wife," Frances S. Osgood, *Graham's Magazine*, December 1843, vol. XXIV, no. 6, pp. 268-271

mercenary motive on his part, she was not less amazed than delighted when, after two or three interviews of the same description, he formally proposed to her father for her hand, and was at once accepted. Exulting in her conquest, yet awed by his distant demeanor, she hardly knew at first whether to be happy or the contrary; but loving and gentle as she was, there was a latent spirit of pride and lofty resolution in her soul, which she had never dreamed of till it was awakened by her present situation.

With a woman's instinct, she learned to read his heart. She saw that the demon Ambition had obscured, without obliterating, its nobler and more tender feelings, and she trusted to time and her own truth to conquer the one and arouse the other.

But in the mean time she would be no pining victim to neglect. Her sweet lip curled—her dark eyes flashed—her high spirit revolted at the thought! She would sooner die than humble herself in his eyes!

She would love him, it is true, dearly, deeply, devotedly; but it should be in the silent depths of a soul he could not fathom. Not till he should own a love, fervent and devoted as her own, would she yield to the tenderness he inspired. Not till then should be unveiled to him the altar on which his image dwelt enshrined like a deity of old, with the breath of affection for its incense, ever burning over and around it, and the fruits and flowers of feeling and of thought—its sacrifice.

She would wed him, because her fortune could assist his efforts for the good of his country and his own distinction. She would have bestowed that fortune upon him without her hand, but she knew his pride too well to dream he would accept it, and her resolution was taken.

For his life Mr. William Harwood could not have told whether his intended bride had any claims to beauty or to talent. He saw that her manners were refined, he knew that her fortune was immense, and he was satisfied. He heeded not—he never dreamed of the riches of her heart and mind. But while ambition and selfishness blinded *his* eyes to her superiority, it was not so with others. A dazzlingly fair complexion, soft, wavy hair, of the palest brown, hazel eyes, intensely dark and fringed with long, thick lashes of the same hue, a straight Greek nose, a mouth of exquisite beauty, in the expression of which sweetness and spirit were charmingly combined, a light and gracefully molded form—these were the least of her attractions. A thousand nameless graces, a thousand lovely but indescribable enchantments in manner, look and tone, betrayed the *soul* within; and yet, with all this, she was so modest, so timid, so thoroughly feminine and gentle in all her ways and words, that the world never dreamed of calling her a beauty, or of making her a belle. It was those she *loved* that she enchanted.

CHAPTER II.

She stood like a beautiful statue by his side. She quelled her tears—she hushed her heart, and spoke in accents calm and cold as his own the vows which were to bind them for life unto each other. She received the congratulations of friends and acquaintances without a sigh, a blush, a sign of emotion—modestly but coldly. Even Harwood himself wondered at her strange self-possession, and while he wondered, rejoiced that she had so little feeling to trouble him with. But when her father approached to say farewell, and lead her to the carriage, which was to bear her far from home, her proud resolve gave way! She threw herself on his breast and sobbed passionately and wildly, like a grieved and frightened child, till her husband, astonished at such a display of emotion in one usually so quiet and subdued, drew her gently away, and seating himself beside her in the carriage, ordered the driver to proceed.

Harriet withdrew from his arm, pleaded fatigue, covered her face with her veil, and soon succeeding in conquering every outward sign of emotion, sat still and silent during the journey.

It was the evening of the wedding-day. The bride had retired to dress for dinner, and Harwood sat dreaming before his library fire, when a note was put into his hand by a footman. What was his surprise at the contents!

"You do not love me!—and no pretense of love which you may adopt from motives of duty or compassion will avail with me. You had your object in proposing this union—I had mine in accepting that proposal. Be content that those objects are gained, and let me be your wife but in name, I beseech you.

"HARRIET
HARWOOD."

Harwood stared at the paper in astonishment at first; but he had always looked upon Harriet as a child, and he soon began to consider this as some childish and romantic whim, which required his indulgence.

Amused, perplexed, and, if the truth must be told, a little piqued withal, he hastily wrote on a slip of paper— "Be it so!" and folding it, laid it on the table by the side of her plate.

Harriet blushed as she entered, but took her seat quietly and silently. She glanced at the paper, and with a trembling hand unfolded it. Her cheek and eye kindled as she read, and her pretty lip quivered for a moment. The next she put the *billet* by, and proceeded, with calm and graceful self-possession, to the duties of the table. And Mr. Harwood thinking to himself, for the first time, that his wife was a remarkably pretty woman, dismissed the subject from his mind, and discussed his dinner with great *goût*, and the political topics of the day with still greater.

Fair reader! you will say that Mr. William Harwood was a most unfeeling person. But that was by no means the case. He had been, from childhood, so devoted to intellectual pursuits, that he had never found time even to think of love. Had his good angel but whispered to him, at that moment, that his beautiful *vis a vis* loved him as her life, and that her full heart was waiting and expecting his love in return, he would have given it as in honor bound, and have wondered that he never thought of it before; but the trouble was, he didn't happen to think anything about it; and I, for one, cannot find it in my heart to scold him, for if he *had* thought I should have had no story to tell.

CHAPTER III.

Seeing Harriet only at meals, and absorbed in his ambitious schemes, Harwood at last almost forgot that he had a wife, and the poor girl strove to content herself in her own silent and secret worship of her husband—

> But love, unloved, is but
> A wearying task at best!
> Better be lying in the grave,
> In dreamless, careless rest!

She mingled sometimes with the gay; but society had no excitement for a mind like hers. She could not long enjoy a conversation in which her heart was not in some way interested. For, while the poetry of feeling was her element, Harriet was not an intellectual person—she was more spiritual than intellectual—her heart supplied the place of a mind.

One evening, at a party, a young English officer approaching Harwood exclaimed, "My dear sir! do you know, can you tell me the name of that beautiful creature leaning by the window? There, that pale, dark-eyed girl in white! You ought to know, for she has been looking at you, with her whole soul in the look, for the last five minutes."

Harwood looked up; he caught the eloquent gaze of those beautiful eyes; he saw her start and instantly avert them, with a sudden blush, as if detected in a crime, and strange and new emotions thrilled his heart. The hour had come. Love, the high-priest, had suddenly appeared at the altar, and the fire was kindled at length, never again to be wholly extinguished. For the first time aroused to a sense of her singular loveliness, for the first time suspecting her hidden passion for himself, he colored, smiled, and seemed so confused that his friend was turning away in surprise. But Harwood recovered himself, and taking his arm, led him forward and introduced him to his wife.

As we have said before, Harwood was by no means without a heart, but his giant intellect and his situation in life had hitherto rendered him unconscious of so valuable a possession. After listening for a few moments impatiently to Harriet's graceful and naive conversation with the handsome young officer, he drew her hand within his arm, and pressing it tenderly, whispered "Let us go home, dear Harriet; I am weary of this scene."

"Dear Harriet!" Was she dreaming! the words, the tone, the look, the light caress, all thrilled to her inmost heart.

Her eyes filled with tears, and trembling with the heavenly ecstasy of the moment, almost fainting, indeed, from excess of emotion, she murmured,

"Yes, let us go at once."

He sprung into the carriage after her, and drew her to his heart. "Oh, William do you—do you love me? Can it indeed be true?"

"*My wife!*"

The scene is sacred—let the curtain fall.

CHAPTER IV.

"More close and close his footsteps wind,
The magic music in his heart
Beats quick and quicker till he find
The quiet chamber far apart."

At an unusually early hour, the next evening, Harwood returned to his now happy home, and, hastening up the stairs, paused at the door of his wife's boudoir, arrested by her voice within. She was singing, in a low and touching voice, and with exquisite taste, a simple song which he had never heard before. Though naturally very fond of music, it had happened by some strange chance that he had not heard Harriet play or sing, indeed he did not know that she possessed the accomplishment. The words of the song went straight to his heart, and thus they ran:

I knew it! I felt it!—he loves me at last!
    The heart-hidden anguish forever is past!
Love brightens his dark eye and softens his tone;
    He loves me—he loves me—his soul is mine own!

Come care and misfortune—the cloud and the storm—
    I've a light in this heart all existence to warm—
No grief can oppress me, no shadow o'ercast,
    In that blessed conviction—he loves me at last!

Echoing, with his rich, manly voice, the last five words, Harwood opened the door and held out his arms, and his happy and beautiful wife flew to his embrace, with a fresh and artless delight, peculiarly fascinating to the world-worn man she worshiped.

CHAPTER V.

For three months, Harwood was a devoted lover and husband, and Harriet was happy in his love; but he could not all at once, and forever, forego the glorious dreams of his youth—and by degrees he returned to his political duties, and grew gradually stately and cold, and apparently indifferent as before.

And now Harriet was more wretched than ever. Now, that she had once experienced the happiness of being loved, caressed, admired, she could not endure life unblessed by tenderness and hope. By nature, ardent, susceptible, dependent upon those around her for happiness, and clinging to all who could offer her affection, it had been only by a violent struggle that she had forced herself into a state of apparent apathy, during the first few weeks of her marriage; but, once aroused from it, she had abandoned her whole being to the enchantment of Love's happy dream, and henceforward life was lost without it.

Her husband's returning coldness and neglect had wounded, but not subdued her heart; and what was the wife to do with all the now unemployed feeling and fancy awakened in its depths.

The interesting young officer, before mentioned, had fallen in love with Harriet at first sight, ere he knew she was the bride of his friend; and, though distinguished in the field by his bravery and skill, *self-conquest* was an art he had neither learned nor dreamed of. Visiting from time to time at the house, he soon saw her unhappiness, and penetrated its cause. His sympathy was excited—his visits grew more frequent—with refined and subtle tenderness, almost irresistible to a heart like hers, he entered earnestly into her pursuits—read with her, walked with her, sang with her—praised her mind and heart—called her "the sister of his soul," and so adapted himself to her tastes and her affections that Harriet found herself on the verge of a precipice, ere she was aware she had overstepped the limits of propriety and discretion. It was a sort of spiritual magnetism, which she tried in vain to resist.

Harriet would never have been guilty of actual crime—she was too proud and too pure for that; but in a soul so highly toned, so delicately and daintily organized as hers, the slightest aberration, in thought, look or deed, from the faith which was due to her husband, produced a discord, involving the loss of self-respect, and consequent misery and remorse.

And now Love and Sorrow swept the strings, and awakened a melody sweet, but plaintive as the sound of an Æolian harp. They had made her a poet, and she poured forth, in frequent verse, the various emotions they aroused.

CHAPTER VI.

Mr. Harwood had just returned from a long journey. He had been unsuccessful in two or three important projects, and, disgusted with the uncertainty attending his pursuits, he had suddenly determined to abandon politics altogether. His heart yearned toward his sweet wife as it had never yearned before. He had been away from her so long! He *needed* her love now, he needed her soft voice to soothe and comfort him, and he came prepared, not only to receive but to give consolation. He entered her boudoir softly, intending to surprise her. She was reclining on the sofa asleep—pale and sad, with tears still lingering on her lashes, and her fair hair streaming from her childish brow—her lips half parted, and sighing as she slept, she looked so enchantingly lovely that he sprung forward to awaken her with a kiss, when a paper, lying loosely in her hand, arrested his attention. He drew it softly from her. It was addressed "To My Husband," and thinking himself thus justified in reading it, he did so, with what emotions may be better imagined than told. It was as follows:

> Oh! hasten to my side, I pray!
>   I dare not be alone:
> The smile that tempts, when thou'rt away,
>   Is fonder than thine own.

The voice that oftenest charms mine ear,
   Hath such beguiling tone,
'Twill steal my very soul, I fear,
   Ah leave me not alone!

It speaks in accents low and deep,
   It murmurs praise too dear,
It makes me passionately weep,
   Then gently soothes my fear;

It calls me sweet, endearing names,
   With Love's own childlike art,
My tears, my doubts, it softly blames—
   'Tis *music* to my heart:

And dark, deep, eloquent, soul-filled eyes
   Speak tenderly to mine;
Beneath that gaze what feelings rise:
   It is more kind than thine!

A hand, even pride can scarce repel,
   Too fondly seeks mine own,
It is not safe—it is not well!
   Ah leave me not alone!

I try to calm, in cold repose,
   Beneath his earnest eye,
The heart that thrills, the cheek that glows—
   Alas! *in vain* I try!

Oh trust me not—a woman frail—
   To brave the snares of life:
Lest lonely, sad, unloved, I *fail*,
   And shame the name of wife:

Come back though cold and harsh to me,
   There's *honor* by thy side:
Better unblest, yet safe, to be,
   Than lost to truth, to pride:

Alas! my peril hourly grows,
   In every thought and dream;
Not—not to *thee* my spirit goes,

But still—yes! still to *him!*

Return with those cold eyes to me,
 And chill my soul once more,
Back to the loveless apathy,
 It learned so well before:

Jealousy, anger, pity, remorse and love were at war in the breast of Harwood; but, with a moment's reflection through the past, upon his own conduct, the three latter conquered, and, kneeling by her side, he pressed his lips upon her brow. She murmured softly in her sleep, "Dear, darling husband! do you love me?" and the color trembled in her cheek like the rosy light of morning on the snow.

Harwood pressed her passionately to his heart, and she awoke terrified, ashamed, penitent, yet happy at length beyond expression, for she forgave and was forgiven. She had overrated, in her sensitive conscientiousness, the extent of her error. Her fancy, her mind, rather than her affections, had been beguiled. Harwood felt at once that the dewy bloom of purity had not been brushed from the heart of his fragile flower, by the daring wing of the insect that had sought it, and henceforth it was cherished in its proper home—his own noble and faithful breast!

The Lady's Shadow[1]

CHAPTER I.

The very shadow cast by thee,
Is lovelier to love and me,
And dearer too, fair lady, far,
Than living forms of others are!

WELL, IT *was* tantalizing, and I don't wonder he grew impatient at last. Yes; all the way up Broadway, that sunny morning, the graceful little shadow of the lady just behind kept close by his side, and he did not dare turn to see who it could be. What a charming shadow she made—the dainty, tipped-up bonnet, with its waving plume—the fairy sun-shade—the rich shawl, folded with such *recherché* elegance! And then he was sure, by the way it moved, that it must have a lovely foot, and the hand that held up the sun-shade was exquisite.

Either a magnetic influence reached him from the fair reality, or Charles Carlton had fallen desperately in love—with a shadow! He, who had never been in love—to his knowledge—in his life before—and he could not conjure up sufficient self-possession to turn and face the foe. All at once he began to walk consciously erect, and to think—what would *she* think of his walk—and at the very moment when he became thus absorbed in himself the shadow suddenly disappeared. The instant he missed it, Carlton started and turned.

It was nowhere to be seen! Shadow and substance had vanished, and the only person near him, just then, was an old apple-woman. Whither had it flown? Perhaps it was a spirit; but spirits don't carry sun-shades! That night he dreamed of an angel-face, looking out of a cloud in heaven, which cloud suddenly took the shape of a white satin hat with a pale, rose-colored plume. The face was after the approved fashion of angels; delicately tinted, with

---

[1] "The Lady's Shadow," Frances S. Osgood, *The Columbian Magazine*, January 1844, vol. I, no. 1, pp. 32-36

beautiful, light waving curls and violet eyes. He had surely seen it before—somewhere; but where he could not remember. The next day at the same hour he took his accustomed walk, and again, just by Thomson & Weller's, that teasing little shadow flitted by his side!—he knew it was the same by the peculiar flow of the feather; not a hat in Broadway could boast so graceful, so cloudlike, dreamlike an accompaniment as that. "Oh that he could see her features!" There was a strange conflict in his soul; courage and curiosity exclaimed "right about face!" but love and sentiment whispered "be quiet; you will make her blush!" At last a bright thought struck him—why hadn't it struck him before? If he could not see her face, he might her form; and he could find out the home of his phantom-love. He slackened his pace to let the lady pass. The shadow seemed surprised; it wavered, faltered, and finally settled into a slower pace also. This was too much to be thus haunted, baffled, mocked—in the public street—in open daylight!

Still he would not turn. It was so pleasant to have an ideal, to love even a beautiful shadow—to imagine her all that was divine—he dreaded to have his dream dispelled; and again his fairy friend vanished from his side, and he had not even discovered where she lived. He turned—the house which he thought she must have entered had the air of a boarding house. If so it would be worthwhile to take rooms there for the mere chance of its being her home, and without a moment's hesitation he rang the bell—was admitted—inquired for rooms—engaged the first he looked at, without asking the price, and agreed to take possession of them at twelve the next day. The landlady looked as if she rather doubted his sanity, and said hesitatingly as he bade her good morning, "if you please, sir, I should like a reference; we never take only the 'fuss' people here."

"Possibly," said Carlton to himself, "she means the first people;" and he continued aloud, laughing as he wrote for her the address of a friend, "Oh don't be alarmed, my dear madam—I assure you I am one of the 'fuss' people."

CHAPTER II.

Some phantom fair we each pursue,
  Fame, pleasure, fortune, power or love,
And each will prove alike untrue;
  The real dwells above.

Patient reader, I am going to moralize—a thing I never did before—at least on paper—in my life! Somehow or other, my stories always have a moral; but how or where they find it, you know as well as I. They come to it, or it comes to them, by mere accident. For my part I forget all about it till the work is finished, and then I am agreeably surprised to find—a pearl in the oyster—honey in the weed! It must be that, with an intuitive perception of right from wrong, I have, as it were, unconsciously brought up my pen in the way it should go, and now it is old it will not depart from it. But now I am going to moralize in good earnest, for the mere sake of variety. I like an episode now and then, especially a moral one; they are refreshing novelties, particularly in a love-story. Don't you think so, Kate? I beg your pardon, reader; I forgot *you*; I was talking to a friend, who is looking over my shoulder. She is a superb creature, whom I mean to "storify" and glorify one of these days. She calls every fresh beau "an episode," and that will account for my question.

Well, Charles Carlton had set his heart upon a shadow. You smile at his folly, and well you may; and yet I doubt if among all the crowd that thronged Broadway that glorious morning, there were many who were not doing the very same thing—neglecting the substance for the shadow—contented with a pleasant illusion and fearing to face the reality—enjoying a beautiful dream, from which they dreaded to awake—watching, playing with, accompanying the sunny delusions of the present, and shrinking from the future, with a vague consciousness of their folly—worshipping the empty and fleeting shapes of time, and forgetting the glorious truths of eternity. The merchant—the statesman—the bigot—the belle and the beau—to what but phantoms did their aspirations tend? Wealth, fame, power, pleasure—the idle form, without the soul of religion—the applause of the worldly and frivolous, drowning the voice of divine love in the heart. Charles Carlton was not the only idle dreamer in Broadway.

CHAPTER III.

> "Oh! give to airy nothing,
> A local habitation and a name!"

> "I can but see thee as my star,
> My angel and my dream!"

> "Go then! if she whose shade thou art
> Forbids thee still to soothe my heart!"
> *Moore.*

> "This world is all a fleeting show,
> For man's illusion given."

The next morning Carlton was comfortably seated in his new apartment, with a book in his hand, every page of which was blurred by the remembered shadow, when, in the next room, the softest, purest, most delicious voice he had ever heard, began to sing—as if it couldn't help it—the following song. He listened in breathless delight.

> They come—the light, the worldly come,
>   With looks and words untrue;
> But unto them my soul is dumb—
>   *Mon ami! ou es tu?*

> My lips, with false and careless smile,
>   Must coldly speak of you,
> But wildly sighs my soul the while,
>   *Mon ami! ou es tu?*

> Where'er I rove, in hall or grove,
>   Thy absence still I rue;
> Ah! what is life without thy love?
>   *Mon ami! ou es tu?*

It was eloquently—almost passionately—sung, and yet with a graceful delicacy of tone and expression that charmed the fastidious taste of our hero. But the voice was hushed, and the shadow resumed its sway.

As Carlton took his seat at dinner that day, he glanced hurriedly round the table; not a soul could be seen that answered to his shadow. There were an old maid and a young man; there were a mother and three children; there was a middle aged gentleman opposite him; there were a widow and a widower; but there was no graceful girl to fit the phantom of his heart! And even if there were, how was he to identify the substance with the shadow! Ah he was sure something within would tell him if he saw the fair reality of his ideal. One seat, beside the middle aged gentleman, was still vacant. "Perhaps," he exclaimed to himself,—but at that moment his neighbor, the maiden lady, addressed him; he turned courteously to reply, and when he again glanced to the other side, the vacant seat was filled! And how? Angels and ministers of grace! was it magic? Enchantment? There—directly opposite him—was his dream! with its soft curls—its faintly glowing cheek— its eyes divinely blue! Ah! was it his shadow too? What would he not give to know!

The young girl blushed deeply as she caught his eye, and the blush was followed by a smile equally beautiful. Poor Carlton all that night his sleep was haunted. First he clasped a shadow; then he pursued an airy voice of sweet enchantment; then he knelt to a blush that was fading in the sky; and last he worshipped a smile in heaven, which, gradually dawning into day, awakened him to find the morning sunshine streaming on his face. Poor Carlton! was he doomed to love and to follow, through life, only these lovely illusions? But he heard a light step in the next room, and a voice softly singing, "*Mon ami! on es tu?*" and he was sure it was time to rise.

CHAPTER IV.

"His blue eye darkened suddenly,
A shadow crossed his heart!"
Old Song.

"Her walk is like the wind—her smile more sweet
Than sunshine."

Barry Cornwall.

That day he missed the shade—it did not come—and he felt irrepressibly lonely. He was angry with himself, with all around, but more particularly with the glaring sunshine, that seemed to mock him with its smile. At last, to beguile the walk, he began to soliloquize in rhyme, to the tune of Bishop Heber's "I miss thee from my side, my love."

> I miss thee, my aerial love,
> I miss thee from my side;
> I look below, around, above,
> To see the shadows glide.
>
> 'Twas Cupid in the sunshine sweet,
> Stole down with treacherous art,
> And threw that shadow at my feet,
> And drew it on my heart.
>
> There, traced in colors soft as those
> That tint the cloud in air,
> In love's daguerreotype it glows,
> A picture pure as rare.
>
> Oh! glide again, my dream, my hope:
> Along my lonely way,
> And "charm the street beneath my feet,"
> And bless the beauteous day!
>
> Steal lightly from thy starry sphere—
> From sister angels part,
> And "do thy spiriting gently" here,
> Thou Ariel of the heart!

And lo! as if obedient to the playful incantation, it suddenly glided again by his side! How fondly he welcomed the dear little faithful visitor, that had now become necessary to his happiness! And this time he was resolved to know where it went; so, as a last resource, he resolutely folded his arms and stood perfectly still. There was a moment's pause; and then with a quick and somewhat haughty step, a youthful form glided by. It was about the same height, and had the same graceful and high-bred carriage as that of his *vis-a-vis*, at table. He should know, if she entered that house. He would watch her closely this time. He could not see her face, but there was the little satin hat of his dream—pure as the snow in hue—and the costly plume of white, blended with rose-color—so softly, slightly tinted, that he could compare it to nothing but an angel's blush—and the superb white cashmere shawl, with its graceful fold; and then the form! the foot! What "a daintily organized" creature she was and the cunning, and prettily gloved hand, that held the parasol! Charles began to think it might be a fairy after all. But while he was thinking so, a richly embroidered Parisian handkerchief fluttered to his feet. He stooped to take it up, and when he raised his head, the vision had vanished again! Fate! Was he doomed to eternal disappointment?

But he had the handkerchief still; a tangible proof that his ethereal beauty, vanish as she would, was neither sylph nor spirit; for gentlefolk of that quality certainly do not send to Paris for embroidery, or to Lawson's for their hats; and he was quite sure he had seen that one at the famous "opening" in Park Place only a week before.

Perhaps the handkerchief was marked. Yes! sure enough, in one corner, in tiny characters, was written, "Fanny Gray." The name thrilled his soul like a strain of remembered music; but he could not think where he had heard it before.

He entered his apartment, pressed the treasure to his lips, laid it next his heart, and then threw himself on the sofa, to dream of his "airy nothing." A low, merry, musical laugh in the next room disturbed his reverie, and then, with the warble of a bird, the gay voice sang again.

> Oh! would I were only a spirit of song!
>   I'd float forever around, above you!
> If I were a spirit, it wouldn't be wrong,
>   It couldn't be wrong to love you!
>
> I'd hide in the light of a moon beam bright;
>   I'd sing love's lullaby softly o'er you;
> I'd bring fair visions of pure delight,
>   From the 'land of dreams' before you!

> Oh! if I were only a spirit of song,
>   I'd float forever around, above you;
> For a musical spirit could never do wrong—
>   And it wouldn't be wrong to love you!

Carlton forgot the shadow, and adored the voice till dinner time, and then the angel-face enchanted him again. Surely that face belonged to the voice, if not to the shadow. There was the same pure and heavenly harmony in its features, that thrilled him in those tones—that reached, and moved to answering music, the finest chord of feeling in his soul.

At dinner the maiden lady informed him that they were to have a little party that evening in the drawing-room, and hoped he would be there. "Now I shall know her name."

CHAPTER V.

> And back with that soft glance and tone,
>   A faint, sweet dream of childhood flew;
> Those eyes before had met mine own,
>   That voice! it was a voice I knew!

How lovely she was in her pretty dress of pale green silk, with her soft hair floating on her neck! The middle aged gentleman having entered very cordially into conversation with him, Carlton at last found courage to ask an introduction to the young lady. "Certainly, sir, my daughter will be happy to make your acquaintance. Mr. Carlton, Miss Gray." He could hardly repress an exclamation of delight! He had found his beautiful shadow at last—the treasure, the idol of his heart!

He had never been so happy in his life. He was the soul of the party that night.

"But surely, Miss Gray," he said, after a few common places of conversation, "we have met somewhere in former years. A mysterious, indefinable dream of the past awakened in my soul the moment I saw you, and now some link in memory's chain is touched by every look and tone—we have certainly met before."

The lady looked up reproachfully. "Have you forgotten little Fanny Gray, whom you used to play with and pet at school in New Hampshire?"

"Ah! forgive me! I remember now! But you know we always called you 'Fanny' then, and if I ever knew your last name, it had slipped my memory. Yes! now my dream is accounted for—and the otherwise unaccountable thrill I felt, when I first saw that graceful shadow in Broadway—and my emotion too in reading the name on the handkerchief."

"Ah! the handkerchief! You must give it me, Char—Mr. Carlton, I mean."

"Oh call me Charlie, as you used to!"

"Mr. Carlton, where is the handkerchief?"

"Here, Miss Gray!" and he drew it from its resting place, unseen by all but her.

Fanny was embarrassed, and wished to change the subject. "I learned for the first time this evening that you occupy the room next to mine. Perhaps my singing has disturbed you; I rise so early."

"It has, indeed, Miss Gray."

"Indeed!" Fanny seemed grieved and hurt.

"Yes: your voice and your shadow have been a spell to me; they have 'roused a spirit from the vasty deep' of my soul which will never sleep again."

"The spirit of revenge, I should imagine."

"The spirit of love, Fanny!"

Poor child! She tried once more to change the subject.

"Will you share a philopæna with me, Mr. Carlton?"

"Certainly! provided, if I win, you will give me whatever I write on this slip of paper."

"I promise, if it can be given with propriety; but on one condition."

"Name it!"

"That you will write on the other side of the paper some impromptu verses—they say you are a poet—begin now; for I am tired of talking."

In ten minutes Carlton showed her the following doggerel:

There's not a sprite that takes her flight,
    At morning through Broadway,
So pure and bright—so airy, light,
    As lovely Fanny Gray!

Her waving plume—her youthful bloom;
    Her foot of fairy size,
Her moonlight tress—all—all—I bless;
    But most—her violet eyes!

Oh! come with me, if you would see
    The evening star, by day,
With smile of glee and footstep free,
    I'll show you—Fanny Gray!

Well! Fanny was doomed that night to trouble. There was no refuge but in flight, and that she took at once. Rising from the sofa, with the innocent smile and artless tone he remembered in her childhood, she murmured, "good night, Charles!" and left the room.

CHAPTER VI.

"Oh! lightly was her young heart swayed,
By just a look—a word."

Carlton was obliged to leave town on business for a few days, and Fanny missed him more than she dared believe. But one evening at the opera, as she sat entranced by that "bird of Italy," the divine Damoreau—her whole soul floating away to heaven on the waves of melody with which the enchantress filled the room—a voice more dear than Damoreau's, a voice of more than music, recalled the truant spirit, while it playfully whispered, "allow me to say, 'philopæna,' Miss Gray."

Sunny and glad as the glow of a summer morning, was the smile that "softly lightened o'er her face," as she exclaimed, in a low tone, "how glad I am you have come back! You have fairly won the philopæna; and now let me see the paper, and know what I am to forfeit."

"Not yet; I dare not show it now."

"But when then will you?"

"When I can't help it."

About a fortnight afterward, they met alone in the drawing-room. They had been much together since the night of the concert, and Fanny looked up archly in Carlton's face and said—

"Can you help it now?"

He placed the paper in her hand. She started as she read the words, "your heart," traced in trembling characters upon it.

"I cannot redeem the pledge," she said gravely.

"Cannot! and why, dear Fanny?"

"Because I lost the article in question long ago, when I was a little girl at school, and I have never been able to find it since. Did you pick it up by mistake, Charlie?"

The lover's heartbeat high with hope. "Then," said he, quickly, "since you cannot pay that forfeit, you will give me something else?"

"And what?"

"Your hand."

"What an unreasonable, ungrateful person you are! did you not take forcible possession of it three minutes ago, and has it not been lying in yours ever since—patient, resigned, submissive, victimized?"

"Oh, Fanny, do not trifle now!"

She raised her speaking eyes full of tears to her lover's face. He did not complain again of her trifling—that day at least.

*   *   *   *   *   *   *   *   *

And Fanny Carlton's shadow still flits at times through Broadway; but now it is almost always linked, arm in arm, with one more stately and tall than her own. The latter belongs to a distinguished lawyer of the city, and what is better still, to the father of a miniature Fanny Gray, who bids fair to be a belle, and whose shadows will, I dare say, one day turn the head of some dreamer like her "dear papa."

Kate Melburne[1]

READER, I am a coward—a coward in almost every sense of the word—I am afraid of horses, cows, cats, and dogs—of spiders, grass-hoppers, wasps and devil's darning-needles—of shadows—of the dark—of strangers, particularly if they are sensible people—of trouble—of pain—sometimes of myself—and just now—of *you*! I remind myself constantly of the immortal Chicken Little who disturbed a whole neighborhood by her foolish alarm. Ah! could I hope to have my sorrows sung by the same inspired pen, which has lamented hers in such "melodious tears," I should not so deeply regret my infirmity.

Lately my friends have taken it into their saucy heads to *call* me Chicken Little, and I really deserved, the name this afternoon, when on returning from a short drive on a remarkably smooth road—in a four wheeled vehicle—with a perfect hack of a horse—quiet, demure and patient as a lamb–after having magnified every rut into a gulley, and every stone into a rock—I insisted upon waiting in the vehicle until the horse was untackled, because I was afraid he would move if I jumped out. I carry my childishness, in this respect, so far that even my youngest girl—a brave little rogue of four years old—said to me the other day with a perfectly serious face when I offered to share her sports, "well, then—you just pretend you was a *lady*!" This cowardice as you may imagine makes me often selfish—unhappy, troublesome and tiresome—and so well am I convinced of its folly, and so anxious to hold its consequences up as a warning to others that I have just determined to illustrate it by relating some events which happened not long since, and in which a young lady figured, who was almost as ridiculously timorous as myself, and even more selfish than I.

---

[1] "Kate Melburne," Frances S. Osgood, *Ladies' National Magazine*, January 1844, vol. V, no. 1, pp. 24-27

CHAPTER II.

"Your fear of ill exceeds the ill you fear!"

"Oh! mercy! hold the horses! Oh! oh! oh! I shall die—I shall fall—I shall be killed—Charles! Kate! driver!"

The horses were standing motionless as statues—Charles Melburne was assisting his sister Kate across the plank to the steamboat, and the driver was hastening forward to perform the same office for Rose, when the outcry we have named burst forth.

"See to Rose, Charlie, do!" said Kate in a sweet, happy voice, "I can take care of myself!" and letting go his arm, she tripped lightly over the plank, while her brother returned for Rose. Kate Melburne had hardly reached the deck when looking back she saw a young woman with one child in her arms, and another clinging to her dress, slowly attempting to cross—Kate ran toward them, and taking the oldest boy's hand, led him carefully over. And now Rose, after sundry little shrieks and almost as many misgivings, had crossed, and was looking round for a comfortable seat in the ladies' cabin. There were two rocking chairs—both of them occupied.

Rose looked very discontented and disconsolate, as if she thought the easiest chairs were made for her especial accommodation; but one of the ladies rising soon after she slipped into the deserted seat, and kept possession until she recollected that she had not chosen her berth. Kate entered at this moment, and Rose saying, "keep my chair for me," left it to seek the stewardess. Meanwhile the young woman whose boy she had assisted came in with her baby crying in her arms, and the compassionate Kate forgetful of her sister's injunction, resigned her place to her at once—and bade her rock the child to sleep. Rose pouted on her return, but did not like to dispute the matter—and after fretting about the inconvenience of her berth went at last quietly to bed.

The Melburnes were on their way to Niagara for the first time. Rose would have been lovely had not an expression of discontent habitually disfigured her pretty mouth and graceful brow. But Kate was a high-bred, distinguished-looking girl, with a superb form, a heavenly face, and a heart and mind to match. Nothing could cloud her sunny and beautiful temperament, for she was above all petty trials, and gloried in braving great ones. Whenever she was at home or abroad she made herself, and tried to make every one around her happy.

Kate preferred sitting up all night and reading to tossing upon one of the close, damp, coffin-like beds of the steamer. She was infinitely entertained by the scraps of conversation which she caught now and then from the different groups around her, and by their doleful arrangements for a comfortable night. A fat lady was making ludicrous attempts to ensconce herself in one of the highest berths—a lean one was telling in a sepulchral voice her religious experiences. At last all was quiet, and Kate comfortably reclining on the sofa, had become deeply interested in Miss Bremer's enchanting *Nina*, when all at once she became conscious (how she knew not) of two eyes fixed upon her face in a most obstinately inquisitive manner. She looked up—the lean lady was sitting upright in her berth, with her cadaverous countenance, looking more sallow than ever beneath the full, broad frills of her *"bonnet de nuit."*

Kate gazed at her and she at Kate for full two minutes before either spoke, and then the hollow voice groaned out—"where was you raised?"

"Oh!" said Kate, laughing, nodding, and laying down her book, for she knew from the nasal Yankee twang the storm of questions that would inevitably follow, and was determined to brave it cheerfully.

"Oh! In America."

"What part?"

"United States."

"What state?"

"Massachusetts."

"What town?"

"Boston."

"What street?"

"Beacon."

Down sunk the *"bonnet de nuit,"* and Kate heard no more till morning, when she was awakened from a short slumber by the same voice—

"Myount! get up! get up, Myount! I never see such a lazy feller—come be a stirring!"

The lean lady had risen betimes, and was dressing one of her four boys, while she thus called to another.

"*What* is his name?" asked a neighbor, disturbed by the noise.

"Myount, ma'am, Myount Libanus. It's a scriptur name. His father likes scriptur names. Come, Shadrack, it's time you was dressing—Abednego here's your trousers. This here little one's named Nebuchadnezzar, ma'am. Fine, long name, ai'nt it? Where was you raised?"

The woman's face, and indeed her figure too were singularly expressive—when she asked a question her whole person appeared to take an interrogatory form. She was an interrogation mark personified. Eyebrows, eyes, mouth and nose assumed "a questionable shape" and throughout all, even in the lightest and most trifling conversation, she kept up a doleful look and doleful twang, which made her irresistibly amusing.

Kate was very sorry to part with her and her four scripture-named sons. But a steamboat after all is a tiresome place. So cross the plank with me dear reader, and meet the Melburnes at the Astor House in New York.

CHAPTER III.

A Hero at Last.

And a princely looking fellow he was. He had been deeply interested in the appearance of the sisters, and had obtained an introduction through their brother, whom he knew. At first, he took a rather fancy to Rose than Kate— and really for a few moments after she appeared on deck in the fresh morning breeze, she looked like a rose-bud bathed in fresh morning dew and sunshine, but the heaven of her beauty soon clouded again and Vincent turned to Kate and forgot in her majestic person, in her fresh, original and high-toned character the lighter charms of Rose.

George Vincent had never been in love, he had an aversion, mingled with a little contempt, for *women*, though he adored *woman* in the abstract with a reverence and a tenderness unlimited and inexpressible. He had seen so much of folly, of coquetry, of selfishness, of deception in the sex, that he had almost forsworn them altogether. In person he was an Antinous—in manner cold, stately and reserved. The women declared he had no heart. Perhaps we shall find him one. The ladies' drawing-room at the Astor was crowded with belles and beaux, and the Melburnes seating themselves in a window, listened to the buzzing tongues around them. A group of old bachelors first attracted their attention.

"And so," said one, "old L— has paid the debt of nature at last."

"Yes!" grumbled a second, "and it's the only debt he ever did pay. He owed me enough."

"They say he was a free thinker," said a third.

"And is not a free thinker the only true thinker?" said a fourth. "You condemn his worldliness. What is religion but other-worldliness?"

"True," rejoined the first, "and as the other world is infinitely better than this, so is other worldliness—religion—better than this worldliness. I consider this world but as man's primer in which he is placed to learn the rudiments only of all knowledge. Volume after volume, each more sublime than the last will be opened to him hereafter—and step by step, from one glorious orb to another will his mind roam through eternity toward the spiritual sun of the universe, the author of the vast folio of creation."

"Mr. A— must have introduced the subject for the express purpose of making that speech, and he has had to smuggle it in after all," said a satirical looking youth to a lady on the other side of the Melburnes.

"Perhaps so," replied the lady, in a low voice, "but do, Mr. Lawson, manage in some way to stop that poor girl's thumping on the piano. She positively imagines herself playing and singing some of the divine airs from *Norma!* Did you ever hear such sanguinary execution? It is downright murder—and then that delicious Italian so vandalized. I asked her this morning after suffering an hour's unheard of misery from her tones of lengthened sweetness long drawn out, how long she had required to become a proficient in the language."

"Oh! about a fortnight," said she, with the utmost *sang froid.* "I could have boxed her ears with right good will—she could not take my hint, broad as it was."

"And no wonder," replied Mr. Lawson, "a hint is but a jog on the mental elbow, and the poor thing *has* no mind—to take it."

The tremendous thunder of the dinner gong here overpowered even Miss Brown's meritorious, but astounding efforts to make a noise in the world, and the Melburnes joined the throng in the ladies' ordinary; Kate started as she took her seat, for directly opposite were the dark, proud eyes of George Vincent in a reverie. A smile of pleasure illumined his noble features as he recognized her.

"Allow me to help you, madam," said Mr. Lawson to a stranger, who was trying to reach the castor.

"Well! I don't care if you do—thank ye, sir. Was you raised in these parts?"

Kate Melburne turned, and there sure enough was the *bona fide* lean woman of the boat, with Shadrack, Nebuchadnezzar and Abednego on one side, and Mount Libanus on the other.

"Here! what's this ere—here—young man (to the waiter) I want some of that are," and she pointed to the list and read aloud precisely as it was spelt, *Pommes de terre a la Rouenaise*, "some outlandish thing or other, done to ruination, I suppose, but that shan't deter me from trying it, I tell you!"

And with a curiosity perfectly shocking to Rose's refined nerves, the lean lady asked in turn for every French dish on the bill of fare with the same remarkable pronunciation by which she had honored the potatoes. Before she had finished nearly every waiter and guest at the table were in a fit of irresistible and irrepressible merriment, which was, however, soon diverted from the mother of Mount Libanus to a would-be literary lady with bright red corkscrew ringlets, surmounted by a pink and picturesque turban, who took a book from her pocket between the courses, and read for her life, apparently.

"Oh! Miss Brown," exclaimed a very soft, die-away voice from a Miss Edwin, "I am going to a ball to-night, don't you think!"

Miss Brown complied with this very unreasonable request in the most amiable manner—and *didn't* think for the next half hour—at least she *looked* perfectly blank for that space of time, and so we may fairly suppose her a very accommodating young person in spite of her barbarous assassination of the innocent Italian airs.

CHAPTER IV.

More Confessions for the Reader's Private Ear.

Reader! dear reader! it is of no use! I have done my best to brave it out, but I give it up. I thought I had a story to write—and so I have, but I can't—you see how haltingly it goes—you see how many fibs I have told in order to spin it out—I am in despair. I promised to tell you what a little selfish coward Rose Melburne was, and I have only made her scream once in a carriage!

Reader! let there be confidence and kindness between us—let me speak to you for once out of the fullness of my heart, and not, as usual, out of the vacuum of my mind. Let me confess to you in a whisper as to a brother or a sister my predicament, and for the sake of the frankness of that confession, forgive the fault which compels me to make it. If my story is not finished in a few hours it will be too late for the magazine. I don't feel the least like writing it—I haven't the shadow of a plot in my head. The truth is I had rather be scribbling verses. Prose is not my forte. A thousand fair aerial visions—a thousand angel images have floated through my mind since I began, to music fitful, faint and sadly sweet as the voice of an Æolian harp—I am pining to grasp the "airy nothings" by the wings, and give to them "a local habitation and a name"— but I mustn't stop to do it.

My mind is coined for my daily bread,
And how can it soar above?

Mr. Peterson wants a story, and so I must resolutely shut my soul's eyes upon the beautiful pictures, and let them go; but cutting the muse's acquaintance don't help the prose a bit. What shall I do? What shall I make my poor Rose do? Help me, dear reader! She was a coward: Ask Kate and Charlie if she wasn't. She plagued them at every stage of their journey with her fears, her exactions, her nerves, and her nonsense—and she lost a lover by it as you will see in the sequel—but I don't want to tell you all about it! It will tire me and you too!—You will take it all for granted, won't you? and let me skip it over and jump to chapter fifth and last. If you are willing Mr. Peterson will be—won't you, Mr. Peterson? and just to relieve my mind I will scribble down here a few of those haunting verses, which you must kindly look upon as an agreeable variety—will you? If you will I will bless you and do my very best next time.

TO—

Away! away! this glorious day
  I give to idle pleasure,
You frown and say, "let children play,
  But time to us is treasure."
I'll be a child, in frolic wild,
  What's age to hearts so glowing?
Old Time may blight my locks with white,
  My *soul's* beyond his snowing.
This light is love—the air is balm,
  The morning smiles divinely,
'Twere to fly dear Nature's charm
  To turn a sentence finely.
You ask me if the piece is done
  You say 'tis time 't were going
Let *me* have peace—and hold your own!
  And hear my verses flowing!
I cannot stoop to plot and plan,
  I dread the task—the story!
If fame and riches wait *such* work,
  Good bye to wealth—to glory!

CHAPTER V.

Kate's Portrait and Niagara's.

Niagara, queen of the world of waters, was in her glory. Crowned with the soft and luxurious rainbow which gleamed like a jeweled tiara on her awful brow, her magnificent veil of mist floating around her, and softening the light of her radiant and majestic beauty, and the melodious thunder of her voice rolling on in a sublime anthem "from morn to night, from night to dewy morn," with a glorious monotony which never palled upon the ear. Kate was awed by the scene, and returning to the hotel, gave utterance to her thoughts in the ensuing verses.

> She walks in beauty like the moon
>   When blushing at a world's delight,
> Her misty wimple half withdrawn,
>   She dawns upon the gazer's sight.
>
> The dainty rose upon her face
>   Doth ever lightly come and go,
> The smile and blush each other chase
>   As Love and Joy alternate glow.
>
> But more than beautiful is she—
>   Her blue eyes tell of holier things,
> Of generous feeling, warm and free,
>   Of fancy's wild and Genii wings.
>
> "She walks in beauty" and in grace,
>   She speaks with low, melodious tone,
> And o'er her form and in her face
>   His dearest magic Love has thrown.
>
> But flattery's voice has not beguiled
>   Her lofty soul to selfish art,
> For never throbbed in Nature's child
>   A warmer, truer, happier heart!

"Yes! They are all alike—one is as good as another after all—and as I am resolved to marry now I have set about it—by Jove, the first woman I meet the morning, whoever she may be, I will propose to—and take my chance of happiness in the lottery life."

Mr. George Vincent was in a pet. He had had some little misunderstanding with Kate, and was desperate in consequence, as you may imagine from the above awful soliloquy and resolution.

"Oh! I am afraid! nothing would tempt me It is a cold and winter night, to go—it is so dangerous!" exclaimed Rose Melburne on that ever memorable morning—"you go Kate! and tell me about it."

Considerate Rose! Kate ought to be very obliged to you for sending her into a danger you dread so much yourself. But Kate went—and now let *us* go back to our hero.

George Vincent in his most reckless and impetuous mood was dashing over the perilous steps beneath the falls, when he suddenly overtook in the dark a lady following a guide—"a lady!" He admired courage and energy in woman, and he could just see by the faint and fitful light that her form was graceful and noble. His heart be high—his vow flashed upon his mind. This was the first lady he had seen since he made it. Without a second's pause for thought in the strange excitement of the time and place, he drew her hand gently through his arm. It was very soft and it trembled—Vincent was half in love already. She seemed grateful for the support, for she was in some danger at the moment—and then without a suspicion, hardly a care of name or station, he poured fourth in a torrent of eloquence almost as irresistible and overpowering as that beneath which they stood, the love he had been hiding in his heart for Kate for the last three weeks. The lady faltered—paused, and would have fallen had he not thrown his arm around her—she hardly resisted his caress—how *could* she be! If she would but speak!

"Answer me dear one! I implore you! Say I am yours forever, and let me glory in your prize."

"I am yours forever!" murmured the musical voice of Kate Melburne, and at that moment the light of day flashed suddenly upon her beautiful countenance bathed in blushed and tears. They paused—entranced, overwhelmed by their own powerful emotions, and by the magnificent beauty of the scene around. It was a fitting place for the sublime union of two immortal souls—and Vincent as her head turned from Nature's face to hers, reverently thanked God in his heart that his reckless folly had led to so unlooked for—a happy result.

I saw a miniature George Vincent the other day—I wonder if he was christened with the waters of Niagara!

Rose Melburne had fallen, no, *risen* in love with Vincent's princely person had chivalrous demeanor, and she was very much surprised and disappointed when Kate blushingly claimed her congratulations.

Reader! let *me* claim yours! The story, such as it is, is at your service. Good bye.

It is a cold and winter night
The freezing ice-winds blow—
The distant moon looks palely bright
Upon the paler snow.

Newport Tableaux[1]

"EVELINE, ALLOW me to present my cousin, Mr. Gardner—Miss Willis, Howard."

Miss Eveline Willis looked down and smiled, and made as graceful a courtesy as the circumstances would allow, and Mr. Gardner bowed—I cannot say to the ground, though he probably would have done so had there been any ground to bow to—but it so happened that, at the time this introduction took place, both parties were nearly over head and ears—not in love, but in water—bathing in the glorious surf at New Port, Rhode Island; and there they stood, face to face, uncertain whether to laugh or to blush, but very much inclined to fall in love at first sight at any rate—both of them—for Howard looked singularly handsome and picturesque, with his corsair-like scarlet bathing-dress, to which his black hair and eyes, and dark but soul-lighted complexion, formed a fine contrast; and as for Eveline, she seemed a very sea nymph—an Oriental one—in her tunic and full pantaloons of light green flannel, with her pale, golden hair, glittering in the sun, and clinging in wet masses to a throat as white as the driven snow; and so they stood, for a full minute, looking into each other's eyes, and then Eveline, in her embarrassment, turned for relief to her frolic-loving friend, Harriet Grey; but she, the witch, had already vanished, and, for a moment, Eveline thought her lost; the next, however, a voice, too gay and sweet to be mistaken, was heard at a distance singing—

"A life on the ocean wave,
    A home on the rolling deep,
Where the scattered waters rave,
    And the winds their revels keep."

Far away in the surf—too far for the timid Eveline to venture—the spirited girl was trying to dance in spite of

---

[1] "Newport Tableaux," Frances S. Osgood, *Graham's Magazine*, January 1844, vol. XXV, no. 1, pp. 19-24

the roaring waves, which almost overwhelmed her, and so Eveline turned once more to her new acquaintance, and this time they both laughed; but in the midst of their mirth an enormous wave overtook them ere they were aware, and the lady would have been drowned had not the gentleman supported her in time; as it was, she lost her consciousness for a few moments, and was borne by him insensible to a vacant car, where her friends soon gathered to her assistance, and thus ended Miss Willis' first attempt at bathing.

CHAPTER II.

Eveline was no beauty; but her blush and smile were bewitching, and her eyes, darkly and divinely blue, were so seldom fully seen, shaded as they were by remarkably long and drooping lashes, that when she did list them, they almost startled the beholder, and delighted him too, as much as if he were a second Columbus and had just discovered a new world; and so he had, a world of fresh thought and emotion, ever changing and ever beautiful. She was graceful and spirituelle. Every thing she did was done in a way of her own, and a peculiarly charming way it was. She was a constant study not only for a painter, but a poet; for the poetry of feeling breathed in every word and look.

As she entered, after dinner, the drawing-room of their boarding house, with her uncle and Harriet Grey, all eyes were turned upon the new arrival; and one stout, but very romantic-looking, young lady, in a thin white dress, long flaxen curls, sky-blue eyes and sash to match, all innocence and simplicity, as her mother was fondly wont to say, started with clasped hands from the sofa and caught our heroine in an unexpected and therefore embarrassing embrace.

Eveline, mute with wonder, suffered herself to be drawn to the sofa and seated upon it, and then quietly releasing her form, asked her new friend to whom she was indebted for so warm a welcome. Tears, not, we fear, "unbidden," rushed into the sky-blue eyes—"Ah, unkind! do you not remember your old schoolfellow, Heavenlietta?" This was said in a tone so tremulously imploring, that Eveline felt it would be the height of barbarity *not* to remember, if she possibly could, and so, at last, she did recollect that at school, when only fourteen years of age, Miss Heavenlietta Waddie was in the daily habit of bringing herself and her sensibilities before the general eye, in some such manner as she had done just then.

For instance, one day in passing the desk of the teacher, who was a young and interesting man, for the express purpose, as her observant and amused companions mischievously asserted, of obtaining his notice, just then abstracted by a poem, she brushed off a book, apparently by accident. The noise it made in falling at once aroused his attention, and Heavenlietta, instead of quietly apologizing, affected to be overpowered by terror and remorse, and throwing herself on her knees before the astonished master, raised her blue eyes and clasped her delicate hands, calling Heaven to witness that her fault was involuntary, and imploring his forgiveness, in a voice almost inaudible from emotion!

"Rise, Miss Waddle!" said he, as soon as he could sufficiently command his countenance and voice to speak without betraying his keen sense of the ridiculous in her position, "Rise, Miss Waddle, and read no more romances, till you can cease to imagine yourself a heroine in distress."

"Ah! my beloved friend!" murmured Heavenlietta, as soon as she found herself recognized—"At length then I have found a congenial soul! 'Soul!' did I say? The people around us have *no* souls!"

"No souls!" exclaimed our Eveline, trying to look as solemn as the occasion seemed to require, "No souls! you alarm me!"

"Ah yes! *you* can sympathize with me; for sensitive as you are, you must often have suffered as I have. Can you imagine a suffering more exquisite?"

"Are you in pain, Heavenlietta?"

"In pain! No! why do you ask?"

"Oh! you spoke of suffering, and I thought you looked as if you had the tooth-ache."

"Eveline!" said Miss Waddle solemnly, with a sublime pathos of voice and manner, "the agony to which I allude is of a more terrible nature!"

Eveline was really frightened now—"What agony, my dear Miss Waddle?"

"The agony of being constantly misunderstood by the heartless, thoughtless, frivolous beings around me. Gifted as I unhappily am by nature with a sensitiveness the most exquisite, and affections the most ardent, they are wounded at every turn."

"But is it possible that *all* the ladies and gentlemen present are thoughtless, heartless and frivolous?"

"All!" averred Heavenlietta, with a mournful shake of the head; "All but Mr. Maynard," she added, suddenly assuming her sweetest smile, and looking up confidingly in the face of a young man who now sauntered toward them. Mr. Maynard threw himself on the sofa in a lounging attitude, showering by the movement, as he did so, a mass of long hair all over one expressive eye, probably with the intention of doing, like Moore's Eastern beauty, "all the mischief he could with the other."

"You are more animated than usual, Miss Waddle," said he.

"Ah, my friend, believe me!

The cloud but leaves the laughing eye
    To brood more darkly o'er the soul,
And lips may smile while dark within
    The tempest raves beyond control!"

"Don't, Miss Waddle, I beg of you! You look altogether too Sidonian for my nerves. However, that is a pathetic verse; but why not make it rhyme. How much better it would read thus—

"The cloud but leaves the laughing chin," etc.

"Ah! now you are quizzing me! I don't believe but what you are. Are you not, now? Tell me candidly do! I implore! I entreat! You are! You are trying not to laugh! Positively I won't stay another minute: I won't, indeed; so you need not urge me;" and, playfully tapping his cheek with her fan, the too sensitive Heavenlietta waddled from the room.

Mr. Maynard had his peculiarities, as who has not? He was, however, agreeable, intelligent and interesting—rather too Childe Haroldish perhaps, at times, in his views of men and things; but that is often the case with young persons of his age and sensitive temperament.

Harriet, who had met him before, now joined them and introduced him to Eveline, whom he amused until tea-time, with information as to the place and the persons she would be likely to meet.

"The four principal boarding-houses here, Miss Willis, have been nicknamed the Nunnery, the Funnery, the Factory and the Pottery. The first is kept by a cool and economical Quaker lady, who has a virtuous horror of music and dancing, and has lately expelled from the public drawing-room a piano-forte, which had been smuggled into it. Some of the rebellious boarders, for want of more rational and elevating amusements, have betaken themselves to cards, which I have seen in play so early as ten in the morning.

In the intervals of whist, tongues and netting-needles are set in motion—the tongues go rather the fastest of the two, and if a *lapsus linguæ* could be as easily remedied as a slip of the needle or a false stitch, the spirit of Harmony might still reign triumphant in the house, in spite of its anti-melodious landlady's prohibition. By the way, how will the poor Quakers endure the music of the spheres, to which, as we are taught, the spirit's ear will one day wake in Heaven?

There are many interesting persons at the Nunnery— "*black* spirits and brown, *white* spirits and gray"—there is a little gem from the South, a dark-eyed Carolinian, graceful, delicate and *spirituelle* as Shakespeare's Ariel, in the *Tempest*; but *my* favorite—for I've not been introduced to the gem—is a frank, quiet, cheerful, sensible girl from P—, whose beauty is forgotten in her goodness and her truth. She shows off every one but herself, and has always a kind word for the present and a charitable one for the absent.

The Funnery takes its name from the gayety of the bright and beautiful spirits who lead the sports at M's. The Factory is that long, light green house, all windows and no blinds, which you passed on your way hither. It is said the entertainments there are neither few nor dull, and that the queen of the revels is fair as the fabled nymphs of Diana. The Pottery is the house we are in. It takes its name from its proprietor, and is one of the pleasantest in the place. That remarkably stout lady, who is just entering the room, with a little girl clinging to her dress, is Mrs. Waddle, the mother of our friend. She approaches, I must resign the sofa to her. She will inevitably occupy all but the small space which you have appropriated. Listen to her and command, if you can, your countenance."

The stout lady sat down panting and fanned herself. Eveline, who was very fond of children, held out her hand to the little, sallow, glum-looking thing, with large, staring, black eyes and curly hair, who still clung obstinately to her mother's gown. The child was dressed in a still, blue silk, with a gold chain and locket, coral bracelets, and a pink ribbon round her head—

"Go to the lady, Azurelina," said Mrs. Waddle. "I named her Azurelina, ma'am, because I was in hopes she would have had blue eyes. They *were* blue when she was born. Isn't it a pity that they turned out black after all? However, I can hardly have the heart to regret it, since they are so beautiful now. By the way, ma'am, speaking of beauty, I have a particular favor to ask. We never allow ourselves to tell Azurelina how remarkably charming she is. I must beg of you, therefore, to control your admiration before her. We wish her to be modest, as she is lovely and graceful. Dear little pet! Go to the lady, Azurelina, and give her a sweet kiss, there's a love!"

All this was said in a tone sufficiently loud for the "little pet" to hear, and not only the "little pet" but every one else in the room. Why is it that if a child happens to have large black eyes and curly hair, no matter how dull and inexpressive the former may be, nor how dry and ill-colored the latter, it is always taken for granted, at least by the parents, that she is a beauty? Miss Azurelina Waddle, unmoved by flattery and coaxing, resisted all her mother's efforts to draw her out.

"Go to the lady, pet, and you shall have a piece of candy."

"Two pieces!" said "pet."

"Ah! the rogue! Well, two pieces then."

"Three pieces!" said "rogue."

"*Two* pieces, darling; candy isn't good for little tot, you know. Two *great* pieces!"

"No, no, no!" screamed "little tot," "three pieces! I *will* have three pieces!"

"Well, there! three pieces, and that's all! not another one, sweet!"

"Three great big pieces!" said "sweet."

"Yes, yes! now go!"

"Little tot" then allowed Eveline to kiss her thick lips, and instantly turning to her mother exclaimed—"Now give me my candy!"

"Yes! I'll go right up stairs and bring it if you'll just make one *tableaux* for the lady—just one, and then you shall have it."

"Little tot" pouted and shook her shoulders for a few minutes; but at length, overcome by the promise of four sticks of candy, she consented, and kneeling down in a most awkward fashion, and looking more sullen than ever, she put one foot out behind, and one hand above her head, and, rolling up her eyes, made what her foolish mother was pleased to dignify by the appellation of "*tableaux vivant*;" though "*tableaux mourant*" would have been a more appropriate phrase for the exhibition.

"Now give me my candy!"

"Yes! by and by, after tea—there, run away and play—you'll spoil my dress."

The modest, lovely and graceful Azurelina Waddle set up a roar, which nothing but the sight of an enormous paper of candy, all of which was devoured before dinner, could quiet.

Eveline sighed, and turned toward Mr. Maynard, who stood near with a smile of quiet satire upon his countenance. "Let us change the subject," said he, as Mrs. Waddle left the room with her interesting charge. "We are expecting here a poetess of some celebrity. Many conjectures have been formed of her character. Most of the boarders expect an acquisition in her as a talker; others dread her for the same reason. Shall I tell you what *I* anticipate? I imagine her a bold, loquacious, pedantic, independent, unfeminine sort of a person, about forty years of age, full of pretension in dress and manner, putting herself forward on all occasions, and looking down with infinite contempt upon all the commonplace people around her, as she will term us poor inoffensive mortals."

At this moment a graceful, modest-looking girl entered the room with a timid and unobtrusive air, and gliding to a corner began to sew very industriously. She was dressed in the becoming costume of the time. The snowy Persian cymar of delicate linen peeped beneath the loose sleeve and above the high, closely-fitting waist of her light gray silk robe, and her dark-brown hair, loosely braided, was confined by a comb of jet. Her face was not what the world calls beautiful; the features were irregular and the clear cheek was colorless as marble; but her large black eyes were gloriously eloquent, with sorrow and love and earnest thought, and the expression of her full, soft mouth was ineffably sweet and touching.

"I must go and talk to that lady," said Maynard. "She looks shy and sorrowful; she is ill, I think, and must be very lonely; for no one knows her or speaks to her. She always sits in that quiet corner and sews as if her life depended upon it. Will you go with me?"

"Certainly," said Eveline rising, "and we will introduce each other."

The youthful lady looked up as they approached, with a tranquil smile, yet with a shade of reserve and embarrassment in her manner, which wore off by degrees as they conversed.

"I have been giving Miss Willis a description of a certain poetess, who is daily expected, as she exists in my imagination," and he repainted, with additions, his former picture of the blue.

"And why do you judge so hardly of her?" said the stranger, in a low, musical voice. "Have you ever read her writings?"

"Not I! I have something better to do."

For an instant the lady raised her strange eyes to his with a sad, sweet smile, and then silently resumed her work.

"Most of my lady acquaintances," said Maynard after a pause, as he watched her slight fingers in rapid motion for a moment—"Most of my lady acquaintances are of those who sew 'not wisely but to well;' I do not think *you* are liable to that censure," and he smiled at the long stitches she was taking.

"Oh! don't look at it!" she exclaimed, blushing and laughing. "I only sew here because I don't know what to do with my eyes among so many people. I *can* work well sometimes, but this does not require it. I think a great deal of time is wasted in sewing too nicely."

While they were thus conversing, a group near them listened to a Mr. Brown, who was reading aloud a New York paper. "Ah!" said he, as he turned the paper, "here, I see, is a paragraph concerning Miss N—, the poetess, whom we are expecting, and, by the way, why don't she come? But let's see what they say about her," and he read an extravagant puff with great "goût."

The stranger gazed for a moment, like a startled fawn, at the reader as he commenced the paragraph. As he read on, she looked down, colored, smiled, and then rose to leave the room; but, at the door, a visitor intercepted her, and exclaiming "My dear Miss N—I am delighted to meet you"—drew her arm within his and led her back to the sofa, "the observed of all observers." The new comer was no other than our friend, Howard Gardner, and the quiet young lady was the poetess herself, Genevieve N—, of C—. Mr. Maynard stood aghast and tried to recall every word he had said about the literary lady; but, in the midst of these confused cogitations, he caught again those soft, dark eyes, and there was so much of kindness in their look that he felt himself forgiven and was reassured at once.

CHAPTER III.

Come with me, dear reader, to the drawing-room at Potter's, and let us join the gayest group within it. Eveline, Harriet Grey, Howard Gardner, Maynard, Miss Waddle, and Miss N—, were seated at that nice promoter of sociability, a round table—making charades, reading or repeating scraps of poetry, and playing Consequences. Did you ever play Consequences, reader? Let us try it with them. Maynard writes, on half a sheet of paper, a gentleman's name, folds it down and passes it on; the next, without seeing what has been written, writes a lady's name—the next, the name of a place—the next, a gentleman's speech to a lady—the next, a lady's reply—the next, what were the consequences, and the next, what the world said about the matter. Each person hides what they have written by folding the paper. Maynard then unfolds the paper, and reads it with a demure face and much expression, filling up at will.

"Howard Gardner, Esq., one pleasant evening, was so fortunate as to meet Miss Eveline Willis in Purgatory. He exclaimed, kneeling as he did so, 'Dearest, I love but thee!' and she replied, with a bewitching smile, 'Oh! I am so glad!' The consequences were an elopement to Paradise, and the world said 'You don't say so?'"

Poor Eveline blushed and laughed, and pretended to be busily occupied with a purse she was knitting. Howard gazed upon her with an earnest smile, and Miss N—'s pale cheek colored suddenly with a crimson light, and then grew white as death. The next instant, however, she subdued, with a strong effort, her emotion, and turning, with a gay, almost wild smile, to Maynard, began to banter him upon his morning's embarrassment.

Mr. Brown now joined the circle and the conversation. "We are very apt," said he, "to do that sort of injustice to literary ladies. I will show verses somewhat *apropos* to the subject" from his pocket-book and read as follows:

THE HOLY STOCKING.

I went a poetess to see,
I thought to find her lying,
In languid grace, with tresses free,
And robe all loosely flying;

But oh! she wore a common dress
Of silk, a little faded,
And oh! each smooth and silken tress
Was fashionably braided!

And worse than this, if worse can be,
The very thought is shocking!
While talking sweet romance with me,
She calmly *darned a stocking!*

Amazed, confounded, "What!" I cried,
    "Is this a poet's duty?"
"My task," she tranquilly replied,
    "To *me*, is full of beauty

I dream, while thus the rent I close,
    My precious needle plying,
Of him, who wore the silken hose,
    Upon my skill relying;

And when he, trustful, draws them on,
    And finds them nicely mended,
A smile upon his face will dawn,
    Of love and pleasure blended."

While thus she said, so glad her look,
    So calm she bore my mocking,
The act, a nameless beauty, took
    Then graced the holy stocking!

A general laugh followed the reading of these in the midst of which the party broke up.

CHAPTER IV.

"Ah! thus to the child of Genius too,
    The rose of beauty is oft denied;
But all the rich, that high heart through,
    The torrent of feeling pours its tide,
And purer and fonder and far more true.
    Is that passionate soul in its lonely pride!"

A soft, impassioned voice is murmuring in the moonlight. Let us listen!

They are singing—they are happy!
    They have joyous hearts and light!
For them—for them! oh! not for me,
    This starry eve is bright!

For me, in all the wide, wide world,
    No answering heart throbs high;
For me there is no love, no trust,
    No hope, save one—to die!

No hand clasps mine in tender truth,
    No soul-look meets mine own,
My heart is rich in ardent youth,
    And yet—I am alone!

With a heart overflowing with tenderness, yet shy to almost painful timidity, Genevieve N—, an orphan at thirteen, had been thrown unprotected upon the world. With that rich and glowing heart, thrown back upon itself, chilled, disappointed, yet still confiding as a child, and grateful for every look and tone of sympathy or love, we see her at twenty, as we have described.

While she leans absorbed from the window, let us turn over her portfolio. It is one of a story-teller's countless privileges, you know, so it need not shock your delicate sense of propriety, dear reader. We will read some of her verses. Poor child! a vein of subdued and sorrowful tenderness runs through them all.

And wealth seems worthless in mine eyes,
    And power a weary task,
Even wayward fame may sound my name,
    Nor I the echo ask.

Then say no more I love too much!
    All else to me is vain;
I cannot live unless I love,
    And am beloved again!

Here is another—softly! lest she hear us—

And gayer friends surround thee now,
    And lighter hearts are thine;
Thou dost not *need*, beloved and blest,
    So sad a boon as mine!

But in my sorrowing soul for thee,
    Love's balmy flower I'll hide,
And feeling's tears shall keep it fresh,
    Whatever tale beside;

Then, when misfortune's winter comes,
    And frailer love takes wing,
All pure and bright, with hope's own light,
    Affection's rose I'll bring;
And thou shalt bless the simple flower,
    That keeps its virgin bloom,
To charm thy soul in sorrow's hour,
    With beauty and perfume!

CHAPTER V.

Hops, pic-nics, riding parties, tableaux, acted charades, &c., followed each other in brilliant succession at the Pottery. The season was a grayer one than has been known for many years; for the ruling spirit of the scene was one who never failed by his kindness, genius, and ready wit, to enliven the dull, and inspire the intelligent.

One evening, when Eveline was dressing for a hop, Harriet Grey, a lovely, joyous, thoughtless child of sixteen, ran into the room, with her pretty, blue eyes full of tears, exclaiming, "Oh! Eveline! After all, I have left my box of ornaments at home, and have nothing to wear in my hair!" Eveline kissed the tears away, and clasped around the graceful head a costly pearl chain which she had intended to wear herself.

Harriet clapped her little hands in an ecstasy of childish delight, as she saw herself reflected in the glass, looking more lovely that ever; but suddenly a cloud came over the sunny face, and she turned to her friend, "But what will *you* wear, Eveline?"

"Oh! my white wreath will do nicely for me."

Harriet threw her arms round her neck, thanked her, and ran to find her fan and bouquet. She had hardly gone when a knock was heard at the door, and Miss Waddle entered in great trepidation. "Miss Willis, you *must* lend me something for my hair—you must indeed! Will you? Oh! what a lovely wreath! that is just the thing;" and she caught it up, wound it round her head and waddled to the glass.

"How does it look? Is it becoming? May I wear it?"

"Certainly!" said Eveline, "you are quite welcome to it;" and Heavenhetta disappeared with the wreath.

Eveline had wished, she hardly knew why, to look particularly well this evening; perhaps it was because Howard Gardner was to see her for this first time in full dress. However, with a passing smile and sight, which ended in a laugh at the loss of her wreath and chain, she simply wound her soft hair about her classic head, and, in pure white, without any ornament but her own native grace and sweetness, descended to the drawing-room.

Harriet Grey looked enchantingly beautiful in her pearls and lace dress. She was decidedly the belle of the evening. But Eveline danced twice with Howard, and talked with during all the waltzes in which neither of them joined, and she was happier than she had ever been before in her life. Happier and lovelier too; for joy and affection illumined and softened her countenance, and Howard thought her, when she blushed, the most beautiful woman he had ever seen.

And where was Genevieve? She had wandered miles away in the moonlight, with a little brother, and was sitting in a wild nook among the cliffs called Conrad's Cave, listening to the sublimest voice in the ever-sounding anthem of nature—the soft, yet majestic melody of the ocean surf as it dashed up the beach at her feet. A spirit floating by in the moonlight might have heard another tone, inaudible to earthly ears, yet strangely and sweetly harmonizing with the music of the waves—the moaning of a human soul for sympathy, lie the sea-shell asking for the waters that should fill it.

CHAPTER VI.

"What a fearful chasm!" exclaimed Eveline, as she stood at sunset the next day alone with Gardner gazing down full fifty feet into a dark and fathomless abyss, formed by an enormous rock which had been cleft in two probably by some violent concussion of nature, and in which the waves boiled and hissed and maddened as they rose, like the waters of l'hlegethon around the guilty and condemned.

"What do they call it, Mr. Gardner?"

"Purgatory, Miss Willis."

Eveline started and would have lost her footing on the dizzy height, had not her companion caught her in time.

She remembered the game of Consequences, and blushed deeply as she turned from Howard's ardent gaze.

The declaration, which had been prophesied in sport, was made in earnest, and though the maiden's faltered reply was lost in the roar of waters, yet, as he kissed an answer from her eyes, it did not matter much.

The lovers extended their walk around the beach, and came suddenly upon a party of their friends, enjoying a pic-nic, in a wild, rocky, and grandly beautiful scene beneath a grove of buttonwood trees. The warm glory of the setting sun lay like a delicate golden web upon the whole living and ever changing picture; tree, wave, and rock and distant spire gleamed softly beneath the transparent veil of light, and the subdued and murmuring melody of the waves might have been mistaken for the harp of a wandering angel, it was so spiritually soft and clear!

"Oh!" cried our heroine, charmed by the picturesque magnificence of the place, "there should be some appropriate name for a scene so lovely as this!"

"It is called Paradise, Eveline," whispered Howard. "Do you remember the Consequence, dearest? Love will make a paradise of any place with thee!"

But let us back to Purgatory.

CHAPTER VII.

"What an entrancing spot!" exclaimed Heavenlietta Waddle, as she stood gazing down into Purgatory with an honest young sea-captain, whose heart the sky-blue eyes of the sash to match had taken by storm, and to whom she had been betrothed for three days.

"Now, Nehemiah, if you love me, prove your love!"

"Haven't I proved it already by asking you to be my wife, Heavenlietta?" asked the sailor, with an involuntary sight at the recollection; for he was beginning to see into the innate selfishness of her character through the flimsy veil of sentimentality which affection had thrown over it.

"Yes, Nehemiah, you can truly exclaim, with the poet—

"By thy dear side the pilot, Love, has moored it safe and fast,
Dropped anchor at thy fairy feet, and furled its flying sails.'

"But this commonplace. I require a more chivalric proof of your devotion. Leap for my sake this awful chasm, and I'll believe you love me."

"Leap that chasm! You are mad!—it is ten feet wide!"

"And can you hesitate?" cried Heavenlietta, in a pathetic voice. "Then are you no lover of mine, and here we part forever." With one reproachful look from the sky-blues, she turned away.

"Stay, Miss Waddle—are you in earnest?"

"Nehemiah, I am!"

"Then here goes!" And, receding a few steps from the edge of the precipice, with a resolute but somewhat disdainful smile, he took the fearful leap. But stay—where is he going? Instead of springing back to claim the reward he deserves—a kiss from those sweet lips—he neither turns nor pauses, but runs on and on in the opposite direction, nor heeds that tender call—"Nehemiah, Nehemiah! whither do you fly? Come back! come back! I am frightened. I don't know the way home. Oh! Nehemiah, Nehemiah!"

As is pursued by the furies, Nehemiah ran on. The louder she called, the faster he flew. Away, away—he is gone—he is out of sight! Heavenlietta glanced round despairingly, but it was not worthwhile to faint, for there was nobody near to see her, and so she waddled home as fast as she could, wiping the sky-blue eyes with the sash to match, and murmuring as she went—

"She never blamed him, never,
    But received him when he came,
With a welcome kind as ever,
    And she tried to look the same!"

Alas! confiding, but deluded girl! He *did not* come! She never saw him more!

CHAPTER VIII.

The events I have related occurred in the early part of August. In October, the following paragraphs, in a southern paper, caught my eye:

"Married, at Philadelphia, on Thursday morning, by the Rev. Mr. F—, Howard Gardner, Esq., of New York, to Eveline Willis, daughter of the Hon. George Willis, of this city."

"Died, at Charleston, of consumption, on Thursday morning, Genevieve N—only daughter of the late William N—, of Charleston."

A Match for the Matchmaker[1]

WHEN THE time for his examination drew near, Malcolm Malcolmson made up his mind to go somewhere to read by himself. He feared the attractions of the seaside, and also he feared completely rural isolation, for of old he knew its charms, and so he determined to find some unpretentious little town where there would be nothing to distract him. He refrained from asking suggestions from any of his friends, for he argued that each would recommend some place of which he had knowledge, and where he had already acquaintances.

As Malcolmson wished to avoid friends he had no wish to encumber himself with the attention of friends' friends and so he determined to look out for a place for himself. He packed a portmanteau with

> The blessings of the skies all wait about her;
> Health, grace, inimitable beauty wreathed
> Round every motion: On her lip the rose
> Has left its sweetness—(For what bee to kiss?)
> And from the darkening heaven of her eyes
> A starry spirit looks out: Can it be Love?
> *Barry Cornwall.*

CHAPTER I.

It was the misfortune of Eleanor Howard to have no protector but a manœuvering aunt, and a great misfortune it is to a girl so sensitive, so high-souled as was our heroine. Mrs. Howard, herself a leader of the town, was determined her niece should make a brilliant match, and she spared no pains to bring it about; but the more she tried to show her off, the more she kept her on; for Eleanor was a girl of spirit as well as delicacy, and though her aunt had managed repeatedly, by dint of the

---

[1] "A Match for the Matchmaker," Frances S. Osgood, *Graham's Magazine*, February 1844, vol. XXV, no. 2, pp. 53-56

most dainty manœuvres, the most skillful generalship, to bring an "eligible" to her feet, Eleanor, with a quiet dignity peculiar to herself, invariably bade them rise, and gave them to understand that they had mistaken themselves and her.

Mrs. Howard was in despair; not that Eleanor was a burden to her—by no mean! She was no dependent—she had a little income of her own; and was moreover a gay and charming companion for the sometimes lonely widow.

But the lady flattered herself she had a natural talent—she certainly had a natural *taste*—for matchmaking. Indeed she had never known it fail before. She had married off three nieces in as many years, neither of them half so interesting as Eleanor, and she was more vexed at her want of success in this instance than she chose to avow. The men were astounded, the women amazed and incredulous. Both saw through the designs of the aunt, and half suspected the niece of partaking them, until her repeated refusals of rank, wealth and fashion convinced them in spite of their spite to the contrary.

CHAPTER II.

In the meantime, Eleanor chatted and laughed, and sang and danced as gaily and sweetly as ever, and looked as bewitching as possible, and did everything she could to please her indulgent aunt, except—"the one thing needful." She *would* wear all her dresses clasped at the throat—though her neck had the dazzling tint of alabaster—she *would* sing her gayest songs when she ought to have sung the most tender ones; and she would smile just as enchantingly on a penniless poet as on a haughty millionaire. What was to be done with the proud and willful maiden? Was she looking for a coronet? We shall see.

About this time an English nobleman arrived in New York, and a succession of parties were given in his honor by the elite of the city. Rich, elegant and fascinating, he was caressed and flattered by mammas, and smiled and blushed at by daughters, till his handsome head was almost turned.

"Now!" said the aunt, "if I can only bring him to the point, I am sure of her. She must be marble to resist him." And so she laid her plans; but unfortunately for her, Lord F— had laid his plans also. He had his "mind's eye" wide open, although he pretended for the joke's sake to have it shut; he saw at a glance her aim, and believed that the charming Eleanor, with all her pretended nonchalance, shared in it fully. He fancied them both fair game, and resolved to amuse himself with, to use his own words, "their absurd expectations." And Eleanor thought it perfectly natural, this youthful love of amusement—she liked a joke herself, and had not the slightest objection to the gentleman having his; but not at her expense, oh no! So she, too, laid her plans.

"My dear aunt," she said one morning, coaxingly, and with a demure archness of manner, which rather puzzled the person addressed; "my dear aunt, leave *this* one to me."

"I do not understand you, child!"

"Let *me* manœuvre *this* time. I promise to succeed. He shall propose in six months. Please, aunt?"

"You are a saucy girl, to intimate that *I* have ever manœuvered—but have your own way—I give it up," and, with an approving simile that quite contradicted her first words, Mrs. Howard continued to herself, exultingly, "The bird is caged at last!"

CHAPTER III.

Left to herself, unrestrained by her aunt's surveillance—by cautions, hints and praises—unhumiliated by the consciousness of being nightly "shown off." Eleanor was more enchanting, more lovely than ever. If ever a delicate touch of coquetry was excusable in any case, it certainly was in this. Lord F— was caught in his own net, ere he was aware of his danger. Now with a proud and almost imperial dignity repelling his advances, and now with sportive playfulness replying to them—at one time sad, shrinking and sensitive, at another joyous and frank as a child, Eleanor, with exquisite tact, out manoeuvered her aunt and her lover at once, without in the least compromising her maiden delicacy; for she never for a moment gave what any one but a very vain man would have dared to call encouragement to his devotion.

Yes! Lord F— was caught in his own net, as he deserved to be, and he had no alternative but to lay his hand, heart and fortune at her feet.

Eleanor listened in tranquil silence till he had finished, and then, calmly adjusting a bracelet on her arm, told him very gravely that she had made a resolution never to marry a title.

Lord F— looked at her in profound amazement, and it required all her self-possession to subdue the smile which was trying to play round her lips. After a few moments' pause he resumed, with a half-suppressed sigh at his own magnanimity,

"And if, for your sweet sake, dearest, loveliest! I renounce my title, then?"

"Oh! Then I should be exceedingly obliged to you; but the truth is, I have solemnly determined never to marry a man of wealth."

Lord F— was confounded. His very eyebrows "rose to reply." But he conquered once more his dismay and surprise, and, gazing passionately on her beautiful downcast face, where the rosy light of love seemed dawning into day, exclaimed with renewed fervor,

"And what are riches in comparison with you—with *your* love, my treasure? Henceforth I am penniless if that will please you. I will endow hospitals, churches, universities, asylums, poor-houses, libraries. I will do any thing you wish."

Eleanor began to be alarmed. "What am I to do with him?" she said to herself—"whoever heard of such an accommodating man? It is very vexatious!" And then her conscience reproached her a little, and, touched by the ready generosity of her lover, her eyes filled with tears of self-reproach; but a timely recollection of his supercilious manner on their first acquaintance restored her native pride, and, smiling through her tears, she replied,

"I thank your lordship for your preference of myself to so many more worthy of you in rank and fortune; I appreciate your disinterestedness and grieve for your disappointment, but—"

His eyes flashed impatiently. But what, Miss Howard?"

"I have made a vow never to unite myself to a foreigner on any account whatever."

The Englishman sprung to his feet and left the house in a rage. It was too bad—was it not? His title, his wealth, his birth-place, all of which would have been so many passports to the favor of most young ladies in her situation, were here used positively as reasons for declining his addresses! It was indeed too bad.

CHAPTER IV.

The truth is, Eleanor loved, devotedly, fondly, but in secret, a young Southerner, a Georgian, who had appeared in New York about the same time with Lord F— And to conceal this love she assumed a gayety, a dainty and refined coquetry of manner which was intended to deceive, not only the object of her affection, but all the fashionable world beside.

Ernest Cuthbert was the only person, in the circle of her acquaintance, who thoroughly understood and appreciated the noble and proud nature of our heroine. He read her soul like a book—a rich and rare missal which was locked to all but him. It was the magic key of sympathy which thus revealed to him the lights and shadows, the deep and mysterious harmony of her high-toned character. He loved her with all the fervor and earnest enthusiasm of a young and passionate heart, and sometimes he fancied that she returned his love. He perceived that she was humbled and vexed by her aunt's constant endeavors to make her display her graces and accomplishments; he admired her sensitive pride, and he let her see that he felt with her and for her.

And now Mrs. Howard, driven to desperation by Eleanor's refusal of Lord F—, renewed her efforts with redoubled vigilance. Ernest Cuthbert was one of the first matches in the country—she must on no account let *him* slip through the toils prepared for him.

"Eleanor, love, I have told Florette to take out your embroidered satin dress and the diamond spray for your hair. You know young Cuthbert will be of the party."

Half an hour afterward, "Eleanor, love" entered the drawing-room, in a plain white robe of linen cambric, with her graceful hair simply, almost carelessly arranged, and without a single ornament. But she looked so bewitchingly beautiful, with the blush coming and going on her cheek, and the half-tearful smile in her eloquent eyes, that her aunt could not find it in her heart to scold.

"Eleanor, dear, sing Mr. Cuthbert that song you composed yourself. It is so touching! Let me see, what is the first line?—'My heart is like a—'"

"Eleanor, dear" sportively drowned her aunt's memory and her voice too in a spirited waltz, and then began to sing the gayest and least sentimental song she could think of.

"I see you are determined," said Cuthbert, smiling as he leaned over the instrument.

"Determined on what, Mr. Cuthbert?"

"To make me respect even more than I love you, if that can be!" he whispered passionately, forgetting, in the entrancement of the moment and in the charm of her presence, that he had chosen a very awkward time and place for a declaration.

Involuntarily Eleanor raised her eyes, filled with tears of blended sorrow and delight, to his face; the next moment she smiled, shook her head playfully, and finished the song.

CHAPTER V.

"What is the matter, Nelly," said her aunt, the next morning as they sat together in the library; "you have neither smiled nor sung to-day! I do believe you are in love at last."

Eleanor had been sitting for half an hour with her graceful hand over her eyes, and she did not remove it as she answered in a low, faltering voice,

"Dear aunt, I am not quite well to-day."

"But I know by your voice you are crying, Nell. Tell me what troubles you."

"Mr. Cuthbert, ma'am!" said a servant, opening the door; "shall I show him in?"

"Yes, John, certainly; and, John, order my carriage round directly. Can I do any thing for you, Eleanor? I am going to shop."

Eleanor did not hear her. The carriage came, Mrs. Howard departed, and the lovers were left alone.

"And now, my poor Eleanor, now you *must* say 'yes.' There is no chance of escape this time. You love him and he worships you. Be a good child now, and don't make a fuss about it."

And Ernest told his love with all the eloquence of which he was master. There was no reply. The hand was still over the eyes that he wanted so much to look into, and in trying to withdraw it he discovered that she was weeping.

"Tears, Eleanor!—and for me! Speak to me, dearest! Do not keep me thus in suspense. Once more, will you be mine?"

"No!"

Cuthbert started as if a thunderbolt had fallen at his feet—though her voice was scarcely audible.

"No, Eleanor! What does this mean? that you love me—"

Eleanor sobbed passionately.

"Are you resolved to deny me?"

"I am!" This time the tone was distinct and firm.

"Then, Miss Howard, I must wish you a very good morning," and with a stately step he left the room.

And the proud maiden, pressing her hands convulsively on her heart, listened to his receding footsteps and murmured, "Dear, dear Ernest! Thank God it is over!"

Before Ernest had walked the length of one square from the house, a new light flashed upon his mind. "That's it, by Heaven! She is a noble creature, and she shall be mine yet, if misfortune can make her so."

"What, *he* too!" exclaimed her aunt and the world the next day when they heard the news; for the lover had purposely spread it. "The girl is perfectly possessed!"

CHAPTER VI.

Three months went by and Eleanor Howard, pale, but still very lovely, was yet seen at times, though seldom, in the gay circles of which she had been once the brightest ornament.

One evening, at a musical *soiree*, she was turning over some engravings on a table, when a lady near her exclaimed to a neighbor, "Look! There is Ernest Cuthbert just entering! How he has altered! How pale he looks! He has just returned from the South, where he has been to settle his affairs. I am told that he has lost all his property; that one night in a fit—some say of derangement, some, of intemperance—he staked his whole estate upon a single throw, and lost! And now he has nothing to depend upon but his talents as an author."

Eleanor cast one hurried glance toward the door— Ernest was gazing at her with a look so full of sorrowful interest that she could not meet his eyes again, and she soon afterward took her leave, her heart throbbing with mingled anguish and joy. As she passed her lover, she said, in a low, hurried tone, inaudible to all but to him, "Let me see you to-morrow, Ernest!"

She did not see the glow of happy exultation which lighted up his handsome features as she spoke; for she dared not raise her eyes, lest she should betray her emotions to the crowd around.

The morrow came—the aunt and niece were again in the library.

"Well, Eleanor," said Mrs. Howard, "so it seems Mr. Cuthbert has lost all his property."

"Yes, thank Heaven!"

"Thank Heaven! What a heartless creature you are, Eleanor! I really thought you loved that man."

"And so I did and do! Oh! aunt, you cannot guess how fondly, how truly I love him! Would to Heaven he would renew his proposals—I would not hesitate now to accept him."

"Now! Penniless, and through his own imprudence! You, who have refused *such* offers! Eleanor Howard, you are mad!"

"And it was precisely because they were such offers that I did refuse. I have made a vow never to marry a rich man."

"But what can have induced you—"

"Mr. Cuthbert, ma'am. Shall I show him in?" said a servant opening the door.

"Yes, John," said Mrs. Howard, with a sigh, and this time she did not order the carriage.

After a few moments' restrained conversation, Eleanor looked up frankly and bravely in her aunt's face, and said, with a sweet and maidenly dignity which few could resist, "Aunt, I wish to have a few moments' conversation, alone, with Mr. Cuthbert. Will you permit it?"

"Certainly, niece, of course if you wish; but I must say that it is very strange—very!"

And the lady sailed out of the room in a stately pet.

For a moment the young girl's embarrassment and agitation overcame her, and she buried her face in her hands; but, recovering herself, she turned to Ernest and said, softly, "Ernest, do you love me still?"

"Love you! Oh, Heaven—too much—too madly! But I am no longer worthy of your acceptance. You have heard of my losses, Miss Howard; why do you mock me thus?"

"Mock you, dear Ernest!" She laid her little hand timidly in his, and with modest firmness continued,

"Mr. Cuthbert, ever since we first met I have loved you. I refused your proposal because—because—nay, it does not matter why. But now, if this hand and the heart that must go with it can console you for your loss, forgive this unmaidenly boldness and—take them if you will."

She hid her face upon his shoulder, and Ernest Cuthbert, with his whole soul in the embrace with which he held her to his heart, bade Heaven bless her for her truth.

CHAPTER VII.

One morning, a week after the wedding, as Mrs. Cuthbert was sitting at work in her simply furnished apartment, and her husband preparing to go out, a middle aged gentleman, with a benevolent aspect, entered the room, and, walking straight up to the bride, kissed her gravely on both cheeks. For a moment she was confounded, but seeing Ernest smile at her surprise, she said, laughingly, "Ah! I know—it is your kind, generous uncle, whom you have talked so much about!" and she welcomed him with such graceful cordiality that his heart was won at once.

"And now," said he, after a little pleasant chat, "I have a story to tell you both, so sit down, nephew, and listen.

"About six months since, I met, one morning, a young man rushing impetuously round the corner of Washington

Square. He grasped my hand as he passed, exclaiming, 'Don't stop me now—I am in a desperate hurry.' 'So I should suppose,' said I. On he went, and I turned and followed him—he entered a gaming-house, I was astonished. It was the first time in his life, and I knew that something of consequence must have occurred to induce him to take such a step. I followed unperceived. He ascended the stairs. I borrowed a common cloak and a large hat from a waiter, slouched the latter over my eyes, and, thus disguised, entered the room above. I saw that he was bent on high play, and I determined to be his opponent. By a little management I gained my object."

"Uncle!" exclaimed Ernest, "was it indeed you?"

"Be quiet, sir, and hear me out! He was evidently desperate, and determined to risk all in the contest. He played with the strangest recklessness—I knew not what to make of him. I have since heard that a little, self-willed, romantic girl, who had turned his head and her own too with her sentimental nonsense, had refused him for a most absurd reason—you will hardly believe it, Mrs. Cuthbert—you, who appear to be such a sensible and rational woman."

"And what was it!" asked Eleanor, blushing and laughing at the look of comical meaning he favored her with.

"Oh! he was too rich, she said, and so he adopted the shortest method he could think of to rid himself of his troublesome estate. I won it all for him before we had been seated ten minutes. He looked quite relieved when my throw decided against him, as if a load had been taken off his heart, and, seizing my hand, he thanked me with as much politeness and warmth as if I had made him a valuable present."

"Oh, Ernest! Oh, uncle!"

"Hold your tongue, you gipsy! I will be heard. I have now come to restore him the deeds, which were immediately made over to me under a feigned name, and to wash my hands of the whole ridiculous affair."

Ernest embraced his uncle in silent gratitude, and Eleanor pouting, amidst tears and smiles, declared that she was cheated, betrayed, that she would not submit to such a shameful imposition, that she would have a div—: but here her vehement protestations were stopped by a kiss from Ernest, while the good uncle laughed and rubbed his hands and swore that she was the most amusing woman he ever saw in his life.

The Poet's Metamorphosis[1]

Gifted and worshipped one! Genius and grace
Play in each motion and beam in thy face!

SHE WAS just your ideal, dear reader, of all that is noble and lovely in women; with wealth, beauty and goodness for her dower, she might have chosen a husband from the very élite of the land, yet she folded up that blossom of purity and truth, her heart, from the gay and bold insects, bees, wasps and butterflies, that sought its treasures and turned away "in maiden meditation" still. But she shut up within it one image—the image of a singing bird, that had often hovered round but never yet dared to alight. This bird was a poet, deaf, ugly, lame and poor, although Grace Carroll blindly persisted in thinking and declaring him rich, handsome, graceful, in spite of his red hair and sallow complexion, in spite of his halting walk, in spite of his shabby coat; yes, in defiance of friend and foe, in the very face of fact, handsome, rich and graceful he was, and should remain!

"But, Grace, his face is not handsome surely," said her friend Madeline.

"It is 'the divine beauty of his *soul*,' I see."

"He is not *graceful*, at any rate."

"Yes, Madeline, his looks, his tones, his actions, his words are all graceful and tasteful to me."

"Not *rich* then?—you cannot make him rich!"

"Now, Madeline, for shame! What call you wealth?"

"*Is* he, rich, Grace?"

"Yes, rich and noble too: why he has genius, a king would drain his realm to buy."

"What *do* you mean?"

"Genius and honor—hope, truth, love! A heaven in his heart, an empire in his mind. What is your gold but dross to these?"

---

[1] "The Poet's Metamorphosis," Frances S. Osgood, *Ladies' National Magazine*, March 1844, vol. V, no. 3, pp. 73-76

"But then—of such low birth."

"Low?—with the noblest!"

"Ha, ha, ha! Give him a patent of nobility and be done with it—do."

"He has it now—I've read it."

"What!—where?"

"In his eyes, Madeline, and on his noble brow—'t was writ in heaven. You smile—but I tell you that a single word of praise or blame from that high-hearted being would affect me more than the applause or censure of a whole world beside."

"Grace! are you possessed?"

"Yes, *self*-possessed, Madeline, as yet, thank heaven! So pray don't imagine me *in love* with Horace Herbert."

"Well, you can't deny that he's deaf as a post sometimes."

"I'm glad he is. Deaf to all the idle, heartless, noisy buzzing of this frivolous and wearisome world, whose clatter might otherwise drown the music to which his soul still listens."

"And what is that?"

"The voice of God! the voice of divine love! the melody of heaven, which he echoes in his beautiful songs."

They were standing, Madeline and Grace, near a curtained window apart from the other guests at Mrs. Harvey's—and neither dreamed that they were overheard; but behind that curtain was a young man, who had apparently just entered from the garden through the open window. Too agitated—too deeply absorbed in the conversation to think of avoiding the part of a listener, he had stood trembling till it was over, and then, instead of re-entering the room, he rushed once more into the open air to give free vent to the passionate emotions of his soul.

"Thank God! thank God!" he cried, in a voice half chocked by feeling, and tears uncontrollable rushed to his eyes as he spoke. "Thank God, she knows me—she sees me as I am—no, not as I am, but as I might, as I ought to be. She looks into my soul, 'thro' the rose-colored glass' of her own divine imagination, it is true; but I am more worthy of her praise and love than of the ill-concealed aversion of those around her. Blessings on the beautiful— the noble girl! What a lofty and luminous soul lighted up her face as she spoke—and I have deceived even her—but oh! what a triumph to know that it is my genius, my mind, my heart she loves. denied that she loved me. Perhaps— but there is yet hope! She will, she must, she shall," and with a proud and dignified mien, which, in spite of his limp, impressed almost all who beheld him with a sense of his superiority, he re-entered the brilliant drawing-room of Mrs. Harvey, and stood with folded arms apart, gazing upon the object of his long concealed affection, until she caught his gaze, and blushed beneath it as she never blushed for others.

"Oh, Mr. Herbert, you must come and sing for us. You must, indeed—one of your own songs, won't you?" And a bevy of beautiful and highborn girls approached him.

There was no reply; Herbert stood perfectly unmoved. "You forget he is deaf," said Mrs. Harvey, and she wrote their request on a tablet.

"Pardon me, ladies, I am not in the mood just now; my mind is out of tune—and you know how I frightened you the other day with my terrible discord, because I sang when I didn't want to."

The young ladies looked disappointed. "Oh, Grace, *you* ask him. He always does what you wish."

Horace could always hear Grace Carroll's voice, that is if it was *very near him*; and yet she never raised her tone; perhaps it was on that very account—her voice was peculiarly clear and soft, and it seemed to reach his soul instead of his ear. And now she stole timidly to his side and put her sweet mouth close to his face. How his heart beat.

"Do sing for us, Mr. Herbert—just one song." Herbert did not turn—he could not—that tone always roused in his soul an emotion he dared not betray; but he obeyed at once the spell of his enchantress, and sang in a rich, mellow, manly voice—while his dark face lighted up into almost inspired beauty, the following impromptu verses:

> Speak no more! I dare not hear thee!
>   Every word and tone divine
> All too fatally endear thee,
>   To this daring soul of mine.
>
> Smile no more! I must not see thee!
>   Every smile's a golden net:—

> Heart entangled! what can free thee?
> What can soothe thy wild regret.
>
> Speak again! smile on forever!
> Let me in that music live;
> Let me in that light endeavor
> To forget the grief they give.
>
> Thrill my soul with voice and look, love,
> Like the harp-tone in the air,
> Like the starlight in the brook, love,
> They will still live treasured there.

As he finished Horace bent his dark eye earnestly on the fair and drooping face of Grace Carroll, and again it crimsoned as she felt the look.

CHAPTER II.

> I give thee, maiden, faith and love,
> The richest gifts that be.
> *   *   *   *   *   *
> I'll serve thee in the noblest waye
> Inglorious man can finde,
> And struggle for a conqueror's swaye
> Upon the field of minde.
> *   *   *   *   *   *
> And tho' no prowde ones thronge thy gate,
> Nor mean ones courte thy viewe,
> Thou shalt have reverence from the greate,
> And honor from the true.
>
> J. M. H.

Our hero only a short time previous to the scene related in the last chapter, had suddenly appeared in the fashionable circles of B—, introduced by some one, it was believed; but by whom or how, or whence he came, the gossips of the clique declared they could not imagine. Every one was interested in him: how could they help it? He was so peculiar, such a bundle of contradictions! Giving evidence at times in his writings and conversation of a lofty and brilliant genius, he was generally reserved,

silent, haughty, "incomeatable," if I may borrow a word
from a light friend of mine. Shabby in apparel and lame,
there was, nevertheless, a certain nobleness, dignity and
grace in his mien and address, which some few in the
circle could discern and appreciate.

His hair and whiskers of a fiery red, contrasted
strangely with his superb eyes, intensely beautiful in
depth and hue, and full of eloquence in expression. His
face was one of those which light up in emotions of joy,
anger, or love, all the more gloriously from being usually
cold, still and dark. It was generally supposed that he was
of low, or at least obscure birth; but however that might
be, his sentiments, deportment and language were always
elevated and refined.

At any rate, in spite of his red hair, his eccentricity, his
poverty, his defect of hearing, his limp and his reserve,
Horace Herbert was a very fascinating person to those he
chose to fascinate. The Carrolls happened to be boarding
that winter at the same hotel with him, and they had thus
become intimate.

One rainy morning, just after breakfast, when the
ladies' drawing-room was more than usually crowded,
Herbert had seated himself on a sofa near Grace, who was
netting, rather apart from the rest of the company, and
taken up a news' paper. Encouraged by her kindness, and
the subdued softness of her manner toward himself, to
hope for at least indulgence, if not return to his love, he
had been wishing for several days to converse with her in
private; but she was generally so surrounded by friends
that it was impossible, and even now it would not do to
whisper, for that would attract attention and subject her
to remark.

"Won't you read me the news, Mr. Herbert?" said Grace,
leaning toward him, that he might hear—"there is no one
near enough to be disturbed by it." This was just what he
wanted, and he gravely began, commencing every
sentence with one of the items common to newspapers,
and finishing it in his own way, preserving the same
monotonous and quiet tone throughout.

*"An alarm of fire was given last night about nine
o'clock*—I beg you will listen to me calmly for a few
moments, Miss Carroll—go on with your netting; no one

will notice that I am not reading from the paper all the time."

Grace could not repress a laugh at this novel mode of conversing, and the three watchful maiden gossips on the opposite sofa could not imagine what there could be so very amusing in an alarm of fire. Herbert went calmly on.

"*Lost on Saturday morning*—I cannot endure this state of suspense any longer."

This time Grace blushed. "Well!" said one gossip to another, "any one would think it was her heart or his that was lost from the way she colors about it!"

"*Anyone leaving it at this office*—I am obliged to leave town to-morrow for a few weeks."

And now tears stood in the dark and lovely eyes of the listener, as she raised them for a moment to his and dropped them again to her work.

"What in the world does *that* mean?" wondered the puzzled old maids, "crying because a reward is offered! I don't understand it at all."

"*We regret to announce the death of the Hon.*—I shall have no other chance to speak to you before I leave, or I would not enter upon so serious a subject in this apparently trifling way. You must have been aware, long ere this, of my devoted attachment."

A smile so radiant, so ecstatic, illumined the face of Grace Carroll at this moment, that the gossips almost started from their seats in a fidget of surprise and curiosity. Rejoicing as she evidently did over the announcement of a death! Had the deceased left her a legacy? What a heartless creature she must be.

Herbert's voice began to falter—"*We are gratified in being able to state*—oh, Grace! I cannot go on—not here—not now! How dare I hope for such a blessing as your love? But do not—do not quite condemn me for my presumption! Without the advantages of wealth, rank, beauty, or—"

"Nay!" said Grace aloud, looking half in play, half in earnest over his shoulder—"I am sure, Mr. Herbert, you are not reading that sentence rightly—let me finish it myself"—and she began the paragraph again in a low, but distinct voice—"*We are gratified in being able to state that*—you must not go till I have seen you again. Believe me your love is appreciated—valued, returned. Would that you read my heart instead of the paper. But here are some verses you must read to me, Mr. Herbert," and she drew back blushing from his side.

"Is this the poem I must read?—oh, it is an old song of Moore's, I see."

> "'Tell her oh! tell her the lute she left lying
>   Beneath the green willow, is still lying there'—
> Grace! all my soul is with gratitude sighing,
>   While your soft whisper replies to my prayer!
>
> 'Tell her, oh! tell her, the tree that is growing,
>   Beside the green arbor she playfully set'—
> Little those maidens, tho' wondrously knowing,
>   Dream *of the news* I am telling thee yet!
>
> 'So while away from that arbor forsaken,
>   The maiden is wandering—oh! let her be'—
> Meet me to-morrow when first you awaken,
>   Here, and meanwhile take my blessing with thee!"

"That is a touching and beautiful poem, Mr. Herbert— the last lines have found an echo in my heart; but I must bid you good morning now," and Grace Carroll, with her fair cheek flushed, and her lip trembling with subdued emotion, glided from the room.

"What does it mean? What does it mean?" murmured all three of the gossips in a breath—"how she colored—an echo in her heart! Let us look at the song, Mr. Herbert," some of them said, speaking aloud, "be so good as to lend me the paper a moment. I want to see what the play is."

"What the *by*-play is, you mean," said Herbert to himself; but at the same time he looked as if he had not the most distant idea that he had been spoken to.

"Dear! I forgot he was deaf! How stupid the man is!" She rose, and with a significant look laid her hand upon the paper, which Horace immediately resigned. They turned eagerly to the last verse of the song—

> "True as the lute that no sighing can waken
> And blooming forever unchanged as the tree!"

"an echo in her heart! does she mean that *her* bloom will last forever, and that his sighing can never affect her? Well! did you ever? such vanity! Oh! that's it undoubtedly."

CHAPTER III.

"I give thee all I can no more,
Tho' poor the offering be;
My heart and lute are all the store
That I can bring to thee!"

The next morning before breakfast Grace entered the drawing-room with a beating heart. A young man, a stranger, occupied a sofa near the fire, from which he courteously rose as she came in. Grace thought she had never seen so handsome and distinguished-looking a man. He made a singular impression upon her mind, for which she knew not how to account. His carriage was noble and easy—a pale complexion, intellectually pale, set off to advantage his hair of glossy black, and eyes of the same deep hue, glistening with the fire of genius and feeling. Grace had naturally a passionate love of the beautiful in all its varieties, and this person's beauty was of so high an order, so classic and so noble, that it fascinated her in spite of herself.

Besides it seemed to her that they must have met before, though where she could not imagine. After pacing the room for a moment or two, he went out, and immediately afterward Horace entered, and with only half a sigh at the contrast, Grace soon forgot the handsome stranger, in listening to the eloquent outpourings of his generous and pure soul; but while frankly owning a return to his affection, the happy and agitated girl overlooked the probability of her friends objecting to his poverty and his obscure origin; and when she did remember this, it was with some trepidation that she referred him to her father, and bade him "good bye" for the present.

CHAPTER IV.

That Herbert had more than satisfied Mr. Caroll was very evident, from the earnest manner in which the latter congratulated his daughter upon the subject,—and when Horace returned from his journey the wedding took place quietly, without any of the untasteful parade usual on such occasions.

Grace was very happy. She had but one trouble—the image of the handsome stranger would every now and then force itself upon her mind. It was very wrong, very improper, she said to herself, to bestow a thought of the kind upon any one but her noble, her devoted husband; but how was she to help it, poor child! when that husband himself by something indefinable either in manner or expression hourly recalled the image? And she found herself involuntarily constantly comparing the two;—"Horace would be handsome—he would resemble *him*, if he had only black hair instead of red! I must confess my folly to my husband—I shall not be happy till I do, and when I have once relieved my mind by owning it, perhaps I shall forget that singular person," and so one morning about six weeks after the wedding poor Grace confessed to Herbert that she feared she did not love him as he ought.

He did not look quite as miserable as she had imagined he would at this terrible announcement; but merely saying, "then it is high time I should bid you good morning," walked quietly out of the room.

In the evening Mr. and Mrs. Carroll, Mrs. Harvey, Madeline, and a few other intimate friends came in. Horace had not returned, and Grace was restless and disturbed. All at once, as she was adjusting a braid at the mirror, she saw—could it be—yes! in the very centre of the room, conversing with her father, and apparently perfectly at ease, the very person whose appearance had so strangely infatuated her fancy! As she turned from the glass he approached her and raised her hand to his lips, ere she was aware of his purpose. Grace was confounded, indignant.

"Sir!" said she with dignity, "your unasked intrusion here and this unwarrantable insolence must be explained to my husband." Mr. Carroll laughed, and the rest of the company opened their eyes.

"Madam," said the new guest, with a saucy smile, and the voice was strangely familiar, "you are tired of your husband's red hair. Does mine suit you?"

More and more amazed, Mrs. Herbert turned impatiently to her father. He was laughing heartily—and Grace echoed the laugh; for as she turned she faced the glass again, and saw the stranger hastily adjusting over his dark and curling locks the stiff red wig and whiskers of Horace Herbert himself! The amazed company joined in the merriment occasioned by this sudden metamorphosis, and Grace snatching the false hair playfully from him, threw it into the corner of the room.

"And the limp, Horace? ruse?"

"A poetical license, Grace."

"And the deafness, too?"

"Ah! let me still be deaf to all but you, sweet wife!"

> SWEET notes, to all but him unspoken,
>   Attuned to bliss a poet's thought;
> He grasped the lyre, the strings were broken,
>   And silence hid the strain he sought.
>
> A longing heart would fain have given
>   A nobler life to mortal things;
> But found that earth will not be heaven,
>   Nor lyres resound without the strings.
>   STERLING.

Virginia,
the Little Match-Girl of Kentucky[1]

"SIX FOR a fip! Six for a fip! Matches! matches!" The voice was clear and glad as a bird's, and Russell Hartley turned to see from whence it proceeded; a little, bare-footed girl, about ten years old, with the sunniest, sweetest face he had ever seen, was tripping just behind, and, as he turned, she held up her matches with such a winning, pleading, heavenly smile in her the eyes, that he bought nearly all she had at once.

Her fair hair fell in soft light waves, rather than coils, nearly to her waist, and a hole in her little straw hat let in a sunbeam upon it that turned it half to gold.

In spite of the child's coarse and tattered apparel, in spite of her lowly occupation, her manner, her step, her expression, the very tones of her voice unconsciously betrayed a native delicacy and refinement, which deeply interested the high-bred youth whom she addressed. Impelled by an irresistible impulse, he lingered by her side as she proceeded. "What is your name, my child?" he asked.

"Virginia, sir. What is yours?"

"Hartley—Russell Hartley," he replied, smiling at her artless and naive simplicity; "and where is your home?"

"Oh! I have no home, at least not much of one. I sleep in the barns about here," and again she looked up in his face, with her happy and touching smile.

"And your mother?"

In an instant the soft brow was shadowed, and the uplifted eyes glistened with tears.

"I will tell you all about it, if you will come close to me. I don't like to talk loud about it," she replied, in low and faltering tones.

---

[1] "Virginia, the Little Match-Girl of Kentucky," Frances S. Osgood, *Graham's Magazine*, March 1844, vol. XXV, no. 3, pp. 133-135

Russell Hartley took her little sunburnt hand in his, and bent his head in earnest attention.

"We had been in the great ship ever so many days, mother, and father, and I, and all the other people, and one night we were in the room they called the Ladies' Cabin, and mother had just undressed me, and I was sitting on her knee singing the little hymn she taught me, and she had her arm round my neck—mother loved me— oh! so dearly—and she was so sweet and good!—nobody will ever be so good to me again!" and here the little creature tried to repress a sob, and wiped her eyes with her torn apron. "Well, and so I was just singing my pretty hymn,

> I'll know no fear, when danger's near,
> I'm safe on sea or land,
> For I've, in heaven, a Father dear,
> And He will hold my hand;

"All at one, there was a dreadful, confused sound, a rumbling, crashing, shrieking noise—a terrible pain, and then—I woke up, and there I was on a bed in a strange room, and some people standing by the fire, talking about a steamboat that had burst her boiler the day before, and I found that I had been washed on shore, and that Mr. Smith had found me, and taken me home to his wife, and she had put me into a warm bed and tried to rouse me; but she couldn't till I woke up myself the next day. And when I cried for my own sweet mother, they looked sad, and said she was drowned, and I should never see her again! And then I wanted to be drowned too, but they said that was wicked, and I was sorry I had said so, for I would not be wicked for the world! Mother always loved to have me good; and so I tried to be happy as they told me I must; but I couldn't—not for a great while—I used to pine so at night for her dear arms round me! At last, I found a little comfort in doing just as I knew she would like to have me, and in knowing she could see me still, and in talking to her; and I used to sing my little hymn to her up in heaven, just as I did when I sat on her knee, and I sing it now every night. Mr. Smith and his wife both died and left me all alone again; but I am hardly ever sad now, for I am almost always good, and you know good people must not be unhappy," and the beautiful, loving smile shone again through her lingering tears, as she finished her simple story.

Russell was touched to the heart. His own eyes were moist, and, bending down, he kissed the innocent cheek of the little orphan, and bade her go with him, and he would give her money to clothe and feed herself. But the child drew gently, yet somewhat proudly, back and said, earnestly, "Oh I never take money *as a gift;* mother would not like it." Then, kissing tenderly the gentle hand, that still held hers, she tripped lightly round a corner, and, a moment after, Hartley heard her soft, silvery, childish treble, far in the distance, singing, "Matches, matches! Six for a fip! Who'll buy my matches—matches, ho!"

Russell Hartley kept that sweet picture in his soul, undimmed, through years of travel and change and care. He visited, with enthusiasm, the noble galleries of painting and sculpture in England, France, and Italy, and many a gem of art was enshrined and hallowed in the mosaic tablets of memory, but there was none to rival the *gem of nature*—the matchless little match-girl of Kentucky! with her fair hair streaming on her scanty red cloak, the glad and innocent smile in her childish eyes, and the lovely sunbeam stealing through the hole in the old straw hat to light, as with a message from Heaven, the lovely head of the orphan girl.

That beautiful ray of light!—made more beautiful by its chosen resting place, giving and receiving grace!—it seemed a symbol of the Father's love for the poor little motherless wanderer. It was only the *hole* in the hat that let in the sunshine—it was her *poverty* and her lonely, lowly state, that made her especially the child of His divine pity and tenderness; and they, like the sunbeam, changed to gold her daily care, and smiled through every cloud that crossed her little heart.

Seven years flew by-on butterfly wings to joy and thoughtlessness, on leaden ones to sorrow and "hope deferred"—and our little Virginia, now a lovely girl of seventeen, had earned money enough, by her bewitching way of offering matches for sale, to introduce herself as a pupil into one of the first boarding-schools of the country, not to commence, but to *finish* her education; for, with a passionate love of books, she had found means to cultivate her tastes and talents in many ways.

The lovely and lonely little orphan had struggled with hunger and cold and fatigue, with temptation in its most alluring and beguiling forms, with evil in a thousand shapes, yet had she kept the heavenly sunshine of her soul pure and unclouded through it all. She had never taken money as a gift, nor as a bribe. She had assisted, from her little store, many a child of misfortune, still humbler and poorer than herself; and, with faith, truth, and purity—an angel guard around her—by the light of her own innocent smiles, she glided, like a star, through the gathering clouds unharmed, unstained, unshadowed. In the words of our beautiful poet—

> "Peace charmed the street, beneath her feet,
>   And honor charmed the air;"

and music—the music of her own sweet heart and silver voice went always with her through the world.

It was on the evening preceding that on which the annual ball of the school took place. The young ladies were discussing, round the school-room fire, the dresses they were to wear. Virginia, a little apart, listened to them, and half wished she had a fairy godmother, like Cinderella's, to deck her for the festival. "Pearls, diamonds, japonicas! Satins, laces, velvets! She, alas! had none of these! She had only the plain, white dress in which she had been crowned Queen of May the spring preceding. It was so very plain, not even a bit of trimming round the throat."

"And what are you to wear, Miss Lindon?" said one of the aristocrats of the school, turning, with what she fancied an imperial air, toward the young stranger.

Virginia blushed, and said, simply, "My white muslin."

"And what ornaments?"

Virginia smiled. "Oh, I can find some bright autumn leaves for a wreath."

Imogen Grey would have given her diamond necklace for such a blush and smile; for her own sallow cheek was never so illumined; but she sneered nevertheless at the white muslin and the garland of leaves, and deigned no further question.

Virginia's delicate and sensitive spirit felt the sneer intensely, and she left the room with a swelling heart and tearful eyes. Once safe, however, in the asylum of her own little chamber, peace descended again a dove into her soul, and, after undressing, she knelt in her night-robe, by the side of her bed, and said prayer, and sung her little childish hymn—

> Of old th' Apostle walked the wave,
>   As seamen walk the land,
> A power was near him strong to save,
>   For Jesus held his hand!
>
> Why should *I* fear, when danger's near?
>   I'm safe on sea or land;
> For I've in heaven a Father dear,
>   And He will hold my hand.
>
> Though on a dizzy height, perchance,
>   With faltering feet I stand,
> No dread shall dim my upward glance,
>   For God will hold my hand.
>
> But oh! if doubt should cloud the day,
>   And sin beside me stand,
> Then firmest, *lest I lose my way*,
>   My Father! hold my hand!

Doubt, and danger, and sin, were nearer than she thought, but her little hand was held by One Who *would not let her fall*. As she rose from her devotions, she saw, for the first time, a box on a table by the bed. It was addressed on the cover simply to "Virginia." She opened it, wondering, and found a set of exquisite pearl ornaments, for the arms, neck and head. Her little heart beat with girlish delight. She hurried to the glass and wound around her hair a chain of snow-gems, less fair and pure than the innocent brow beneath. Next she bared her graceful arm and clasped a bracelet there. How exquisitely delicate ornaments became her childish loveliness! She thought she had never looked so pretty—not even when she used to deck her hair with wild-flowers, by the clear pool in the woods. And she could wear them to the ball! But who could have sent them? Again she looked at the box, and this time she saw a note peeping beneath the cotton wool on which gems had rested. Virginia's fair cheek flushed as she read—

"Let Innocence and Beauty wear the gift of Love.
                    HOWARD GREY."

Had the bracelet been a serpent, with its deadly sting in her arm, Virginia could scarcely have unclasped it with more fearful haste. The chain too was snatched from her head, and both, with the note, replaced in the box; and then the fair child threw herself again on her knees and buried her face in hands. After a silence of some minutes, broken only by faint sobs, she sung once more, in low and tremulous tones, the hymn, which seemed to her a talisman for all evil, and then calmly laying her head on the pillow, and, murmuring the name which was music to her soul, sunk into the soft and deep slumber of innocence and youth.

For nearly a year had the young libertine, Howard Grey, pursued her with his unhallowed passion, aided as he vainly imagined by his costly and tasteful gifts; but there seemed a magic halo around the young Virginia, through which no shadow of evil could penetrate. Besides the native purity and delicacy of her mind, there were two other influences at work in the beautiful web of her destiny, to prevent any coarse or dark thread from mingling in its tissue: one was her spiritual communion with her mother, and the other, her affectionate remembrance of Russell Hartley—the only being in whose eyes she had ever read the sympathy for which her lonely and loving heart yearned always.

It was evening again. The young ladies had assembled, dressed for the ball, in the drawing-room—all but Virginia. "Where is the sweet child?" asked an invalid teacher, to whom she had endeared herself by her graceful and affectionate attentions.

"She was so long helping me and sister dress," said a little shy-looking girl, "that she has been belated."

"I will go and assist her myself," said the principal of the school, pleased with this proof of kindheartedness on the part of her new pupil.

She softly opened the door of Virginia's room, and almost started at the charming picture which met her eye. Robed in white, with her singularly beautiful hair falling in fair, soft curls around her face, which was lighted up by a smile of almost rapturous hope and joy, the young girl stood in an attitude of enchanting grace, raising in both hands to adjust, amid the braids behind, a half wreath of growing and richly tinted autumn leaves.

"Let me arrange it for you, my child," said the lady approaching, and Virginia bent her fair head modestly to her bidding, and then, hand in hand, they descended to the drawing-room. Many of the company had arrived—the doors leading to the ball-room had been thrown open, and Virginia was almost dazzled by the splendor of the scene into which she was thus suddenly ushered. She blushed beneath the eyes that were riveted upon her as she passed.

"An angel!" "A grace!" "A muse!" whispered the gentlemen to each other. There was one among them—a noble, chivalric—looking man-who did not speak his admiration! An indefinable something in the heavenly beauty of that face had touched, in his soul, a chord which had not vibrated for many years before. Virginia knew him at once. The rich chestnut curls of the boy of twenty had now assumed a darker tinge, the eyes a somewhat softer fire, and the youthful and flexile grace had given place to a manly dignity of mien; but there was no mistaking the soul in the glance of Russell Hartley.

And Virginia was decidedly the belle of the ball. Gay, but gracefully so, for her sportive mood was softened and restrained by a charming timidity that enhanced her loveliness tenfold, she looked and moved like one inspired. She had met Hartley's admiring gaze; she was almost sure he would ask an introduction, and she felt as if her feet and heart were suddenly gifted with wings. She floated down the dance like a peri through the air, and then Russell approached and was introduced.

The sunny smile of the little match-girl shone in her eyes, as she accepted his arm for a promenade. "Surely I have seen that look somewhere before!" he exclaimed, half aloud. "Matches! Matches! Six for a fip!" murmured Virginia, looking archly up in his face, and the mystery was at once explained.

Imogen Grey's diamond necklace was worthless dross in comparison with the wreath of autumn leaves, which Hartley laid beneath his pillow that night, and all her brother's costly offerings could not have purchased the smile which accompanied the gift.

Reader, if you ever go to Kentucky, come to me for a letter of introduction to Mrs. Russell Hartley. She is looked up to, respected and beloved by all the country round, and I am sure you will enjoy her graceful and cordial attention, and the luxuries of her elegant home, all the more for remembering that the distinguished and dignified woman to whom you are making your very best bow, was once the little match-girl of my story.

Feeling Versus Beauty[1]

CHAPTER I.

"BUT, SYBIL, you have something better worth than beauty—you have genius, feeling, grace, and gifted thus you cannot fail to win him."

Sybil's dark eyes filled with tears, and, clasping her hands with passionate earnestness, she exclaimed—"And what are they all without it? All men shrink from genius in a woman, and they never give an ugly one credit for *feeling*. As to grace, there is not one in a thousand of them that has taste enough to appreciate that divine emanation of the soul. No, no, Eleanor, beauty and good temper are all they ask in us—gifted with more or less we only annoy or repel them. And yet—yes—I will—I must believe that Hamilton is an exception to the general rule. His letters are so filled with lofty and generous sentiment. They are so noble, so chivalric! He must be superior to all I have seen and known as yet."

Sybil Stanley's eyes were superb—her mouth affectionate and sweet; but she was not beautiful—not even handsome—and yet the color went and came in her cheek with such bewitching unexpectedness that her face was always interesting, and those who saw it once were sure to look again. She had been betrothed in childhood to her cousin Hamilton Herbert, at the wish of his dying father, and she had not seen him since he was a boy. He had been educated in Europe but was daily expected home. During the past year the cousins had carried on a playful and affectionate correspondence, of the latter part of which we will make some extracts.

---

[1] Feeling Versus Beauty, Frances S. Osgood, *Graham's Magazine*, June 1844, vol. XXV, no. 6, pp. 274-276

Herbert to Sybil.

Do not tell me, Sybil, that I must not expect to find you beautiful. The soul that glows in your letters must speak in your face also. It must talk in changeful and ever eloquent blushes on your cheek, in radiant glances from your eyes. It must express itself in a graceful and noble bearing—it must lend its rare, rich music to your voice, its purity to your smile—I don't see for my part how you can help being lovely, and I will not believe you to be otherwise. For years you have been my ideal, my star, my dream, "my beautiful hope." I have compared with the sweet picture in my heart the charms of every land through which I have passed—the languid and voluptuous grace of the Spaniard—the impassioned loveliness of the dark-eyed Italian—the light, buoyant, spirituelle daughter of gay and gorgeous France—the high-bred, blooming English belle—all yield the palm to you; for I imagine that in you are combined the enchantments of each—grace, feeling, refinement, vivacity and wit—they must all meet in my Sybil. . . . .

Sybil to Herbert.

Hamilton, I implore you not to come to me with that false and fatal dream of beauty in your soul; it cannot be realized in me, and your disappointment will destroy your love. I wrote this morning some playful verses on the subject—but though written half in jest, you must read them in earnest—

Oh! come not to me, if you watch the glow stealing
   That 'neath the lash lightens, in Beauty's blue eye,
I have naught but affection, true, timid and tender;
   If this be not dear to you—*all* to you—fly!

Oh! seek not my side, if the grace of a ringlet,
   That goldenly floats, too beguiling can be;
A love such as yours is can ne'er want a winglet;
   Go! wave it o'er others—but come not to me!

Oh! come not to me, if you watch the glow stealing
　O'er Beauty, like rose-light of morning on snow;
No bloom warms my cheek, save the wild-rose of Feeling!
　If this be not dear to you—*all* to you—go!

Sybil was dancing through the garden, with her little baby brother mounted on her back and clinging with his dimpled limbs around her—her classic head half turned to meet the happy smile of her playmate, her dark curls floating from her forehead, her eyes, cheeks and lips kindled with the glow of exercise, and the grace of her fine form charmingly developed by the attitude—she met the gaze of a young man who was just entering the gate—her heart told her at once who it was, and lightly swinging the child to the ground she stood for an instant perfectly still, with locked hands and drooping head, in an attitude of enchanting timidity. Hamilton Herbert sprung forward with a smile, which gloriously illumined his dark and noble face, and exclaimed—"Sybil! It *is* Sybil, is it not?" The clasped hands were placed frankly and affectionately in his, and, for a moment, there was an eloquent pause of wordless emotion.

Preparations were making for the wedding, when one morning Sybil received a letter from a young cousin, reminding her of a promise made years before, that she should be her bridemaid. A shadow crossed the frank, sweet face of our heroine when she read this epistle. "I am so sorry," she exclaimed, as she placed it in her lover's hands.

"I see nothing to be sorry for, Sybil," said he. "It is a very sweet, simple, affectionate letter, rather too sentimental perhaps; but the love she evidently feels for you would redeem a graver fault than that. Is this her real name—Zephyrine?"

"Oh no! she was christened Nancy, after my aunt; but she adopted this years ago, and insists upon her friends calling her so."

Herbert smiled—"And why do you regret her coming?"

Sybil colored and was silent—but there was an expression of pain on her ingenuous face which interested and surprised her lover, and he repeated his question more earnestly.

"I will tell you, Hamilton," she said, raising her eyes to his, "at the risk of being misunderstood. I will tell you frankly, because I think it my duty. My cousin is exquisitely beautiful, and I dread the effect of her beauty upon you."

"Sybil! can *you* be so weak?"

"I dread it for my own sake, cousin—still more for yours. If you trust her—if you love her, you are lost!"

"Oh, Sybil! her letter is simplicity itself, and she seems to worship you."

Sybil burst into tears.

CHAPTER II.

Heed not her sigh,
      'T is Falsehood's breath;
Trust not her eye,
      Belief is death.

It was winter—the wedding was to take place in three weeks. The Stanleys had returned to New York from their country seat, and Herbert one evening was alone in the conservatory attached to Sybil's sitting-room. A Croton fountain played in the centre. He was leaning against a pillar, and gazing down into the marble basin, when suddenly a face, delicately beautiful, smiled from the water and vanished. He started and turned. A slight rustle among the plants, as of some one gliding swiftly away, was all that betrayed the presence of another. He returned to the sitting-room, restless and wondering; but Sybil came in, looking paler than usual, and the trouble in that dear face recalled him to himself.

"What ails you, dearest?" he asked.

"Nothing!—but—she has come!" said the poor girl in a low voice, then, passionately clasping her hands, she bent an earnest, almost imploring, gaze upon his face.

"Who, Sybil?—who has come?"

"My cousin."

"Zephyrine?"

At this moment the door softly opened, and a light, airy-looking creature—lovely as a dream—stole into the room, sunk upon a footstool at Sybil's feet, and, leaning her head on her cousin's lap, looked up to Herbert through the soft fair curls that fell over her face, and said, in a voice bewitchingly, childishly sweet, and with a naive and simple earnestness of manner—

"Are you my Cousin Hamilton?"

The words were nothing, but the enchanting melody of her tone, the exquisite, childlike grace of her attitude, the ineffable expression of those lovely eyes, all told upon his heart, and for a moment he was perfectly bewildered with delight, surprise and admiration. He gazed from one to the other.

"Yes, Zephyrine," said Sybil, very quietly; "this is our cousin, Hamilton Herbert."

The beauty put up a little hand dazzlingly white, drew back the curls from her eyes and said, with an arch smile, "Why don't you ask me how I do?"

Gifted with a rare and peculiar charm, her voice and manner lent a grace to these simple questions which Hamilton knew not how to resist.

With a woman's instinct, Sybil saw that the spell was at work. She dared not remain lest she should betray her feelings, and, coldly releasing herself from Zephyrine's embrace, she left the room.

The young girl remained seated on the footstool at Herbert's feet, and, raising her eyes full of tears to his face, with a touching expression of sorrow, she said—"I wish I knew how to make Sybil love me as I love her. She is so good and so intellectual—so superior to me—she is just such a friend as I need, for I am very wild and inexperienced. I want some one to guide me and to teach me. But she is always so cold that I am afraid of her. I lost my mother when I was very young, and I do a thousand things I ought not to—will *you* be my friend, Cousin Hamilton?"

There was no resisting this appeal—so artless, so confiding, so tender. Hamilton replied to it with affectionate fervor, and the cousins were sworn friends from that hour.

"Do go away, child," exclaimed Zephyrine, and her delicate cheek flushed with anger as she spoke, for little Willie, Sybil's brother, attracted by her beauty, had climbed the sofa by her side, and was stroking her lovely hair. "Go and play—do, I can't bear children." Willie gazed at her for a moment, with his large eyes full of sorrowful wonder, and then slowly returned to his playthings on the rug at Sybil's feet.

A well-known step was heard on the stairs. Zephyrine sprung from the couch, and, flinging her fairy form on the floor by his side in the most picturesque manner imaginable, began to caress the boy with great apparent fondness.

"What a charming *tableaux!*" said Herbert, as he entered. "Isn't it, Sybil?"

"Very," she replied, with a slight curl of her graceful lip.

Herbert looked surprised and displeased at her tone, but Willie withdrew from Zephyrine's embrace, and, nestling close to his sister, said simply, "Just now, cousin, you pushed me away from you, and said you could not bear children, and I don't want you to play with me if you don't love me."

The discomfited beauty colored, but exclaimed, "Willie what a fib you are telling!"

"Sister," said Willie, "what does 'fib' mean?"

"It means an untruth, dear."

"But I have not told an untruth, Sybil."

"No, darling."

Zephyrine hid her face in her hands, and *seemed* to be weeping—her sweet voice faltered as she exclaimed, "Oh, Sybil, how unkind you always are to me! You know I was only in play when I pushed Willie."

Sybil was silent and the beauty sobbed audibly. Hamilton, touched by her sorrow, could not help saying, "You are indeed ungenerous, cousin. Do you not see that you have deeply grieved her?"

Sybil resolutely shut her eyes to hide the tears that anguish forced into them, and, with a slight quiver of her lip, bent over her work—but Willie, with the instinct of a loving heart, felt that she was suffering, and, springing into her arms, put his round her neck.

"Let us go up stairs away from them," he whispered.

And again Herbert was left alone with his dangerous companion, and again was he beguiled into sympathy and confidence by the alluring grace and pleading tenderness of her manner.

Thus it went on—the lovers gradually and almost imperceptibly estranged from each other, and Zephyrine winding herself like a beautiful serpent around the heart of her victim.

One evening she tripped into the room where Herbert and Sybil were sitting, dressed for a fancy ball, in the becoming costume of a Sicilian boatwoman. Her beautiful hair, partly confined by a net whose crimson tassels mingled on her cheek with a rich profusion of golden curls—the small black hat placed coquettishly on one side—the short, full, gray petticoat, striped with red—the bodice of green velvet—the little dainty slippers, with crimson lacings crossed and recrossed over her delicate ankles—and the light, shining over, which she held with graceful ease—the whole was exquisitely picturesque. She was singing gaily a boat-song, as she came in, and Herbert, more than ever enchanted, playfully joined in the chorus.

> Oh! share my bark—the night is dark,
> And wild the wintry weather;
> And Love will light his taper bright;
> We'll gaily row together!

"Cousin Hamilton, I came to persuade you to go to the ball with me. You are not obliged to be in costume—do come! there's a dear cousin," and, leaning on his arm, she looked up coaxingly in his face.

"Sybil," said Herbert, hesitatingly.

"Do not hesitate on *my* account, cousin," said Sybil, proudly.

Herbert went, and, on his return home at night, found in his room a letter, which almost brought him to his senses.

"Dear cousin—It is time I should free you from an engagement, which is evidently a restraint to your heart. I do it cordially. Farewell! and may God be with you! Your sincere friend,

"Sybil Stanley."

Such was the letter which the proud girl wrote to her lover, but the following lines, written in a journal and blotted with tears, are a better transcript of her feelings at the time:

> Go, then, forever! since your heart
>   Can stoop to one so light, so vain,
> Though Hope must perish if we part,
>   With calm resolve I break the chain.
>
> Go, then, forever, at the shrine
>   Of Beauty bend that noble brow,
> Pour forth the love *I* dreamed divine,
>   And *more than waste* wild Passion's vow.
>
> Yes, yes! Her eyes are stars of night—
>   Her cheek, a rose in dainty bloom—
> Her radiant smile, the morning's light—
>   Her sigh, the violet's soft perfume.
>
> Go, then forever! Leave the soul
>   From which your lightest look or tone—
> As zephyr o'er the air-harp stole—
>   Could wake a music all your own.
>
> Leave, leave me with your breaking heart—
>   If Greif would let me, I could smile.
> To see an idle toy of art,
>   So grand a soul as yours beguile.
>
> But when, through Beauty's veil of light,
>   You seek in vain for Feeling's fire.
> Remember one—whose day in night—
>   Who breaks, for you, her heart and lyre!

Herbert came the next day to remonstrate with Sybil—whom he still loved—to own his momentary infatuation and to implore her to forgive it; but he had hardly seated himself to await her coming, when Zephyrine, in her childish morning dress, looking fresh and sweet as a rosebud, came dancing into the room, and, seeing his look of sadness, flew to his side, laid her light hand upon his forehead and asked, in a voice of touching tenderness, if he were ill. With a moment's struggle, Herbert yielded once more to the strange charm of the little enchantress. Poor Sybil was again forgotten, and Zephyrine was listening, "with downcast eyes and modest grace," to a fervent declaration of love, when a voice, which made her start with clasped hands from the half embrace in which he held her, was heard in the hall.

"T is he!—he has come!" she exclaimed.

"He! Who? What do you mean, Zephyrine?"

"Hush!" said the little actress, placing her finger on her lovely mouth, in a listening attitude.

A young, dissipated-looking man entered the room.

"How are you, Zeph?" said he, coolly drawing her toward him, and imprinting a kiss upon her cheek.

"Oh! Charles! I am so glad you have come at last! I have been so unhappy! Why did you stay so long? Mr. Murray, Mr. Herbert."

It was evidently an engagement. With one reproachful look to the beautiful coquette, whose only reply was a light laugh and a graceful but saucy shake of the head, Herbert left the lovers to themselves.

Sybil had long ago discovered the utter heartlessness—the consummate duplicity of Zephyrine's character. She had known more than one noble heart victimized by her fascinating arts, and had therefore dreaded her power upon Herbert. She was aware of but had thoughtlessly promised to keep secret, her engagement to Murray, who was a handsome, good-natured, but shallow-brained and shallow-hearted youth, very rich and very dissipated.

The reader must guess if Sybil forgave her lover. I can only say that the last time I saw her, she was smoothing, with a mother's care, the silken curls of a beautiful little girl, whose dark eyes were very like those of a certain wight we wrote of by the name of Hamilton Herbert.

Valentine's Day;
or a Lover's Reminiscences[1]

You say each soul, in realms above,
  Will seek with faith divine
The twin-soul it was formed to love;
  Ah! then—will yours seek mine?

THEY CALLED her a sad coquette; but they were mistaken. A proud, pure and earnest spirit like that of Mary Maclane could never stoop to the trilling arts by which too many of her sex secure the conquest of an hour. I cannot tell whether Mary was pretty or not. In her presence there was no time to think of beauty. I am not sure that I could tell even the color of her hair or her eyes; though I think the latter were of a deep violet hue, veiled by remarkably long and jet-like lashes. I have a faint impression that her mouth resembled a dewy crimson rose-bud more than anything else; and I believe her form was perfect. I suppose it must have been, from the piquant reply a witty poet made to her one day, after begging her to give away the dress she wore, because it did not become her—

"To whom shall I give it?" she asked.

"Oh! to the Venus de Medicis, of course! It would fit no one else."

As I said before, in her presence there was something besides beauty, and more than beauty to think of Grace, gayety and sweetness, with the indescribable but exquisite charm of *naïveté*, in manner, look and speech, combined to render her irresistible. The envious or ill-judging of her own sex declared her eccentric, and therefore affected. She *was* eccentric, if to act herself—a self so different from the commonplace, stereotyped people around her—was to be

---

[1] "Valentine's Day; or a Lover's Reminiscences," Frances S. Osgood, *Graham's Magazine*, July 1844, vol. XXVI, no. 1, pp. 23-25

so. Frank, truthful, trusting and nobly independent, she retained the beautiful simplicity of childhood, with the dignity and spirit of a woman, true to herself and her divine destiny. Affected it was all the rest of the fashionable world who were affected, not she. It was they who belied their own natures, who assumed a manner, who molded their dress, their attitudes, their tones, even their smiles, to the one model of the day. She trusted her own soul and uttered it in mien and look and word. She revered too deeply the divinity within, to hide, to smother or deny it. She was as natural, and simple, and incapable of art or affectation, as the birds and the flowers which she loved, and which loved her in return.

And they called her a coquette! because affectionate, and confiding, pining for sympathy and tenderness, she looked for good in all around her—and finding it, for who would not have been good for *her* and to her. She imagined the perfection of her ideal in each new suitor for her love, and in turn in each was disappointed.

"I will not," said Mary, in a letter to a friend, "cannot compromise my sympathies. I cannot sacrifice my integrity of heart to the opinion of the world, which pronounces me a coquette because I have been deceived. Though I die single, I will be true to the divine sentiment of love within me, which will be ratified, if not in this, surely in a future life. I will keep my soul virgin till it meets the twin-soul which is its destiny. It is not I that these men love. They have no knowledge of *me*. They have taken a fancy to my looks, my tones, my manners perhaps; but they are strangers to my *heart*. Were there one among them destined for that heart, believe me, Clarice, in the words of a dear friend—

"It would spring like a falchion bright, glowing and true,
To the hand that its worth and its temper best knew.'

"When some affectionate and judicious visitor kindly tells me that I am called a flirt, I think of the lines I read to you once; perhaps you do not remember them.

> "They tell me I was false to thee;
> But they are false who say it;
> The vow I made was pure and free,
> And time shall ne'er betray it.
>
> "'I laid my heart on virtue's shrine,
> I loved truth, honor, kindness;
> I love them still, I thought them thine,
> Too soon I wept my blindness.
>
> "'T is *thou* wert false, to them and me,
> My worship still I cherish,
> My love, still true, has turned from thee,
> To find them or to perish.'"

I felt interested in Mary Maclane before I saw her. It was her voice that first magnetized my heart. She had arrived the day before at the hotel where I was staying. It was said she had just dismissed a wealthy suitor, who had received encouragement sufficient to warrant his expectations in proposing. I had heard much of the Kentucky belle, and while dressing for dinner was resolving that I would avoid an introduction; for I had an unaffected dread of a coquette. The tones of a guitar from the next room broke in upon my reverie, and the next moment a sweet, pure voice commenced the following song—

> I loved an ideal,
>   I sought it in thee,
> I found it unreal,
>   As stars in the sea;
>
> And I shall I, disdaining
>   An instinct divine,
> By falsehood profaning
>   That pure hope of mine?
>
> Shall I stoop from my vision,
>   So lofty, so true,
> From the light, all Elysian,
>   That round me it threw?

> Oh! guilt, unforgiven,
>   If false I could be,
> To myself and to Heaven,
>   While constant to thee!

> Ah, no! though all lonely,
>   Oh earth be my lot,
> I'll brave it, if only
>   That trust fail me not;

> The trust that, in keeping
>   All pure from control,
> The love that lies sleeping,
>   And dreams in my soul,

> It may wake in some better
>   And holier sphere,
> Unbound by the fetter
>   Fate hung on it here!

The deep feeling that thrilled through the voice, the high and pure sentiment of the song, affected me strongly, and when, in the evening, an interesting and distinguished-looking girl, a stranger, whose name I had not learned, was led to the piano, I was not surprised to hear the same clear tones which had so enchanted me before.

I begged an introduction to the lady, and almost started back in dismay when it took place. It was Mary Maclane herself.

The instant our eyes met, hers seemed to fill visibly with light, and then the long lashes drooped suddenly over a cheek that had grown strangely pale with that momentary emotion. An evident effort restored her, however, immediately to her wonted graceful self-possession, but I could not so easily recover mine. I felt at once that the good or evil genius of my life was before me, embodied in that slight girl.

Was I in love?—at first sight! I, who had always avoided a flirt as I would a beautiful serpent—to whom the *rattle* of the former seemed almost as fatal to moral safety, as that of the latter to physical.

Weeks flew by, and we became intimate friends. Mary knew that I loved her, although no word had betrayed it, and I was sure that she returned my love. She was surrounded by distinguished and wealthy admirers, who had not my reasons for silence on the subject; but, though courteous to all, her soul remained loyal to mine. Mine was the sudden and beautiful blush, and mine the endearing smile; her sweet voice faltered only for me, and ever took a deeper and fuller tone when replying to my own, for then her heart was in it.

But I was too proud to marry a rich woman, and too poor for a poor one, and so, as Mary was an heiress, I cherished my love in silence. Fatal mistake! Had I possessed but half her generous and noble independence, I should have thrown pride, that petty pride to the winds. I should have been ashamed to name it in the same breath with my love, even to myself; for was it not a profanation of *her* to give a thought to her paltry wealth?

Now and then I could detect a tearful wonder in her suddenly uplifted eyes because I did not corroborate by words the affection which almost every look and act involuntarily betrayed, and so, to relieve in part my own feelings and to soothe hers, which I feared were wounded, I sent her, on Valentine's Day, some verses; the handwriting was disguised, but I said "if she loves me as she should, she will feel that they are mine"—and so she did. I was present when the servant handed them to her. A soft blush burned in her delicate cheek as she read; her eyes filled with tears, and, averting her face from my gaze, she hastily wrote something beneath them with a pencil.

Instantly I feared that I had gone too far, and asking to see the lines, I coolly read them aloud, ridiculing both the language and the sentiment, as I went on, with a criticism so calm and so severe, that poor Mary seemed utterly at a loss what to think. From that moment, however, she assumed toward me a dignified and distant demeanor, avoiding me as much as possible, and, though I think suffering intensely, preserving an outward serenity which I would have given worlds to imitate. The verses were as follows:

TO MARY.

Rare bird of the West! where the pride of the prairie
    Can boast of no blossom to rival your blush,
Oh! fold for one moment your wing wild and airy,
    And, while I sing to you, your sweet warble hush.

Fair bird of the West! where the sky bent above you,
    So fondly it lent half its light to your eye,
Where the wild-flower you tripped over looked up to love
you,
    And the happy wave paused o'er your picture to sigh.

You dreamed not, while sporting in freedom and pleasure,
    Of cages and nets that would setter your wing,
But oh! let me warn you—too rare is the treasure—
    The fowler, the hunter have both heard you sing:

They are up, on the track–oh! be prudent and wary–
    They have nets, they have cages, of iron and gold;
Look well to your pinion, sweet bird of the prairie,
    And shame, with that blue eye, the false and the bold.

There is one who would cherish, and love the least ringlet
    That floats o'er your young cheek, or kisses your neck,
Who would guard every wave of your exquisite winglet,
    And toil for earth's treasures your beauty to deck;

But he has no claim to your lightest smile, Mary,
    He can but sing truly, though may be too bold;
Look well to your pinion, wild bird of the prairie,
    Beware of their cages of iron and gold!

    Beneath them Mary had traced, in a trembling,
delicate hand, the following verse:

Je ne chante que pour toi!

I fold my wings; I heed not now
  The idler's gaze, the flatterer's tone;
I turn from every lighter vow,
  I sing for thee alone!

Soon after this Mr. Maclane's affairs became deeply involved, and unable to meet his engagements, to avoid public disgrace he urged to his daughter the necessity of marrying one of her wealthy suitors, who had offered on that condition to assist him. Mary had but an hour to decide, and her reply was the following letter to her father:

"I have had a severe struggle, but I feel that in complying with your wishes I can wrong only myself; for a man, who can be willing to accept a reluctant hand without a heart, and who can make such the condition of his aid to a friend in the hour of need, is not worthy of a thought. He can have no heart to wrong. Were he a better, a nobler being, I should refuse him; for I should feel that I could have no right to injure and betray a pure soul by linking it for life to a mere *name*, even to save your honor, my father.

"As it is, I accept this man; but, in so doing, I shall explain to him, as frankly as to you, my feelings with regard to him. It will make no difference to him; for he cares, not for my heart, not for my love, or my respect, but for my capability of ministering to his pride, of ornamenting his establishment. He will show off whatever of beauty, wit, or grace, I may possess, as he would his fine pictures, or his spirited horse. I accept him, then, but upon one condition; I choose to be wedded—no not wedded, I will not so profane the word—I choose to be bound to him by a magistrate, not by a clergyman; no man of God, for me, shall thus belie his holy calling, his sacred office, and the divine institution of marriage. Where love hallows the tie, let religion sanction it also; but in this affair of barter and exchange, the civil law will be all sufficient surely."

Mary was right; it did make no difference to him—to the soulless fool who bought her. So they were wedded, and by a magistrate too. In this she persisted, in spite of her father's remonstrance, "for the poor, craven bridegroom said never a word."

The world inveighed against the heartless coquette, as it persisted in calling her, and declared that I had been shamefully treated; that I had at first been led on by the freest encouragement, and then deserted for a wealthier man.

And Mary smiled serenely at the slander, and years since I sent Mary the first Valentine I ever wrote. I now send her the last. It is a song, which I once heard, and which impressed me deeply at the time.

> "Oh! call it by some better name,
>   For Friendship is too cold,
> And love is now an earthly flame,
>   Whose shrine must be of gold;
> And Passion, like the sun at noon,
>   That burns o'er all he sees,
> Awhile as warm, will set as soon,
>   Oh! call it none of these!
>
> "Imagine something purer far,
>   More free from stain of clay,
> Than Friendship, Love, or Passion are,
>   Yet human still as they;
> And if thy lip, for love like this,
>   No mortal word can frame,
> Go ask of angels what it is,
>   And call it by that name!"

The Flower and Gem;
or the Choice of Grace Gordon[1]

I am not sure, dear reader, that you would have called Grace Gordon beautiful. *I* used to take it for granted she was, because I never could keep my eyes or my heart from her when she was present. Grace was a brunette. Do you like brunettes? I hope you do; if you don't you won't "take an interest," as my little sister used to say, when she had newly arranged her baby-house; she would tottle to the head of the stairs and call out, in her little shrill, bird-like voice, "Father—mother—Fanny!—come and take an interest!" I wish my call to you would be answered as promptly as hers always was.

At any rate, if Grace was not a beauty, she was a darling; a wild, sweet, sunny, frolicsome creature, with great, shy, antelope eyes, that wouldn't look up when they were wanted, and a mouth whose smile was bewildering. I loved Grace for a thousand reasons, but chiefly because she was once the cause of my being, in my own private opinion, a heroine. From a child I had always had an ardent desire to be a heroine, in some way, I hardly cared what. I was a pet, and was seldom crossed, and therefore to be crossed was my chief ambition. At three years of age, I used either to try to be naughty or pretend to be, for the express purpose of *enduring* the punishment. Then I was a martyr, and I gloried in it.

But let us return to Grace. I will tell you a secret, sweet reader; but you must promise not to betray me; for worlds I would not confide it to any one but you. May I trust to your honor? Well, then, I had a lover once! That is, I imagined him a lover; it was a poetical license on my part; for, to tell the truth, I don't suppose he cared "an individual straw," to quote from a quaint friend at my elbow, about me.

---

[1] "The Flower and Gem; or the Choice of Grace Gordon," Frances S. Osgood, *Graham's Magazine*, August 1844, vol. XXVI, no. 2, pp. 63-64

He was a tall, dark, mysterious-looking, Lara-like man, whom I adored, or fancied I did, for no earthly reason, that I can remember, except that he was poor,—that his name was Percy, and that he had a Byron mouth, a stern, deep voice, which used to thrill me with fear and delight. Well, I was only fifteen years old and he was thirty, and, I suppose, he looked upon me as a mere child, for he used to pet me, and bring me sugar-plums, and call me his "little humming bird." I was proud of his attentions, and fancied I had an exclusive right to them. Alas! I was dolefully deceived.

> He did not say he loved me;
>   Yet, oh! he used to bring,
> To deck my braided tresses,
>   The fairest flowers of spring!
>
> He did not say he loved me;
>   But, in his earnest eyes,
> I thought I saw the secret,
>   A thousand times, arise.
>
> He did not say he loved me;
>   He did not breath a vow;
> I needed no confession;
>   I read it on his brow.
>
> I met it in his glances;
>   I heard it in his tone;
> I asked not if he loved me;
>   I *felt* he was mine own!
>
> He did not say he loved me;
>   Yet, oh! he used to sing;
> Such songs as thrill the spirit,
>   While feeling tunes the string!
>
> But false his dark eye's smiling,
> And false my dream as brief;
> Alas! for man's beguiling!
> For woman's fond belief!
>
> He did not say he loved me;

> Why did he ever bring,
> To braid amid my tresses,
> The token-flowers of spring?
>
> Why did he looks so fondly?
> Why did he speak so low?
> Oh! if he did not love me,
> He should have told me so!

Grace Gordon came to our village on a visit, from her home, in the far West; a party was made for her the night after her arrival, and every one was charmed with the young stranger. Beautiful, witty, affectionate and gay, she was the very being to bewitch my grave and dignified cavalier; and the moment I saw her I felt a presentiment of evil. He was introduced, and oh! how my childish heart ached as I watched his noble head bending over her chair, and heard the low tones which I knew were thrilling her soul. Yes! I knew it by the sudden lifting and dropping of those lovely, yet unfathomable eyes, by the alternate dimple and blush deepening on her cheek, and I went home with a soul full, as I fancied, of anguish, pride, passion, and grandly beautiful resolve. Percy was poor and so was L—.

Miss Gordon was comparatively rich, and had many influential friends, who might be of service to him in his career. It would be a capital match; every one had said so at the party; and I would do all in *my* power to bring it about. He came as usual the next day. In his manner toward me there was more "empressement" than before, and, from the way in which he spoke of Grace, I found that my imagination had gone too far—that she had not made so deep an impression as I thought; but I had made up my mind to be a heroine, and I was not to be cheated out of my position in that way. I had determined to be great, and great I was. I assumed a gayety and indifference I did not feel; I called his attention to a thousand little graces in my rival which he had not thought of before; I told him anecdotes of her wit and generosity which charmed him; lastly I took him to see her, and afterward avoided him as much as possible. To complete the romance, I thought myself in duty bound to compose some

heart-rending on the occasion, which, if I rightly recollect,
ran thus:

> I cannot forget him!
>   I've locked up my soul;
> But not till his image
>   Deep, deep in it stole.
>
> I cannot forget him!
>   The Future can cast
> No flower before me,
>   So sweet as the past.
>
> I turn to my books;
>   But his voice, rich and rare,
> Is bent with the genius
>   That speaks to me there.
>
> I tune my wild lyre,
>   But I think of the praise,
> Too precious, too dear,
>   Which he lent to my lays!
>
> I cannot forget him!
>   I try to be gay,
> To quell the wild sorrow
>   That rises away;
>
> But wilder and darker
>   It swells, as I try;
> If *Heaven* could forget him,
>   So never can I!
>
> I cannot forget him!
>   I loved him too well!
> His smile was endearment,
>   His whisper a spell.
>
> I fly from his presence;
>   Alas! it is vain;
> I see him—I hear him—
>   He's with me again!

He haunts me forever;
I worship him yet;
Oh! idle endeavor!
I cannot forget!

Grace and I became very intimate, and the affair went charmingly on, until a rich and fashionable admirer of hers, by the name of Walters, followed her to the village. Then I perceived an indecision, a shade of coquetry, in her manner which alarmed me. Percy was too proud to bear with caprice, and I trembled lest his rival should carry off the prize.

One evening I called for her on my way to a party. She was standing, half dressed, at the glass, and turning toward me as I entered, she said, half in sport and half in earnest, "Fanny, which shall I wear?" In one hand she held out a half-blown moss-rose, in the other, a magnificent wreath of leaves, formed entirely of emeralds and gold.

"Oh! the moss-rose, dear Grace, by all means," I replied.

"You little know, Fanny, how much depends upon my choice!—-but I will hesitate no longer," and, laying down the jewels, she twined the flower in a rich, dark braid that fell upon her neck. I had unconsciously sealed my own fate—the rose had been sent by Percy, the emerald wreath by his rival, and the former was accompanied by the following lines,

TO GRACE.

If o'er your cheek the blush that plays,
When he who loves you dares to praise,
Be sent by 'wakened Feeling there,
Nor bloom to win the worldling's gaze
Oh! deign my simple gift to take,
And braid it in your lustrous hair!
For mine, dear Grace, and Love's sweet sake,
Beside the blush, rose-bud wear!

> If, in your voice, the cadence low
> That, soft replying, falters so,
>   Be taught, by Truth and Love, to thrill,
> If from your *heart* its accents flow,
> The deign my token-flower to take,
>   And wear it with a gracious will!
> Oh! flower of flowers! For Love's sweet sake,
> Be tender and be truthful still!
> But if the tone, the blush, be part
> Of changeful woman's wily art,
>   If that soft smile, so fond, yet shy,
> Speak not the language of the heart,
>   If that dark lash droop not to hide
> The tell-tale, Love, within thine eye,
> Then give to air the blossom's pride,
> As I, the hope, thou doom'st to die!

Grace wore the rose; and oh! how enchantingly she blushed, as she caught Percy's dark and eloquent eyes bent fondly upon her, on entering the room, at Mrs. Hall's. He was by her side in a moment, and one glance at the pair, as he led her to a seat, showed me my doom was sealed. Never before or since were my spirits so buoyant, so strangely wild and light, as on that eventful evening, and never before or since has my smile been assumed to hide a heart so dark and sad.

I was bridemaid at the wedding; but it was so long ago that I had forgotten I was ever in love with Percy Howard, until last night, at a gay party given by his wife, she pointed out to me the emerald wreath, worn in the fair hair of Mrs. Walters, the bride for whom the party was made—a pretty, but insipid-looking girl—and whispered, as she did so, "I would not give my withered rose—I have it now, dear Fanny for all the gems she wears!"

"Grace, dear Grace," I exclaimed, clapping my hands with delight, "it is just the thing! May I put you in a story? I must write one for Graham tomorrow, and I want material sadly."

"And I am your 'dernier resort?' Well, Fanny, victimize me if you will; but don't tell for the world that I gave you leave to do it!" Dear reader, keep her secret.

The Soul Awakened; or Which Shall Win Him[1]

CHAPTER I.

There bloomed beside thee forms as fair,
   There murmured tones as sweet;
But round *thee* breathed th' enchanted air,
   'T was life and death to meet!
And henceforth thou alone wert fair,
   And though the stars had sung for joy,
   Thy whisper only sweet.
Bulwer.

PRECIOUS READER! please shut your eyes and dream that you are with me at one of Ole Bull's concerts. I want you to mark those three *distingué* (I am so tired of that convenient word!) girls on the front seat—Violet, Blanche and Eleanor Elwell;—because that intellectual-looking young man behind them has rested the decision of an important question upon the manner in which they meet this melodious miracle. They are all lovely, graceful and intelligent; but Edgar Stanton is in search of a soul, and he trembles lest his choice should fall upon some beautiful temple, destitute of the divinity within.

This very morning, they have all betrayed their preference for him, and each in a different and characteristic manner.

Blanche, the romantic, capricious, petulant, but beautiful Blanche—she with the long gipsy curls and white shoulders—sung with her sweet, faltering voice,

---

[1] "The Soul Awakened; or Which Shall Win Him," Frances S. Osgood, *Graham's Magazine*, October 1844, vol. XXVI, no. 4, pp. 152-154

> Go! let me pray,
>   Pray to forget thee!
> Wo worth the day,
>   Dear one, I met thee!
>
> Ever till then,
>   Careless and free, love,
> Never again,
>   Thus shall I be, love.
>
> Calm in my soul,
>   Love had been dreaming,
> Veiled visions stole,
>   Light round him gleaming.
>
> One smile alone,
>   O'er his rest glancing,
> One only tone,
>   Low and entrancing.
>
> Soft, through that sleep,
>   Thine the voice breaking,
> Long shall I weep,
>   Weep his awaking.
>
> Weep for the day,
>   When first I met thee,
> Then let me pray,
>   Pray to forget thee!

Eleanor—stately and statue-like—she with the classic head, the cold, bright eyes and exquisitely chiseled mouth—asked which he thought most becoming, the blue or the white cashmere, which had been sent home for her inspection, and on his expressing a preference for the white, had calmly arranged its rich folds around her Juno form, and requested his attendance in a walk.

But the prettiest and most graceful little token of interest had been given him by Violet—the child Violet— the simple, earnest, sensitive, affectionate girl, who seemed to look up to him with the trustful and truthful tenderness of a younger sister, who confided to him all her gay and all her sorrowful emotions—who asked his advice about her studies, and made him tell her fairy tales, and listened when he read—as if the harps of Heaven were playing to her and who would sit sometimes for hours on a little cushion at his feet motionless, almost breathless, with—what? Could it be love?

But Violet was so wild, so shy, when he tried to sound the depths of her heart, that he could not fathom it. He could not tell if she had a soul, that would answer his, or if she were merely a pretty, thoughtless, loving child. If she had one, where was the key to it? Time would show, and he would wait and watch. Now and then a flash from her dark, purple eyes, like summer lightning through a cloud, told that the spirit, which had slumbered since it left its divine home, was dreaming beautiful dreams, and was near its waking. That she had fancy and feeling, her playful wit, her caressing looks and manners, her pity for the suffering showed. But it was more than fancy and feeling that he wanted; it was sympathy with himself that he looked for. That virgin soul, when it did awake from its pure and happy sleep, would it wake for him? Would it chord with *his*? Would

> *"the same touch*
> *Bid the same fountain flow"*

in both? Would the same airs of heaven that sometimes played over his, like the south wind over an Æolian harp, bearing on their wings the odors of celestial flowers, the tones of angel-voices, which he had loved "before his birth below," and filling his soul with an intense yearning for its holier home, would they waken in hers, too, the music of hope and memory?

Violet had taken a snow-drop from its fellow flower— her bosom—and given it to him, "with a flitting blush;" and when another gentleman present complained of her partiality, instead of taking one from her own bouquet, she stole a yellow rose from her mother's and presented it to him, with an arch smile, which *he* thought very provoking.

Now then—let us watch them, while the Bulbul, as dear Mrs. Child calls him, is echoing the choral hymn of Nature. That man's soul, like the ocean-shell, which has caught and kept, even in exile, the melodious murmur of the waters sweeping for ages through its cell, must have learned and borne away into this life, from the shores of eternity, the music of its ever sounding waves.

But let us return to the ladies. Eleanor adjusts her ruby bracelet and whispers with the exquisite beside her; Blanche droops her graceful head upon her hand, and closes her eyes—she has lovely long lashes—in the most picturesque attitude she can think of. But dear little Violet heeds neither bracelet nor beau. Her soul is awakened by the magic-music of that wonderful master of sound; for the first time it feels its immortal wings, and unfolds them, in tremulous and timid delight; and now it is up and away with that of the Bulbul, soaring, "singing at the gate of Heaven!" Her dark eyes, full of tears, are reading the music in his; but her first impulse, when he pauses, is to search, with one eloquent glance, for sympathy in those of Stanton. That mutual look was enough; it was the key-note to the melody Love was playing in their hearts, and Edgar felt that their whole beings harmonized with each other.

> "The Venus rose from out the deep
> Of those inspiring eyes."

CHAPTER II.

Still art thou all which thou wert when a child,
Only more holy, and only less wild!
Hervey.

Violet, Blanche and Eleanor had each a little boudoir attached to her chamber, and the peculiar taste of each was in no way more characteristically displayed, than in the adornment of these pet rooms. Eleanor's was gay and elegant; filled with a profusion of the richest bijouterie, mirrors, curtains of sea-green and gold, and sofas, ottomans and cushions of crimson velvet. The romantic Blanche had chosen curtains and furniture of the palest rose-colored damask; covered the walls with sentimental second-rate pictures, and the tables with flimsy annuals and magazines. But Violet's room was a little fairy paradise. The full, snow-white muslin drapery, gracefully shading the windows, let in the sunbeams on the rich carpet, on the exquisite miniature groups of sculpture in alabaster, the classic vases filled with rare and delicate flowers, and the few richly bound books of poetry, philosophy and romance which lay around.

A figure of Cupid in flight, bearing a watch on his pinions, was the tasteful design of a timepiece, singularly in keeping with the tone of the place, where Love must have ever "lent wings to Time." There were but three pictures, but they were chef d'oeuvres of a master in the art. One was the Virgin, another a lovely landscape, and the third a sleeping child. On the marble mantel-shelf, on either side of the time-piece, were two lamps of exquisite workmanship, in white marble, one borne by a Psyche, bending over her slumbering lover, the other by Gulnare at the couch of Conrad. Three little French lounges of black walnut and green velvet, a luxurious arm-chair and an embroidered cushion, the favorite seat of Violet, completed the *coup d'œil*. And Violet sat there, the morning after the concert, on that low cushion, looking as fresh and pure, in her gray, transparent muslin robe, as the dewy moss-rose on the stand beside her. She held to her lips a tiny porcelain vase, beautifully painted, filled with lilies of the valley, and in the other hand, which rested on her lap, was an open paper containing the following lines.

TO THE LILY'S SISTER.

This morn, when Aurora above the lake bent, love,
    To tie up the braids of her pale, golden hair,
While the gleam of her curls, to its small ripples lent, love,
    Looked just like a star, broke and fallen in there,

Away from their banquet the fairies I frightened,
   For I shook, from a wet spray, a shower-bath of dew;
And their luminous winglets all quivered and
lightened,
   Like fire-flies, round me as swiftly they flew.

Their cut-diamond dinner-set with them departed;
   But one painted vase-full of lilies was lest—
Their stateliest treasure—forgot when they started—
   I stole it and rail—oh, forgive me the theft!

And take it, dear maiden! and while you are stealing
   The sigh that my fairy bouquet breathes for you,
Remember the flowers of Fancy and Feeling,
   We've twined in bright hours, too fleet and too few!

Violet wore but one ornament that evening, at the *soirée* they gave—it was the fairy bouquet from the porcelain vase. Were the flowers really enchanted? Had they borne with them, to her bosom, the spells of fairy-land? Were their tiny bells, unheard by all but her, ringing a choral peal of light and dainty music, such as in Titania's realms is signal for the dance? What else could have brought that divine rose-hue to her delicate cheek? What else could have kindled in those drooping eyes the light their lashes could not hide? Ah! it was love had charmed the flowers— 't was he that rung the fairy bells! And though Eleanor shone like a star amid the crowd, with her dark hair wreathed with gems, Stanton saw but his own little lily of the valley—for henceforth she "alone was fair," her "whisper only sweet." And though Blanche sung, softly and meltingly, the following pathetic song—

A pride I would not alter,
   Forbids me to reveal,
Howe'er my soul may falter,
   The wretchedness I feel!

And so, with idle laughter,
   I while away the hours,
And weep in secret after,
   O'er memory's buried flowers.

They say I'm all too wild,
  They chide my reckless joy,
They call me but a child,
  That plays with every toy:—

A child they little know
  The woman-woes, I've proved;
Too wild! 'tis but to show
  A soul by grief unmoved.

And so, with seeming laughter,
  I while away the hours,
And weep a moment after,
  O'er memory's buried flowers.

Yet I was once all glee, love,
  A singing bird in the spring,
My spirit fluttered free, love,
  On light and sportive wing.

But Fate his arrow sent,
  And broke the buoyant wing,
And changed to wild lament,
  The song I used to sing.

And now with mocking laughter,
  I chase the weary hours,
And weep in anguish after,
  O'er memory's buried flowers.

As she only wept in *song*—melodious tears—they did not have the effect intended, for ere the moss-rose faded in the bower, our Violet knelt at the alter beneath the bridal veil, with Stanton at her side.

The Magic Lute[1]

CHAPTER I.

My beauty! sing to me and make me glad!
Thy sweet words drop upon the ear as soft
As rose-leaves on a well.—*Festus.*

ON A low stool at the feet of the Count de Courcy sat his bride, the youthful Lady Loyaline. One delicate, dimpled hand hovered over the strings of her lute, like a snowy bird, about to take wing with a burst of melody. The other she was playfully trying to release from the clasp of his. At last, she desisted from the attempt, and said, as she gazed up into his proud "unfathomable eyes"—

"Dear De Courcy! how shall I thank you for this beautiful gift? How shall I prove to you my love, my gratitude, for all your generous devotion to my wishes?"

Loyaline was startled by the sudden light that dawned in those deep eyes; but it passed away and left them calmer, and prouder than before, and there was a touch of sadness in the tone of his reply—

"Sing to me, sweet, and thank me so!"

Loyaline sighed as she tuned the lute. It was ever thus when she alluded to her love. His face would lighten like a tempest-cloud, and then grow dark and still again, as if the fire of hope and joy were suddenly kindled in his soul to be as suddenly extinguished. What could it mean? Did he doubt her affection? A tear sell upon the lute, and she said, "I will sing

---

[1] "The Magic Lute," Frances S. Osgood, *Graham's Magazine,* November 1844, vol. XXVI, no. 5, pp. 214-216

THE LADY'S LAY.

The deepest wrong that thou couldst do,
  Is thus to doubt my love for thee,
For questioning that thou question'st too,
  My truth, my pride, my purity.

'T were worse than falsehood thus to meet
  Thy least caress, thy lightest smile,
Nor feel my heart exulting beat
  With sweet, impassioned joy the while.

The deepest wrong that thou couldst do,
  Is thus to doubt my faith professed;
How should I, love, be less than true,
  When *thou* art noblest, bravest, best?

The tones of the Lady Loyaline's voice were sweet and clear, yet so low, so daintily delicate, that the heart caught them rather than the ear. De Courcy felt his soul soften beneath those pleading accents, and his eyes, as he gazed upon her, were filled with unutterable love and sorrow.

How beautiful she was! With that saint color, like the first blush of dawn, upon her cheek—with those soft, black, glossy braids, and those deep blue eyes, so luminous with soul! Again the lady took her lute—

For thee I braid and bind my hair
  With fragrant flowers, for only thee;
Thy sweet approval, all my care,
  Thy love—the world to me!

For thee I fold my fairest gown,
  With simple grace, for thee, for thee!
No other eyes in all the town
  Shall look with love on me.

For thee my lightsome lute I tune,
  For thee—it else were mute—for thee!
The blossom to the bee in June
  Is less than thou to me.

De Courcy, by nature proud, passionate, reserved and exacting, had wooed and won, with some difficulty, the young and timid girl, whose tenderness by her noble lover was blent with a shrinking awe, which all his devotion could not for a while overcome.

At the time my story commences, he was making preparations to join the Crusaders. He was to set out in a few days, and brave and chivalric as he was, there were both fear and grief in his heart, when he thought of leaving his beautiful bride for years or perhaps forever. Perfectly convinced of her guileless purity of purpose, thought and deed, he yet had, he thought, reason to suppose that her heart was, perhaps unconsciously to herself, estranged from him, or rather that it never had been his. He remembered with a thrill of passionate grief and indignation, her bashful reluctance to meet his gaze— her timid shrinking from his touch—and thus her very purity and modesty, the soul of true affection, were distorted by his jealous imagination into indifference for himself and fondness for another.

Only two days before, upon suddenly entering her chamber, he had surprised her in tears, with a page's cap in her hand, and on hearing his step, she had started up blushing and embarrassed, and hidden it beneath her mantle, which lay upon the couch. Poor De Courcy! This was indeed astounding; but while he had perfect faith in her honor, he was too proud to let her see his suspicions. That cap! that crimson cap! It was not the last time he was destined to behold it!

The hour of parting came, and De Courcy shuddered as he saw a smile—certainly an exulting smile—lighten through the tears in the dark eyes of his bride, as she bade him for the last time "farewell."

A twelvemonth afterward, he was languishing in the dungeons of the East—a chained and hopeless captive.

CHAPTER II.

"Ah! fleeter far than fleetest storm or steed,
    Or the death they bear,
The heart, which tender thought clothes, like a dove,
    With the wings of care!"

The sultan was weary; weary of his flowers and s fountains—of his dreams and his dancing-girls—his harem and himself. The banquet lay untouched before him. The rich chibouque was cast aside. he cooling sherbet shone in vain.

> The Almas tripped, with tinkling feet,
> Unmarked their motions light and fleet!

His slaves trembled at his presence; for a dark cloud hung lowering on the brows of the great Lord of the East, and they knew, from experience, that there 'ere both thunder and lightning to come ere it dispersed.

But a sound of distant plaintive melody was heard. A sweet voice sighing to a lute. The sultan listened. "Bring hither the minstrel," he said in a subdued tone; and a lovely, fair-haired boy, in a page's dress of pale green silk, was led blushing into the presence.

"Sing to me, child," said the Lord of the East. And the youth touched his lute, with grace and wondrous skill, and sang, in accents soft as the ripple of a rill,

THE VIOLET'S LOVE.

> Shall I tell what the violet said to the star,
> While she gazed through her tears on his beauty afar?
> She sang, but her singing was only a sigh,
> And nobody heard it, but Heaven, Love and I;
> A sigh, full of fragrance and beauty, it stole
> Through the stillness up, up, to the star's beaming soul.
>
> She sang—"Thou art glowing with glory and might,
> And I'm but a flower, frail, lowly and light.
> I ask not they pity, I seek not thy smile;
> I ask but to worship thy beauty a while;
> To sigh to thee, sing to thee, bloom for thine eye,
> And when thou art weary, to bless thee and die!"

Shall I tell what the star to the violet said,
While ashamed, 'neath his love-look, she hung her
young head?
He sang—but his singing was only a ray,
And none but the flower and I heard the dear lay.
How it thrilled, as it fell, in its melody clear,
Through the little heart, heaving with rapture and
fear!

Ah no! love! I dare not! Too tender, too pure,
For me to betray, were the words he said to her;
But as she lay listening that low lullaby,
A smile lit the tear in the timid flower's eye;
And when death had stolen her beauty and bloom,
The ray came again to play over her tomb.

Long ere the lay had ceased, the cloud in the Sultan's
eye had dissolved itself in tears. Never had so moved his
soul. "The lute was enchanted! The youth was a Peri, who
had lost his way! Surely it must be so!"

"But sing me now a bolder strain!" And the beautiful
child flung back his golden curls—and swept more
proudly than before, and his voice took a clarion-tone, and
his dark, steel-blue eyes flashed with heroic fire as he
sang

THE CRIMSON PLUME.

Oh! know ye the knight of the red waving plume?
Lo! his lighting smile gleams through the battle's wild
gloom,
Like a flash through the tempest; oh! fly from that
smile!
'T is the wild-fire of fury—it glows to beguile!
And his sword-wave is death, and his war-cry is doom!
Oh! brave not the knight of the dark crimson plume!

His armor is black, as the blackest midnight;
His steed like the ocean-foam, spotlessly white;
His crest—a crouched tiger, who dreams of fierce joy—
Its motto—"Beware! for I wake—to destroy!"

And his sword-wave is death, and his war-cry is doom!
Oh! brave not the knight of the dark crimson plume!

"By Allah! thou hast magic in thy voice! One more! and ask what thou wilt. Were it my signet-ring, 't is granted!"

Tears of rapture sprung to the eyes of the minstrel-boy, as the sultan spoke, and his young cheek flushed like a morning cloud. Bending over his lute to hide his emotion, he warbled once again—

THE BROKEN HEART'S APPEAL.

Give me back my childhood's truth!
Give me back my guileless youth!
Pleasure, Glory, Fortune, Fame,
These I will not stoop to claim!
Take them! All of Beauty's power,
All the triumph of this hour
Is not worth one blush you stole—
Give me back my bloom of soul!

Take the cup and take the gem!
What have I to do with them?
Loose the garland from my hair!
Thou shouldst wind the night-shade there;
Thou who wreath'st, with flattering art,
Poison-flowers to bind my *heart!*
Give me back the rose you stole!
Give me back my bloom of soul!

"Name thy wish, fair child. But tell me first what good genius has charmed thy lute for thee, that thus it sways the soul?"

"A child-angel, with large melancholy eyes and wings of lambent fire—we Franks have named him Love. He led me here and breathed upon my lute."

"And where is he now?"

"I have hidden him in my heart," said the boy, blushing as he replied.

And what is the boon thou wouldst ask?"

The youthful stranger bent his knee, and said in faltering tones—"Thou hast a captive Christian knight; let him go free and Love shall bless thy throne!"

"He is thine—thou shalt thyself release him. Here, take my signet with thee."

And the fair boy glided like an angel of light through the guards at the dungeon-door. Bolts and bars fell before him—for he bore the talisman of Power—and he stood in his beauty and grace at the captive's couch, and bade him rise and go forth, for he was free.

De Courcy, half-awake, gazed wistfully on the benign eyes that bent over him. He had just been dreaming of his guardian angel; and when he saw the beauteous stranger boy—with his locks of light—his heavenly smile—his pale, sweet face—he had no doubt that this was the celestial visitant of his dreams, and, following with love and reverence his spirit-guide, he scarcely wondered at his sudden disappearance when they reached the court.

CHAPTER III.

"Pure as Aurora when she leaves her couch,
Her cool, soft couch in Heaven, and, blushing, shakes
The balmy dew-drops from her locks of light."

Safely the knight arrived at his castle-gate, and as he alighted from his steed, a lovely woman sprang through the gloomy archway, and lay in tears upon his breast.

"My wife! my sweet, true wife! Is it indeed thou! Thy cheek is paler than its wont. Hast mourned for *me*, my love?" And the knight put back the long black locks and gazed upon that sad, sweet face, Oh! the delicious joy of that dear meeting! Was it *too* dear, too bright to last?

At a banquet, given in honor of De Courcy's return, some of the guests, flushed with wine, rashly let fall in his hearing an insinuation which awoke all his former doubts, and, upon inquiry, he found to his horror that during his absence the Lady Loyaline left her home for months, and none knew whither or why she went, but all could guess, they hinted.

De Courcy sprang up, with his hand on the heft of his sword, and rushed toward the chamber of wife. She met him in the anteroom, and listened calmly and patiently as he gave vent to all his jealous wrath, and bade her prepare to die. Her only reply was—"Let me go to my chamber; I would say one prayer; then do with me as you will."

"Begone!"

The chamber door closed on the graceful form and sweeping robes of the Lady de Courcy. But in a few moments it opened again, and forth came, with meekly folded arms, a stripling on a page's dress *crimson cap!*—the bold, bright boy with whom he had parted at his dungeon-gate! "Here! in her very chamber!"

The knight sprang forward to cleave the daring intruder to the earth. But the stranger flung to the ground the cap and the golden locks, and De Courcy fell at the feet, not of a minstrel-boy, but of his own true-hearted wife, and begged her forgiveness, and blessed her for her heroic and beautiful devotion.

The Little Lost Shoe; or
Fielding in Search of a Foot[1]

CHAPTER I.

WHAT A musical shriek! Henry Fielding was wandering through a noble western wood, at sunset, when the sound startled him from a profound reverie, and looking up, he beheld at a distance a young girl, motionless with terror, gazing, as if fascinated, upon entering the stagecoach, which was just ready to an immense snake, apparently just coiled for a spring.

Harry raised his hunting rifle, aimed, fired, and the monster lay writhing in the agonies of death. But whither had the wood-nymph flown? She was nowhere to be seen; and vexed and disappointed the young man wandered on. He had caught but a glimpse of a youthful and picturesque-looking creature with wild, gazelle-like eyes and parted lips, her soft, dark hair and snowy robe floating in the breeze, and her hands clasped in terror.

He hurried forward, hoping he might overtake her. Suddenly he sees a prize in the path, and stoops to take it up. What can it be? Is it a bracelet? A ribbon? A ring? No, gentle guesser, it is a little black kid slipper, of the daintiest and most graceful proportions imaginable. Harry was sure now he should overtake her, for she must limp, poor thing! With that little shoeless foot; unless, indeed, she had wings, which he was almost afraid she had.

Suddenly he came upon two paths, diverging from the one he was in. Here was a dilemma–which should he take? The right or the left? There was no time to lose. He chose the right, which proved the wrong after all; for it led straight to a great pond in the depths of the wood, and left our unlucky friend but one of two alternatives, to drown his disappointment in the tempting water, or to retrace his

---

[1] "The Little Lost Shoe; or Fielding in Search of a Foot," Frances S. Osgood, *Graham's Magazine*, December 1844, vol. XXVI, no. 6, pp. 287-291

steps and try the other. With an enlightened wisdom, and a profound moral courage, which did him honor, our hero chose the latter, and that led to his own home in the village, where he ought to have been at least three quarters of an hour before, and not have kept everybody waiting for dinner. Upon the whole, though, it would have been better if he had stayed away altogether; for he poured the water into his aunt's plate, instead of her tumbler, and put mustard into her tumbler, instead of her plate, and when she asked to look at the newspaper, took out of his pocket the poor little shoe, and placed it gravely in her outstretched hand.

"Harry Fielding, what upon airth ails you, and what in the world is this?" exclaimed the astonished old lady, peering into his face with her little gray eyes, from which she had removed the spectacles to wipe them.

Harry replied by seizing the shoe and rushing out of the house. On he went, up one street and down another, looking in vain for the fairy foot of the forest Cinderella.

As he approached the inn of the village, he saw entering the stage-coach, which was just ready to start, a lady thickly veiled, in a very elegant travelling-dress. Harry ran forward with a sudden misgiving. One little foot, in its neat black gaitor-boot, was already on the step—she sprang lightly in—the door closed—the driver cracked his whip, and ere our hero reached the spot, the coach was half-way down the street.

It was she! he was sure of it. She had gone, perhaps forever! and Henry Fielding sauntered listlessly on, humming "What's this dull town to me?" and looking as if he had not a friend in the world.

CHAPTER II.

"Are you looking for anything, my dear fellow?" said Charles Seaton, meeting a friend in Chestnut Street, about a month after the occurrence of the incident mentioned in the last chapter.

"What large feet you Philadelphians have!" was the rather irrelevant reply.

"Large! *au contraire*—they are famous for their small ones."

"Well, here is *my* model," said the other, sighing deeply, and taking from his pocket a tiny kid shoe.

"That is, indeed, 'a trifle light as air!' exclaimed Seaton. "Introduce me to the sylph who owns it and I will take you to see *la belle* Julie this very evening."

"Hang *la belle* Julie! Haven't I been wasting a whole month in search of the foot to which this little slipper belonged?" And Fielding proceeded to relate the history of his adventure with the wood-nymph.

"And you acknowledge you have wasted a month in this ridiculous search? Take my advice, Harry, resume your law studies at once, and forget your wood-nymph as fast as possible. What would your father say if he knew of this romantic folly?"

Harry colored a little at this frank reproof from his open-hearted friend; but after a moment's pause, he replied sadly—"You are quite right, Charles; but if you knew what a beautiful dream I resign, in adopting your advice, you would not wonder at my reluctance."

He did resume his studies; but he could not quite forego the lone and lovely hope which gleamed like a morning-star in the heaven of his future, and now and then a vision of an exquisite little foot, pure and white as alabaster, would glance across the dull, dry page of Coke upon Littleton, or put even Blackstone to the blush.

CHAPTER III.

"Mamma! darling mamma! you are suffering for a thousand things—do let me go."

"Yes, my sweet child, you must indeed go now. I fear I have already delayed it too long. But you will have a quarter's salary in advance, and that will more than discharge the few debts we have incurred. Go now, dear, while I dare let you go."

Julia St. George repressed her starting tears, tied on her little crape bonnet, (she was in mourning for her father,) kissed the pale cheek of the invalid, and set forth on her errand with a beating heart. She had been offered the situation of governess in the family of Mrs. Beaumont, a banker's widow, and she was now going to accept it.

Mrs. Beaumont received her with a cold hauteur, calculated to chill her into humility. Her eldest daughter, a delicate, aristocratic-looking beauty, languidly raised her glass—surveyed her for a moment—then let it drop, and resumed her book. But both felt, in an instant, the superiority, the innate nobility of the person upon whom they affected to look down

Dressed in deep mourning, and with the most tasteful and graceful simplicity, her dark hair parted plainly on her brow, her beautiful face radiant with spirit, feeling and intellect, Julia St. George walked calmly up the room, bending her head with perfect self-possession, in return for the haughty greeting of Mrs. Beaumont, while the slightest perceptible curve of her lovely lip betrayed her consciousness of the manner in which she was received. The lady pointed to a chair—the visitor seated herself with provoking composure.

"You have come, I presume, Miss St. George, to say you accept the situation I proposed to you.

"I have, madam," was the reply, in a low, calm, but most musically modulated voice, "and I should like to enter upon my duties at once, if agreeable to you."

Mrs. Beaumont hesitated—Miss St. George was evidently not a person to be put down—and her serene dignity, the result of a self-respect, which that lady could neither understand nor appreciate, might possibly prove troublesome—but then, on the other hand, the example of her evident high-breeding would be invaluable in forming the manners of her hitherto untamable little Angela, while her attainments were such as were rarely to be met with, even in a governess.

"I will let you know in the course of a week," she said at last."

"I am sorry, madam, to disoblige you," replied Julia, as quietly as before; "but I cannot wait a week for your decision. It is necessary that I should secure a situation of some kind immediately."

"Oh, very well: if you are in such haste, perhaps you had better look elsewhere."

"Good morning, madam," said Julia, rising at once.

"Stay!" said the lady hastily, "Upon the whole I think you will do. You may come to-morrow if you like."

Miss St. George calmly bowed her assent and was about to take leave, when a wild, graceful, little creature burst into the room, exclaiming—"I will see the governess!" Her white, embroidered frock was torn and soiled, a profusion of soft, glistening, amber-colored hair, in the utmost disorder, clustered round a pale, but singularly lovely countenance. The large, dark, Oriental eyes were instantly cast down on meeting those of the stranger, their long jet-black lashes resting with a slight curve on the colorless cheek beneath; the full, yet delicate lips were of the richest red imaginable, and her attitude of unconscious, childish grace was charming, as she stood for a moment, silently twisting in her pretty fingers the ribbons of a gipsy hat.

The next instant, however, she looked up again into the eyes which had awed her at first, for Julia had lingered in the room absorbed in surprise and admiration, and seeming to gather courage from their expression of earnest interest, the child went timidly up to her, and climbing into her arms, whispered half aloud—

"Will you love me very much, and praise me all the time; and never, never punish me?"

"I cannot promise *all* you ask, darling—began Miss St. George—

"Angela, I am ashamed of you!" exclaimed Mrs. Beaumont; "you are always making scenes! Go to your room and have your hair brushed, and your dress changed, immediately."

Angela pouted and clung to the neck of her new friend; but Julia kissed the pout away, and putting her gently down, repeated her good-morning to the stately lady of the mansion and her indolent daughter, and departed.

CHAPTER IV.

"Oh, mamma! she is beautiful, and so affectionate—I shall be very happy, I know."

"Is she, dear? Then I must confess I am agreeably surprised. I have always understood that she was very cold-hearted, and any thing but beautiful."

"What! Angela?"

"Who is Angela? I was speaking of Mrs. Beaumont."

Julia laughed and shrugged her pretty shoulders; she had forgotten all the unpleasant occurrences of the morning, in the delight with which she thought of the lovely and loving little girl who was to be confided to her care.

CHAPTER V.

"If you can manage *that* child," muttered the nurse, as she consigned Miss Angela to her new governess the next morning, "you will do more than anyone else ever did—that's all *I've* got to say."

"I will tell you a secret, if you will promise *never* to tell," whispered the child to Julia, as the door closed upon the nurse.

"But I cannot promise never to tell, dear, for that would be wrong."

"Well, then, you *may* tell, if you like; but I know you won't. You see, the reason they can't manage me is because I *try* to be naughty before mamma and nurse!"

"Oh, Angela! I am sorry for that. Why do you do so?"

"Because they make such a fuss about every little thing. I like to hear them scold—it's so funny. Besides, they never let me have any peace except when they shut me up, and then I have real good times, all by myself, in the little bed-room next to the nursery. They shut me up once in a dark closet, but I didn't like that, because I couldn't do anything there; so I screamed just as loud as I could, and they thought I was frightened, but I was not a bit; and now they always put me in the little room, and I pull the clothes off the bed and make it all up again nicely, and then I take off my apron and dust the chairs with it; and sometimes I climb up on the bureau, and play 'fish' with a bent pin and a piece of thread. Oh! it's real fun to be punished! I wish mamma would punish you and me together sometimes, and we'd have grand times playing fish! But I suppose grown up people never *need* punishing. They are always good—ain't they? Mamma never seems to think she ought to be shut up. Did you ever play fish?"

"Yes, dear, when I was a little girl. But can't you have good times, without being naughty first, Angela?"

"No, indeed! They won't let me do *any*thing I want to. They say I mustn't climb, for fear I shall tear my clothes; and I must not run, for fear I should get heated; and I mustn't read much, for fear I should make my head ache; and I mustn't sew, for fear I shall stoop. They don't want me to do *anything* out of school hours, but just sit up stiff, 'like a lady.' Why should I be like a lady, when I ain't a lady? I'd rather be a child, and be *like* a child—hadn't you? I don't think ladies are half as happy as children—do you? Oh, dear! if I only had something to do, all the time, I don't believe I should *ever* be naughty, or unhappy either—*that's all* I want, *something to do!* Do all little girls have a mamma at home, that keeps plaguing them and fussing over them?"

Alternately surprised, amused, and grieved as the little indefatigable chatterbox thus ran on, Miss St. George saw the difficulty of the task before her. She saw the weeds and flowers struggling together in that rich but neglected garden, her pupil's heart; and she felt how difficult it would be to destroy the one without injuring the other. But she resolved to lend her whole energies to the work, and she was sure to succeed in time.

In the course of two or three months the little Angela visibly improved. Her hair and dress were not often out of order; she was seldom disobedient, or disrespectful, to her mother or her nurse; and, if she were *ever* so, a word, a look from Julia had the desired effect. Passionately fond of books and of her teacher, there was no fear that her intellect would be neglected. The great difficulty seemed to be to keep her ever-restless imagination in, check; without any companions of her own age, she was in the habit of surrounding herself at her studies and her play with the creations of her fancy, to whom she gave the most romantic or high-sounding names she could make up at the moment. These little visionary friends she would address in terms of endearment, reproach, or expostulation, reply for them, and carry on the conversation until she forgot that they were unreal.

One morning she was sitting in the school-room, surrounded by empty chairs, in each of which she had placed a little invisible schoolmate, and was asking them, in turn, to spell all the hard words she could call to mind, when her sister entered to speak to the governess, and, ignorant of the mischief she was doing, seated herself in one of the "tabooed" chairs. The little girl, excited by her interesting play, burst into a passion of tears, exclaiming, "Get up, quick! quick! You will kill that darling Cariella!"

and, flying to her astonished sister, endeavored to pull her from the chair.[2]

Julia now saw, for the first time, the evil tendencies of this habit, and, fearful almost for the reason of her charge, begged Mrs. Beaumont to allow the child real flesh and blood playmates.

CHAPTER VI.

But what have we done with our hero? Has he found the little lost foot yet? No! he has almost given it up; but he has become an attaché to a foreign embassy, and is quite a pet among the higher circles in Europe, where a true, frank, honorable and intelligent American is always received with favor.

Mrs. Beaumont, her daughter, Victoria, and her niece, Miss Adelaide Sinclair, were in "perfect ecstasies," for George, the only son, who had just returned to England, from a continental tour, was expected home, to pass the Christmas holidays at their country seat, and was to bring with him the wealthy, talented, and distinguished Henry Fielding, and his pleasant friend, Mr. Seaton.

Julia St. George had gradually become a favorite in the family. Once secure of a position among them worthy of her talents and refinement, she was quite willing and ready to unbend, and to make herself agreeable and obliging to all. The young ladies soon discovered that nothing could be done without the assistance, the advice, the sympathy of little Angela's tasteful and kind-hearted governess, and even the cold and stately mother felt her heart soften toward one who had devoted herself so tenderly and so successfully to the improvement of her child.

On the day of their arrival, the young men did not linger long over their wine after dinner; for George was anxious to renew an old flirtation with his spirited cousin; Seaton had heard much of Victoria, and Fielding always enjoyed the society of an intelligent and interesting woman more than anything else.

---

[2] A fact.

Adelaide Sinclair was a brilliant, playful, pretty and saucy coquette. Her cousin, Victoria, a dainty and delicate creature, indolent, graceful, and gentle, partaking somewhat of the cold and calm pride which was the prevailing characteristic of her mother. When the gentlemen entered the drawing-room, Adelaide was arranging a ringlet at the glass, Victoria, half reclining on a sofa, embroidering a velvet slipper, and, in a distant corner, looking over a book of prints, the governess and her young charge, who had been allowed to sit up in honor of her brother's arrival. Mrs. Beaumont had retired, fatigued with the unusual excitement.

Fielding seated himself near Victoria, and admired her work. "It is for a friend," said she; "isn't it a tiny shoe?"

"I think I can show you a smaller one," said Fielding, and, impelled by a sudden impulse, he drew from his bosom the little kid slipper of his wood-nymph.

Adelaide caught it playfully from his hand. "A prize—a prize!" she exclaimed, trying to hold it up out of his reach. "As I live, here are verses, on the sole of it! Listen, good people," and she began—"Little treasure, light and—"

"Nay!" remonstrated Fielding, in the same gay tone, "no one shall read the verses who cannot wear the shoe."

Adelaide's satin slipper was off in a moment, but the shoe was too small; she tried in vain to squeeze her pretty foot into it.

"Come, Vic," said her brother, "let me try it on you—if it don't fit somebody, we shan't have the verses."

Victoria languidly put out her foot, but in vain, it would not fit.

"I know somebody it will just suit," exclaimed little Angela, in an eager tone. "Miss St. George has the cunningest foot in the world, only she never shows it." Fielding drew the beautiful, earnest child toward him, and Adelaide, flying to the governess, dragged her forward, laughing and blushing, into the circle.

"*La belle* Julie! by all that's wonderful," exclaimed Seaton, in a low tone, as they approached.

"Hang *la belle* Julie!" murmured a sweet and playful voice, and the next moment the young governess was cordially shaking hands with her well-remembered friend, Mr. Seaton, who could scarcely believe his eyes or his ears.

"Introduce me," whispered Fielding.

"Miss St. George—Mr. Fielding. Years ago, in America, my friend was promised this introduction."

"Yes, and I happened to hear his polite reply to your proposition," said the lady, laughing.

"What was it?"

"To the best of my recollection, it was, 'Hang *la belle* Julie!' I walked into a shop to avoid hearing the rest of his courteous adjuration. What had I done to deserve hanging, Mr. Fielding?" she asked, turning gaily toward him, with her lovely smile.

"Oh! stop! no matter what you had done. Don't you see that the poor man is out of his wits with consternation? Try the shoe at once—there's a dear!—and let us hear the verses. They ought to begin—'Sole of my soul,' but men so seldom pay a graceful compliment."

Fielding was perfectly enchanted with "*la belle* Julie." He gave but one sigh to his wood-nymph and, almost sure that his verses were safe, for many a belle had tried the shoe in vain, he said, "Yes, Miss St. George, prove that you generously forgive my thoughtless folly, by putting on the slipper."

As Julia took the shoe from his hand, she started, colored deeply, and gazed from it to him with a bewildered look, which was infinitely amusing to as but our awakening hero.

"That look!" He felt a strange thrill as he met it! Could it be? "Pray try the shoe at once," he exclaimed in an agitated voice.

Miss St. George had recovered her self-possession. Seating herself, she drew the shoe with graceful ease upon her perfect little foot, and looked up into Fielding's eyes; such a look! so eloquent, so full of wonder, joy and gratitude, that his wild hope changed at once into conviction. He had found her at last! His wood-nymph! his Cinderella! his morning star.

Adelaide clapped her hands in ecstasy. "The verses— the verses! read the verses, Miss St. George. It fits exactly. I should think it was made for you! The verses!—we *will* have the verses!"

And poor Julia was obliged to read, in her low, soul-tuned voice, the lines on the sole of the shoe.

Little treasure! light and airy.
　　Didst thou clasp the dainty foot
Of a wandering woodland fairy,
　　Flying from a sylph's salute?

Or did some young mortal lace thee,
　　Tripping with elastic tread,
All too softly to deface thee,
　　Where the sweet, wild fancy led?

Tell me what the woman-passion?
　　Was 't to bend the graceful sole,
In the gay saloons of fashion,
　　While along the dance she stole,

Or, through upland glen and valley,
　　Hast thou pressed the happy flowers?
Tell me, did she love to dally,
　　Mid the fragrant woodland bowers?

Did the prairie blooms caress thee,
　　Breathing balm around they tread?
So the *heart* where now I press thee,
　　All its wealth for her shall shed.

"I should judge from all I see and hear," said Seaton, in a sly, demure tone, "that Miss St. George could show, if she chose, the mate to the wonderful shoe."

"Oh, what is it?" exclaimed the lively Adelaide. "There is some romance attached to it, I know. Tell us all about it, Mr. Seaton—there's a nice man."

The story was told, the mate was brought down, and slyly exchanged in the course of the evening with Fielding for that he had cherished so long, and Julia was persuaded, ere many months had elapsed, to leave her pet Angela, and reward her with her hand, and "her heart in it," the untiring devotion of her lover.

The Soul Mirror[1]

IT WAS ten o'clock; the lights and the ladies were trimmed for the ball; the band and the belles were ready to strike up, and young Rudolph Werner stood near the door watching the brilliant and beautiful creatures as they glided in on the arm of parent, brother or friend, till his heart was in a whirl, waltzing away to the tune of "Love's Young Dream," as if it never would stop. The belle, why they are *all* belles. Every new face was naturally or artificially radiant—with purity or pearl-powder—with rapture or rouge, and how could *he* tell the difference—he, an unsophisticated student, who had never heard of white paint, and would as soon "doubt that the stars are fire," as dream that the graceful, golden tress which kissed the swan-white neck of Araminta Martin, was but a transient guest "far from its native home exiled."

"My dear Miss Brown," murmured a pair of rosy lips in the most dulcet of tones, "you must allow me to admire your beautiful dress. You do look sweetly to-night. Forgive my frankness, I cannot help telling you so." It was Araminta who spoke—Miss Brown simpered with delight, and Rudolph gave up his heart without a struggle. Such a voice—such a mouth—and such an enchanting softness of manner—what a kind, frank spirit must be hers.

Poor Rudolph, five minutes afterward he heard the same low and tender tones again. "Do look at Miss Brown, Mr. White, old as *she* is, to dress in that childish style— what a pity some friend will not tell her to cover her thin, freckled neck. I wish *I* knew her well enough to advise, I would not permit her to make herself so very ridiculous. It is *too* bad poor thing, isn't it?"

Rudolph involuntarily shut his eyes and would have stopped his ears, but for the awkwardness of the movement necessary to such a result. Gradually as he listened to the conversation around him, and watched more closely the faces he admired, he began to awake

---

[1] "The Soul Mirror," Frances S. Osgood, *Ladies' National Magazine*, January 1845, vol. VII, no. 1, pp. 1-4

from his dream of woman's perfection, and sighed as he did so. He now noticed, for the first time, a quiet girl who stood near, without any of the dazzling attractions of the fashionable women around him, but distinguished from them by the freshness, simplicity and unconscious grace of extreme youth and innocence. Rudolph gazed at her for some time, but said to himself as he turned away—"She too, lovely as she looks, is probably heartless and insincere like the rest. I will go back to my books and my ideal."

As he spoke he sauntered into an unoccupied apartment leading to the supper-room, and threw himself fatigued upon a sofa. He lay for some time dreamily gazing upon a large, old-fashioned, quaint-looking mirror, the silver frame of which, on one side, was supported by a beautiful marble figure holding a lamp, which threw a clear, brilliant light upon the glass. As he gazed he heard the rustling of silks and fans, the murmur of voices at the door, and looking round observed that the company were passing through to the supper-room. Araminta was tripping in on the arm of an officer, bending her blue eyes to the ground with the prettiest air of timidity imaginable. Rudolph turned impatiently away, and again his eyes fell upon the mirror, just as Araminta raised hers to steal a self-approving glance at the reflection of her exquisite form.

Rudolph started in amazement and dismay. The image in the glass was that of a shadowy spirit—its wings drooping heavily, ruffled and dim—its eyes gleaming with malice, envy and worldly pride, while a sneer distorted its thin and pallid lips. For an instant the apparition gleamed in the magic mirror was gone. But the next moment, upborne on wings of light, its angelic face beaming and glowing with love, purity and truth, a shape of heavenly loveliness flitted across the glass. With a prophetic throb at his heart, Rudolph turned again and saw the modest and youthful maiden whom he had noticed just before leaving the ballroom, and as he followed her with his eyes through the door, he thought the marble figure bent toward her with a benign smile on its beautiful features.

But a hand at that moment was laid upon his shoulder, and the beautiful voice of his host was heard, exclaiming—"asleep, Rudolph! What are you dreaming about? Why don't you follow the ladies to supper?" He rubbed his eyes—was it indeed a dream? The mirror was still there; but he did not dare to look in it as he passed.

"Come, Rudolph," said his host, as he approached the table, "take this seat between my niece and me, and let me introduce you to each other—Miss Lucy Courtland, Mr. Werner."

If our hero and his interesting neighbor had not exactly "the feast of reason," they shared at least "the flow of soul;" for they were friends in ten minutes, and before the fourth course was removed, had confided to each other all their pet plans and most profound secrets. Some writer has said, "it is the peculiar charm of frankness that it calls mind in contact with mind, and does the work of years." And Rudolph and Julia, (as their mammas and elder sisters called them,) were both as artless and candid as children; for neither of them had been long enough in what is called the gay world to learn that early lesson of its votaries, how to hide with a dazzling smile the involuntary tear, and to veil with light and careless words the deep emotions of the heart.

CHAPTER II.

"Fair as a being of heavenly birth,
But loving and loved as a child of the earth."

If Lucy Courtland did not shine the "star of stars" at the festival, she was the "flowers of flowers" at home; and as Rudolph became more acquainted with her, he caught many a glimpse of the beautiful vision which had been once reflected in the soul mirror.

Lucy had a fidgety father—a manœuvring mother—a selfish sister, and a bear of a brother. Yet she moved above the discord like a halcyon on the deep, and calmed the troubled waves and smoothed "the raven down of darkness till it smiled."

"Lucy," said her father, "don't be eternally reading that confounded poetry!—Can't you find something sensible, child?"

Lucy laid down her book and took up the newspaper. "Shall I read you the deaths and marriages, father?" she asked, with an arch smile dimpling her delicate cheek, and playing stealthily through her long, drooped lashes.

"Yes, and the marine intelligence too, Lucy—there's a good girl."

And Lucy read her father to sleep.

"Lu!" said her sister Helen, "why can't you let *me* wear that bird to-night? You have so much hair you don't need any ornament in it."

And Lucy cheerfully took the golden humming bird, with diamond crest and emerald wings, from the rich, dark braids in which it nestled, and with which it contrasted so beautifully, like "a star in the midnight heaven," and placed it with her own gentle hands in the scanty, red locks of her sister.

"Lulu," said Mrs. Courtland in her blandest tone, "if that young Werner presumes to ask you to dance to-night, you will certainly refuse—will you not, my love?"

The tears trembled in Lulu's dark blue eyes as she murmured,

"Yes, mamma."

"Luce!" said the bear, "do leave off squalling that stupid love-song, and sing something worth hearing—can't you? Sing the 'Rover's Barcarolle.'"

And Luce stopped short in the very first line of "Teach, oh! Teach me to Forget!" and sang in her best bravo style.

"THE ROVER'S BARCAEOLLE."

How gaily o'er the waters stole
The Rover's ringing barcarolle,
While every wave that sparkled round
Seemed dancing to the joyous sound!
Give her sail to the breeze and her prow to the wave!
Though she toss like a toy, still the tempest we'll brave,
And the wilder the wind is the greater our glee;
For danger is dear to the "Rover at sea!"
Yes! softly o'er the waters stole
The Rover's ringing barcarolle,
While every wave that sparkled round
Seemed dancing to the joyous sound!
Oh! well have we named her the Cygnet, my boy!
For she breasts the wild waves like a bird in her joy,

With her white wings unfurled, full of grace and of glee,
She glides in her glory—a queen on the sea!
    Still faintly o'er the waters stole
    The Rover's ringing barcarolle,
    While every sunlit wave around
    Seemed dancing to the joyous sound!
Look—look! 'tis a sail! 'tis a foe! and in chase!
Hurra! let them come! all their fury we'll face.
Let our flag wave defiance!—the flag of the free!
For our swift-winged "Cygnet" is queen of the sea!

"Luce, you're a real, good girl—if you'll look on your dressing-table, you'll find some wild flowers, which I picked for you this afternoon." The bear was a lamb to Lucy!

CHAPTER III.

Oh! gaily fled the laughing hours,
For Love, with fettered wings, in play,
Was pelting them with fragrant flowers,
And singing, "Still delay!"

"You are looking at the magic mirror, Rudeli," said Lucy—"would you like to hear the legend connected with it?"

"Yes, Lulu."

Miss Courtland was passing a week with her uncle, who had persuaded his sister-in-law, Mrs. Courtland, to consent to the betrothal of the lovers in consideration of his having procured a lucrative office for his young friend, Werner.

"Yes, Lulu."

"Well, then—if you'll promise not to twist my hair out of curl any more, I'll tell it you. Do you promise?"

"Yes, Lulu."

"Then why don't you leave it at once?"

"Because it won't *come* out of curl if I *do* twist it. Don't you see how tenderly it twines of its own 'sweet accord' round my fingers? How much expression there is in hair!—no one, with a hard or cold heart, ever has tresses of this soft, yielding, flexible quality that yours has, darling. But tell me the legend, sweet one."

THE LEGEND OF THE MIRROR.

"Once upon a time, about a century ago, there lived a proud and beautiful lady, an ancestress of mine, whose name was Isabel Courtland. From childhood Isabel's greatest delight had been to gaze in the great mirror which hung in her chamber. Her soft, dark hair, changeful as the wing of the golden pheasant, her rich, gazelle-like eyes, her lovely mouth and perfectly rounded form were all flatteringly reflected in the glass, and made in it, as she thought, the prettiest picture in the world. She was never tired of looking at it. But while her person grew in beauty and in grace, Isabel forgot that she had a mind and heart to take care of. To lace the slipper on her dainty foot—to zone with graceful care her robe—to braid her hair with gold and gems:—these were her dearest employments, and thus she grew to womanhood, selfish, high-tempered, willful, wayward and vain.

"Isabel's superb beauty procured her many suitors; but weary at last of her caprices and her haughty bearing, one after another retired, till only Percy Howard, the noblest of them all, remained; and him she loved with an ardent devotion which her inordinate pride would not allow her to betray.

"Percy returned her love, and had set his heart upon 'taming the shrew;' but the shrew would not be tamed, at least by him.

"Isabel often saw, or fancied she saw, behind her image in the mirror, two dim, unearthly shapes, perhaps her good and evil angels; for one was fair, benign and lovely, the other dark and lowering—and she noticed that when she approached the glass in an angry mood of mind, the bright one retreated with a sorrowful pity in her earnest face, and gradually faded in the distance, while the dark and threatening one bent forward as if to embrace her. On the contrary when her better nature prevailed, the fair spirit looked on her with loving, smiling eyes, and bent caressingly above her image in the mirror.

"One day, when she had had a quarrel with her lover, in which she had wantonly wronged his generous heart, she threw herself grieved and penitent upon a sofa, fronting the glass, and exclaimed with tears—'It is thou, beguiling mirror, that has been the evil of my life! It is thou that hast nourished with thy flattery the pride which is my curse. Oh! for a glass that would reflect the soul, that I might see myself as I am. But thou, at least, false friend, shall deceive me no more—no longer shalt thou minister to the sinful feelings which I have too long indulged.'

"She rose with a calm and high resolve on her beautiful brow, and taking a heavily bound missal from the table, deliberately dashed the plate to pieces: and forth through the empty frame stepped the good spirit, arrayed in garments of celestial light, and beaming with angelic loveliness and grace. In her arms she bore a glass which she placed before the wondering girl, and thus she spoke—

"'Maiden! thy wish is answered. Behold the mirror of the soul!' and Isabel looked and saw her soul's image in the glass, and bitterly she wept to see how dim was the light on its downcast face, and how feeble the wave of its faint, yet fluttering wings. But she thanked the kind, guardian angel for her gift, and day after day she consulted her new treasure, and found the image slowly assuming a fairer, purer and lovelier shape. The wings grew bright and waved with a freer and lighter play, and the softened eyes looked up with a frank and grateful smile—for Isabel was gradually subduing her wayward temper and becoming gentle and generous and affectionate.

"Percy Howard watched her with wonder and delight, and at last won from her the secret of the magic mirror. It was he who caused the beautiful marble figure of Truth, with her lamp, to be sculptured, and to support the silver frame, and on her wedding day he led his lovely bride toward it, and bade her see how fairer far 'than any mortal mixture of earth's mould' was the 'divinity within' when once allowed to have free play, unclouded by the petty cares and vain desires of a selfish and worldly life.

"I have finished and you will laugh at my idle legend, love; but of this I am certain—the mirror is more than true. It must be enchanted in some way; for it exaggerates all the deceptions with which art would conceal the defects of nature or the ravages of Time, so ludicrously that many of our friends involuntarily shudder and turn away whenever they are obliged to pass it."

"Lulu!" said Rudolph, drawing her closer to his heart, and imprinting a kiss upon her pure forehead, "you have inherited more than the looking-glass from your ancestors. Her beauty and her virtue are yours; but let *me* be *your* soul mirror, darling!—will you not? I will promise to be faithful in my reflections and true to my trust—and I too shall grow pure in time 'by being purely shone upon.'"

Florence Errington
"An O'er True Tale"[1]

"He entertained an angel unaware."

"A STORY for Graham! Oh, Caroline! you dark-eyed rogue! you little Oriental beauty, 'with sleep in your eye and passion in your heart!' Oh, Anna! with your Siddons lip and glance of fire! do something ridiculous, or pathetic, or sublime, and furnish me material for a story! You are either of you quite pretty enough to follow the whispers of your own sweet will. Do take compassion on a poor storyless author, and give the reins to whim and wonder forthwith!"

Upon this hint, Anna dons at once a boy's cap and cloak, in which she looks bewitchingly beautiful, springs into the street, and shouts at the very top of her rich, musical voice, just as the torch-light democratic procession turn the corner—"Hurrah for Harry Clay!" Three or four indignant torches, with boys attached, sprang after her, but she reached the shelter of the house in safety, and reappeared at the window, beaming with smiles, and looking as innocent and unconscious as if she had never seen a cap or a cloak in her life.

"But, Anna, that won't make a story!"

"Listen to me, Fanny," said a friend, who had overheard my first pathetic adjuration—"I cannot *do* a story; but I will tell you one. So just take your pet seat on this tabouret at my feet, and look right up in my eyes, and leave off turning that restless little head about in every direction, to see what other people are doing, and for once listen quietly and patiently without interrupting me; and pray don't, as you usually do, burst into tears when I expect you to smile, or laugh, and set every one else laughing, just when I think I have touched that sickle,

---

[1] "Florence Errington 'An O'er True Tale,'" Frances S. Osgood, *Graham's Magazine*, February 1845, vol. XXVII, no. 2, pp. 54-56

'will-o'-the-wisp' heart of yours, that never knows what to do with itself. Do you hear me?"

"Yes, darling, I do—and I will be good!"

"Well then—I begin"—

The first time I saw little Florence Fearing she presented as lovely a picture as the imagination of painter or poet ever conceived. She was leaning over the vine-covered balustrade of a balcony, resting one hand upon it, holding a pipe, and with the other shading from the sun her large, light gray eyes, in order to gaze after a brilliant bubble which she had just set floating overhead.

She was the most delicate, ethereal-looking creature I ever saw. The bubble itself seemed hardly more frail or more beautiful. The inmost leaf of a white Provence Rose has sometimes the faint, soft coloring that warmed her delicate cheek; but her lips were red as the wild wood-berry, and her fair hair, of the very palest golden hue, fell round her snowy shoulders like a veil woven of the starlight. So light, so pure, so airily graceful did she look, that I almost trembled lest she should suddenly spread a pair of hitherto invisible wings and vanish from my gaze.

But the bubble burst, and little Florence started and let fall the pipe; it lay shivered at her feet, and the child flew, in tears, to confide her first grief to her mother.

Ah, Florence! many a radiant hope, in after life, sent from thy heart into the sunny world—beautiful and frail as that soaring "circlet of light"—was destined like that to die!

She grew up lovely, loving and beloved; but still so tender and so delicate, that all who saw her trembled. At the age of seventeen she was wedded to the man of her choice. Henry Errington was young, handsome, intellectual and affectionate, although too much a man of the world to be a suitable husband for her. He regarded his wife with fondness and admiration; but she was far too pure, too aerial, too finely organized for his rougher and warmer temperament.

He did not understand her. He did not know what to make of the exquisite fragility, the timid sensitiveness of the creature confided to his keeping; he had wooed and won and wedded the first being that caught his fancy, and now that the plaything was all his own, he could not tell what to do with it. If he had caught a Peri and caged her he could hardly have been more at a loss. Every flutter of her spirit's wings frightened him, as that of the Peri's would. He could learn in time, by constant study, how to *feed* and *clothe* his dainty captive sprite; but there were "immortal yearnings," to which he could never minister.

If his manly voice took unconsciously a colder or more careless tone, those great gray eyes would be raised pleadingly, imploringly to his, slowly filling with "unbidden tears." If he breathed a word of praise, a quick, vivid blush would burn and fade in her pure cheek so suddenly that it startled him. If he frowned, the graceful lip would quiver, and the soft eyes close, as if to shut out some terrible and overwhelming spectacle.

At last he wearied of being kept so constantly on the "*qui vive.*" He tried to persuade himself that his lovely, innocent and affectionate wife was a very unreasonable person, a petted and spoiled child, whom he ought, for her own sake, to discipline a little. And so, gradually, he became careless, and frequented his club, and grew fond of gay parties, and willfully blinded himself to the fact, that his Peri was perishing of cold, and starving for want of food, or, in other words, that his wife's heart needed sustenance and attention and care, quite as much as her physical frame. If "the winds of Heaven should not visit" the *latter* "too roughly," neither should the chilling blasts of neglect or unkindness from her other heaven, himself, be suffered to fall upon the former. But men forget that hearts can break, and that Peris were meant to fly.

In the gay world he met one night a brilliant and impassioned creature, to whom he was, at her own request, introduced. Henrietta Harley had been in early life a warm-hearted, generous and guileless girl; but, disappointed in her dearest hopes, she had become almost reckless of her future fate. She was now, at twenty-five, a gay, witty, capricious and captivating woman, who seemed to have but one object in life—excitement for her restless mind—and that she was determined to obtain at any cost.

Henry Errington was just in the mood to be caught by this contrast to his trouble at home, and he was soon a willing victim to the beautiful and gifted coquette.

The slighted wife caught now and then an echo of the rumors which were circulated concerning them; but she resolutely shut her senses, her heart to the fact, and would not doubt. What could doubt have been but death to one so constituted?

One day an anonymous letter was put into her hand, by a person who hinted that it enclosed one from her husband to the lady in question. With a flash in her eye, unwonted there, and a curve of disdain on her beautiful lip, she tore the packet, sealed as it was, into atoms, and flung them from the window where she stood.

But the poor child was destined, in spite of herself, to know all that she dreaded but to dream.

At a birth-day *fête* given at the country-seat of one of their friends, Florence was wandering alone through the grounds, when she suddenly heard the voice of her husband in a shaded walk close by. "My own beautiful Henrietta!" it passionately began. Florence would not for worlds have heard another syllable. She glided swiftly away by the nearest path, and locking herself into her chamber, gave way to a wild and long-suppressed burst of feeling, so violent that her frail frame shook beneath it, like a flower in an autumn storm.

She never betrayed, by word or sign, the cause of the intense suffering which from that hour was visible in every look. It was only by her private journal that the terrible secret was long afterward revealed. But, day after day, the faint color paled in her youthful cheek—day by day, the spiritual eyes grew more spiritual, and the slight form wore away. Yet she was still exquisitely fair and graceful, and her husband, proud of the wonderful and unearthly loveliness, which attracted all eyes, and thinking that she needed excitement, urged her into society, for which she was little fitted to exert herself.

Ignorant that she was aware of his heart's transient infidelity, he did not think it necessary or beneficial to tell her that he had broken with the brilliant and dangerous woman who had so lightly lured him from his allegiance; but he was now devoted to his evidently suffering wife. The sight of that patient suffering, by touching his pity, had re-awakened his love, and he watched over her as fondly, as tenderly as a mother over her first-born babe.

But the shaft had flown and could not be recalled; the heart was breaking silently, yet surely, and the pure spirit within was already pluming its wings for a flight through eternity.

One night, reluctantly yielding to his wish, which she never dreamed of disputing, she had consented to take part in some tableaux, which were to be represented at their own house. Florence had all day a presentiment that some awful event was about to happen, and as evening approached, she grew more and more timid and nervous, and would have given worlds to have lain her weary head on her husband's bosom in peace and quiet—to have told him once more how fondly, how dearly she loved him—to have thanked him for his tender care, and slept or died, she scarce cared which; but she had not strength to reason with him upon her fears, and so she allowed herself to be dressed, like a victim, for the sacrifice.

She was to appear in the last *tableaux* as the Peri at the gate of Paradise, and in the one immediately preceding, Henrietta Harley was to personate Cleopatra at her toilet, attired by Charmion and Iris.

A brilliant and fashionable circle, of which I was one, had assembled to witness the tableaux, and all had now been represented but the two last.

The curtain suddenly rising revealed the gorgeous chamber of the Egyptian queen, and gloriously did the graceful Henrietta personate the character.

Arrayed in a rich undress, she lay luxuriously pillowed on a splendid couch, with her rich black hair unbound, and partly gathered in the hands of a dark but beautiful girl, who was braiding it with jewels, while another knelt by the couch and tied the sandal on a foot of exquisite proportions. Magnificent drapery, flowers and gems were lavished in rich profusion around, and the whole scene was redolent of beauty, grace and splendor.

"The rare Egyptian" lay in attitude of charming languor. Her dark, eloquent eyes, where love seemed to be dreaming, were half closed. Her full, crimson lips were parted slightly, and her clear brown cheek, "most passionately pale," was pillowed on an arm round and graceful as that of Juno. But the lightly veiled bosom was seen to heave, and, as the first symptom of restlessness, on the part of the performer, had been agreed upon as the signal for dropping the curtain, the radiant vision vanished from our view.

Again the curtain rose. The whole stage was in profound darkness, except just in the centre, where a flood of rosy light from some invisible source illumined a shape, that I held my breath to see. Attired in a transparent, flowing robe, with drooping wings and hands clasped languidly before her, while her fair shining hair fell waiving to her waist—the graceful Peri leaned against what seemed to be a cloud, bending her head and listening with her large lustrous eyes upturned as if in wondering rapture, while a strain of low, delicious melody rose softly on the air and died away, and came again and went, till our very souls came and went with it almost! Never to my dying day shall I forget that thrilling moment! You could have heard your heart beat, so profound, so wrapt was the stillness that prevailed. But at last delight and wonder changed to awe, so motionless, so statue-like she seemed! Not a breath—not a sigh. It was too perfect! almost painfully so. We longed to speak and bid her move! No!—still the vision remained, without the slightest perceptible change.

Bathed in that pale, rosy light, soft, radiant, aerial as a dream of heaven, there was a superhuman loveliness in the picture which might well make us tremble. Suddenly, with a sharp, agonized cry, her husband sprang from his seat and rushed toward her. The terrible truth flashed at once upon us all. She was dead! Life had left her even as she stood "the observed of all observers!" Her husband took the inanimate form in his arms, staggering beneath its light weight, in the enfeebling anguish of the blow. The curtain fell, and we saw her no more till we saw her in her shroud.

Dear, lovely Florence Errington! Thou wert admitted sooner than they dreamed "beyond the gate" where thou hadst stood "disconsolate!"

Mabel.
A German Legend.[1]

LITTLE MABEL'S mother had gone long since to the great fatherland of the universe, and the child, frail and delicate from her birth, pined for the sweet caress and the fond smile that had been the light and the blessing of her infant hours. One day her father—a poor woodman, sad and weary at his work—became impatient as he listened to the moans of the little, discontented girl, who lay at his feet on the moss, with her blue eyes following the clouds that floated overhead, as if asking of them for the spirit of her lost mother. There was a strange, sad, unearthly charm about the child—a timid earnestness in the dark eyes—a grieved, but sweet and tender expression on her lovely mouth, which touched all hearts. Her fair hair was beautiful as moon-light and made a sort of misty halo round her face, and her voice was an Æolian harp, plaintive, pleading, yet passionate in its wondrous and even musical modulations.

"Hush thee, darling!" the father said, "thy cries disturb my soul."

But still the child moaned on.

"See, love, the flowers I give thee! thou shalt braid a garland for thy head."

But the child wept over the flowers, and cried—

"Mother! mother! come down and deck your Mabel's hair."

"Hush thee, sweet," the father said, "I cannot bear thy tears."

But still the child moaned on.

"Look! I have found a bird's nest, and in it are three little ones—the mother bird has flown—take it, my Mabel, and be still!"

---

[1] "Mabel. A German Legend.," Frances S. Osgood, *The Columbian Magazine*, February 1845, vol. III, no. 2, pp. 70-72

"Mother, sweet mother! Come back and bless your little bird. She cannot sing or fly without you. Mother, sweet mother, come back!"

And still the child moaned on. And the father, sad and weary, became angry at last. Still and forever fretting!" he cried in a momentary passion—"the evil spirit take thee, peevish child! Thou makest me weary of my life."

Instantly he felt passing him a mighty rush of invisible wings through the air. Then there was a wild, unearthly shriek that thrilled the father's heart, and Mabel vanished from his bewildered sight.

A low, musical murmur of voices, strangely sweet, awoke the child from the trance into which she had fallen, when the spirit bore, her away. She opened her eyes, but the light dazzled her, and shutting them again, she lay and listened to the song which innumerable voices were warbling all around.

Fair and sorrowing child,
Hear the song we sing thee!
Pleasures bright and wild,
Joyously we'll bring thee.

Would'st thou slumber deep?
Clouds of soft vermillion,
Curtaining all thy sleep,
Drape thy light pavilion.

Fairy wine we'll bring,
In a charmed chalice;
Music sweet shall ring
Through thy golden palace.

Soft Æolian notes,
From our air-harps stealing,
Every tone that floats,
Some fond thought revealing.

Would'st thou gaily ride?
Steeds of spirit fire,
Rich in grace and pride,
Wait thy first desire.

In a chariot proud,
From a glowing cloud
Wrought with magic power,
Thou at midnight hour,

With the reins of light,
In thy snowy fingers,
Swift shalt speed thy flight,
Where the morning lingers;

There thy coursers curbed,
While some wandering mortal
Sees, with soul disturbed,
That resplendent portal.

Dreams his eye can trace
In thy cloud delaying,
Some young angel's face,
From its heaven-home straying.

Fair and sorrowing child,
Hear the song we sing thee,
Treasures rare and wild
Joyously we'll bring thee.

But the light was so dazzling around her that little Mabel could not open her eyes—her heart was home-sick, and she could only murmur in her soft, sighing voice, "Let me go home! let me go home!"

Then she felt a fragrant breath upon her eye-lids, and she lifted them, and looked around, and the sunbeams hurt them no longer. She was in a vast amber palace hung with clouds. Innumerable spirits that seemed to be made of light were about her. Some were bending over her beautiful face and gazing with breathless wonder and delight; others, linked in loving embrace, were floating idly through the air. One graceful group reclining on a cloud were weaving a glorious rainbow of many-colored, luminous flowers.

Their own radiant smiles seemed to lend light to the task, and when it was woven, they rose and flew lightly and swiftly away with it, through a dark vapor beneath them. Mabel looked down and saw them suddenly pause in their flight, to suspend the heavenly wreath for a moment in the air. Mortals beheld and praised its glorious and transparent beauty; but they would not have forgotten it so soon, had they seen, as Mabel did, the benign beings who stood smiling beneath its arch—it was an air *tableaux* which she remembered forever.

Another band of these aerial creatures, with glittering hair and glowing cheeks, were bending round a vast, dazzling urn, full of liquid fire which seemed like the setting sun, and filling little transparent vases with the light. These they bore away, each to a separate place in the sky, and Mabel saw that whenever they paused in their flight, a star suddenly appeared, until the sun had sunk, and the whole heaven was illumined. These airy lamplighters amused the little girl for a while, but she could not forget her home, and still she murmured,

"Let me go!"

Then the spirit, in whose arms she lay, bent on her a look of ineffable love and pity, and breathing on her eyelids, which closed involuntarily, she bore her far away. Softly, like a dream, they descended, and Mabel heard the plash of waters around her, but she felt nothing save the tender, twining arms of the protecting spirit. At length they paused, and the child again awoke; and now she was in "a city of the sea," in a floating palace of red coral, whose pillars, formed of shining "mother of pearl," were wreathed with graceful, petrified flowers of rich and various colors.

The soft murmur of the tranquil waves, as the fairy dwelling glided on its way, blended melodiously with the choral lay of the sea-sylphs—and this was the song they sang:

> Gliding through the waters,
> Singing soft and low,
> Ocean's spirit-daughters,
> Ever gay we go.
>
> Where the sea-star ranges,
> With the gold-tish bright,
> Where the dolphin changes
> In its own strange light,

We'll perfume thy pillow
With our wondrous flowers,
Beaming through the willow,
From enchanted bowers.

We will deck thy ringlets
With our purest pearls,
We will weave thee winglets,
Like our ocean girls'.

Many a strange, sweet vision
Thou shalt smile to see,
Many a dream Elysian,
Night shall bring to thee.

Music wild, entrancing,
From our sea-shells wound,
Timed to light feet, dancing,
Soft shall echo round.

Stay, oh child of sorrow!
Share our glorious glee!
Every hour shall borrow
Some new joy for thee.

But Mabel could not forget her home, and she murmured still—"Oh let me—let me go?" Then there was a low sigh of disappointment around her, and again she was borne away.

This time she opened her eyes upon a superb hall carved in the heart of a solid rock. A chandelier, formed of a single dazzling diamond, hung suspended from the dome and lighted up the interior with a strange and beautiful glory. This dome was supported by columns of jasper, chrysolite and other precious materials, on which, from the capital to the base, were suspended garlands of glittering gems. Countless little dark creatures, with eyes that gleamed like fire, were rustling about—some piling up heaps of diamonds, rubies, emeralds, &c., some dancing fantastic measures on the smooth and glistening floor; some playing ball with jewels of immense size and value, and others, holding small wands of burning gold, muttered mysterious words over bits of some dark substance, which gradually changed beneath the spell into diamonds of rare brilliancy. They did not sing; but they stared now and then at Mabel so wildly with their gleaming eyes that the poor child was frightened, and cried in a voice of grief,

"Take me hence. Let me go to my father!"

But no one answered, and she lay trembling with fear. The child seemed wonderfully lovely in that strange light. Her soft hair shone like amber, and her fair complexion and childish grace contrasted strongly with the swarthy skins and antic gestures of the little imps around her. By and by they began to approach with softened eyes, and they laid their richest treasures at her feet, but she shook her head mournfully and wept. One bound her brow, her arms, her neck, with jewels—another wrought with lightning rapidity beautiful toys of gold and gems— baskets, vases, birds, flowers, cups and urns, and laid them in her lap; but she shook her head mournfully and wept. Mabel was in despair. How should she ever escape from this wild place Oh! if she were only at home once more she would never trouble her poor father again,

"Father! dear father!" she sighed, "where are you?"

Then a soft voice, of heavenly harmony, that sounded like her lost mother's, murmured, "Pray!"

And the fair child knelt in that magic light, with the dark gnomes all around her, and said her simple prayer, and ere the last words trembled on her lip, she was in her own home—in her father's house! with her arms around his neck—blessing and blessed!

The poor man had been severely punished for his momentary sin, for he had passed three days and nights of anguish; but now he wept tears of joy in gratitude for his restored treasure, and Mabel pined no more; but all her life she bore a fairy charm about her; her dreams at night were ever beautiful, and through the day she heard at times such strains of ravishing melody as nothing mortal could breathe.

From cloud and wave, from shell and flower, soft tones stole out, and sunny faces smiled, and bright wings gleamed and vanished seen by no eye but hers. And as she grew in goodness and in grace, it was whispered through the land that her physical and her spiritual nature were ministered to by her viewless fairy friends.

Her being so harmonized in its purity with the natural world around her. The sighing music of the breeze and wave was in her voice—the soft, blue depths of heaven in her eyes—"the wild gazelle of Judah's hills" stepped not with more elastic grace, and the last faint hues of rosy light that decked the dying day were less pure, less lovely than her blush.

Carry Carlisle[1]

CHAPTER I.

"DESCRIBE HER?" I shall do no such thing. Why don't you ask me to describe the enchanting scene before us now, with all its combinations of glory, grace and loveliness. The gorgeous sunset on one side—the perfect rainbow, so delicately brilliant that we tremble every moment lest it should fade—on the other, the soft, balmy, gentle shower, kissing the earth between them. And the tender, golden light, that glistens over all—sleeping, dreaming on the slowly moving cloud, dancing on the distant wave, and clothing wood and wold with ever changing beauty.

No! I will not attempt to describe her—Willis might do it with that tasteful, graceful, dainty, inimitable pen of his; but I "hide my diminished head." Ask *him* if she was not bewilderingly beautiful, with a smile like a sunbeam, a voice like a lute-tone, and a step like the ripple of a wave. She was not made to be described, any more than the sunset shower. Like it, her beauty was rather felt than seen, with all its shade and shine, its smiles and tears, its glow, its grace, its harmony and truth.

> "One shade the more, one ray the less,
> Had half impaired the nameless grace
> That waves in every raven tress,
> Or softly lightens o'er her face!"

I am not going to tell you her real name, she would scold me if I did. I wish you could hear her scold. She does it to a charm! She curls her beautiful red lip with such dainty disdain, and tosses her head with so airy and saucy a grace that you would be half tempted to tease her for the sake of seeing it. But I gave her my word that I wouldn't tell her name. So we must make one up for her.

---

[1] "Carry Carlisle," Frances S. Osgood, *Graham's Magazine,* March 1845, vol. XXVII, no. 3, pp. 128-130

Let us see–Carry Carlisle, will that do? Well then, one moonlight evening Carry Carlisle was leaning languidly against a pillar in the piazza of the Ocean House, at Newport, surrounded by beaux and belles, as usual. Her dress—I am afraid my friend is a little coquettish about dress. She likes to have it correspond with the tone of her feeling—and her usual choice in summer, is a plain, white muslin; now and then as her mood varies, it is a pale rose, or violet, or blue, always exquisitely simple, but that night it was all black. The sleeves reaching just below the elbow were edged with a narrow frill of black lace, and the same trimming was round the top of the dress, which was cut low enough in front to show a throat and part of a neck of dazzling whiteness. It was clasped on her bosom by a golden bird of rare workmanship, and a braid of black velvet confined the knot of lustrous, jet-like hair behind.

"Have you lost a friend?" whispered one of her devotees.

"Yes" she replied with a sorrowful smile, "one whom fought to have valued, and whom I shall never meet again. I have lost *a day!* I have done nothing but dream and sing, and dance and strive for the last eight hours, and now I am weary and sad, and cannot talk any more," and half closing her eyes, which were full of tears, the turned away.

"A rose-bud for your thought, fair lady!" exclaimed Henry Vaughan, a handsome Virginian, shrewdly suspected of being a prime favorite with the beauty.

"It should be a pure white one, then," said Mr. Charles Courtland, half aside.

"And isn't it?" asked a young Irish officer, as Vaughan placed the fair flower lightly in the velvet braid.

Caroline raised her drooping head, blushing and smiling through her tears, like a wild rose through the rain, as she replied, "It was a foolish, idle thought, and is not worth your beautiful bribe, Mr. Vaughan; but you shall have it, such as it is. I was wishing for a fairy to wait on my will, and to bring me some new delight."

"Name your desire, and let me be your fairy!" said Vaughan.

Carry laughed and shook her head. "Oh! you cannot! for I want to be queen of beauty at a tournament, this very night."

The Virginian's dark eyes flashed with the light of his sudden and happy thought.

"And so you shall, this very night. It shall be a tournament of mind. We'll lay the lance of thought in rest. Our will shall enter the lists, and tilt in your honor, sweet queen, and the victor's prize shall be that golden bird! Is it a bird of paradise? It has lighted in Eden just now."

"What made the gold wings flutter, Carry? Was it the beating heart beneath?"

"Come, Courtland," he continued, "you must tune your light guitar. Two hours hence we are to reassemble in No—, each of us prepared to sing or recite an original song or poem, in honor of our sovereign lady."

"No, no!" Mr. Vaughan, said Carry gaily. "You are not to have it all your own way. You lords of creation may appropriate the field of battle to yourselves, but on the 'field of mind', woman shall be your competitor. If any lady-bird can, and will sing, she shall and there shall be no queen, except the queen of song. A wreath of flowers for the lady victor, and the golden bird for the gentleman, the latter to present the crown, and the former the bird, their claims to be decided by vote. Shall it not be so, ladies?" she asked, appealing to those around.

A unanimous assent was given, and the party separated to prepare for the meeting.

CHAPTER II.

I loose the falcon of my hopes,
    Upon as proud a flight
As those who hawked at night renown,
    In song-ennobled fight.—HOFFMAN.

It was a pleasant and picturesque scene. The room was richly curtained, elegantly furnished, and brilliantly illumined for the occasion. The ladies, in gay and tasteful costumes, reclined on cushioned sofas; the gentlemen sat at their feet, and the signal was given for the trial of skill to commence. A magnificent woman in a robe of purple velvet, a widow, with an eye like a midnight cloud, in which the lightning slept, was first called upon for a song. Her classic head; her bare, and beautiful arms; her full, majestic form, were all displayed to advantage, as she leaned with regal grace toward her harp, and playing a wild and passionate prelude, recited rather than sung—

THE LAY OF THE LADY CORINNE.

Oh! tell me at once that you love me no more!
Oh! say you are weary, and hope will be o'er!
But let me not fruitlessly waste my soul's life,
Between doubt and despair, in this passionate strife!
                      Implora pace!

It is time, Heaven knows, that I turn from my dream,
'T is folly! 'tis madness, tho' sweet it may seem,
And if once from your lips your estrangement I know,
I've a pride still at heart, that would rise at the blow.

By all the true tenderness lavished too long
On your bosom, oh, soul of my thought and my song;
By all the wild worship I've poured at your feet,
Oh! soothe me no more with this fatal deceit!

I seek not your pity; 'twill deepen the grief
That can find but in love all it asks of relief;
But tell me at once that I trusted in vain,
And ne'er be those dear eyes bent on me again!

Yon cannot give back the pure bloom of my soul,
The freshness, the light that my wild passion stole;
You cannot restore me the innocent truth,
That once was the glory and pride of my youth.

They are gone, and forever the joy and the bloom,
They are fled like the withered flower's blush and perfume;
If your love has gone with them, oh! listen my prayer,
Let me rest, tho' it be in the calm of despair!
                      Implora pace!

What had Mr. Charles Courtland to do with "The Lay of the Lady Corinne?" Surely those dark, impassioned eyes were bent upon him more than once during the recital, and the rich voice faltered more and more, the more he tried to avoid them.

A pale, plaintive looking youth came next in turn, and sung—with a sweet, sighing voice, "The Wild Wood Rose," a simple love-song, which brought tears to the eyes of several young ladies.

The wild wood-rose was blushing,
　Beside our sunny way;
The mountain rill was gushing
　In light, melodious play;
When last thy vows I listened,
　When last thy kiss I met,
And then thy dark eyes glistened
　With fondness and regret!

The wild wood-rose, o'ershaded
　By clouds, has lost its bloom;
And Love's soft flower has faded,
　'Neath falsehood, grief, and gloom.
The waves, in winter failing,
　No more to music part,
And I but weep, bewailing
　The winter of the heart!

The wild wood-rose, resuming
　Its bloom and beauty gay,
The fitful gale perfuming,
　Again shall grace the way;
Again the mountain river
　Its melody shall pour,
But thou returnest never!
　And Love will bloom no more!

The next was a bright-eyed school-girl, who blushed as she timidly sung,

Too long have I tuned the light strings of my lyre,
To Love's wayward music that weakens the wire,
And now like a bird from a flower-chain free,
My Country! Its song I devote unto thee,
Nor ask that thy laurel the minstrel repay,
While I wake it once more to a loftier lay.

My country, my country! How sweet are the words,
How soft to that melody thrill the light chords!
Like Memnon's, the harp that is laid on *thy* shrine,
Must be touched from on high by a glory divine,
And sound at the sunrise of Liberty's light,
Its holiest strain for the True and the Right!

And dearer to me, than the smile I adore,
Be my fatherland's honor, and fame evermore!
Tho' not unto woman the glory they yield,
To combat for thee, in the counsel and field;
If her voice for one moment thy fame may prolong,
Be thine, only thine, all the soul of her song!

It was Carry's turn next—how pure and beautiful she looked in her graceful robe of white, as she bent over the quaint old Moorish lute, and murmured in those soul modulated tones—

Would you woo a lady fair!
    Woo her like the knights of old!
Love was then an ardent prayer,
    Now 'tis but a question bold.

Then the boy on battle field
    Won his spurs and wore a *name*,
Ere his lady grace would yield,
    Ere her smile he dared to claim!

Not till glory crowned his brow,
    Not till Fame before him went,
Came he, with impassioned vow,
    With his knee to Beauty bent!

Those chivalric feats are o'er,
    Yet there's still a glorious field!
Lovers! To the lists once more!
    Here are arms you yet may wield.

Fancy's fiery coursers rein,
    Trappings gray and golden bit,
Wheel them to the charge a main!
    Couch the glittering lance of wit!

Hope, the herald, cries "good-speed!"
    Love's light pennon floats on high!
Beauty's smile your dearest need!
    Sound the trump! to combat fly!

And now, Mr. Charles Courtland. You desperate flirt! You gay deceiver! It is your turn—what are you looking at the window for, with that beguiling smile? He touched his guitar with a light, and skillful hand, and sang in a clear, bold voice,

"*Sempre lo stesso!*"—the pure stream of feeling,
    May show on its surface all shadows that pass,
The light summer cloud, thro' the azure air stealing,
    The wild flower that bends like a belle to her glass.

"*Sempre lo stesso!*"—the wave may give back, love,
    The bird's sunny pinion, that gleams and is gone;
The stars' silver glory, the breeze in its track, love,
    The faint smile of twilight, the gray mist of morn!

"*Sempre lo stesso!*"—the cloud and the rose, love,
    The skies' changing beauty, the wing's glowing tint,
Break not for a moment the stream's pure repose, love,
    They touch but the surface, and leave not a print.

"*Sempre lo stesso!*"—deep, deep in its bosom,
    Where the world's fleeting pageants ne'er ruffle the tide,
It hoards, like a miser, its own gem and blossom,
    And sings to itself all the love it would hide.

The young Irish officer followed with—

THE LORD OF DELMAINE.

The heiress was lovely, the heiress was bright,

But the heiress was cold as the winter-moonlight,
And she cared not a straw for the penniless wight,
    The gold-hunting Lord of Delmaine!

'T was night, and the lady had gone to repose,
Who sings 'neath her window! "Thy dark eyes unclose!"
With a smile on her lip, Leonora arose,
    For she guessed 't was the Lord of Delmaine.

She leans from the lattice, enraptured he sings!
But hark! On the pavement what love-token rings?
Oh! spirit of mischief! a *penny* she flings!
    Thy guerdon—young Lord of Delmaine!

"Poor, wandering minstrel! For the serenade,
My thanks, with the copper!" gay Leonora said;
He gazed at the money, he gazed at the maid,
    And away stalked the Lord of Delmaine.

And then, Henry Vaughan, leaning on the back of the
sofa where Carry reclined, gave with exquisite taste,

THE FAIRY IN THE SHELL.

Listen what the fairy sings,
    The lost fairy in the shell,
Clear and sweet, her warble rings,
    If you listen right and well!

"Lady, in the coral hall,
    Of my ocean home afar,
Where the waters softly fall,
Where the gold-fish seems a star.

"While the sea-sylphs rocked their child,
    Listen, lady, what befell!
Came the waves with cadence wild,
Whispering round my winding shell.

"Wondrous sweet the tunes they played,
    Well I learned ach soft refrain,
    Mingling in a music-braid,

Half of joy and half of pain.

"Now from the dear home exiled,
It is life and light to me,
Still to sing the music wild,
Born of ocean's grief and glee!

"Lady, when in cradle light,
You, a dreaming baby lay,
Angels floated through the night,
With your smile of love to play.

"Hymns of Heaven they warbled low,
Lady, now, when grief is wild,
Sing to soothe your woman-wo,
All they taught the cradled child!"

The last of the competitors was a noble-looking Spanish boy, who sat at Carry's feet and gazed admiringly upon her half-averted face, while he sang to spirited air on the guitar the following song—

The rose—bring the rose breathing sweet thro' the dew!
The shell—bring the shell, with its soft, carmine hue:
Bring the blush from the cloud beneath morn's beaming eye,
I will show you a blossom of a lovelier dye;
It is Love's dearest flower, and it blooms to beguile,
It was born on the bright cheek of Carry Carlisle!

Let love tune the lute to a light, dainty lay,
Or soft o'er the wind-harp, the southern wind play;
Let the mountain-rill's low, mellow ripple be heard,
Or the faint-warbled trill of the far forest bird;
To music more graceful I listen the while,
'T is the soul-thrilling laugh of sweet Carry Carlisle!

Bring the rarest and purest of gems from the mine,
In the depths of whose heart plays a lightening divine;
Bring the soft ray that beams thro' the blue mist of morn,
Bring the star-illumed wave ere its glory is gone;
I will show you a purer and lovelier smile,
Beneath the dark lashes of Carry Carlisle!

By an almost unanimous vote, the bird was awarded to Mr. Henry Vaughan, and the wreath to Carry.

And as the former—after crowning the graceful girl—bent on one knee to receive from her his reward, their eyes met, and revealed a story which only the little bird heard, and told again to me.

Once More[1]

CHAPTER I.

Oh childhood! frolic childhood!
How beautiful thou art!
With the smile upon thy face
Of the morning in thy heart!

"ONLY ONCE more!" exclaimed the eager boy, as he broke from the fond, imploring clasp of his little playmate—"there is a flower I did not see." And seizing again the yielding branch, which swayed beneath his weight, he swung himself out over the water, and caught with one hand the golden-hued blossom which smiled so temptingly in a cleft of the rock beneath; but just as he seized it, the faithless branch cracked and gave way, and the boy fell backward into the waves, with one despairing look to the shrieking child whose entreaties he had so recklessly disregarded. Suddenly Mary hushed her cry, and fell upon her knees.

Bathed in the soft light of the setting sun, with her hands clasped in speechless prayer, and her fair hair falling over her pure, white dress, she seemed a child-angel, who had folded her wings for a moment to rest upon the earth. And not in vain she knelt. Heaven heard and answered the prayer of that loving and innocent heart. A large Newfoundland dog dashed over the rocks into the sea, and seizing the body, as it rose for the third time, struggled with it to the shore and laid it safely at her feet, with the golden flower half crushed in its cold and clammy hand!

---

[1] "Once More," Frances S. Osgood, *Graham's Magazine*, July 1845, vol. XXVIII, no. 1, pp. 4-5

CHAPTER II.

Oh! lightly was her young heart swayed
By just a look—a word!

Mary Grey and Frederick Lansing, the rash, impetuous little hero of the foregoing chapter, went to the same school. One morning Mary sat, as usual, in her place on the small bench, apparently conning her lesson, but there was a cloud on the fair, childish brow, and the pretty little tender mouth quivered, while she spelled half aloud the words which were too hard for her to read without spelling. At last a tear fell upon the leaf. Frederick, who had been watching her from his desk in another part of the room for a long time, saw the tear, and hastily tearing a scrap of paper from his writing-book, scribbled a few lines with an agitated hand. But how was he to send it? He began to look thoughtful—to plan—to calculate.

"Master Lansing will do his sums correctly to-day, for a wonder," thought the teacher, as he glanced for a moment from his book around the room. A minute afterwards a nut-shell fell in Mary's lap. She started, blushed, and drew from it the tiny scrap of paper; on it was written—"I am sorry I spoke cross to you, darling, forgive me!"

Mary raised her head for one moment, and glanced toward the writer. A sweet smile lightened through her lingering tears—a soft color played on her pale and delicate cheek, and then she bent again over her book, and Frederick resumed his sums, in which he made worse mistakes than ever.

And so dawned the day of a holy and beautiful love—a day that still must set "in clouds of tears," yet "lovely to the last," and rise again in other climes, the purer for that weeping.

CHAPTER III.

"Farewell! a word that hath been and must be!"

They stood together at the gate of that humble, yet picturesque, cottage, wreathed by the honeysuckle, and shadowed by the elm—the noble boy of nineteen, and the fair orphan girl, and the old and sorrow-stricken woman.

"God bless you, my boy! since you will go," murmured the mother, while the slow tears trickled from her faded eyes.

"It is for you I go, mother, and for my precious Mary," exclaimed the boy, struggling with the emotion which almost unmanned him; "a year will soon pass—"

"With *you*, my child, for you are young and full of hope; but with *me*!—" she sighed deeply—pressed her thin lips once more to his—laid her trembling hand upon his head, and turned into her now dark and desolate home.

"Come, Mary!" said the youth, repressing a sob—and together they went to the rock, where she had knelt six years before, with the rosy flowers which he had found for her fallen from her clasped hands, and her eyes raised in childlike trust to Heaven—and there they stood, pressed heart to heart, and took their mute farewell.

CHAPTER IV.

Oh! faithless heart—oh! idle vow!
Beloved to-day—betrayed to-morrow!

Years rolled by, and Frederick Lansing, the young merchant from Maine, had realized a little fortune in New Orleans. Love, too, it was said, as well as Fortune, smiled upon his path. The soft eyes of a beautiful Creole—the wife of a planter—has charmed his ardent heart. Letter after letter had come from his mother, imploring his return, and every stroke of the weekly guided pen betrayed and trembling hand of age and suffering.

"You send me gold; but is it *you* I want. It is your warm and manly heart to rest upon—your gentle hand to guide me down the dreary hill of life. Oh, Frederick! is your mother—is your Mary forgotten?"

On the receipt of such letters, again and again had he resolved to close his business concerns, and return to those whom he had so long neglected; but some new and dazzling speculation would lure him to a longer stay.

"For *their* sakes"—he would say—"It is to place *them* in affluence; and a few months cannot make much difference." But now he no longer made that excuse to himself. The dark eyes of Adèle Delorne, a creature of exquisite grace and loveliness, had fatally infatuated him, and his pure-hearted Mary was indeed forgotten.

CHAPTER V.

Dear reader, look with me through the half-closed blinds into this luxurious apartment. Adèle—the graceful, gifted and impassioned child of the South—is sitting at the feet of her lover—her beautiful head resting on his knee—her black hair unbound, and falling in glossy masses over his caressing arm—a magnificent shawl thrown carelessly around a form as flexile in its willowy wave as the spray that bends to the lightest breeze, yet perfect in all its delicate proportions as that of Hebe at the feet of Jove. Hark! she is singing, and he bends to hear the low Æolian tones—

> Ah! let our love be still a *folded* flower,
> A pure, moss rose-bud, blushing to be seen
> Hoarding its balm and beauty for that hour
> When souls may meet without the clay between!
>
> Let not a breath of passion dare to blow
> Its tender, timid, clinging leaves apart!
> Let not the sunbeam, with too ardent glow,
> Profane the dewy freshness at its heart!
>
> Ah! keep it folded like a sacred thing
> With tears and smiles its bloom and fragrance nurse;
> Still let the modest veil around it cling,
> Nor with rude touch its pleading sweetness curse.

Be thou content, as I, to *know*, not *see*
The glowing life, the treasured life within—
To feel our spirit-flower still fresh and free
And Guard its blush, its smile, from shame and sin!

Ah! keep it holy! once the veil withdrawn—
Once the roses bloom—its balmy *soul* will fly,
As fled of old in sadness, yet in scorn,
Th' awakened god from Psyche's daring eye!

CHAPTER VI.

"We repent—we abjure—we will break from our chain—
We will part—we will fly—to unite again."

One day as Frederick Lansing was about to leave his counting-room, for a visit to his bewitching friend, he received what he supposed to be a letter from home, directed in his mother's hand. He opened the sheet. There was not a line of writing; only, on a small piece of paper enclosed, a rude drawing of the old homestead—the cottage, with its vine—the elm—the wicker-gate—the old well—the little garden at its side.

Frederick passed the touching memento passionately to his lips, his eyes, and wept bitter and burning tears of mingled shame, remorse and tenderness—"My mother I will—I will return!" he exclaimed. And instantly seating himself at his desk he wrote to his lawyer, giving him the charge of his affairs, and requesting him to settle them in his absence. He then went to a wharf and engaged a passage in the steamboat which was to leave next day, and afterwards returned home, resolved not to expose his heart again to the dangerous influence of his enchantress, lest she should charm him from his purpose. But the next morning, when all was ready for his departure, and he had still an hour on his hands, he had time to think of her love—her beauty—her distress—and his stern resolution gave way.

"Only once more!" he said, as he took the road to her dwelling.

He stood by her side. Almost buried in rich and downy cushions—robed in muslin, whose loose folds fell with a wavy, careless grace over her charming form, her black hair braided and bound with gleaming gems—her languid eyes, in which love and sorrow had softened the fire, half shut—a tear still lingering on the glossy lash—thus lay Adèle, half murmuring, half singing, in a tone of touching and upbraiding sadness, the following words:

'T is gone—all gone!—the charm, the dream, the glory!
  Passion has dimmed the light in Love's pure eyes;
Thus was it ever, in all olden story—
  Warned by the flame, the rose too early dies'

I read it in thy tone so light, so altered—
  I see it in thy look, so soon grown cold;
Oh! hadst thou heard the prayer I wildly faltered,
  Love yet awhile his angel-wings might fold.

Could we have kept unstained those glorious pinions,
  Like the pure bird of Paradise, whose flight
Is ever *near* the sad earth's dark dominions,
  But stoops not, lest he soil his plumes of light;

Could we have kept undimmed their primal glory,
  Nor lured to earth the beauteous bird of Heaven;
Ours had been then a proud and peerless story,
  And love so pure had surely been forgiven!

Softened by her unwonted sadness—bewildered by her rare and captivating beauty—Lansing knelt beside her as she sung, and forgot home-duty–mother—all—in the intoxicating enchantment of her presence. The French time-piece struck the half hour. He started up—"I must go, Adèle! I must leave you! oh God! forever!"

With a wild shriek, she threw herself at his feet, and wound her white arms round him with the miraculous strength of passion and despair; but the next instant she relaxed their hold, and fell senseless to the ground, the life-stream trickling from her lips. She had burst a blood vessel! He stooped to raise her—

"False-hearted betrayer! defend yourself!" shouted a voice in his ear. A pistol was pressed into his hand; he raised it mechanically—stunned into unconsciousness by the sight of the ruin he had caused—and fired without an aim. A bitter laugh was heard—a bullet whistled through the air—and Frederick Lansing fell dead at the feet of the injured husband of Adèle.

Ida Grey[1]

As the lone dove to far Palmyra flying
   From where her native founts of Antioch glean
Weary, exhausted, painting, sighing,
   Lights sadly at the desert's bitter stream—

So the worn soul, along Life's wayside faring
   Love's pure, congenial spring unfound, unquaffed,
Suffers, recoils, then helpless and despairing
   Of what it would, descends and sips the nearest
draught.

Mrs. Brooks.

NO—I will not attempt to deny it. She was a coquette—a desperate one—a coquette by nature—yet wild, reckless, wayward and often heartless as she appeared—everybody seemed to love her, and to be happy in her presence. How could they help it? She was the merriest sunbeam that ever gladdened the weary, weary world with beauty and with light. You would hardly have wondered, as she glided by you—"with the step of a fawn and the glance of a star"—to have seen fresh flowers spring suddenly up in the way—

> "Wherever on the happy earth
> Those fairy footsteps fell."

She was a privileged person, too, and was not to be judged by common rules. Everyone was willing *she* should be a coquette—just as they would look indulgently, because of its beauty and its grace, on a lovely, petulant, impetuous and happy little hummingbird, as it darted from flower to flower, sometimes nestling tenderly within them, and sometimes tearing them mercilessly into atoms.

---

[1] "Ida Grey," Frances S. Osgood, *Graham's Magazine*, August 1845, vol. XXVIII, no. 2, pp. 82-84

She was a hummingbird to *hearts*—and nobody could find fault that what all were willing to give, she should be willing to take. The mischief was, that when the pet was disappointed, and did not find all the treasures she expected, the poor heart had to suffer for it like the flower. But then she was so bewitching, so sportive, so affectionate, so radiantly beautiful, that you could not help letting her have her own way with you and everybody else. But I am not going to describe her. I shall merely remark—*en passant*—dear *Mr.* Reader, to *you*, that she bore a decided and remarkable resemblance to your latest idol. And to you, dear *Miss* or *Mrs.* Reader, that she looked exceedingly like—yourself.

And now, of course, you are both satisfied that she must have been the most enchanting woman in existence—if not, the fault must lie in your taste, and not in my spirit of accommodation. After all, if she let too many love her, and shared with too many her heart, it was because she had more heart to spare than most people, and did not grudge it where it could give pleasure.

Oh! but it was very idle, and foolish, and mad, and indiscreet, and improper, and undignified, and unwomanly! I do not deny it. I do not attempt to defend her. But I pity her from my soul. Poor little thing! Poor, dreaming, deluded little humming-bird! She had not found the right flower yet, and so she wasted, ray by ray, and tint by tint, the light and bloom of her existence—with an ineffable yearning in her soul, constantly asking for something purer and holier and deeper and mightier than all the love she found.

Unhappily she seemed to think that the whole world was made for the accommodation and amusement of her own sweet self. And the world returned the compliment, and insisted that she was made for it. Both were mistaken—particularly the world. Never was there a being less fitted for its heartless conventionalisms than she. She ought to have been hidden in a sea-shell, singing the music taught her by the winds and waves, or shut up in a Night-Blowing Cereus, only when day had gone down to steal out and commune with the stars and her own soul. Then, perhaps, she would have found out what she was made for, before it was too late.

Ah! well, dear Ida! we will not blame you now. You have rued too dearly the folly, the recklessness, the waste of heart and time, which were your sin.

At twenty-four she was a widow, and still a child in heart and manner. There was no teaching her to grow old—to be sedate like other folks. There was no scolding her into propriety—a child she was, and a child she would remain. An impulsive, thoughtless, passionate and charming child—utterly incapable of stopping to think long enough to look forward or back; living, loving, laughing, in the present, a light and willing "waif upon the stream"—without a fear or care, but with a heart and mind that needed and waited only the divining-rod of that subtle enchanter Love, to yield up treasures untold, undreamed of; and he, the enchanter, was near—nearer than she thought.

She had loved her husband in her way—that is, with that playful, caressing, yielding, docile affection which she seemed ready to bestow on all who awoke her gratitude by kindness. But he was a sort of cypher in the world— scarcely more a cypher dead than alive. She could not rest upon his heart or look up to his mind, and when he died, she wept inconsolably for a week, and in a fortnight seemed almost to have forgotten that she had ever been married. Ah! now, don't call her names! I know you are doing so and it seems to me as if I had cruelly put her own helpless little self upon the paper, and thus exposed her to your harsh censure—and I feel an almost irresistible impulse to put my hand tenderly and cherishingly over what I have said of her—the darling little humming-bird!— and so guard her from your cold rebuke!

I cannot help it! In spite of her coquetry—her folly—her vanity—her sauciness—she was just the dearest, loveliest and most winning creature that ever breathed the breath of life! It is a fib the sages tell, when they say everything has its use. There were some things intended by nature to be utterly useless—for instance, the butterfly and Ida Grey. They were just sent into the world to be happy and beautiful—"only that and nothing more." There are useful people, and grave people, and sensible people enough in the world already. Let the butterfly and Ida go! We will not clip *their* wings. Ah! if only *Love* had let her go!

I have thus far written of her as she appeared to the little world of friends of whom she was at once the idol, the pet, the torment. How little did we guess the strange, wild, passionate inner life, which that seemingly light and gay child of frolic and caprice was leading?

The last time I saw her in the gay world, was at a small but brilliant party, given by her friend Mrs. M—, about eighteen months after the death of Ida's husband. That night she was in one of her wildest moods, and as her soft joyous laugh,

> "without any control,
> Save the sweet one of gracefulness, rang from her soul,"

all eyes were turned toward her, for all acknowledged a magic music in that laugh, which was perfectly irresistible. But afterward, as I sat watching, in the dance,

> "Her airy step and glorious eye,
> That glanced in tameless transport by,"

I saw her suddenly pause—the jest died on her lip—her gaze was riveted for an instant on a distant part of the room—and then blushing deeply, and faltering some hurried excuse to her partner, she left the dance and took a seat by my side. There she remained still and pale, looking down upon the rich bouquet which lay in her hand upon her knee. I asked if she were ill. She shook her head but did not speak. About fifteen minutes had thus passed, when our host approached with a remarkable looking man, whose face once seen could never be forgotten, so wonderfully spiritual was its expression. As Mr. M— asked permission to introduce his friend, Ida raised her head—

> "Bloom to her cheek—fire to her eyes—
> Similes to her lip—like magic rise!"

I never saw so sudden and so lovely a change, except perhaps of a mid-summer's afternoon, in heaven, in the midst of a shower, when the glorious sunlight suddenly slashes out through the clouds, lending then all a radiant rosy hue, and filling the whole atmosphere with beauty and with joy.

Only a few, formal words passed between Ida and her new acquaintance; but I remarked that his keen gray eyes were bent with singular earnestness upon her face, and though his manner and expressions were merely and coldly courteous, there was a peculiar *depth* in his tone, which only some strong emotion could have given it.

From that evening Ida Grey was seen no more in society. She shut herself up in her little study, and read and wrote, and saw only her most intimate friends, for six months, and then she entered the convent at —. On parting with her friends she gave to each some graceful token of affection—and with me she left the dearest of all, her journal, some extracts from which will best illustrate that inner life of which I have before spoken.

"I have seen him at last!—him of whom I have read and heard so much. For several days before our introduction there had been a presentiment at my heart that stilled and awed it—a presentiment that something was about to happen which would affect my whole future life, here and hereafter—the *one event* of that life—and when we met I was so strangely affected that I could hardly speak. His own manner, cold and calm yet courteous, only added to my embarrassment. I knew that he had heard much of me, and had sought an introduction, and I cannot tell why, but I was foolish enough to expect that he would meet me frankly and cordially, and that we should be friends at once. But no! he was strangely distant. We spoke but a few formal words, and then we parted— parted! ah no! we shall never part again! Our souls are one forever! Yes! cold and careless as he seems, he loves me—or *will* love me! I feel it in my heart. He belongs to me, to me alone. I do not care to see him again in this world. It is better not, for his earthly nature is another's. He is married. His wife, they say, is cold and does not love him. They need not have told me this—I should have known it; for I believe that a true, heaven-inspired love is always met by its counterpart. If destiny had willed her to love him, he would have loved *her*—and do I not know that he is *my* destiny? She will find hers hereafter. No we will not meet here anymore, or if we do we will not reveal our souls. I can wait—for have we not eternity before us—and here there would be so much to alloy the poetry and beauty of our love. Eternity, what a sense of weariness that word has always until now conveyed into my soul! Impious as it may seem, I could almost feel it stretch its wings and yawn in an involuntary and prophetic fit of ennui at the thought; for I could not conceive—since in this world I so soon weary of everything and everybody—since I had never known a pleasure which I cared to have last, and had never been contented in my life—I could not, I say, imagine how, in another world, I was to employ eternity so as to be happy and contented. But now I see clearly that there is indeed a heaven for me as for others. Ah! not even eternity can be too long for our love! My soul has so much to say to his, and his so much for mine! and we shall have so much to do—for, blest ourselves, we shall then feel the sweet necessity of blessing others—and so much to learn, too. He, with his wonderful, lightning intellect, which even *here* seems godlike, will there receive all those divine truths of which this world is but the primer, so much faster than I, that he must needs teach *me* himself! Ah! will not that be the true luxury of heaven? to love and to learn of one who loves me! I do not think I ever *felt* my soul before—and now all life but the soul-life is nothing to me. How purely intellectual and spiritual is the beauty of his face and head! He thinks, he talks, he writes, he looks as never did man before!

. . . .

"We have met again. I am grieved. I am not so happy as I was. He has written to me words of almost divine passion. Ah! why did he do this? Why could not he too wait—as I would have done—with that serene and dear consciousness in my soul, that we are, not 'all the *world*' but all *heaven* to each other? And yet it is sweet to read those thrilling words. He feels, as I knew he felt—that God has sent him to me—to calm my heart—to spiritualize my being—to wean me from the world. How perfectly already he sees into my soul. He understands, he appreciates me as no one else does or can. He sees at once all my faults, all my errors, all the good, all the beauty that is in me— and to him alone of all the world would I wish or dare to confide the secrets of my past life. It is his fate to love me—it is mine to love him—and we can and must forgive all the past in each other, for the sake of the sweet present and the glorious future. How utterly has he merged all self in his beautiful and happy love for me! and what an exulting consciousness is mine that I am worthy of it! in spite of all the past. Ah! if I were not worthy, Heaven would not suffer him to love me—to sacrifice that proud and noble and mighty heart upon a false and worthless shrine! Yes, darling of my life! soul of my soul! you do me that justice—you believe, you know, as I do, that my nature is pure, and that even were it not, your love and mine would make it so! Yes! he has generously forgiven me for all the wrong I did him ere he came; for all that levity in my past life which was treachery to him; and every tone of pardon and of love, and every glance of his soul from those dark, keen, eloquent eyes, melt more and more my heart, and make it more and more worthy of his own. . . . . .

"He bids me tell him that I love him, as proudly as if he had a right, an unquestionable, an undoubted, a divine right to demand my love. Ah! with what grand and simple eloquence he writes! Yet I would that he had spared me until our spirits meet in Heaven!"

I shall make but one more extract from this singular journal—it is a poem, dated several weeks later than the above.

If our poor little Ida could only have been allowed to remain in that soul world into which her pure aspirations had wasted her—to remain there with her one hope for the sustenance of her spirit—she might yet have been happy; but the following verses will show that her divine nature at times "bent to its clay," like others.

TO—.

Had we but met in life's delicious spring,
   When young romance made Eden of the world,
When bird-like Hope was ever on the wing,
   (In *thy* dear breast how soon had it been furled)

Had we but met when both our hearts were beating
   With the wild joy—the guileless love of youth—
Thou a proud boy—with frank and ardent greeting—
   And I, a timid girl, all trust and truth:

Ere yet my pulse's light, elastic play
    Had learned the weary weight of grief to know,
Ere from these eyes had passed the morning ray,
    And from my cheek the early rose's glow;

Had we but met in life's delicious spring,
    Ere wrong and falsehood taught me doubt and fear,
Ere hope came back with worn and wounded wing,
    To die upon the heart she could not cheer;

Ere I, love's precious pearl had vainly lavished,
    Pledging an idol deaf to my despair;
Ere one by one the buds and blooms were ravished
    From life's rich garland by the clasp of care.

Ah! had we *then* but met—I dare not listen
    To the wild whispers of my fancy now!
My full heartbeats—my sad, drooped lashes glisten—
    I hear the music of thy *boyhood's* vow!

I see thy dark eyes lustrous with love's meaning,
    I feel thy dear hand softly clasp mine own—
Thy noble form is fondly o'er me leaning—
    It is too much—but all! the dream has down:

How had I poured this passionate heart's devotion
    In voiceless rapture on thy manly breast!
How had I hushed each sorrowful emotion,
    Lulled by thy love to sweet, untroubled rest:

How had I knelt hour after hour beside thee,
    When from thy lips the rare, scholastic lore
Fell on the soul that all but deified thee,
    While at each pause, I, childlike, prayed for more.

How had I watched the shadow of each feeling
    That moved thy soul, glance o'er that radiant face,
"Taming my will heart" to that dear revealing,
    And glorying in thy genius and thy grace:

Then hadst thou loved me with a love abiding,
    And I had now been less unworthy thee,
For I was generous, guileless and confiding,
    A frank enthusiast—buoyant, fresh and free.

But now, my loftiest aspirations perished,
    My holiest hopes—a jest for lips profane,
The tenderest yearnings of my soul uncherished,
    A soul-worn slave in Custom's iron chain,—

Checked by those ties that make my lightest sigh,
    My faintest blush, at thought of thee, a crime—
How must I still my heart, and school my eye,
    And count in vain the slow, dull steps of Time.

Wilt thou come back? Ah! what avails to ask thee,
    Since Honor, Faith, forbid thee to return?
Yet to forgetfulness I dare not task thee,
    Lest thou too soon that *easy lesson* learn!

Ah! come not back, love! even through memory's ear
    Thy tone's melodious murmur thrills my heart—
Come not with that fond smile, so frank, so dear—
    While yet we may—let us forever part!

Leonora L'Estrange[1]

CHAPTER I.

The Question.

"MAMMA–MAMMA!" cried little Rose Russell, a beautiful child of nine years old, scampering into the breakfast-room, with her blue gingham sun-bonnet in her hand, and her satchel on her arm—"mamma, you said I should have the fancy-ball, if I brought home the History medal to day!"

"And so you shall, my precious child—but let me put on your bonnet quick, or you will be late to school!" and the fond mother smoothed back the glossy, golden, clustering curls, tied the strings under the dimpled chin, kissed the sweet, smiling mouth held up to her, and bade her darling hasten on her way.

Little Rose's heartbeat quick that day as she took her place at the head of her class in History; but unfortunately, in her eager agitation, she missed—as they say at school—in the very first question put to her. The question passed on unanswered, till it reached the last child in the class. It was a new scholar—a plain-looking little stranger, in deep mourning, with large, wistful, dark eyes, sallow complexion, and straight black hair, hanging neglected about her ears.

As she gave the answer promptly and correctly, the wild eyes lighted up, and a faint tinge of red stole into the hitherto colorless cheek; but, directly, the lashes drooped again—the light—the glow faded as suddenly as they came, and she took her place at the head with an air of listless languor, for which the other eager little aspirants tried in vain to account.

Poor Rosy's blue eyes sparkled through their tears with momentary resentment at what she looked upon

---

[1] "Leonora L'Estrange," Frances S. Osgood, *Graham's Magazine,* October 1845, vol. XXVIII, no.4, pp. 151-154

almost as an usurpation of her rights; but when she saw the sorrowful expression in her school-fellow's face, her ready sympathies were at once excited in her behalf, and before the lesson was finished, she found herself almost as much interested in her rival's success as in her own.

At the last question, Leonora, the young stranger, hesitated—evidently, for the first time, at a loss.

"Now," said Rose, to herself, with a triumphant glow on her fair sweet face, "I shall be at the head again—and I shall have the ball!"

She looked up eagerly, exultingly to her companion. Leonora's cheek was intensely pale—her lips trembled, and her dark eyes flashed with the earnest excitement of the moment.

The fresh, young heart of Rose was touched and awed, she hardly knew why, by this strange enthusiasm in one so little older than herself. With a generous impulse of interest and pity, she suddenly cast down her eyes, and softly whispered the answer to her companion.

But Leonora L'Estrange, young as she was, had too proud a spirit, and too noble a nature, to avail herself of such assistance—and while tears of gratitude sprang to her eyes at this proof of interest in the lovely little girl by her side, she instantly requested the teacher to pass the question to Rose.

CHAPTER II.

The Ball.

A child's fancy-ball! What a scene of enchantment it was! There was the gay and beautiful Rose, sportive and happy as a butterfly, flitting through the throng with silvery wings and snowy robe, in personation of the fairy queen Titania, surrounded by her elfin court. There was her modest little cousin Lucy Howard, with her lovely auburn curls and hazel eyes, dressed as "Little Red-Riding-Hood," and there, too, was the handsome and graceful Henry Herbert, an English boy of sixteen, in a sailor's costume. But who was the little gipsy-girl, with her wild elf locks, and lustrous eyes, and picturesque attire?

It was the orphan, Leonora L'Estrange. Harry had just laid his hand in hers, to have his fortune told, when I entered the room, and in a sweet, earnest voice, the child-sybil murmured the following words:

In youth's most rare and radiant hour,
    Ere thou hast learned the world's cold art,
Thou 'lt press Love's glowing passion-flower
    Close to thy proud and ardent heart.

But round the high-born English boy,
    The world shall weave a thousand wiles;
And faithless to that flower of joy,
    Thou 'lt lightly leave its tears and smiles.

"Come and waltz with me, you little gipsy wonder!" said Harry, laughing, as he withdrew his hand to wind it round her waist, and away they whirled to the bewitching tune—Titania with the saucy Puck, Red-Riding-Hood with a Greek Brigand, and the dark eyed Gipsy with the Sailor Boy. Pair after pair tripped after them—but suddenly the waltz changes into a march, to which they move to the supper-room—and there, on the centre-table, stands a noble Christmas-tree, lighted with colored lamps, and hung with bon-bons and *bijouterie* of all descriptions, all of which are to be drawn as prizes in a lottery.

Before the party broke up, I observed that Harry and Leonora had exchanged prizes. He had placed upon her slender finger a little emerald ring, and she had twined, in the button-hole of his sailor's jacket, a beautiful flower of colored spun glass.

"But I must have a kiss from my fairy-queen before I go," exclaimed the bold and light-hearted boy, as he lingered behind the departing crowd. The little coquette in miniature showered her sunny hair over her eyes, and put her dimpled hand upon his lips—but Harry stole the kiss from her glowing cheek nevertheless.

The gipsy girl looked back from the open door in time to see the accident, and her little heart heaved, she scarce knew why, as if the slighted flower had been itself.

CHAPTER III.

L'improvisatrice.

With her dark locks flung recklessly back from her forehead; her cheek colorless as that of a statue: her large, black, glittering eyes raised wildly to his own, and her proud lip curled, yet quivering with irrepressible emotion, Leonora L'Estrange stood by the side of her high-born lover, and listened to the hesitating avowal of his engagement to one of wealth and station far superior to her own.

For a few moments after he had ceased to speak, she remained motionless, almost breathless, overwhelmed by the suddenness and intensity of the blow. Gradually her eye and cheek kindled into a wondrous and passionate beauty, and snatching a guitar, which lay by her side, she threw herself on a low cushion at his feet, and, after a wild and faltering prelude, poured forth the following song, in a voice whose power and melody thrilled his very soul:—

> Dost deem my love so light a boon,
>   That thou mayst throw it idly by—
> As winds may waft a flower at noon,
>   And leave it low at night to die!
>
> By all my spirit's pain and strife,
>   By all the hopes that now reward thee,
> Thy proudest boast, in after life,
>   Shall be that I—*that I adored thee!*
>
> Not mine the brow to droop in grief,
>   Not mine the soul to pine alone!
> The pang, though passionate, is brief—
>   The doubt is o'er—the dream as flown!
>
> The love of one so light of heart
>   Were scarcely worth one fond regret;
> All is not lost, although we part,
>   The pearl in Life's cup sparkles yet!

Some cords there are in Love's sweet lyre.
    Thy false hand knew not how to play:
Some gleams remain of Feeling's fire—
    Thou couldst not all my heart betray!

I'll win a name from wayward Fame.
    That thou sha't bear with fond regret;
The heart thy tablehood left to shame,
    Shall find some glorious solace yet!

Yes! By this moment's pain and strife,
    By all the vows I have restored thee,
Thy dearest boast, in after life,
    Shall be that I—that I adored *thee!*

A mere child in years—she was but sixteen, and without beauty or culture—there was still a magic about the youthful improvisatrice, which was almost irresistible to one of Herbert's ardent temperament. It was the magic of genius and feeling and untaught grace, acting upon a soul fully capable of appreciating those rarest, richest gifts of Heaven.

Leonora's mother—an Italian—had been very beautiful; but her child, born in the ungenial north, seemed only to have inherited the impassioned poetry of her mother's southern heart, without that glowing loveliness of countenance which had won the vows of L'Estrange. It was only when inspired by the enthusiasm of genius, that her sallow cheek and large dark eyes kindled into the lustre and bloom which had charmed all hearts in her mother's classic face. Her hair, black and glossy, but short, hung in wild, gipsy locks about her ears, and her plain and simple dress was too carelessly arranged to be becoming.

In spite, however, of these disadvantages, Herbert was charmed again to his better self, as he met those eyes flashing through indignant tears, and heard that full, rich, sweet, yet faltering voice, where Love and Pride seemed striving for the mastery, like the lute and the nightingale in the olden play. He drew closer to her side, and, as she finished, would have pressed her to his heart; but Leonora repelled him with a look, and, rising suddenly from her seat, was gone ere he could speak.

And so they parted—he to his wealthy bride, and she to her poor and widowed mother—he to meet the world's applauding smiles, and she to struggle with its frowns, with a heart wrung but roused, and a genius that needed but the impetus given it by pride, and the lesson taught it by grief, to soar and sing even at "the gate of Heaven!"

CHAPTER IV.

A Mystery.

Years had gone by. Herbert had left the city to pursue his profession, the law, at the South, where the fair rival of Leonora resided; but his engagement to her was of only short duration. Some gambling debts, which he had rashly contracted, had come to the knowledge of the father of his betrothed, and that gentleman had forbidden him her presence, until he could bring proof that they had been paid, and that he had wholly given up play for a year's time. Hoping to settle the debts at once by some fortunate throw, and not content to wait patiently until the profits of his profession had enabled him to pay them, he had gradually become still more deeply involved, until at last, wretched, restless and humiliated, he returned to his lodgings one night with a desperate resolve, and was about to raise to his lips the fatal draught, which would have sealed his guilt, when his eye was caught by a packet lying upon the table. Hoping, he scarce knew what, he opened it and found—a receipt in fall from his creditors—accompanied by the following note, in a carless, but peculiarly graceful handwriting:

"From one, who will not claim repayment, until Mr. Herbert's professional prosperity shall be such as to warrant it."

Now, indeed, he had incentives to energy and industry. Love, honor, gratitude, and an earnest desire to know to whom he was so deeply indebted, all were at work to prompt his future course.

He made a solemn vow, and kept it—that he would never gamble again. He returned to his profession with renewed ardor, and soon became distinguished for his talent and integrity.

Could he have forgotten his first love—(and who ever forgets it?)—he might have been happy in hope, honor and prosperity—but the shadow of Leonora L'Estrange still darkened his heart at times, and not even the glad and beautiful image of his betrothed could rouse him from the trance of sorrow and remorse into which Memory threw him then.

CHAPTER V.

Rose Again.

Beneath the vine-wreathed veranda of a house in a far southern city, leaned a fair and graceful girl, with her pale, golden hair looped in picturesque waves around her head—in earnest converse with our hero.

"And oh, Harry," she exclaimed, in soft, yet eager tones, "you have made us all so happy by your return! Father seems to love you again just as well as ever, and I—" the sweet voice trembled, and the dark blue eyes raised for an instant to his own, were obliged to finish the sentence. "But stay!" she continued—"I have a note to show you. It is from an old school-fellow of mine, who, with her uncle, Count Vellino, has lately taken up her abode among us, and whom, as she was out when we called, I have not yet seen—but of whose wealth, and wit, and grace, and goodness, we hear most wonderful accounts. The poor in the neighborhood look up to her as to some divinity; the exclusives pronounce her the most recherché being in their circle; and the most intellectual men of the day throng around her with the worship they would pay to Minerva, if she were suddenly to appear in the midst of them—"

"You little enthusiast! show me the note."

"Here it is."

And Herbert read as follows:—

"I was grieved that I did not see you, dear Rose, and should have returned your visit to-day, if it were not one of my dark days. Do come to me this evening! If you are as happy a little humming-bird as you used to be, I am sure you will hum away my heart-ache. You will meet only a few mutual friends. Bring any of yours you choose.

"Yours faithfully,

"L."

Herbert grew pale and red by turns as he read these simple lines. They were in the same handwriting that had accompanied the receipt from his creditors, twelve months before!

"Tell me her name, dear Rose!" he said, in as calm a voice as he could assume.

"Ah, no! I shall do no such thing—for you must go with me, and see if you will recognize her. I should be too jealous to let you go, if she were not engaged to Mr. —, the distinguished senator from —. I don't believe you have seen her since she was so high!"

And Rose playfully held her little hand about two feet from the ground. Herbert caught the hand—kissed it, and hurried away to prepare for accompanying her.

CHAPTER VI.

The Meeting.

In the softly lighted reception rooms of Count Vellino, the rarest and richest gems of classic art were arranged with a taste so pure, so faultless, that it was evident a woman—and a woman of genius, and of exquisite refinement—had presided over the decorations. As our hero entered, with the fairy Rose Russell on his arm, the grace and harmony of the "*tout ensemble*" so affected his mind, ever alive to the poetry of nature and of art, that he heaved unconsciously a wistful sigh of pleasure, and of undefined regret.

The count came courteously forward, and led them toward a lady, who was so absorbed in conversation that she did not notice their entrance. She was gloriously beautiful! Her black hair was braided into a graceful crown above her brow; her large, dark eyes were full of fire; a rich yet delicate color played upon her cheek; while her queenly form was displayed to advantage in an enchanting attitude of languid repose. As she turned, and Herbert met the full glance of those magnificent eyes, his heart told him at once who it was. Wondrous as was the change in the face and form before him, there was no mistaking the eloquent and inspired beauty of expression which had won his boyish fancy, years, long years ago. It was, indeed, his early love—the gifted Leonora L'Estrange. And she, too, recognized him, and, for a moment, seemed disturbed; but she recovered herself, and, after affectionately greeting Rose, she gave him her hand with a quiet dignity, which at once and effectually checked all outward show of emotion on his part.

She soon after introduced, to them both, the gentleman to whom she was about to be married, a nobly intellectual person, who commanded respect and admiration from all around him.

Herbert stood apart, living over again his last interview with Leonora, and listening once more to the song she had sung in her passionate grief and pride—when the playful voice of Rose recalled him to himself—and with one half-smothered sigh to the irrevocable past, he started from his reverie.

In the course of the evening he had a *tête-à-tête* with Miss L'Estrange, in which he referred with great embarrassment to the generous assistance which had saved him from dishonor and death.

She could scarcely restrain her emotion as she listened; and when he had finished, smiling through her tears, she said—

"Do not talk of it anymore! You shall give the sum to my pet-school, since you insist that you owe it to me; but you are very vain to suppose that I could take such an unwarrantable interest in your welfare!" and, with a faint blush, she glided from his side.

Soon after, she was led by her uncle to the harp, to "improvise" a song, and oh! with what a charming expression and grace she breathed the simple words which follow:

> I have been true to all I loved—
> To Honor, Love and Truth!
> These were the idols of my soul,
> In my believing youth—
>
> And these I worship fondly still,
> With vows all pure and free;
> Alas! that truth to *them* involves
> Unfaithfulness to *thee*.

CHAPTER VII.

The Emerald Ring.

And years again flew by. Herbert had married his blooming Rose, and was now a lonely widower, and Leonora had long been the idolized wife of Mr. — when one night, as the former sat by his desolate fireside, musing sadly over the past, a little sealed packet was handed to him. He opened it with a strange and sorrowful foreboding. It contained only a little emerald ring—a child's ring! He remembered all. He thought of the lovely flower of glass, which had been shivered at his feet by his own careless impetuosity, and a tear, which he did not care to check, fell upon the gem—the token of his boyish love. The next day the papers announced the death of the beautiful and accomplished Leonora —, aged 28.

Kate Carol;
or
Glimpses of a Soul[1]

I SHALL, let Kate speak for herself, reader mine, in a letter to Grace Greenwood. You know Grace!—no? Well at all events you have read and heard of her; for she is just now the pet of Fame;—and well does she deserve of that most capricious of goddesses all favor and all honor,—the darling!

KATE TO GRACE.

I promised you a letter, Grace, and thanks to a large organ of conscientiousness, a promise always haunts me like a spectre until it is performed. I wonder what form a fib will take in Heaven. You know I am *almost* a Swedenborgian, and fully coincide with that wonderful being in his belief, that all our thoughts, wishes, purposes and emotions will take a shape there, fair or foul, from their own beauty and deformity:—that we shall thus create our own scenery, architecture, and surroundings, and that these will vary according to our moods,—that they will grow more and more beautiful and grand as our souls progress in wisdom and in goodness, and vice versa—in fine, that we shall each be in our element. Ah! how grateful is that thought!—that there we shall do what we will and not what we *won't!*—that there, if we *choose*, the atmosphere around us shall be all love and loveliness and divine harmony:—and what *woman* will not choose? I have met with *men*, who owned that they did not care for music, and others, who professed to hate children, and others still who did not need to be loved. But I never met a woman, who had so fatally lost the silken clue, which is to

[1] "Kate Carol; or Glimpses of a Soul," Frances S. Osgood, *The New York Illustrated Magazine of Literature and Art*, March 1846, vol. III, no. 3, pp. 33-36

guide us back to our divine home, and so I reverse the Oriental creed, which supposes that there are no women in Heaven, and believe—don't you?—that there are none in Not-to-be-mentioned-in-ears-politedom, to use your own funny word.

Was it in print that some gentleman gave, as a reason for the former belief, the passage from Scripture,

"And there was silence in heaven for the space of half an hour," and that a lady archly replied, "That must have been because there were no men to talk to?"

Yes—there we shall do what we will. For instance if my spirit longs intensely to pour forth its voice in a paean of love and joy and thanksgiving, I shall not be obliged, instead, to "cabin, crib, confine" it in a love-story for a magazine,—"to coin my mind," as your friend Willis happily says, "for my daily bread." I need not grind a hand-organ, while I pine to be playing the lyre;—I need not chirp in a cage, when I want to be waving my wings in the free air and pure light of the Empyrean—I need not grovel as a glow-worm, when I am burning to beam as a star;—I need not "*come*" at the bidding of a pump-handle, when I am crazy to *go*—a mountain-spring, dancing, laughing, talking to myself, in short having my own way in the woodlands.

What misery, what humiliation to be forced to measure "thoughts that breathe and words that burn," like a rose-colored ribbon, by the yard-stick of a publisher to weigh a "sunbeam of the soul" against a guinea—and—to be "found wanting!"

Ah, Grace! Necessity is indeed "the Mother of Invention" in my case,—and a cross, old, tyrannical curmudgeon of a mother she is!

"Oh, I see her old and formal, fitted to her petty part,
    With a little hoard of maxims preaching *down* a
daughter's heart."

Why, she positively forbids her restless and impulsive child the recreation she especially covets—a frolic with the fairies by moonlight, and keeps her confined to fashionable saloons with her hair braided and a Polka bow, or to a Chesnut street promenade with a *sack* on!

Does *your* Muse wear a *sack?* —"No, indeed!" I hear you exclaim, with an indignant curve of that Sybil lip.

I envy *you*, Grace. I cannot say as you did, so charmingly in your last letter—do you remember? I will recall the whole passage, for I love to recall it,

"With an 'intense and burning,' almost an unwomanly ambition, I have still joyed in your success and gloried in your glory, and all because Love laid a reproving finger on the lip of Envy. I cannot tell you now much this romantic interest has deepened—

> Now I have looked upon thy face,
> Have felt thy twining arm's embrace,
> Thy very bosom's swell,
> One moment leaned this brow of mine
> On Song's sweet source and Love's pure shrine,
> And Music's magic cell."

What a beguiling little flatterer you are! No—I cannot deny it,—I *do* envy *you;*—for your Muse "wanders at her own sweet will"—by mossy rock and murmuring rill,—while mine is only a trained carrier-dove, with a *billet doux* tied to her wing, and all because I am poor and have others dependent upon my talents. I do not sympathize, Grace, in your disdain of riches. No! I would have wealth,—limitless wealth!—that not a low or sordid care might be upon my mind,—that I might give—give—give—(oh! that luxury of luxuries!) forever!—that I might surround myself and those I love with all that is rare and beautiful and glorious in Art and Nature, and that I might have time and leisure to think,—time to be good and great,—that my soul might, as far as possible, be ministered to in all its diviner wants and instincts, and grow like a flower beneath the lavish sunbeams and showers of Summer.

I have been called too dainty—"*too particular,*" as the landladies say. I do not see how any one can be too much so. I own myself excessively fastidious in all my tastes and wishes, even in my food;"—yet in this, as in dress and in all things else, there must be, to please me the most perfect simplicity. I would have life a dream of poetry, a strain of tender and entrancing melody,—yet would I not that it should be wholly free from sorrow and trial;—ah no!

but the suffering should be that of the spirit, which purifies, and not of the body, which vexes and humiliates, not those petty, wearing, degrading cares, which make us feel our insignificance, but some glorious grief, some tempest of thunder and lightning in the soul, which shall test its godlike strength, and for which it must put on all its divine panoply—of Power and Purity and Truth; or else some sorrow—still and calm and deep as night—through which shall steal serener lights than that which gilds the gaudy of Pleasure and Prosperity.

But to go back—on paper—to the heaven of Swedenborg. Have you not, dear one, when in the neighborhood of the *evil eye*, felt your heart instinctively shrink and shut like a flower at the approach of rain, and have you not found your spirit withering, wasting, starving, hungry and cold and forlorn, when surrounded by those, who did not care for or sympathize with you? *There*, Grace, we shall be irresistibly drawn into a sphere, to which only those, whose souls chord with ours, can be admitted, so that Life will indeed be music there.

A friend of mine has sent me a beautiful gift,—an inkstand. On a white marble pedestal are two vases of blue porcelain, each surmounted by a golden bird, with wings unfurled for flight, and behind these vases rises a graceful branch of leaves, in carved gold, among which was placed the following very complimentary poem, by the giver, entitled,

KATE'S INKSTAND.

This azure well hides many a sprite,
Unseen by aught but poet's sight,
And waiting for the poet's spell,
To draw them from this azure well.

With playful din, the airy rout
Are softly warbling "Let me out!"
And ope' and shut their plumes of light,
On tiptoe for expected flight.

Hush, hark, dear Kate! How sweet they pray
That thou'lt let loose each prisoner fay!
They vow they'll dance a gay quadrille
Around your pen's tip, if you will.

Now Fancy to the brim springs up,
While rainbows wreathe the graceful cup,
"Twas from my wing," she whispers low,
"You stole that fairy pen, you know!"

While Beauty o'er the dark, blue water
Floats as of old,—Heaven's radiant daughter!
Love bends his rose-wreathed bow at me
And Grace demands her *home* in *thee.*

Wit speaks and diamonds fall, for words;
And Music tunes her sweetest chords;
And Feeling's tear bedews thy pen;
And Truth, her mirror, mends again.

With such a troop thy will to wait,
Oh! tune thy lute, with heart elate!
And gay or sad its music be,
The world will share its grief and glee.

Isn't it pretty and fanciful as the gift which accompanied it?

And so, Grace, you are sitting for your portrait to our gifted friend—and I am to have it? What a treasure! Be sure you look up with those superb, Spanish eyes, just as you do while reciting. Let "the queen in your nature now put on her crown," and twist your dark hair *a la Sybil,*—and love me dearly, and believe me

Always your own

KATE CAROL.

GRACE IN REPLY.

Thanks, dearest Kate, for the glimpse you have given me into the inner life of your ever fresh and beautiful nature; for I will not call what you have written me, a *letter.* It were blasphemy against the young Deity, Love, and the nine heavenly damsels.

And so you are about to be enveloped in the rosy cloud of Swedenborgianism. I regret to acknowledge myself in a pitiable state of ignorance, as to this modern faith. I only know it to be something exceedingly beautiful and poetical. There is a sort of intellectual aristocracy about it, that somehow impresses me. I think that you can safely trust to your heart's own free impulses in this matter. Only let all inquiries be made in the spirit of meekness, and be sure and forsake not the altar of youth, till the ashes of its extinguished fires are scattered by the winds of unbelief. This is comparatively a new doctrine, but if it fills the yearning void in your nature—satisfies your spiritual want, receive it, joyfully and fearlessly. Old creeds are too often as iron zones about us, restraining the very heavings of our free-born hearts,—and creed-makers have too often presumptuously said to the soul, with all its divine energies and glorious aspirations, "thus far shalt thou go, and no farther."

> See yon bold Eagle toward the sun
>   Uprising free and strong—
> And see yon mighty river roll
>   Its foaming tide along!
> Ah, yet *near earth* the Eagle tires,
>   Lost in *the sea*, the river;
> But nought can stay the human mind.
>   'Tis upward, onward ever!
> It yet shall tread the star-lit paths
>   By highest angels trod,
> And pause but at the farthest world,
>   In the universe of God!

This, can I say,—I have seen the faith of Swedenborg, sitting as a quiet angel in the inner sanctuary of many pure and lofty natures. Not they whose wisdom and greatness are lauded by the world, but

> They upon whose daily paths
> God's smile serenely lies,
> They who can look up into heaven
> With clear, unquailing eyes.

With such I should not grieve to see you classed.

Ah, no, dear Kate, the "male malignants" couldn't shut us out of Heaven if they would, and wouldn't if they could. Only think what kind of singing they would have, forever without the air!

Oh ho, what odd ideas of the next world people have, commonly. "Heaven lies about us in our infancy," says Wordsworth, "and we *lie* about Heaven in our maturity," adds a facetious friend of mine. Some Theologians bolt and bar the gates of Paradise, never allowing a poor mortal a peep into its hallowed precincts; while others condescend to be very communicative, and tell us all about it, just as though they had sometimes been sent for, Mahomet-like—been on an exploring expedition through the promised land.

As for me, I have scarcely yet shaken off my early ideas of a state of eternal fixedness—a dull "Sabbaday," with no play after sundown; a vast court, paved with gold, where good people sat in high-backed chairs, and solemnly repeated the Westminster Catechism, varying the exercises occasionally by singing "Old Hundred."—But I am dwelling on a delicate subject—what would our minister say!

Ah, how cruelly you flatter me—how unmercifully you pelt me with roses! You say you envy me, that my muse "wanders at her own free will," &c. Alas! my dear lady, I have no muse, now-a-days. I have let her out, to a gentleman that writes poetical advertisements for a tailoring establishment. Why, bless your heart, I had no use for her—no one heeded her harpings.

But I will dismiss this wild humor, and write with a more becoming seriousness. Under your own playful words lies a world of deep, sad meaning. Heaven comfort its own stray bird, with the earth-fettered wing!

Would you learn how another has known the wellsprings of her mind's young existence dried up before the time;—has seen her sun of hope, not set in night, but clouded at its rising?

Well, there was one who at early womanhood, felt her entire spirit pervaded with an ever-growing sympathy, a devoted love for her kind;—within whose heart a thought of freedom, universal, God-given freedom, burned like living fire! There were those who told her that she possessed a nature volcanic in its fervent and passionate power. Then she resolved to heed not the allurements of ambition—to silence the soft pleadings of selfishness, and lay all her gifts on the altar of a pure and holy philanthropy.

She heard the fearful whispers of the oppressed—the low murmurs of "God's poor," and sought to give them free, and bold, and startling utterance in strong and indignant verse. She saw a band of true, brave spirits, who disdaining to barter honor for base gold, or to kiss the dust for popular favor—seeking not to be blest of those whose blessing is a curse, cheerfully and earnestly offer their lives at humanity's great need. They were few, and their mode of warfare somewhat rough; they fought rather with the battle-axe of Richard than the sword of Saladin.

> Their music was no lulling strain,
> Drawn from a silken chord—
> Their light no moonbeam, that wakes not
> The insects of the sward,
> But the thunder of high Heaven,
> And the lightning of the Lord!

It was for a while the joy and glory of her, of whom I have spoken, to weave the battle-song, and the prophetic lays of victory for the great moral warfare of our time. But suddenly she beheld those she loved standing aloof–many hearts turned from her, and she was named stern, harsh and unwomanly. They told her that she had resigned a world of light and beauty, for a realm of dreams and glooms and shadows. They saw her sitting in the night of a high and solemn thought, but they marked not its stars— they heard not the singing of its nightingales! But in their blindness they prevailed, and that one pure purpose was crucified.

Then came to her another hope, less lofty, but still most dear. She would pour her soul out in song—song which should live in her country's heart, and whose echo should linger around the grave where moldered the breast from whence it sprung, the lips through which it flowed.

Then did she weave a wreath of soul-flowers—Lilies, pale with the intense passionateness of an over-tasked spirit—Roses, tinged with "ruddy drops," wrung from a wounded heart—Star-flower-hopes, Violet-remembrances, and young love-buds, just glowing into warm life. With those, she sought the shrine of Poesy—sought it throughout her land, and found it not, and the wreath withered on her hands.

Then they came to her and said that she must steep her words in honey, and array her thoughts in silk, and pen soft love-tales for the frivolous and the shallow. Well, she yielded again, and bowed her proud neck to the yoke appointed for that poorly-paid, slightly esteemed, servant of servants, and American authoress. Now, school-girls may shed their ever-ready tears over her pages, and interesting young gentlemen may sonnetize her, but she may scarcely hope that the mourner will look heavenward, cheered by her life-giving words,—or that the heart of the strong man may thrill as her bold, free thoughts flash before him like swords, out-leaping from their scabbards!

But I have written myself into a sad humor, and for fear that I breathe into you the breath of my blue mood, will say *adieu*! Let us part as we oft have parted. There— your spirit's arms are thrown close, close around me! I *felt* that spiritual kiss! 'Twas given half lovingly, half playfully, as though some mischievous Fay, in flitting by, had lightly touched my forehead with a rose-bud.

GRACE GREENWOOD.

Glimpses of a Soul.
----No. II.[1]

DO YOU know, Picciola, I almost tremble as I write. There is some conspiracy against me. I scribbled in all faith to Grace Greenwood the other day, and she, as usual, replied at once in an impromptu sunbeam of a letter—when lo and behold! both epistles in print in a magnificent Monthly in New York! Had they been sent by Magnetic Telegraph, I should have accounted for this miracle, by supposing, either that Mr. L. L. had been cutting the *conductor,* or that the lightning messenger had been *cutting capers* and got *off the track,* gliding into Messrs. Taylor & Co.'s office by mistake or invitation, instead of soberly pursuing "the even tenor of its way;"— but they were *not:*—they were sent by the regular honest, decorous, old fashioned, well-behaved mail,—the mail, that, everybody knows, is always true to its *post;*—the *only* male indeed that could ever be depended upon for faithfulness and sobriety of conduct,—and how, in the world, they came into the *devil's* hands, at the printing office,—the—"devil only knows." That *sounds* naughty; but it isn't.

However "let bygones be bygones"—we will manage better this time;—we will send ours by express, and if they get *in* press, why—we will "submit, with a *good Grace,"* literally;—for has not Grace Greenwood submitted.

But I have a thousand things to say to you and only an hour to say them in. There ought to be a heart daguerreotype for our letter-writing, Picciola, and the sunbeams of Love and Truth should be its calligraphists. There *is,* in heaven, I suppose; for the things of earth are but shadows of those there, and Monsieur Daguerre probably saw, in a dream, I speak in all reverence,—some

[1] "Glimpses of a Soul.----No. II.," Frances S. Osgood, *The New York Illustrated Magazine of Literature and Art*, June 1846, vol. III, no. 6, pp. 83-84

seraph adjusting the glorious lens in the celestial machine, and took his idea from that.

I *do* believe, dear, that all beautiful and noble inventions and discoveries, as they are called, are thus originated, thus heaven-inspired,—Don't you?

And by the way, this theory, that everything in Heaven has its symbol upon earth,—that all that is and all that happens in this world has a spiritual significance, has suggested to me a singular similitude.

You know, it is said, that by a sort of daguerreotype process, our persons and actions are constantly being painted on the walls around us, and that there may be *made,—how* is not yet known,—some chemical composition, which, properly applied, would bring to light apparitions of ourselves and others, that would teach us lessons more impressive, than all the sermons of Experience;—a sort of external conscience, which by bringing our portraits in various moods and employments hourly before our eyes, would force us to—"walk chalk"— as they say out West. Now I sometimes have a nervous fancy, and it recurred this morning, that each individual among us is surrounded by just such a wall,—only spiritual and therefore invisible,—which, by the agency of spiritual light, is silently and incessantly absorbing impressions not only of our actions but our thoughts, wishes, emotions—to be, in another world, by an instant's magic power, perhaps by a glance from God, revealed to us and to the assembled hosts of Heaven! Ah! if only that spiritual light, that sunbeam from the source of all Beauty and Truth would keep whispering "a chiel's amang ye, taking notes!"—*Wouldn't* we be good, Picciola? *Would* we ever be cross, or spiteful, or jealous, or weak, or—or— anything that a child of Heaven should not be?

Could I have heard that "angel's whisper" yesterday,— what a storm of sorrow and indignation might have been lulled within my soul, by the "still small voice" of its divine reproof! Would to Heaven, sweet Halcyon, that you could impart to me the secret charm of your unchangeable serenity of soul!

Now, with your wonted, loving interest in all that concerns your wayward friend, I hear you ask—"And what, my Kate, could have caused so wild a tempest?"

I won't answer that imagined question; but I will sing
you, instead,

A LOVE SONG.
From the Arabic.

"To night I'll wear around my hair,
   This string of fragrant beads," I said;
I loved to breathe the enchanted air,
   That o'er thy gift, in perfume, played!

The only amulet were they
   I cared to keep, all ill to charm:
Within that magic round, could stray,
   One only wrong, one only harm!

One only wo, they could not ward,
   One only wrong, they could not right!
It was—thy falsehood, my adored!
   And *that,* ah, Heaven! I learned to-night!

I tore them madly from my hair;
   I slung the faithless token by;—
Yet still its fragrance fills the air,
   And still I breathe its perfumed sigh!

And thus I flung from off my soul
   Those vows too sweet—those chains too dear;
And thus their memory backward stole,
   To bind my heart and charm mine ear!

Somebody, looking over my shoulder, suggests that
"walk chalk" is a slang expression and therefore vulgar. I
deny the "*therefore*"—and to me, do you know! the phrase
sounds rather poetical than otherwise from the quaint
picture it presents to my mind as I have used it. I don't
know what was meant by it originally; but *I* mean *this—I*
fancy the Powers Supreme having chalked out, on the
great map of Life, the "way we should go," and I fancy
innumerable beings trying to keep to the mark,—as I have
seen children at play try to step on certain figures all over
a carpet, and avoid others, their touching which would

oblige them to pay a forfeit.—That's what I mean by "walk chalk"—and I think it a pithy and not inelegant expression.

I have been re-reading some of Mary Hewitt's classic and beautiful poems. Their memory lingers in my mind like that of a graceful marble statue or an exquisitely cut cameo. I was about to say that I wondered she was not more popular as a writer, but I do not; for as the cameo and the statue could find but few in our as yet *raw* country, with taste sufficiently cultivated to appreciate them,—so must she, at present, appeal only to the few for a just acknowledgment of her genius. How like her poetry she is! As a friend of mine said of her—she looks "up to an Epic" and she has the majestic tread of a Juno.

A mutual acquaintance sent me yesterday some verses addressed to her, which I will copy for you below:

> "Dear Mary, it was *almost worth the storm,—*
> Whose earliest breath turned weaker hearts away
> Like weather-vanes,—to test how true, how warm,
> How noble was thine own,—that in the fray
> Still rallied, with most loyal trust and truth,
> Firm at my side, 'mid wrong, reproach, and truth!
>
> Too pure to doubt,—too strong to swerve or change,
> How should *they* blush before thy friendship's power!
> Serenely true,—the clouds, that they estrange,—
> To *thee endear* the shrinking, drooping flower;
> And Sorrow's storm across my bright day thrown,
> Makes the grieved heart *more* cherished by thine own."

But what a letter! Punish me by writing a still longer one, darling, and I will "kiss the rod." Heaven be with you.

Always your
Kate

Philadelphia, Nov., 1846

Glimpses of a Soul.
----No. III.[1]

KATE CAROL TO -----

MY FRIEND of friends, please let your heart submit to become "the ocean to the river of my thoughts," while I tell you of a new pleasure, which I have just experienced. A distinguished editor from your city, the most original of originals, at our first meeting this afternoon, charmed and alarmed me by a quiet but severe lecture upon not calling things by their right names. You know how utterly indifferent I have always been to the praise of the press unless certain of it's emanating from a candid critic whose judgment I could respect. You know how heartily tired I am of newspaper *puffs* and drawing room flattery. Imagine then my mingled delight and dismay—when I spoke of some one's kind notice of a "poem" of mine—to hear the refreshing tirade which followed—"Did he call *that* a poem! Then he is doing all he can to corrupt the public taste. What right has he so to confound names? I thought Milton's "Paradise Lost" and Homer's "Iliad" and Byron's "Childe Harold" were *poems*. I thought *Shakespeare* was a *poet*.

Is there to be no distinction between them and the pretty versifiers of the present day! *I* have written verse. But I do not presume therefore to call myself a poet—and when asked 'by the Editor of the Poets and Poetry of America,' *which* of my poems he should insert in that preposterously misnamed book, I replied, 'I do not come under that head, sir. I am not a "poet of America."'

So he went on fixing upon me all the time those cool, serene, blue eyes, in the most tranquil manner imaginable. But instead of being confounded, as he perhaps intended I should be, I clapped my hands in

---

[1] "Glimpses of a Soul.----No. III.," Frances S. Osgood, *The New York Illustrated Magazine of Literature and Art*, September 1846, vol. III, no. 9, pp. 135-138

ecstasy at the novelty of being for once "cut up," and, thanking him with all my heart, promised with due solemnity not to "corrupt the public taste" any more.

Do you know, dear one, this epistle is a bit of generosity at the expense of justice, for I don't owe *you* a letter, and oh! I am as said even to *look* in my writing desk, there are so many unencumbered ones, ready to stare me out of countenance there. The truth is, I don't feel in the mood to-day for any being in the wide world but just your own individual darling, genial self and nobody else shall have me by—but it's vulgar to swear even *our* graceful and classic oath.

When I last looked into the said repository there was one letter in the elegant handwriting of sweet Mrs. S.— full of sportive tenderness and grace, in which, among other kind and playful things, she says, "I miss you much, my Kate. I miss your laugh and your love. I miss your books and your beaux. I miss your inconsistencies, which were yet so very consistent. I miss your talk which was so different from everyone else's."

Isn't it delightful to have one's *inconsistencies* missed? Then there was another from Mary —, redolent of her own truth and nobleness—and another from our American Di Vernon—G. G.—all fire and dash and spirit and irresistible fun, where she complains so drolly of having to *help* at home that I could not help laughing in spite of my sympathy with the poor little murmuring muse condemned for a time to fold her wings and become a reluctant Cinderella. She closes her complaint characteristically as follows—"Let Patience have her perfect work—I wish she had *mine!*" There is another still from the P. o C. I., who somewhat saucily says—"Your letter in the H. J. was *you* talking—but I don't like to have you talk to all Loaferdom."

"Sir! it was to *Japonicadom* I talked!"

There are more letters—more reproachful spirits still in that haunted desk—and sometimes my troubled conscience hears a low, confused and tender murmur of complaint issuing thence that chides my long delay, but they shall all be appeased by and by. And last not least there are some graceful stanzas accompanying a New Year's gift—a rich case containing a very beautiful pen and paper-knife. I must copy the verses; for all, that pleases your Kate, pleases you.

TO KATE.

When in thy hands, this happy knife
  Divides some poem's precious leaves,
Disclosing dreams of cloudless life,
  Such as thine own pure genius weaves,
Ah! let thy soul's celestial smile,
  Like light, around my image play,
And bless my lonely wanderings, while
  They brighten in that heavenly ray.

Thus, as the Persian poet sings,
  A happy clod of humble earth,
Perfumed the air with fragrant wings,
  Which all believed of roseate birth.
A passer by in wonder cried
  "Some Rose—transformed by magic—blows!'
"An no!' the modest clay replied,
  "But I have once been *near* the rose!"

I am sad to-day, my friend!—Who, that pauses in the whirl of Life to *think,* can be otherwise? I believe, if it were not for the dear ones around me, I could brave all trouble—all sorrow—with an unbroken spirit; for mine is one of those yielding hearts, that, like the reed, is swayed and bent by every breeze—and *therefore* breaks not. But when I think of *their* future, in this hard, cold world, I tremble and shrink and shut my eyes with a feeling almost of terror. Daily, nightly I pray that God, in his infinite mercy, may spare those sensitive and pure hearts the ordeal that all must pass, who live to maturity—that He will transplant those delicate buds while yet their dewy bloom is fresh and bright, ere yet the worm has found the core, that so they may blossom in Heaven undimmed by the earth-stain of remembered infirmity and grief. Is the prayer a vain and almost impious one? And ah! if it *be,* will He not forgive it for the sake of the wounded spirit, from which it arose?

To me, the Shunamite's reply to the question of the man of God—"Is it well with the child?" would be no effort of Piety and Duty. I could answer—"It *is* well!" with a grateful and unfaltering heart.

Last week, for the first time, I saw "Ion" performed. How exquisitely beautiful it is both in design and execution. I would rather have been the author of that poem than of any that I have ever read. Not by any means that I think it the greatest or most powerful; but that it could only have emanated from a mind pure, noble, and unworldly. The part of Ion seems to me almost too perfect, too sacred for any mere mortal actor to assume. Anderson, however, appears to appreciate it, and certainly performs it better than any other *man* now on the stage. Were I a young actor, I should want to keep myself "unspotted from the world," were it only for the express purpose of fitting myself to represent that lovely and noble character.

Sivori, too—the enchanter has been here—and somebody sent him the following impromptu on his magic violin:

A Dryad's home was once the tree,
    From which they carved this wondrous toy,
Who chanted lays of love and glee,
    Till every leaflet thrilled with joy:
But when the lightning laid it low,
The exiled fay flew to and fro,
Till finding *here* her home once more,
She warbles softly as before!

You have heard I suppose that Miss Barrett—the poetess of the nineteenth century, the sainted recluse—the unapproachable sensitive plant—is *married*!! and married to Browning too—the wonderful poet! What a beautiful union, and yet what an astounding piece of intelligence!—They say he is the first gentleman she has seen for years; for you know she has been long a secluded invalid. It reminds me of the Arabic tale of "the fated fairy prince," who was permitted to break the chain and to wake from her wondrous trance the enchanted child of the palace. By the way Miss Barrett owes me a letter, and now she can never pay the debt, since, in becoming Mrs. Browning, she has

"Suffered a soul-change
Into something new and strange."

You have never read Browning's poems I believe. I would hand you my treasured copy which our friend W— sent me from England only that I want to be with you when you read them and share your wondering delight. There now, don't raise your dark eyes so appealingly to Heaven—I plead guilty—I *am* selfish—but that lovely drama—the "Blot on the Scutcheon," is too exquisitely touching for one soul alone to bear the burden of its beauty. It would overwhelm you—you *must* share it with me. But meanwhile I will treat you—now and then—to a taste—rich and rare of this delicious poetry—this Helicon of the heart. Just try this—from "Pippa Passes" the first poem in the volume. Pippa a young girl of Asolo employed in the silk mills, springs from her bed, on New Year's morning, and thus closes a beautiful apostrophe to Day— that day, which is to her the only holyday in the year:

"Day! if I waste a wavelet of thee,
Aught of my twelve hours' treasure—
One of thy gazes, one of thy glances,
(Grants thou art bound to, gifts without measure,)
One of thy choices, one of thy chances,
(Tasks God imposed thee, freaks at thy pleasure,)
Day, if I waste such labor or leisure
Shame betide Asolo, mischief to me!
But in turn, Day, treat me not,
As happy tribes—so happy tribes! who live
At hand—the common, other creatures' lot.—
Ready to take when thou wilt give,
Prepared to pass what thou refusest;
Day, 'tis but *Pippa* thou ill-usest
If thou prove sullen—*me*! whose old year's sorrow,
Who except thee can chase before to-morrow!
Seest thou, my Day? Pippa's, who means to borrow
Only of thee strength against new year's sorrow!"

How inimitably naive and tender and simple is the whole sportive appeal! how playfully earnest! how touchingly childish and sweet!—"See'st thou, my Day?"—

Can't you hear the eager little darling—with her silver voice and lovely smile! Could the day, so appealed to, have helped being beautiful and gracious?—Could it have helped falling in love with the maiden? Did not its smiles and blushes burn in the air as it passed, and did it not linger long and lovingly in the west ere it looked its last farewell? I will give you another sip from our Ganymede's god-given chalice in my next.

Yes! the soul of Browning is a fitting mate for that of Elizabeth Barrett. There must have been a conjunction of two glorious stars in Heaven on their wedding-day. I have been reading "Lucretia," and I deeply regret having done so. The character is a most horrible and unnatural one, and not all the enchanting grace and purity of the two youthful lovers, Perceval and Helen, can compensate for the unpleasant impression it leaves upon the mind.

"The New Timon" is a more genial and satisfactory work—unequal indeed, and at times prosy in expression, but abounding in gem-like lines of exquisite beauty and finish. It contains passages too of great power, and of rare pathos and truth.

Have you seen that singularly brilliant and melodious yet most unaccountable poem, "The Flag-Star of Even?"

"With her sails, wet with glory, her cordage of light,
Oh! bravely she rides on the billows of Night!"

As dear Mrs. Child says, "The loveliest dew-drop may reflect the loftiest *star*," so I suppose I may be allowed to quote. Are not the following lines very beautiful?

"Hark! soft to mine ear from the Flag-star of Even,
The sweet and unwritten Ionic of Heaven
Like the footfall of Thought in the halls of the soul,
Like the coming of twilight upon me it stole!
Like the music of wings it filled all the air,
And I knew in my soul that a spirit was there!
As glistens the dew in the heart of the flower,
So deep in My heart lies the thought of that hour."

All this certainly gives most delicious "promise to the ear"—but hardly keeps "it to the sense." I wonder if Mr. Ernest Dillaye takes opium. I wish he would give us another exquisite poem and take the trouble to find out just what he means by it beforehand. With a little *more* of *"earnest delay,"* he might make a sensation.

By the way—the *Home Journal*—which copies this "Flag-Star of Even" is becoming quite a starry paper. It is decidedly the most brilliant weekly going—don't you think so? I do selfishly hope that Morris and Willis may live forever, (at least *my* forever,) and always edit a paper. The former is inimitable, unapproachable, in his dainty dashes and flashes of wit and sentiment, and the latter, apart from his own talent, must certainly have some magnetic attraction for genius in our sex—for the more spiritual stars in the literary firmament—the Marys and Graces, the Fannys and Annies—seem to cluster around him as their prototypes do around the great luminary of Heaven.

I have just heard a good anecdote, which I have never seen in print. George the Fourth's upholsterer refused to work for him on Sunday. His Majesty, with whom he was a favorite, asked him his reasons. "Because," said he, "to-day I have an order from the King of Kings." George appreciated the beauty of the sentiment, and the principle of the man, and rewarded him accordingly.

I took our little dark-eyed M—, cold as it was, to Fairmount yesterday—we had a glorious walk. On our return at dusk, suddenly M— exclaimed—"Oh! look, Mamma! its just beginning to *star!*" The gypsy has always an idiom of her own. I am told she strongly resembles in every way the youngest child of Fanny Kemble Butler—and gifted as she is with genius and its invariable accompaniment, sensibility—she almost frightens me at times, not more by her strange and wayward willfulness and recklessness of character than by the impulsive and impetuous fervor which her every word, look and action betrays.

D— asked me to-day for a love-song to set to music. I had been reading a French story, the heroine of which interested me very deeply—and I wrote the following lines suggested by her fate.

CORINNE TO HER LOVER

Had I essayed, with wanton art,
To lure you and ensnare your heart,
Your falsehood would but justice be,
That now is treacherous wrong to me;

But well you know I shrank, in fear,
From tones that grew too deeply dear,
Your falsehood would but justice be,
That now is treacherous wrong to me;

But well you know I shrank, in fear,
From tones that grew too deeply dear,
And trembled with prophetic dread,
When Passion warmed the words you said!

And you recall my shame and awe,
When first your burning dream I saw,
And how I turned nor dared to look,
The soul of fire that lit your look;

And how I struggled day by day,
With love that won too wild a sway,
And how at last before his shrine,
My very *soul* I dared resign.

And *you* betray me! *you,* for whom
I braved that saddest, darkest doom;
Oh, God! take hence thy child, nor spare!—
Thy wrath,—*not his,*—my heart may bear!

"Don't *wish* but *do*"—said a capital book to me today, entitled "Dignity of Human Nature," by —, I have forgotten whom; but what an invaluable aphorism is that for us dreamers by daylight! "Don't wish but do." Every separate letter should be formed of diamonds, set in a tablet of gold and worn upon the heart as an amulet against Idleness and Discontent:—yet if *I* wore it, I should wish, and oh!—

If I were a bird, that sings,
    In the joy of a spirit free—
If *wishes* were only *wings,*
    How soon I would be with thee!

As the lark soars at sunrise alone,
    While the air with his rapture rings,
Thy smile I would meet, mine own,
    If wishes were only wings!

It is only when sorrow like this,
    A shade o'er my spirit flings,
It is only when thee I miss,
    That I wish—my wishes were wings!

Lately I have tried to *wish* less and to *do* more. I feel that there is a nobler, loftier poetry in action than in thought. By the way, you must read that thrilling poem by Anne C. Lynch, in the *Opal*, entitled, "Wasted Fountains," and let me meanwhile quote to you my favorite stanzas,—

"Up and onward! toward the East,
    Green oases thou shalt find,
Streams, that rise from higher sources,
    Than the pools thou leav'st behind;

Life has import more inspiring,
    Than the fancies of thy youth,
It has hopes as high as heaven,
    It has labor—it has truth

It has wrongs, that may be righted,
    Noble deeds that may be done;
Its great battles are unfought;
    Its great triumphs are unwon.

There is rising, from its troubled sleep,
    A low, unceasing moan;
There are aching, there are breaking,
    Other hearts beside thine own!"

Isn't that noble poetry? I promised to send you the additional verse to my "*Laborare est orare.*" It is the only poem that I ever bestowed any *labor* upon—and the only one that I ever rewrote with corrections—with one exception. As it is appropriate to the present subject, you shall have it, tho' it is bad policy to give it now, after *hers.*

Labor is Health! Lo! the husbandman reaping,
How thro' his veins goes the life current leaping!
How his strong arm, in its stalwart pride sweeping,
True as a sunbeam the swift sickle guides!
Labor is wealth—In the sea, the pearl gloweth,
Rich the queen's robe, from the frail cocoon, floweth,
From the fine acorn, the broad forest bloweth,
Temple and statue—the marble block—hides!

Droop not tho' shame, sin and anguish are round thee;
Bravely fling off the cold chain that hath bound thee;
Look to yon pure heaven smiling beyond thee;
Rest not content in thy darkness a clod!
Work—for *some* good—be it ever so slowly!
Cherish some flower—be it ever so lowly!
Labor—*all* labor is noble and holy;
Let thy great deeds be thy prayer to thy God!

I had a strange dream last night of the "Day of Judgment." I thought that Time, for the first and last *time,* appeared in Heaven amid the assembled universe. The Shape was shadowy yet sublime, with an expression of profound resignation on the pallid and majestic features, and in his hand he carried not the scythe which was his attribute on earth, but a vast and wondrous Magic-Lantern, and from it, as one by one the people came up for judgment, on those adamantine walls of Eternity were reflected in successive pictures "the deeds they had done in their time;" and when *my* frail shape appeared, magnified upon that stupendous tablet, I trembled and turned one imploring look upon the Father,—a silent prayer that I and those who loved me might be spared that sorrowful sight!—then, feeling that the fearful review was inevitable, I covered my face with my hands, but an Almighty and invisible power drew them away and with a shriek of intense suffering I awoke. Ah! how thrilling was that dream!—Is Memory indeed to be our punishment hereafter? I think I could prefer *any* other. Will there be no

"Letheon" *there*? No "Nepenthe" for the *soul*? But *you* will love me, dear one, whatever revelations of my life that awful Lantern may show—and so with a blessing, good bye!

KATE CAROL.

Athenais[1]

[1] "Athenais," Frances S. Osgood, *Graham's Magazine*, September 1846, vol. XXX, no. 3, pp. 141-143

CHAPTER I.

In her utmost lightness there is truth—and often she
speaks lightly;
And she has a grace in being gay—which mourners
even approve;
For the root of some grave earnest thought is
understruck so rightly,
As to justify the foliage and the waving flowers above.
E. B. BARRETT.

WHAT COULD he wish for more? The girl was graceful,
high-bred, intellectual, and singularly beautiful, and yet
Mr. Sydney Hazard was not satisfied; only because his
kind uncle had chosen for him, instead of allowing him
the right of judging for himself; and therein did Mr.
Sydney Hazard's uncle show himself an exceedingly
impolitic and injudicious old gentleman. He should have
let the wayward youth alone, and ten to one he would
have fallen desperately in love with the very being whom
he now vowed he would not so much as look at—because
he was sure beforehand that she would not please him.
The truth is, our Sydney had some very romantic
dreams about love and courtship and marriage, and the
idea of proposing to any given person, because his uncle
happened to think it expedient to do so, was utterly
repugnant to the tastes of a poetical, high-toned being like
him. In the meantime, his newly arrived cousin—Honora
Revere, the lady in question—assumed, whenever he
approached her, an air alternately of the most provoking
indifference or the most chilling hauteur—so different
from what our "conquering hero" had been accustomed to,
that he might easily have been piqued into the required

passion, but for the officious zeal of the well-meaning old gentleman.

It was the more vexatious, because with others she seemed the very soul of gaiety and sweetness. She was a rare creature, too. In the very wildest excess of spirits, when her dark magnificent eyes seemed absolutely on fire with excitement, her voice never lost for a moment its "low, liquid contralto," her attitudes and movements never their soul-born majesty and grace.

Sydney began to feel quite provoked with her for being so wonderfully enchanting. Nay, he caught himself once or twice wishing that the old gentleman had been in Guinea before he had sworn to disinherit him in case he did not propose to her within a year, because otherwise he might possibly have condescended to take the trouble to admire the lady; but now, of course, the thing was impossible. "Besides," he said to himself, "she is a mere coquette after all; for, did she not jilt poor Seymour, whose attentions she certainly permitted, if not encouraged!"

At last, what with the lady's nonchalance, and the gentleman's obstinacy, matters came to such a pass that they scarcely spoke to each other, except when common courtesy required it, and then in the coldest and briefest manner possible.

At this delightful crisis our hero, fortunately for his resolution, met with a new interest in another quarter, which threatened quite to supersede, at least for the present, all thought of the haughty Honora.

In carelessly glancing at the contents of a new magazine, his eye was arrested by the following verses, under the signature of "Athenais:"

TO——.

Upbraid me not, that having taken thee kindly
   Into my earnest heart, and finding still,
There where I throned thy spirit, somewhat blindly,
   A depth, a height, which thou hast failed to fill—
That finding this—my faith I disavow,
And seek a nobler, holier love than thou.

That my soul asks it, pleads for it forever,
   Proves it a claim divine, and not a *wrong*.
Stay the wild rush of yon impetuous river,
   Not the upsoaring of a spirit strong;
For I were wronging *thee* to meanly tame
Each winged impulse unto thy light claim!

Thus would our natures both be chained, degraded—
   Be ours a larger, nobler, loftier care!
The flowers, with which yon summer bower is braided,
   Plead always wistfully for light and air;
So grow *thy soul*—from love to love ascending—
Not to its mortal clay ignobly bending!

Something in the sentiment of this little poem touched his fancy—nay, his heart—and, with nothing better to do, the whim of the moment prompted a reply to it.

CHAPTER II.

We should see the spirits ringing
   Round thee—were the clouds away!
'Tis the child-heart draws them, singing
   In the silent-seeming clay—
Singing! Stars, that seem the mutest, go in music all the way.

            E. B. BARRETT.

A lovely girl, half asleep in a fautueil, lay languidly turning over the leaves of a magazine. Suddenly she started; a soft bloom dawned and deepened in her cheek, and her dark eyes dilated with surprise, not unmingled with pleasure. It was the romantic young dreamer whose verses had attracted the attention of Sydney Hazard, and it was his reply, addressed—"To Athenais"—and signed simply "Vivian," that had so startled her from her reverie. Listen to her, dear reader, as with a faltering, subdued, but exquisitely modulated voice she reads the lines aloud.

TO ATHENAIS.

A pilgrim here—with waiting heart—
  I've passed by many a blooming shrine,
And some were wrought with rarest art,
  And some were touched by light divine.
Why won they not the gift—the prayer?
My soul would fain have worshiped there—
But something whispered still—"Beware!"
        Not *these* are thine,
        That dream resign!
Nor thus profane th' appointed hour
When blooms for thee thy promised flower!

And calmly then I went my way;
  Too sacred glowed the fire I nursed,
To blend with any but the ray,
  The one dear ray—the last—the first—
The only one, reserved to share
My path below—its joy—its care—
And that sweet life in Aiden, where
        Each radiant dream,
        That lends its gleam,
A glimpse of Heaven our earth to give,
Will take its own bright shape—and *live!*

Speak, lady, did I wait in vain—
  In vain reserve the sacred fire?
Must Love, beneath thy far disdain,
  Make of this heart his funeral pyre?
A soft light dawns upon my way—
A flower unfolds, my steps to stay—
I hear a heavenly harp-string play!
        My soul and lute,
        Till now so mute,
In one wild thrill, respond to thine!
Bid me not, sweet, "*that* dream resign!"

This was Romance indeed! Oh! if she could but dare
reply! It would be so beautiful—this enchanting mystery—
this spiritual love! Besides, it would keep her mind from

wandering to a certain haughty and indifferent person, who did not deserve a look, a thought from her—and yet who, somehow, contrived to occupy a prominent place in every dream by night and reverie by day.

"I *will* reply," murmured Romance—"there can be no harm in it, for he can never discover me."

But then womanly delicacy and pride began to remonstrate—and a week—almost a fortnight elapsed, ere she could decide.

I can't help blushing a little myself, dear reader, while I am forced to acknowledge that—wild, wayward, thoughtless, willful, dreaming Romance won the day, and sent the following response to the Magazine.

THE SLEEPING HOPE.

Yes—in my soul, with folded wing,
    A pure and happy hope is sleeping,
While Love low lullabies doth sing,
    His vigil o'er it keeping.

A hope, divinely beautiful,
    With wings in rosy splendor gleaming;
It dreams of Heaven—it dreams of *thee*—
    It smiles in that sweet dreaming!

I dare not name its name to thee,
    No, not in softest, faintest sigh—
For oh! if once betrayed by me,
    'T would wake and weep and fly!

No earthly care or grief shall wave
    Its cold and blighting pinions o'er it—
For Love shall guard my spirit-hope,
    Till Heaven dawn before it.

Then let it sleep—profane it not—
    That slumber soft and light and holy!
The dearest joy—the fairest thought—
    That lights my lot so lowly.

Ah! let it sleep, with folded wings,
   Till when the angel Death shall free it—
At Heaven's own glorious gate it sings—
   Then shall *thy spirit* see it!

CHAPTER III.

"And her smile—it seemed half holy,
As if drawn from thoughts more far
Than our common jestings are.

"And if any painter drew her,
He would paint her unaware,
With a halo round her hair."

Sydney Hazard read the reply of Athenais with a glow of rapture that was new to him, and from that moment the correspondence went swimmingly on.

In the meantime, a strange change had come over Honora—an unwonted light was in her eyes—a new and ever changing glow upon her cheek. She seemed to be ever in a waking trance—to be gazing at some unseen form, and listening to music inaudible to those around. She might have passed for a Greek sybil—so beautiful, so melancholy, so inspired was her look. And young Hazard watched her with an increasing interest, which he struggled in vain to subdue.

Not that he was inconstant for a moment to his worshiped Athenais—his spirit-love. Oh, no! but he found himself hoping one morning, much against his will, that she might resemble Honora—in person and manner—in *mind* he was sure she did.

He began earnestly to long for an interview with his fair incognita. She, in the wild poetry of her womanly faith, had wished that they should never meet on earth, and had repeatedly described the glorious visions she cherished of a life with him in Heaven.

But our less spiritual friend Sydney could no longer content himself with this sublime state of things, and he wrote her a passionately eloquent letter, earnestly imploring an interview.

Poor Athenais! How could she resist such musically worded entreaties? It was true, to grant them would put to flight the ideal dream which she had lived upon so long. But then she was too unselfish not to sacrifice even that to *his* wish—and so the meeting was appointed—a meeting at her friend's, May Mortimer's—a lovely little arch imp of mischief, who knew a great deal more about the whole affair than either of the lovers. She had discovered Athenais's secret long ago; and now, at last, partly by accident, she had found out who "Vivian" was. But she kept the precious knowledge to her little wise self, and patiently and demurely awaited the denouement.

Sydney was an old friend of May Mortimer's, and he was quite surprised when he found that his unknown poetess knew her also. He was rather annoyed, too, that he should be obliged to reveal himself to her, as a party to this ultra-romantic appointment. But there was no help for it—so he put a bold face on the matter, and walked straight to her house.

May showered her fair soft curls over her eyes to hide the mischief in them, as she curtsied demurely on his entrance. She was alone, and Sydney almost felt relieved to find her so, for his heart throbbed half painfully at the thought of what was to come. But May would not let him long enjoy his reprieve.

"My friend is in the conservatory," she said. "We did not expect you quite so soon," and she glanced archly at a French time-piece—a figure of Cupid running away with a watch.

Sydney bit his lip—for he saw that, in his eagerness, he had anticipated, by ten minutes, the hour appointed.

"Will you seek her, Mr. Hazard—or shall I bring her here?"

"Oh, don't let me give you that trouble, I beg," he replied, and, glad to escape the playful malice of her smile, he hurried to the conservatory.

A lady, with her back to the door, was bending over a beautiful camelia in full bloom. The majestic form—the superbly classic head, with its mass of dark, glossy hair, wound in a careless, simple, yet perfect wave of grace around it! How like Honora Revere!

Startled by his step the lady turned—and at the same moment the gay, light tones of May Mortimer were heard

from the hall, exclaiming, as she tripped up stairs—
"There, Honora! how do you like your Vivian?"

She stood for a moment a very statue of amazement!
Then a rush of mingled emotions—shame—love—and,
shall we confess it?—an indefinable rapture, came over
her heart—and hiding her burning, drooping face with
both her hands, she would have fallen had not our
astonished, yet equally delighted hero, recovering his self-
possession, sprang forward to sustain her.

"Honora! Athenais! my precious angel-love! Look up to
me! Speak—speak but one word! Oh, God! this ecstasy is
too divine!"

Slowly the color stole back to her hueless cheek—
slowly she unclosed those beautiful, humid eyes, and
meeting his ardent gaze, hid them again on his shoulder.
It was enough—their cup of happiness was full.

Of course, Romance and May Mortimer were altogether
to blame in the affair, and they ought to have been
ashamed of themselves for their conspiracy against two
such dignified and determined personages as Sydney and
Honora—had tried to be. But the delighted old gentleman
thought otherwise, it seems—for as he clasped, on the
wedding day, a costly cameo bracelet around the dimpled
arm of the bridemaid, he whispered in her ear—

"We have had our own way with them, after all—
haven't we, May?"

Le Porte-Bouquet, or
Genius and Ingenuity
An Incident in Fashionable Life.[1]

CHAPTER I.

"Oh! sweet, pale Margaret!
Oh! rare, pale Margaret!
From the evening-lighted wood,
From the westward-winding flood.
From all things outward, you have won
A tearful grace, as tho' you stood
Between the rainbow and the sun."—
TENNYSON.

A RARE and queenly creature was Margaret Leslie, with her dark blue "luminous eyes," and the superb hair that swept in wavy masses round her brow. She had been passing a few weeks in the country, with a fair cousin of hers—sweet little Lizzie Leroy. And the two beautiful girls stood at the white gate of the pretty cottage, clasped in a farewell embrace, for the carriage was waiting to convey our heroine to the neighboring city. It was a graceful and picturesque tableaux—Lizzie in her girlish frock of white muslin, and Margaret in a dark travelling dress, with a straw hat hanging on her arm, bending that noble form till her pale cheek rested amid the golden-hued curls of her younger companion.

Suddenly Lizzie withdrew from her arms, and searched eagerly in the little garden for a flower, as a parting token of tenderness; but the search was vain, and Margaret, who had watched her with a loving smile, as she flitted like a

---

[1] "Le Porte-Bouquet, or Genius and Ingenuity. An Incident in Fashionable Life.," Frances S. Osgood, *The Fountain. A Gift: "To Stir up the Pure Mind by Way of Remembrance,"* December 1846, pp. 119-125

sylph beneath the grape-vines, drew out her pencil and hastily wrote on one of the palings of the gate the following impromptu:

"You would speak your farewell by some beautiful flower,
And you grieve that none bloom in the sad autumn bower;
But while, with Love's summer, your sunny heart glows,
Ah! do not regret it!—the *wish* was a Rose!"

And by the way, speaking of impromptus, it was about Lizzie's little hand, playfully placed one day before Margaret's magnificent eyes, that a graceful *jeu d'esprit* was written upon the instant, by one who made no pretensions to the name of poet:

"Those radiant eyes, that charm the soul,
Fear not that tiny hand's control;—
The snow-flake melts before the sun;—
The snow-flake and the hand are one!"

Were ever two women, at once, so skillfully complimented within the compass of a quatrain?

CHAPTER II.

"Unworthy all the homage thou
Art living to secure,
Unlovely in thy inner life,
Though outwardly so pure!

"Thine eyes are full of light, I arty,—
I would they were less bright;
For then the serpents shining there,
Might never pain my sight.

"I would that they were sometimes seen
To shed repentant tears
O'er all the ruin of thy heart,
O'er all the blight of years."

The lady Cleopatra W— was a very remarkable person. With a weak brain and weaker heart, the homage paid to her beauty and grace had turned the one and completely hardened the other. Yet, gifted with consummate art and a wonderful ingenuity—without a ray of genius,—(how often in this superficial world are the glow-worm sparks of the one mistaken for the starry radiance of the other!) she contrived to pass in a certain set for a high-souled and intellectual woman. But her task must have been a painful one; for, to those who watched her at a distance, untrammeled and undeceived by her allurements, her whole existence seemed to be a series of petty and mean manœuvres for power,—and she sometimes stooped so low to conquer, that it was with difficulty she regained her equilibrium. She had in her train a dreamer, who might have attained some celebrity as a poet, had he not lavished the incense of his intellect upon a shrine so poor that the very offering was degraded thereby. This person, a simple-hearted, well-meaning man, lent himself, with an unaccountable blindness to her schemes;—and with a few high-sounding, cant phrases of his at her disposal— phrases which he had repeated so often that he came at last to believe the sentiments they portrayed his own,— with these, I say, and now and then a stray waif of unclaimed poetry, which she greedily appropriated and showed as written by herself, it is not surprising that she dazzled the weak, and deluded the credulous, to her very small heart's content.

Then she had a way of flattering each new individual admirer, (aware that he could not fail to hear abroad stories to her disadvantage,) with the idea that to him alone had love and sympathy unveiled that inner, noble nature, which pride and lofty disdain concealed from the unappreciating world. This was the crowning triumph of her consummate tact, and with this she victimized many a heart that was worthy of a better fate. It has been wisely said, that hypocrisy is the involuntary homage which vice pays to virtue. How must that modest and retiring goddess have been overwhelmed by the perpetual worship of the lady Cleopatra!

In person, she was very tall and very stout:—her shoulders were high, her neck was short; yet she could assume at will a certain voluptuous languor of attitude, which easily passed for grace.—Her face was childishly round and plump, with hair and mouth whose loveliness was indisputable—a singularly bewitching smile—small eyes of greyish green, and a "forehead vacant of all glorious gems." Yet was her manner, when she wished to please, so affable, so caressing, so inexpressibly alluring,—that few could at first resist her. Coarse and mean in mind and heart, illiterate, uncultivated, shocking at times the modest and sensitive of her own sex by her astounding vulgarity of language; yet so enchanting when she chose,—what an enigma she was!

The lady Cleopatra, was dressing with unusual care for a party to which a newly arrived poet,—*the* poet of the day—had been invited, especially to meet her.—A curious wreath composed of those brilliant insects of green and gold, which illumine the dense forests of the South, glanced like a chain of gems amid the soft braids of her luxuriant hair. Her sultana form was robed in dark green velvet, and the least possible touch of rouge relieved the sallow hue of her cheek.

The neck of her dress was somewhat low,—its sleeves were somewhat high, but Fashion sanctioned that, and the lady Cleopatra was a privileged character.

On her toilette table lay some gorgeous flowers, sent to her by the said poet for the occasion, on the strength of a former brief interview during which she had made a certain impression, which it was evident he had not forgotten. How proudly her lip curled in anticipated triumph, as she arranged them in her costly *porte-bouquet*, gleaming with gems and gold, a superb toy fresh from Paris upon which she especially prided herself. Had she known that another and a fairer had received, from the same hand, the same blooming and fragrant token of remembrance, she would have felt less secure of conquest.

CHAPTER III.

"But day by day the flimsy veil grows thin
And clearer shows the worthless waste within;
And one by one the idolaters resign
The wavering fire of their Phihelion's shrine."

The *soirée* had commenced. Our poet stood beside the lady Cleopatra somewhat *ennuyeé* by her flattering expressions of gratitude for his lovely gift, and of admiration for his last poem, when a sudden stir and murmur near the door attracted their attention towards it. A group of ladies and gentlemen were entering—among whom was conspicuous Margaret Leslie in all the glory of her intellectual grace—in all the delicate, yet radiant bloom of her unequalled beauty. She looked like a Greek dryad fresh from the woods; for a garland of many-colored autumn leaves defined the pure and graceful contour of her head, and in her hand she held a rare cluster of flowers, arranged with the perfect taste, not in a vase of rubies, emerald and gold; but in nature's own *porte-bouquet*—a magnificent calla—over the sculptured edge of whose exquisite cup drooped a few, fairy, crimson-tinted bells contrasting brilliantly with the snow-white leaf that sustained them.

The lady Cleopatra was fond of complaining in a lofty tome of the littleness, the petty jealousies, which constantly annoyed her in her own sex; but had any one of her numerous admirers happened to notice the almost demoniac expression which deformed her exquisite lip at that moment, the thought might have occurred to them, that it is not always they who talk most concerning their abhorrence of such feelings, who are least infected by them.

In a voice trembling with restrained spite, yet sweet and bland as Hypocrisy could make it, she said,—"Do you know Miss Leslie? How well she is looking! It is such a pity—is it not?—that with all that talent and beauty 'she has not heart!' I was very fond of her once; but I soon discovered that I wasting all my tenderness, and I gave her up. And yet I cannot but envy her sometimes her want of sensibility."

By how trifling an incident may the destiny of a life be decided! The sight of his graceful gift, so tastefully, so appropriately disposed, enchanted the poet-heart of—— and to the exceeding disappointment of his fair neighbor, who saw herself in all her splendor of attire, in all her panoply of fashionable attractions, at once and completely eclipsed, by the dignified simplicity displayed in the dress and manner of her beautiful rival,—he devoted the rest of the evening to Margaret Leslie.

This happened only last week, dear reader, and that veracious though rather talkative old lady Madam Report already positively affirms that they are to be married in a few months. At all events, of one fact, I myself am cognizant—that the very next morning, Miss Leslie received the following lines entitled—

THE FLOWER SYLPH'S PORTE-BOUQUET.

'T would have fitted a fairy of wood-nymph wild,—
That delicate fancy—thou dreaming child!
Did they pray to thy heart from their balmy bowers?
Did they sing thee a hymn—those pleading flowers?
And thus did it flow—with its cadence low—
Like the music sweet—in the measured beat—
Of a playful fountain's silver feet?—

—"Aye! gather us still with your pure, white hands,
And weave our beauty in blooming bands!
But oh! by the flower-like truth and grace,
That full they spirit and light they face,
Imprison us not—the frail—the gay,—
As Fashion's votaries coldly do,
In a cage as cold and hard as they,
The jewel-light of a *porte-bouquet*
Too soon would wither our bloom and dew!"

'Twas thus they sang—and lo! to the sound
Of a magical melody pealing round,
A flower-sylph came in her white canoe—
The curved Calla of spotless hue—
And moored, by the violet's bank of bloom,
Her graceful bark in its faint perfume,
And as she flew from her golden seat,
A zephyr bore to the pausing feet,
The beautiful scallop in tender play,
And whispered—"*Here* is a *porte-bouquet!*"

Glimpses of a Soul[1]

KATE CAROL. To MARY H—.

"I MISS you, Mary mine, more than I can tell, with this cold pen and sluggish ink. I own I love Right Angledom. After the bustle and *randomness* of life in New York—its straight ways, its quiet and its monotony, are refreshing. I love the Quakers too, with their delicious repose of manner—their low, lulling, musical voices, and their simple truthfulness of character and conversation. Their 'ways are ways of pleasantness, and all their paths are peace.' But I must confess to, now and then, a feeling, I cannot say off home-sickness—for I, wanderer that I am, have no home, unless it be in your heart, and in some few others, a *precious* few, indeed—but a feeling of regret, a pining for the past; for the few true and pure spirits to whom I have dared reveal myself, who *know* me thoroughly, faults and all, and who love me the more for those faults; because love and pity come *together* on their divine mission from the gate of heaven, and walk hand-in-hand, twin children of God, ever tender, and beautiful, and sad, through this clouded vale of tears.

"'Thee knows,' Mary, as a lovely Quaker maiden said to me in a low lute-tone the other night, 'Thee knows the gravel and the gold run together in all characters.' Sweet Lizzie L—, thee does not know how much that simple Orphic saying consoled me. Well, there is *some* gold in *my* character, but it requires the sunbeams of love and sympathy to light it up, and so reveal it; and *they* might change even the gravel to gold in a heart so docile as mine, if they only knew it, and would only take the trouble.

"Thee knows, Mary dear, my invincible aversion to strangers. Gay, careless, confiding, frank, indeed to a fault, among those who seem to love me, I am shy, cold,

---

[1] "Glimpses of a Soul," Frances S. Osgood, *Graham's Magazine*, February 1847, vol. XXX, no. 2, pp. 90-92

dull—nay, worse, I am *wretched*, where I am not sure of pleasing. This is a most unfortunate weakness of mine, and has been the cause of many troubles to me. I recollect once in New York going to a party, which I afterwards heard was made *for me*—made expressly to introduce me to some distinguished authors—and just see, Mary, how badly I behaved; see what a wayward, naughty lion I was.

"Had I only *known* then, as I afterward did, the kind interest that my host took in me, I should have been so happy, so social, so delightful; but as it was, with my usual want of self-confidence, finding myself among strangers, I felt my heart, like the pimpernel on the approach of rain, coldly shrinking and shutting up, leaf by leaf, until I became a statue of *lead*; and on my introduction to those writers, whom I had all my life been eager to see, and whom, if I had only been sure that they would let me, I could have loved at once. I replied in monosyllables, so coldly, so drily, that they left me, surprised and repelled; and my dear, kind, disappointed host, afterward said, in reply to some encomiums by a friend—'Yes, I suppose she is all that, but you must allow that she is very eccentric.' *Am* I eccentric, Mary? Am I anything but foolish and timid, and sensitive to a ridiculous degree?

"Now it was this shrinking of the heart that I felt, when I first took possession of a large, and at first, somewhat dreary room in a Philadelphia boardinghouse. The sister of a dear friend, then in Washington, called upon me, and with a single magical sentence, like a gleam from the lamp of Aladdin, warmed, and furnished, and lighted up the chamber, till it seemed a home even to my lonely and sorrowing heart. She simply said, 'Oh! this is the room that Sophy had!' The following impromptu will show you how fervently I felt the change.

THE ROOM THAT SOPHY HAD.

Though strange and chill at first the room,
  How soon it seemed with comfort clad,
When someone said—and blessed the gloom—
  "It is the chamber Sophy had."

With that sweet word the sunshine stole,
  Around a spirit lone and sad,
A lingering ray from her true soul,
  Still warmed "the room that Sophy had."

And here has beat her happy heart;
  And here have rung her accents glad;
And here the darling mused apart—
  Oh, precious "room that Sophy had."

And here, perhaps, my image stole,
  When care unwonted made her sad,
And whispered love through all her soul,
  And cheered "the room that Sophy had.

No palace-hall a queen may pace,
  With splendor lit—with beauty clad,
Would seem so filled with light and grace,
  As this dear "room that Sophy had."

"You bid me send you all the verses I write. You little dream of the shower that would overwhelm you, were I to comply literally with your request. '*Nulla die sine linea,*' is my motto as well as that of the painter of old, and while I sew, or walk, or ride, or lounge, I am forever singing to myself impromptu love-songs, from imaginary damsels to imaginary youths, set to music by a score written in the air, and invisible to all eyes but mine, while a band of aerial musicians play the accompaniment, with my heart, for the leader, beating time. You shall have one of them, dear, and that, I think, will content you for the present—

Should all who throng, with gift and song,
  And for my favor bend the knee,
Forsake the shrine, they deem divine,
  I would not stoop my soul to *thee*!

The lips, that breathe the burning vow,
  By falsehood base unstained must be;
The heart, to which mine own shall bow,
  Must worship Honor more than me!

> The monarch of a world wert thou,
>   And I a slave on bended knee,
> Though tyrant chains my form might bow,
>   My *soul* should never stoop to thee!
>
> Until its hour *shall come*, my heart
>   I will possess, serene and free;
> Though snared to ruin by thine art,
>   'T would sooner *break* than bend to thee!

"Ah, Mary! if only my dream-opera could play on through life, uninterrupted by the coarser or commoner cares of every-day existence—if the charm of that music, inaudible to others, to which, when I am let alone, my spirit moves, gliding or dancing as the measure chances to be swift or slow, might not be broken by the discord of reality, how light would float the fairy hours, led by that weird and wondrous melody, from 'night to morn, from morn till dewy eve.' But often, just in the midst of my heroine's most impassioned reply to my hero—the bell rings for dinner—or our little Lily-belle wants her robe arranged—or rosy, roguish Mary insists upon playing that she is my mamma and that I am her youngest and naughtiest responsibility; and, after all, the glee that our three loving hearts play and sing together, with now and then a coo from the cradle from our little dove, our precious 'Picciola,' as an accompaniment—if less ethereal—less artistic—is quite as sweet and more spirited than the dream-music that Fancy plays in the air for me. To be sure, I have to be punished and put in the corner by my little tyrant, rather oftener than is convenient or agreeable, and to spell hard words, that I eschewed in my vagrant schooldays some—forty years ago!—if we count time by 'heart-throbs,' as Festus bids us, I have lived longer than that—

"I broke that chain of thought, attracted by the peculiar grace of a compliment paid by a gentleman to a very lovely woman, who is sitting near me, bending a pair of superb Spanish eyes and a graceful Psyche-head over a suspender, on which, beneath her fairy hands a wreath of exquisitely delicate flowers is growing and glowing; all too daintily for the heart it is meant to chain—since that heart is man's—

> For still the fairest, frailest flowers
>   He soonest casts aside!

But the compliment. Someone remarked, that her head would be perfect, were it not that the organ of reverence was entirely wanting in it. 'It has never been brought into play,' was the reply, 'for she has found *no superior* on earth.'

"Last night, as I watched her pensive look, I found myself chanting to myself a song to her lost child—the most divinely beautiful being that I ever beheld. I loved her as my own, and the tears still spring to my eyes whenever I think of her. Will you hear the song, Mary?

TO LITTLE ANNIE C—.

> Thy dark eyes danced in light,
>   And on thy cheek the while,
> Life's morning; rosy bright, Annie,
>   Did softly glow and smile.
>
> A rare and radiant grace,
>   A beauty not of earth,
> Had 'o'erinformed' thy face, Annie!
>   God's darling! from thy birth.
>
> When last I pressed thy brow,
>   There dawned thy soul divine;
> But Heaven has won thee now, Annie!
>   A lovelier morn is thine!
>
> While paled life's early rose,
>   Thy spirit plumed her wings,
> And now—how soft they close, Annie!
>   While God's new angel sings!

"Some time before her death, the dear little child had frequently looked up in her mother's face, and exclaimed, without any apparent or immediate cause—'Happy Annie!' and 'Happy Annie!' was the only epitaph they traced upon the simple slab of white marble that marked her little grave.

"But I shall sing you to sleep, my own Marie, if I give you any more of my verses: so take a spirit kiss, and believe me still

"Your fondly attached,
"KATE CAROL."

Life in New York.
A Sketch of a Literary Soirée.[1]

My own blue-belle!
My pretty blue-belle!
Don't fear that your secrets I'm going to tell;
My wings you view,
Of your own bright hue,
And oh! never doubt that my heart's "true blue!"
THE BUTTERFLY'S SONG.

SOMEBODY SAID of our fair hostess, that she reminded him of a cathedral with a simple, unpretending portal, which gives you no idea of the rare revelations within, and through which you pass to wonders that you did not dream of before. Once within, you are overwhelmed with the grandeur, the beauty, the mystery, the majesty around you—the lofty and magnificent arches, the dim, far-reaching aisles, the clustered columns, the vaulted roof, lost to the eye from its wondrous height—the glorious pictures by the master-hand—the iris-colored light from the painted windows poured softly over all—the silence, the religious calm pervading the place—all combine to awe and elevate the stranger, who has perhaps rashly and unthinkingly entered that sanctuary of the soul.

He was an enthusiast, a noble one, who said this, and I cannot tell if it be true. I only know that she exerts over my individual self a magnetic attraction and influence, which I do not care to analyze or to resist, because it soothes and satisfies me whenever I am with her, however restless and unhappy I may have been the moment before.

---

[1] Life in New York. A Sketch of a Literary Soirée.," Frances S. Osgood, *Graham's Magazine*, March 1847, vol. XXXI, no. 3, pp. 177-179

A pleasant party were assembled in her drawing room. There was the statuesque Georgine—

> —"with stately mien
> And glance of calm hauteur,
> Who moves—a grace—and looks a queen,
> All passionless and pure."

A creature of faultless harmony and grace; but whose perfect repose of manner, attitude, look and language, exquisite as it is, almost frightens you away from her at first. So still, so fair, so pure—like a snow-cloud moving serenely through the silent air. There she sits; with her graceful Greek head bent slightly forward, its luxuriant, light brown hair wound carelessly and wavily around it; her chiseled features serenely beautiful, and her hands, white as Pentelican marble, resting half-clasped upon her knee.

If I mistake not, beneath that snowy crest, there are flowers of fancy and fountains of feeling—all the lovelier and purer for being so guarded, by the vestal from the world.

> Her cheek is almost always pale
> And marble cold it seems;
> But a soft color trembles there,
> At times, in rosy gleams!
>
> Some sudden throb of love, or grief,
> Or pity, or delight,
> And lo! a flush of beauty—brief,
> But passionately bright!
>
> She 'minds me of a rose I found,
> In a far, Southern land—
> A robe of ice its blushes bound,
> By winter breezes fanned.
>
> But softly through the crystal veil,
> That gleamed about its form,
> There came a fitful glow to tell
> The flower beneath was warm

Oh! that all women could thus proudly wear the veil! It is a protection we need so much—that mantle of snow! But there are those (and they most want it) in whose hearts the waves of feeling never rest long enough for the winter crust to form—who never stop to think, to look back, to reflect, to prepare; but dash on to the ocean "over bank, brake and scaur," giving back only half-formed or broken images of the beautiful visions that beam above their way—the bird—the cloud—the flower—the star—now humming a careless carol to the breeze, now murmuring a plaintive chant, now thundering in torrent tones, as they madly leap adown the rocks that would oppose them, and now dancing out of sight into the dim, untrodden forest-depths, where none will dare to follow.

We have seen the statuesque—there were not wanting the "grotesque and arabesque," as well to our literary *soirée.*

There was one unique, whom I hardly dare attempt to describe. In speaking he deals principally in antithesis, and he himself is an antithesis personified. The wildest conceits—the sharpest satire—the bitterest, maddest vituperation—the most exquisite taste—the most subtle appreciation of the delicate and beautiful in his subject—the most radiant wit—the most dainty and Ariel-like fancy—with a manner and a mien the most quaint, abrupt and uncouth imaginable—it is like nothing in nature, or rather it is so exceedingly natural that it seems almost supernatural. His discourse is all thunder and lightning—every play of his impish eye-brows is an epigram, every smile a *jeu d'esprit.* At one time affectionate, confiding, careless, buoyant, almost boyish in his mood; at another, irritable, ferocious, seemingly ready for a tiger-spring upon any foe, and again calm, cold, haughty, and uncomeatable as an Indian of the olden time. Here is a stranger original than any his favorite author ever drew. He is the ideal Yankee of the nineteenth century.

There, too, nestled demurely in a corner of the sofa was that little "will-o'-the-wisp," V—, whom nobody knows what to make of wild, wayward, capricious as an April day—changeable as the light spring-cloud, and restless as the wave—the spoiled child of Fancy,

"Dowered with the hate of hate, the scorn of scorn,
    The love of love!"

To those who care for her, all trust and truth, and poetry and sportive fondness, and deep impassioned feeling—to all the rest of the world proud, still, reserved, dull, apathetic, reckless of opinion and of consequences: a tame Canary-bird to kindness, a lioness to injustice and oppression. Nature, with her sympathetic ink, has drawn pictures in her soul, which seem to the cold and careless only pale, frost-work, wintry views; but which, in the warmth of affection, change to glowing summer scenes, with flowers and foliage, and gleaming springs, shifting clouds, and singing birds and butterflies, all of which were always there, and needed only the summer of sympathy and love to draw them out.

By her side sat the man of exhaustless and most whimsical wit, whom *she* calls the "laughing philosopher," and whom *I* strongly suspect of having found, and selfishly concealed the "philosopher's stone." He is the most refreshing, contented, and sunshiny-looking mortal that ever smiled in this cold world of ours. Ever ready and brilliant, he whispers his irresistible *bon-mots* and his charming *jeux d'esprit*, as if he were ashamed of them, and calls it a breach of confidence if they are repeated aloud.

Next to him sat the stately, intellectual, and warmhearted Mrs. —, who, according to her witty neighbor, always looks "up to an epic." I suppose he will call this a betrayal of confidence; but when these pages meet his eyes, I shall fortunately be far beyond the reach of his cutlass-irony; so spare yourself, till I come back, "most potent, grave, and reverend seignor," and don't "waste your *satire* on the desert air."

In earnest conversation with the lovely and loveable Mrs. S— was young —. His rare and pure intellect; his "Doric delicacy" of taste; his gentle and winning manners; his sensitive, generous, and trustful nature, are best appreciated by those who know him best.

Well—first we played the game of "What is my thought like." Smile not, sagacious reader—Canning did the same. Several good answers were elicited in the course of the game, among which were the following:—

"Why is a dew-drop like Miss R's sash?"
"Because it trembles on a flower."
"Why is fame like a clasp?"
"Because it is all a catch."
"Why is Mrs. — like an omnibus?"
"Because we are all carried away by her."
"Why is my heart like a mirror?"
"Because you can see *yourself* in it."

When the game was over, one of the gentlemen took from his pocket a volume of poems, by that Proteus author, "Anon," of which he happened to have the only copy in the country, and read aloud the following verses, in a voice tremulous with the weight of its own melody and feeling:—

TO—.

You would make hearts your stepping stones to power,
And trample on them in your triumph-hour;
But mine was formed for nobler fate than this.
It knows the treachery of your Judas-kiss.

You talk of "lofty feelings pure and high,
Too pure, alas I" and then you gently sigh;
You mourn the trials, which a soul like yours.
So true—amid the meaner herd endures.

You say 't is sad, but yet you would not part.
For worlds, with that proud dignity of heart!
Now never breathed in woman's breast, I ween,
So poor a spirit, 'neath so bold a mien.

I've learned you well—too well—your serpent-smile
Is fond and fair; but cannot "me beguile."
I've seen it called, and on your soft lip worn.
To win a heart those lips had laughed to scorn.

I've heard that voice—'t is very sweet, I own.
Almost too much of softness in its tone;
I've heard its tender modulations tried.
On one you'd just been slandering—aside.

I've seen you welcome, with that fond embrace.
A friend who trusted in your frank, bright face:
And while her parting steps the threshold pressed.
Her love, her looks, her manners turned to jest.

You triumph in the noble trick you've found,
Of winning love and trust from all around;
While cold and reckless, with a sneer at heart,
You plead, manœuvre, bind with Carce art.

But day by day, the flimsy veil grows thin.
And clearer shows the worthless waste within:
And one by one, th' idolators resign
The wavering flame of their Parhelion's shrine.

The mysterious book was then handed to Georgine, who took it tranquilly, and read in a most musically modulated voice, while a faint rose-color warmed her usually hueless cheek.

TO—.

Ah! do not let us worse than waste,
In idle dalliance, hours so dear;
At best, the light-winged moments haste
Too quickly by with hope and fear.

Be ours to wreath, (as swift in flight
They pass—those children of the sun,)
With Fancy's flowers, each wing of light,
And gems from Reason's casket won.

The Passion-flower has no perfume,—
No soul to linger when it dies;
For lighter hearts such buds may bloom,
But, oh! be ours more proudly wise.

And wouldst thou bind my soul to thine,
Bid Truth and Wisdom forge the chain;
Nor o'er its links, as bright they twine,
Let Folly breathe one burning stain.

Thy mind—so rich in classic lore,
Thy heart, from worldly taint so free;
Ah! let me not the hours deplore,
Which might be all embalmed by thee.

At last the "will-o'-the-wisp" was called upon for a recitation, and after laughing, and blushing, and scolding, and making as "much ado about nothing" as the Lady Heron did about singing "Young Lochinvar," she gave, in her own peculiar way, the following song:

They call me a careless coquette;
    That often, too often, I change; they chide
    Because every being on earth I've met,
    Of the glorious mark in my hope falls wide.

It is only a yearning of soul,
    For the lovely—the noble—the true and pure;
    A fond aspiration beyond my control,
    That was born with my being, and must endure.

But I know that shadow and shine
    Must over this world, float side by side;
    That Reason and Folly still entwine
    Their flowers of light and bells of pride.

And I, in whose heart so wild,
    Too often Love's music in Discord dies;
    Oh! should I not—idle and dreaming child—
    Shrink back from a being all pure and wise?

I will hush in my heart that trust.
    I will hide from the world that daring dream,
    And seek in the sand for the golden dust,
    Since ever they mingle in Life's deep stream.

The gay party separated about 12 o'clock, apparently highly satisfied with each other and themselves. It is to be hoped, they will meet again as "beautifully blue" as ever. And in the meantime, forgive me for having converted *"pro bono publico,"* their classic saloon, into a modern "Ear of Dyonisius."

Kate Carol to Mary S.[1]

VALENTINE'S EVENING, Mary! How I wish I were with you at the gay party in Waverly Place, where C—, the favored priestess of the saint, does the honors with a quiet grace peculiar to herself! Do you remember the party *last* year? Do you remember the beautiful poem from St. Valentine himself, to St. L—? You *should* remember, since it was *yourself* who wrote it; although no one guessed it at the time but I.

Do you remember, too, how tired you were that morning before it was quite finished, and how, after introducing in the poem several of your favorites who were to be present, you suddenly broke down with a provoking headache in the midst of a delightful description of *me,* whom you had reserved till almost the last—probably upon the same principle that governs children who keep their cake till they have eaten all their bread and butter up—and how I happened in just then and you offered me the pen to *finish myself* with, and how, *for the sake of a rhyme,* Mary, I was obliged to flatter myself in a most unheard of manner, and with what a demure countenance I heard it read aloud in the evening, and how that enchanting Mrs. S— S— playfully held her fan before my face to hide my blushes? Ah, Mary! how many sad changes have taken place since then . But we won't talk of them now. Rather will I recall the passage in the poem alluded to. I love to recall *your* praise.

[1] "Kate Carol to Mary S.," Frances S. Osgood, *The Columbian Magazine,* May 1847, vol. VII, no. 5, pp. 203-206

"One wayward heart is here, whose restless beat
Is ever chiding Time's deliberate feet;
Yet, in its guileless movements, you may trace
The good that lends e'en waywardness a grace:
And she who owns it makes her inward life
A charmed dream, with love and beauty rife.
A changeful cloud—n wild bird on the wing
Is not so airy or so bright a thing
As her sweet fancy.—Wild, capricious, gay,
With every flower it sees it stops to play!
Tell her, fair priestess—if she'll stay to hear—
That guardian spirits watch her very near;
That all unswayed by rules of worldly art,
Her truest teacher is her own.

*   *   *   *   *

There, Mary, you were just there when I stole in upon you. How I wish I had stayed away five minutes longer! I should so like to know what you were going to say. *Now*, I fear "I shall never hear the *last of it*," as the man said of his scolding wife's tongue.

I have seen several pretty Valentines to-day, received by some of my young friends. Would you like to hear them? That which follows was addressed to one of the loveliest of beings—lovely in mind, heart and person. The verses convey the impression of some coquetry on her part; but that must be a mistake. That which in a weaker, a lighter or commoner person would be coquetry, in *her* is only a natural and involuntary soaring of the soul from an inferior object to one more congenial to, more worthy of her refined elevation of character. In other words, as her spirit progresses in the path of virtue, and truth, and knowledge, it just takes another step toward Heaven—on a higher heart than that where last it rested. And how is she to help it? What else were men's hearts made for? And if by chance this spirit of light has left a luminous fairy footprint in some soul more than commonly susceptible—that of the writer of the Valentine, for instance—I can only say he ought to be proud of the token, that a creature so exquisite, so dainty and so pure, had deigned to pause there, if only for a moment—if only to plume her peri-wings for a flight to loftier regions. I have no patience with these unreasonable bipeds who carp at woman's caprice!—as if a passing smile or blush were not more than their *share* of Heaven! No, no! thou self-styled "lord of creation!"

Reprove not *me*!—if still I change
  With every changing hour,
For glorious Nature gives me leave,
  In wave and cloud and flower.

And you and all the world would do,
  —If all but dared—the same.
True to *myself,* if false to *you,*
  Why should I reck your blame?

Yon soft, light cloud, at morning hour,
  Looked dark and full of tears;
At noon it seemed a rosy flower,
  Now, lustrous gold appears!

So yield I to the deepening light
  That dawns about my way.
Because *you* linger with the *night,*
  Shall *I my noon delay?*

But the Valentine; here it is:

TO —

You love me no longer! The heart that once listened,
  In passionate joy, to each murmur of mine;
The eyes—the dark eyes—that once tenderly glistened,
  With hope so enraptured and love so divine,

Are turned to another. Why dared I believe them?
  Ah! False as the siren that sings in the sea,
Those spells of enchantment, though lightly you weave them,
  them,
  Though sport to your spirit—were ruin to me!

Another came to our merry little M—. With what a beautiful flash of wonder and joy her dark blue eyes dilated as her sister read it to her. It was dated 1860, anticipating her bellehood. Here you have it.

TO MAY.

I'm lonely, I'm lonely—for on my sad hearth,
No *cricket* is chirping with heart full of mirth;
I've a gold-wired cage—a garden in bloom;
But no bird on the perch, and no rose's perfume.

Blithe cricket! sweet bird! Dainty rose set apart!
Come chirp for me, sing to me, bloom for my heart!
The hearth stone is ready—my spirit is true;
The bird and the rose shall have "sunshine and dew."

That sounds like *you*. Didn't you write it, Mary? Angelica M— received the following:

Had you a fairy god-mother?
If not, who bribed the artist Nature,
That she, to deck you out, has robbed
Each other living creature.

With half your heart and half your mind,
And half the light your eyes illuming,
She might a dozen have designed
Of maidens bright and blooming.

The, lady, out of all your store,
Something you surely may impart,
Suppose—since *mine* is fairly lost—
You let me have *your heart*.

To Miss H— came a most mysterious missive containing these astounding verses. What can they mean? You should have seen her snow-pure brow flush as she read them? Under the leaves of a heart's-ease, raised by a silver thread, we found a golden ring.

TO ROSALIE H—.

I have brought you back your token,
I renounce the vows you've spoken,
And the heart you would have broken,
                    Wanders free!
To another vow as lightly,
To another smile as brightly,
                    As on me.
Never more my heart shall listen,
Never more mine eyes shall glisten,
To those tones in music breathing,
All my soul in rapture wreathing,
                    Rosalie!
Never more to my caresses,
Fondly curl those careless tresses;
Now they seem like silken jessus,
Where the falcon Love was captured,
Where he lightly swung enraptured,
                    Mocking me!
Fare you well! You'll never rue
All the mischief that you do,
While that imp of mischief, too,
Love himself 's in love with you!
                    Rosalie!
You two sprites from fairy land,
                    You and he,
Both together, plotting, scheming,
When you catch a mortal dreaming,
Play into each other's hand,
'Till you have him fast trepanned,
                    Rosalie!
And but few escape, like me,
From your little fairy grasp,
Without leaving in your clasp,
Half a broken heart, to see!
                    Rosalie!

Another to that bewitching woman Mrs. P—, runs thus:

TO FLORENCE.

You bade me go—your accents low
Had less of calm disdain than woe;
You bade me go—yet spite of pride,
A half-checked sigh your words denied;
You bad me go—yet in your eyes
I saw the tears of anguish rise;
Unsay those words! We will not part!
Break *mine*, but not *your own dear heart!*

But the prettiest of all was one which our brilliant friend, Grace Howard, sent to D—. It was an embossed card, in the centre of which an exquisite butterfly fluttered on the heart of a superb passion flower, its wings attached to the flower by a fine spiral chain of gold. As it gently rose to the touch, part of the flower rose with it and revealed, on the page beneath, these words, in the most minute and fairy-like chirography imaginable:

I know that restless heart of thine!
Even now it flutters to be free
To rove where fairy flowers twine
The rose wreath of love for thee.

No longer *I* the wings restrain,
Whose lightest wave my heart could thrill;
But tangled by a *golden* chain,
The *sordid spirit* lingers still.

Away! I will not bind thee thus!
My burning *soul* was naught to thee,
Its rapturous dreams—its truth—its trust,
All wasted—all! Away! thou'rt free.

Grace is an heiress, you know, and has lately taken it into her head that D—'s golden fetter frets him. I have always thought he did not appreciate the true wealth of his lady-love.

Another pretty one was as follows, but I shan't tell you whence or to whom it came.

> Had Greece known thee, there would have been
>   A change in classic lore;
> The Muses would have counted *ten*—
>   The Graces had been *four.*

One more and I change the subject. It was sent by the magnetic telegraph, and contained only the initial letters of five very bewitching words—D. S. L. D. F. I dare say the clerks at the office imagined they were transmitting some important news concerning stocks; but *somebody* knows better.

So much for Valentines.

I have been reading a lovely book by Miss C—, of Boston, called "Studies in Religion." It is brimfull of beauty and truth and cheerful piety. Hear what she says of duty.

"We live God's will in living after our nature. Could we fancy the acorn endowed with consciousness, when it first springs from the ground, a tiny stem and leaf, it might say—"What I am to be I know not—all is dark before me." But urged on by irresistible impulse, it continues to throw forth shoots, leaves and branches, and learns its destiny to become the oak in the fact of becoming it.   *   *   *

But we, instead of seeing what God will make out of us, seek to make something out of ourselves, and so only spoil his work by our foolish intermeddling. Yes! we talk of forming character and lay out, in our own thought, plans of what we will be like, as if the great Artist of all would permit us to mar the smallest detail in his creation by our caricature sketching. We are not willing to be, ourselves, what God meant us to be. Like some perverse oakling, instead of following the tendencies to leaf, to bud, to stem, we insist on running altogether to stem, and so the obstructed leaves and buds wither into knots and gnarls, and the tree is thereby unsightly. Oh it were much if we were to give ourselves up meekly to the sway of our being, to follow the leadings of God in our tastes and talent and convictions—to be willing to be ourselves and none other!"

And again:

"To do the highest we know and feel—and of all that God has given us, impulse, thought, feeling, conviction, capacity—to lose nothing, but to evolve out of it the element of immortality it embodies.   *   *   *   *   *

Sometimes, when the heart has been tired of the signs of premeditated purpose, the din and wear of doing duty, by storm, when the useful, the important things in life have seemed somewhat wearisome and one has bethought him, with a sigh, of those far away lilies, who wore their regal garments without toiling or spinning—then have we come, as it seemed by chance, upon a word uttered by some lowly spirit in its weakness or triumph—uttered merely for the relief of the utterance—or have heard a trait of character mentioned perhaps in condemnation, but betraying that there a human soul was struggling, possibly sinking, and such word or characteristic has stirred the fountain of being to its depths—has made resolve stronger—life clearer—or patience more profound; and supposing these had thus appealed but to one heart—to one immortal being swayed by tenderness and thought, who can measure the good of that word or character, a word spoken to the winds, a character evolved by suffering, perhaps stricken with error?

"Let us distrust ourselves and be very humble when we imagine ourselves doing good; it is as infants, putting their tiny hands to their mother's work, fancying themselves assistants—knowing not that to lie down in quietness beside, or to continue afar off their sports, were to help her the most. Who are the useful—who the important ones of society? Let us keep ourselves from the folly of judging."

After all, I have not quoted to you what I most like in the book; but I happened to open to those pages, and are they not beautiful and true? How many waste a lifetime in trying to struggle out of their element! A true and kind but mistaken friend once wrote to Fanny S—, thus:

"If your other friends are satisfied with you, Fanny, *I* am not. You! who should pass the syrens of life's sea, so absorbed in singing hymns to the gods that you hear not their beguiling strains—how are you won by their light love-lays to forget your diviner destiny?"

And Fanny thus replied—half in sport, half in earnest, yet somewhat ungrateful, as she afterward felt—to that frank and high reproof:

"To me it seems, my Anna, with all due deference to your more profound wisdom, that the sweetest and truest 'hymn to the gods' is that of a pure and joyous life; that the docile heart yielding to every impression of love, sorrow, rapture or remorse—

> That grateful takes the genial light,
> And trustful lets the shadows pass—

can scarce help beating musically in their ears. If I have the 'gift of song,' Anna, I can't always be singing psalm-tunes; I must sing only when my heart asks me to, and *what* it asks; I must interpret its throbs in love-lays or glees or dirges or paeans—as it is swayed in turn by affection, pleasure, grief or exultation. I cannot play the organ forever, I must sometimes tune my little lute and wake a lighter strain. Indeed, to tell you the truth, my friend—a rather humiliating truth, perhaps—I am afraid love-lays are my vocation. At all events the soul of song never rises so buoyantly, so impetuously from the strings as when the theme is love. I don't think Heaven meant me to be sublime or grand. It meant me to be only a light, little, petulant humming bird,

> "To gather honey every day,
> From every opening flower,"

and to fly so fast from one to another that people are rather puzzled to guess what I am or what I am about—to meekly reflect in my wings the beautiful lines of flower, and sunbeam, and cloud, and star—and to *hum,* on earth, the songs that I mean really to *sing* in Heaven."

And Fanny was more than half right; was she not? Fanny's line of *right* is that of *grace* as well. *Beauty* is duty to her. But Fanny has a friend whose line of right goes straight up—never swerves—never bends, like God's beautiful promise of love in the Heavens, which is not the less heavenly because it turns toward the earth, and the hues of which are not the less luminous and lovely because tears are mingled with the light from which they spring. Now Fanny's line winds in and out, in many a graceful sweep and curve—crossing and recrossing the straighter one, thus $. Fanny declares it resembles a vine around a May-pole; but her friend insists that it is more like a glittering and beguiling snake around a lofty palm tree. However that may be, since the aim of both is

Heaven, I dare say Fanny will reach there first, because she glides like a flash of chain-lightning, while the other creeps, and the very exercise, necessary to her longer and more intricate route strengthens her for the journey; perhaps she will go so far that she will have to turn and descend to find her friend the straight line, after all. But enough of Fanny and her friend—"may their lines fall in pleasant places," and may they meet at last where beauty and truth—where grace and good go hand in hand forever.

Good night, my heart's true friend:

Your own

KATE CAROL

Kate Carol to Her *.[1]

OF ALL my friends, I am most *en rapport* with *you* to-day, dear Star of my life; for it is the Sabbath—the day we have most frequently passed together, shut out from the world—with those who are nearest and dearest—forgetting every lighter love—calling *home* our hearts, and living the only true life. And though you are not here visibly, still shall my soul's Sabbath be spent with yon, dearest and best; and I will catch by the wings each butterfly-thought as it flies, and take its daguerreotype for you on paper.— You wish to know all that pleases—all that pains me—and as I would share with you rather my joys than my sorrows, I will relate how pleasantly I passed last evening in my little *sanctum*, which first I must describe.

"Imagination's airy wing repress,"

in other words, let it alight and fold its pinions, if it can, on a fairy boudoir of a room—an oval one—small, but lofty—in which the only furniture consists of a couch, a table, a couple of chairs, a small Turkish divan and an escritoire.

The pattern of the paper which covers the walls is peculiarly delicate. It is this—at intervals of about two feet,—on a ground of pale peach-bloom, arise, from floor to ceiling, columns of silver, wreathed with silver flowers. White muslin curtains, lined with the same dainty peach-bloom hue, and depending in broad folds from a silver bar, are loosely looped by cords of silver to each side of the window, which reaches to the ground and reveals a tempting view of the conservatory beyond. The furniture is of rosewood, and exquisitely graceful and artistic—the deep arm-chairs, and the "many cushioned sofa," are covered with silken damask of dim sea-green. The rich Axminster carpet is also of sea-green, with an arabesque

---

[1] Kate Carol to Her *.," Frances S. Osgood, *Sartain's Union Magazine of Literature and Art*, August 1847, vol. I, no. 2, pp. 55-58

pattern of gold, silver, and pink winding over it, like the graceful convolutions of a serpent. The couch and escritoire are curved to the oval shape of the room. The door directly opposite the window is veiled from the view by the same style of drapery; so that not even a thought of the world beyond, which to me a door always troublesomely suggests, will intrude itself. Only the world of Nature, from which the flowers in the conservatory keep sending perfumed missives of love; accompanied at intervals by a musical message from the fountain; but that I forgot to describe. A large lotus flower springs from the basin, and poised on the flower stands the winged boy Eros; holding with one hand a shell to his ear, while two sea-nymphs in playful strife below seem tossing the water over him, and endeavoring to reach his other hand in order to lure him down to their ocean home.

The leaf of the escritoire, lined with pale-green velvet, is unfolded, and on it are "Kate's Inkstand," (the blue one, you know, with its golden vine and doves), and the daintiest of golden pens—another gift from one she loves—from Mrs. Norton, the noble English poetess. The handle is cornelian, and around it twines a serpent of gold. The dove and serpent! emblems of wisdom and of truth! Ah Kate! why is the lesson lost? Why are not their shadows blended in all that you write?

A MS. lies beside them—her last effusion probably—we will read it by and by. Behind the glass doors of the escritoire are ranged a variety of valuable and tastefully bound volumes, among the more modern of which are conspicuous, Emerson, Carlyle, Browning, Tennyson, Lowell, Barrett, &c. Surmounting the escritoire is an exquisite marble Ariadne on her panther, and on each side of the window, a slab, also of white marble, supports a master-piece of sculpture—one, the three Graces, and the other a nymph asleep, whose cheek a sportive Cupid touches lightly with his feathered dart.—I have named it the Origin of the Dimple.

The beautiful boy stands on tiptoe in the most graceful of attitudes, with the fore-finger of one hand pressed archly to his smiling lip. This is my pet group. On the oval table in the centre of the room, is a small lamp, with a transparent Sevres porcelain screen, representing Psyche bending above her slumbering lover, holding in one hand a lamp, which she endeavors to shade with the other; but she does not quite succeed; for the delicate hand is transparent as the leaf of a lily; the real light is placed just behind her hand, and the illusion thus produced, is very beautiful. The table is covered with delicate and rare *bijouterie*, and a few costly enamels and books of engravings. Above it, attached to a silver chain which is fastened in the ceiling, hangs a large lamp of chased silver in the shape of a boat, with another little Love in it,—(Kate seems to *love* Love.)

> "The poet in a golden clime was born,
>   With golden stars above,
>
> Dowered with the hate of hate—the scorn of scorn:
>   The love of love."

The ceiling is painted in fresco, and represents the reunion of Cupid and Psyche, in the palace of the gods.

And now that you have glanced at my surroundings, behold your Kate on the couch—now drinking in delicious draughts of melody from Norma, Lucia, and Semiramide—warbled in snatches by a superb tenor voice, almost as sweet as Benedetti's—now listening demurely to her own wild love-lays, read aloud by a critic who is too kind to criticize as he ought to—and anon taking from the same generous friend a random lesson in botany, in the languages, in grammar,—in *any* thing; for she is a novice, and he is proficient in all.

But I promised to let you read the MS. upon the escritoire Let us look it over together.

THE MISSING GIFTS.

> You send me back my gifts, you say—
>   And *some* return, I own—
> But these are paltry trifles, sir!
>   Why come they thus alone?

You keep the costlier tokens, then?
    The diamond ring is here;
But with the ring I gave—if I
    Remember right—*a tear!*

The rosy riband too, that bound
    My braided hair, returns;
But the warm blush 't was yielded with
    No more beside it burns!

This golden locket—round your neck
    You vowed the gift to wear;
You *lost* the blended smile and sigh
    With which I hung it there!

And here's a little, dainty note—
    A playful, school girl billet;
But where's the wild, impassioned kiss,
    With which I tried to seal it?

Nay—nay; I wrong your beggar state,
    'T was to a soul I sent them;
In vain my lost gifts sought, in thee.
    The shrine for which I meant them!

(It strikes me, my Kate—if I may be allowed to express an impartial opinion—that you rather borrowed that last stanza. Did you not?) And here is another MS., blotted seemingly with tears.

"I KNEW HER IN HER HAPPY YOUTH."
S. J. H.

You knew me in my "happy youth,"
    Ere care had clouded heart and brow?
Yet even then before me lowered
    The fate that chills my spirit now.

I shrank apart, nor joined the play
    Where others met in careless glee;
I was loo earnest for the gay—
    Too timid for the wild and free.

Yet in my soul a spring of love,
    Of trusting and impassioned truth,
That asked but love's divining-rod,
    Was wasted in my wistful youth.

You knew me in my "happy youth?"
    Ah! *none* could know me then or now!
I dared not—dare not tell the dreams,
    That sent their fire to eye and brow!

I know there *are*, in this rude world.
    Who share these dreams of pure delight;
But fate has parted, from my path,
    The few who'd read my heart aright.

Perhaps in climes of blissful truth,
    Where joy will dry life's last fond tear,
My soul will live the "happy youth"
    That wayward fate denied me here!

Now, Kate, let me read you a lecture. (Kate is my other self, you know, and you will forgive these little episodes to her.) Just "take the good the gods provide," "my superdainty Kate;" you have more than your share already—more, far more than that fickle, wayward, willful, jealous, exacting little soul deserves. Are there not noble hearts that cherish you? Is there not *one* spirit as far above yours, in all true knowledge, and virtue and beauty, as the *star* is above the fire-fly, who stoops to mingle his calm and spiritual ray with your fitful lightning, whenever you need it? Are there not young, human flowers, that look up to you for the sunshine and dew of their existence?

Be quiet about your *fate! Make* your fate *yourself!* "Do the duty that lies nearest to you," and be happy. But you say you would not be happy for the world, for then you would not write poetry! Very well, then—"write poetry," and try to make others happy! Forget yourself and your sorrow; which, after all, are not the two most important affairs in the world, though you would fain make the world believe they are. You "can do without happiness," and the world can do without *you*, "upon a pinch." At all events, you can't make it care "an individual straw" about your "sentimental sufferings." Try, rather, the spells of wit and merriment; for if it don't laugh *with* you, it will be very likely to laugh *at* you, my poor Kate. So be beforehand with it; and, since it has a penchant for "Mothergoose melodies," sing away, and *dimple it with the smile* of your ever-buoyant and sportive fancy! But hush! Mr. G. is singing again an English song; words by Kate Carol, music by himself.

LULI.

I grieve to let you go, Luli—
   I grieve to let you go;
For I shall miss your merry tones—
   Your laugh so light and low—
      So light and low, Luli!
   Your laugh so light and low.

And I shall miss your smile, Luli!
   That dimples as it goes,
Like a zephyr, with a sunlit wing,
   At play around a rose—
      Around a rose, Luli!
   At play around a rose.

And the heart-heaven in your eyes, Luli!
   And the golden cloud of curls;
And the graceful, winsome, cherub mouth,
   Whose poorest words were pearls—
      Whose words were pearls, Luli!
   Whose poorest words were pearls!

And the fairy, frolic step, Luli,
   That seemed to wake the flowers;
And more than all, the soul of song,
   That charmed the changing hours—
      The changing hours, Luli!

That charmed the changing hours.

I *will* not let you go, Luli!
  So fold the wings you hide;
And you shall be my fairy-queen,
  And I'll ask nought beside—
    Ask nought beside, Luli!
  And I'll ask nought beside.

Ah! why, if we must part, Luli!
  Why let me love you so?
Nay! Waste no more your sweet farewells,
  I *cannot* let you go—
    Not let you go, Luli!
  I cannot let you go!

Bravo! bravo! Mr. G—, most charmingly set and sung. By the way, how few can sing the *soul* of music. No one whose heart has not lived intensely, has not passionately suffered and rejoiced—can, it seems to me, modulate the voice to express every fine and delicate shade of emotion in word and note, so that the mingled melody and feeling shall fill the soul of the hearer.

Mr. W— denies this, and brings in support of his opinion, the fact that Barili, who cannot be more than nineteen years of age, sings with the most passionate expression imaginable; but then an Italian girl, at nineteen, is *all* passion and sensibility; and if she have not actually realized the fiery heart-ordeal, hears at least in her soul, a prophetic voice chanting to her, her destiny, and thus learns by institution to express the revelations of the sybil.

"Please, Mr. W—, read us that little poem about the Life-clock," pleads a sweet voice from the divan; and there sure enough half hidden among its silken cushions, is a dainty creature, to whom I forgot to introduce you. I have a sort of misgiving that she does not properly belong here—that she has stolen out of the new planet Leverrier on purpose to bewitch Mr. W—, and that someday she will vanish from our gaze, taking his soul away with her!

By the way, why don't somebody write a sketch called "Life in Leverrier." Rovers in Authorland! don't all speak at once! But if one of the rest of you don't do it, I shall. Dear

"Sinless Child," with your "spiritual grace of thought," how such an "article" from you would *halo* the *Union Magazine*. Darling L. M. C., my "fairy friend," how would your wonderful imagination revel in that field? Somebody wants me to write the libretto for an opera; I think I will "call it by that name." Talking of names, I am about editing (*not* writing) a book to be called "The Nameless Book," and the motto is to be from Moore:—

> "Go! ask of angels what it is,
> And call it by that name."

won't that be nice? And I am collecting for another little book, to be entitled "Rose-leaves," all my fugitive love-lays.

But the lady from Leverrier called for a poem. Go on, Mr. W—.

THE LIFE-CLOCK.

> I mourned that time too swiftly sped,
> I wept that youth was flying;
> "I'll put your Life-clock back," he said,
> "So hush your sad heart's sighing!"
>
> He brought me flowers, to soothe my gloom,
> And stay Time's tell-tale finger;
> For tangled in their wreathing bloom,
> The Life-clock's hand may linger.
>
> And while I turn the treasures o'er,
> And breathe the balm they give me.
> I dream I am a child once more,
> With nought to harm or grieve me.
>
> And answering flowers within my soul,
> The fresh, wild flowers of feeling,
> Wind with them round my Life-clock's hand.
> And stay its onward stealing.

Then if they fade—(ah! *will* they fade?)
 Their fragrance still may linger,
And hallowing Time's sad evening shade,
 Embalm his tell-tale finger!

(Pretty well, Kate, considering it was almost an impromptu.)

Talking of clocks, I forgot to tell you of a little fairy time-piece, sent to me by some unknown friend, which may have escaped your notice among the *bijouterie* on the table. It represents Time as a beautiful youth, bending tenderly over one of the half-blown roses, which spring with other flowers in lavish profusion around him. His sickle is hung upon a myrtle tree; and the face of the watch, which rests also amid the branches of the tree, is marked by flowers, instead of figures.

"For lightly falls the foot of Time
 That only treads on flowers."

If you are not tired, dear Mr. W—, just read *to the divan*, the best verses in that poem you showed me, written by M. G., "A review of the past year." Begin after the allusion to the battle of Resaca de la Palma, if you please. It was written *before* the castle was taken, my dear Star.

Ho! ye who dwell upon the height
 Of Juan D'Ulloa "*Stand from under*!"
From out the clouds, some winter's night,
 Our war-balloon may chance to thunder!

You'll dream, when at a burst revealed,
 That iron storm the sky is shading,
That Satan takes the airy field,
 And stuns you with his cannonading!

Nay, since Invention goes so far—
 Cotton, I mean—all distance scorning—
Suppose we storm the new-found star,
 Or shoot the "man i' the moon" some morning!

> O Science! radiant child of Truth!
>   Aladdin's lamp thy hand has lighted!
> No fairy page may pleasure youth,
>   Like the weird tales by thee recited!
>
> Thou train'st "the fiery bird of Heaven,"
>   Till, tamed, it turns—thy magic minion:
> Along the line the viewless levin
>   Thy Ariel speeds with folded pinion.
>
> Its lightning wand, that, swift as thought,
>   Has traced those words,—fond memory's token,
> O'er countless leagues a wish has brought,
>   That instant felt, that instant spoken!
>
> And like the fisher-boy of old,
>   Who sealed the Genius in the Casket,
> The storm-king thou a slave dost hold,
>   And tam'st his will, that thou may'st task it!

Talking of genius, I heard to-day of the drollest printer's error! in a sentimental poem too! The line read in MS.:—

> Carnations on thy lovely lip!

but, alas! for the lover-poet!

> *Darnation* on thy lovely lip!

appeared in the printed piece!

In one of *my* poems, they made "Beauty *raging* thro' a bower," instead of "ranging!" The deuce is in the devils, seems to me! but I forgot, it isn't they who set up the types.

Speaking of beauty,—I wish people would dress pleasantly, benevolently. I saw a lovely girl today looking unlovely and unloveable, because her muslin dress was stiffly starched, *to keep clean the longer.* My laundress tries in vain to persuade me into the barbarous custom. To my mind, a woman should always look as soft to the touch as a flower, and as pure. All her garments should be made of the finest and softest material possible; material, that will easily dispose itself into folds, falling gracefully around her; and not, by being liable to ruffle at every movement, compel her to stiff attitudes and starched demeanor, denying her all luxury of lounge and loll; why, my very words would grow prim and precise, were I to wear a dress, which depended on flour or potato for its propriety. But I am growing sleepy, and you are tired, are you not, my Star? So I'll wish you "good night," and the dearest of dreams.

Your own Kate.

Violet Vere's Vacation[1]

LETTER FROM VIOLET TO HER COUSIN KATE ELTON.

MY OWN dear Kate:—When I last wrote—on the day that commenced my temporary emancipation from the jurisdiction of Miss Serena Primrose—(you see I am endeavoring to do credit to my respected teacher, by using all the hard words I can think of)—I promised to indite an epistle to you, immediately after my arrival at the paternal domicil.—Oh! a truce to this formal style—I will begin again! My darling Kate!—"Kate, of Kate Hall—my super-dainty Kate"—I am *so* glad to be at home once more! If mamma would only forget that I have grown up, and think a little less of my appearance—of the set of my dress and the turn of my curls—if I could only persuade her to make believe I was a little child again, and had never been to boarding-school, I think I should be perfectly happy. But if ever, for a moment, I yield to the almost irrepressible impulse which prompts a romp with the children, or any other dereliction from the duty of sitting upright with folded hands and parted hair, she is sure to call me to order with some such expression as this:—"Violet, that is not very lady-like; you are altogether too demonstrative; you did not behave so at Miss Primrose's establishment!"

Ah me! what a desperate inclination I feel to reply—"But, mamma, I am *not* a lady—I don't *pretend* to be a lady—I am only a merry-hearted little girl of sixteen, who has come home to have a good time!"

I wonder what Heaven put play into our hearts for, if it isn't proper to play! It is very trying, Kate, to see my little sister and brothers frolicking to their hearts' content, without being allowed to join them. This morning, as I sat with mamma, most especially behaving myself because Mrs. Rattle happened in, there was that rosy rogue Georgy peeping in at the window—there was Will, hiding and

[1] "Violet Vere's Vacation," Frances S. Osgood, *The Odd Fellows' Offering for 1849*, May 1848, pp. 53-62

kicking under the sofa where I sat—and gentle Charlie, and saucy Hal, and dear little Louise, marching to a merry martial tune through the room—and there was poor *I*, pining to jump up and don Hal's soldier-cap and feather, and lead the infantry into the garden;—but no! that would have been altogether "too demonstrative!"

And while I sat there, with my eyes cast down, looking as meek and demure as *you* know I can look, Kate, I heard Mrs. Rattle say to mamma, *sotto voce*—"How much she has improved!—she used to be such a wild little puss. Her air and manner are perfect—that graceful repose is quite the thing!"

Oh, Mrs. Rattle, what conventional nonsense you talk! *Why* is repose "the thing?" Does anything in God's beautiful world set us the example of repose? Does not the brooklet dance and sing, and the spray above it bend to every breeze? Do not the clouds change, and glow, and float away, free either to weep or to smile in the blue and blissful air? Does not the flower accept what hues of light it most desires from heaven, and reject what it loves not, and bloom a jasmine or a snowdrop, a tulip or carnation, as its inner spirit prompts? But we poor fashionable flowers of humanity, pining exotics from the wildwoods of nature into the hothouse of "good society"—we must all be japonicas—cold, white, soulless japonicas—trained, trammeled, bound to grow just so! We must not venture to laugh into life, like the sunny hearts-ease—to blush with love, like the rose—that would be "too demonstrative;"— repose is the *sine qua non* of japonicadom!

> Taught to restrain, in cold Decorum's school,
> The step, the smile—to glance and dance by rule;
> To smooth alike our words and waving tress,
> And the pure heart's impetuous play repress;
> Each airy impulse, every frolic thought,
> Forbidden—if by Fashion's law untaught.

What an unsatisfactory life it is! But when *I am* set at liberty from mamma's *surveillance*, and sent out into the grounds to "*walk* for exercise," *don't* I make the most of it! Do I walk? I should like to see myself doing any such lady- like and humdrum thing! Kate! I have a secret of the utmost importance to impart to you! You know Miss

Primrose recommended me to "pursue my studies during vacation." With your leave, respected Ma'amselle P., I shall do no such thing! I shall pursue any and every thing, *rather* than my studies. I have no idea of wasting this radiant summer in that style. I shan't have time. There are lovely butterflies to pursue! There are wild, sweet woodland paths to pursue! There are charming whims and fancies to pursue! There is my darling little Georgy, who *insists* upon being pursued! In short, I shall not "pursue the even tenor of Miss Primrose's "way," until I am safely shut in Primrose Hall again.

But the secret is yet to be told. Well, Kate, I have not touched a book since I came home. When I say books, I mean things bound in calf or cotton, with rows of black letters on every page; but I have quite a large library out of doors, of "books which are books," printed in letters of light, with rare illustrations, and splendid emblazonings, in the *old style*, which I never am tired of studying. I have just been "turning over a new *leaf*" to-day. That is, I have had a long walk in the woods, and found a new flower.

Oh yes! I *have* read one book in-doors, a novel—only think!—"The Maiden Aunt." What would Miss Primrose say? It is exquisite. It is brimful of poetry, and pathos, and nature, and truth, and quaint humor, and grace, and goodness, and deep earnest, unaffected piety.

There is one little song in it, translated from the German, which is worth all the propriety pieces we had to read at school. It is the daintiest little pearl of poetry that ever memory strung on her rosary of gems. Shall I quote it? I wish I could procure the music also, which a German friend tells me is very beautiful.

> "My heart, I bid thee answer—
> How are Love's marvels wrought?
> Two hearts to one pulse beating,
> Two spirits with one thought!
>
> "And tell me how Love cometh?
> "Tis here—unsought—unsent!"
> And tell me how Love *goeth*?
> That was not *Love* which went."

Isn't the last line perfect in its enchanting quaintness and simplicity, in its pathetic *naïveté*?

And do you know, Kate, *I* have been writing verses. They are brimful of treason to dear mamma's notions of education; so don't, for the world, "let on to anybody," as our Bridget would say, that such is the case. They were composed long ago at school, but I would not dare show them to anyone but you. Here they are;—

THE SCHOOL GIRL'S SONG.

I do not love the teacher,
I do not like the school;
I cannot bear to talk and walk,
To look and smile by rule.

Oh! such a tedious lesson
As I have learned to-day,
About that tiresome prism,
And the sun's refracted ray!

I'd rather watch the rainbow,
In colored light arrayed,
Than study how it came there,
Or how its arch was made.

I'd rather play with flowers,
Beside the fountain bright,
Than search their sweet corollas,
To count the stamens right.

While they drink the golden sunshine,
And breathe the blessed air,
What for their Latin cognomens
Do glowing roses care?

My teacher tears their leaves apart,
Their order, class, to know;
I wonder she can have the heart
To treat a blossom so!

Once, if a flower were dying,
On a sultry summer's day,
I could hear its spirit sighing
Her balmy life away!

And now, alas! must Learning's lamp
The lovely dream consume,
And haughty, humdrum Reason
Must blight my bower's bloom!

I cannot love my teacher,
I hate to learn by rule;
I had a pleasanter governess
Before I went to school.

She taught me prettier lessons,
And easier too, by far;
She bade me think the silver moon
A warbling seraph's car.

And when I saw it gliding slow
The wreathed clouds amid,
And caught the gleam of spirit steeds,
That paced the heavens half-hid;

While round them softly glistened
The starry train of fire,
How earnestly I listened
To hear the heavenly choir.

She called the sunny rainbow
A band of brilliant flowers,
Linking heaven and earth together,
In the lovely, summer hours—

By cherub fingers braided,
In haunts of bliss above,
And flung, in angel play, to earth,
A token of their love.

But now—instead of looking
For the Violet divine,
For the golden Lily's glory,
And the Rose's blush benign,

For the tears and smiles of cherubs,
Shed o'er that garland gay—
I shall think of the rain-drop prism,
And the sun's refracted ray.

Oh! a thousand lovely lessons
My playmate taught of yore,
And a thousand thrilling sights I saw,
Which I shall see no more.

For Fancy was my teacher's name;
A sportive sprite was she!
She bore me on her wings to heaven,
She led me through the sea.

There marked I many a floating hall,
By coral columns graced;
And many a dim sea vision,
Through crystal walls I traced;

I traced them by the dazzling light
Of jewels rich and rare,
That hung in garlands round about,
And made a glory there.

The walls were all of crystal,
The sea-waves were the floor,
And Ocean's daughters floated
Its gleamy surface o'er.

Between the rosy pillars,
Some, gayly gliding by,
In curvéd shells of varied hue
Their shining oars did ply;

And some their tresses garlanded,
With strange and gleaming flowers,
Plucked by the goldfish's fitful light
In Ocean's darkling bowers.

Ah! many a scene beyond the stars.
Of rapture pure and free,
And many a dim sea vision,
Did I and Fancy see.

But we must part forever,
My playmate sweet and I;
She to some heart as wild as mine,
I—to Reality!

Oh, Kate! what an uncon*scio*nably long letter I have written to you; I won't bore you another minute. Good-by! May Heaven love you even more than I!

Your devoted
VIOLET.

KATE'S REPLY.

My dear cousin,—I have read your pleasant letter with much interest, and laughed heartily and sympathizingly over some parts of it; but as I am older than you by two whole months, I may be allowed, may I not? to give you a little sober advice.

It appears to me, from what you write, that you and Miss Primrose are each pursuing an *extreme*; and mamma says that all extremes are injudicious, if not dangerous. Miss Primrose is all for learning and decorum, and you are all for freedom and for play; is it not so? To be sure, it is vacation, and it is quite natural that play should seem to you the legitimate object of your emancipation from the restraints of school. But I think you would *enjoy* your play far more, if you would *sometimes* study and read. Your self-imposed tasks would give a zest to your after-recreations, I assure you.

Ah, dear Violet, make these, in truth, *holy*-days, by rational and elevating employments, out of doors or in; it matters little which.

I, who have never been to school—for you know mamma is my teacher—have never had a fit of ennui in my life, that I can remember.

Shall I give you the history of one of my days? Not in vacation; for I never need, or care to have one.

I rise at five now, (in summer,) and then follows a cold bath; a glass or two of cold water; a long walk; breakfast; a few, light household duties; two hours' study; an hour's play in the garden or gymnasium, with my brother; an hour's practice on the piano; two hours' study again; dinner; two hours' practice; and the rest of the day, from five o'clock, P. M., is quite at my own disposal—to read, to sew, to visit, to dance, to play, or to draw from nature, of which I am very fond.

Try this system, dear Violet, even in vacation, and I think your mother will see so much improvement in you at the end of six weeks, that she will take you from the boarding-school you so much dislike, and let you pursue, not only your butterfly fancies, but your studies at home.

Yours, most affectionately,
KATE ELTON.

Frances S. Osgood
Short Biography[1]

Frances Sargent Osgood was the daughter of Joseph Locke, a merchant of Boston, and was born in that city about the year 1812. Her early life was passed principally in Hingham, a beautiful village on the shores of Massachusetts Bay; and here she early displayed that poetical genius which has given her a place among our best poets for delicate fancy, and ease and naturalness of versification.

Her first printed productions appeared in Mrs. L. M. Child's *Juvenile Miscellany*, when she was about seventeen years of age. Soon after this, she wrote for the *Ladies' Magazine*, edited by Mrs. Sarah J. Hale, under the signature of "Florence." In 1835, she was married to Mr. Samuel S. Osgood, an artist of distinction and of cultivated literary taste, who fully appreciated the genius of his wife. Soon after their marriage, they went to London, where Mr. Osgood received great encouragement in the exercise of his art, while his wife published a small volume called *The Casket of Fate*, and also a collection of her poems, under the title of *A Wreath of Wild Flowers from New England*, both of which were much admired, and favorably noticed in some of the leading literary journals.

In 1840, Mr. and Mrs. Osgood returned to the United States, and, after being some time in Boston, took up their residence in New York. Here she wrote continually for the magazines, and edited "The Poetry of Flowers and the Flowers of Poetry," and "The Floral Offering," two richly-illustrated souvenirs. But her health began gradually to decline, and in the winter of 1847–48, she was so much of an invalid as to be confined to the house. Her husband's health, also, was feeble, and he was advised to seek a

---

[1] *A Compendium of American Literature, Chronologically Arranged*, Edited by Charles Cleveland, 1859, p. 657

change of climate. The next year, as his wife's health improved, Mr. Osgood sailed for California, with fine prospects there in the line of his profession. He returned early in 1850, with his fortunes as well as health improved, but just in time to be with his wife in the last few weeks of her life; for, five days after, she breathed her last, on the 12th of May. Her remains were removed to Boston, and laid beside those of her mother and daughter, at Mount Auburn, on Wednesday of the same week."[2]

---

[2] Of the character of her poetry Edgar A. Poe thus writes: —"Mrs. Osgood has a rich fancy,—even a rich imagination,—a scrupulous taste, a faultless style, and an ear finely attuned to the delicacies of melody. In that vague and anomalous something which we call *grace* for want of a more definite term, and which, perhaps, in its supreme development, may be found to comprehend nearly all that is genuine poetry.-in this magical quality—magical because at once so shadowy and so irresistible,—Mrs. Osgood has assuredly no superior in America, is indeed she has any equal under the sun."

Other Titles by Bottletree Books
BottletreeBooks.com

Leo Tolstoy's 20 Greatest Short Stories
Annotated

"Anna Karenina" and "War & Peace" branded Tolstoy one of the greatest writers in modern history. These novels have been enjoyed by millions. Few, however, have read his wonderful short stories. Now, in one collection, are the greatest short stories of Leo Tolstoy in an annotated edition. They give an important snapshot of Russia and its people in the late nineteenth century. The Tolstoy short stories book includes a fine introduction and annotations of difficult Russian terms. There is also a Tolstoy biography at the start of the book with photos of Tolstoy's relatives. The classic stories include:

A Candle, After the Dance, Albert, Alyosha the Pot, An Old Acquaintance, Does a Man Need Much Land?, Khodinka: An Incident of the Coronation of Nicholas II, Lucerne, Memoirs of a Lunatic, My Dream, Recollections of a Scorer, The Long Exile, The Posthumous Papers of the Hermit Fedor Kusmich, The Young Tsar, Three Deaths, and Two Old Men.

Leo Tolstoy's 5 Greatest Novellas

After reading War & Peace, Fyodor Dostoevsky put the book down and said, "The fool hath said in heart there is no God." Tolstoy's shorter novels (i.e., novellas) are also filled with war, adventure, comedy, religion, tragedy, and Russian tradition that inhabit the longer novels of the Russian bear of literature.

Now the editor of the bestselling anthology, "Leo Tolstoy's 20 Greatest Short Stories Annotated," has gathered the very best of Tolstoy's novellas into one remarkable collection that includes hundreds of annotations of difficult Russian terms and sheds light on historic figures mentioned in the stories. Yet there is much more to this anthology; included a short biography on Tolstoy and a chronology of his life and publications. Read these fascinating stories today:

1) **The Invaders** - A Russian team moves against Shamyl and his Islamic army in the Caucasus, which is based on Tolstoy's military experiences in the 1850s.
2) **The Death of Ivan Ilyich** - When a man who has done good his entire life is stricken with an illness, it makes him question everything.
3) **Two Hussars** - When a hell-raiser takes lodging in a small Russian city, debauchery is inevitable but will it be matched years later by his son?
4) **Father Sergius** - The taboo subject of a priest being subjected to physical temptation is explored in one of Tolstoy's most scandalous stories.
5) **Master & Man** - By the end of this snowstorm adventure, you will be asking yourself, Who is the master and who is the servant?

Edgar Allan Poe
Annotated and Illustrated Entire Stories and Poems

For the first time in one compilation are background information for Poe's stories and poems, annotations, foreign translations, photographs of individuals Poe wrote about, and poetry to Poe from his romantic interests.

"Annabel Lee," "The Bells," "The Black Cat," "[The Bloodhounds]," "The Cask of Amontillado," "The Conqueror Worm," "A Descent into the Maelstrom," "The Fall of the House of Usher," "The Gold-Bug," "The Haunted Palace," "Lenore," "The Masque of the Red Death," "MS. Found in a Bottle," "Murders in the Rue Morgue," "The Oblong Box," "The Pit and the Pendulum," "The Premature Burial," "The Purloined Letter," "The Raven," "Some Words with a Mummy," "The System of Doctor Tarr and Professor Fether," and "The Tell-Tale Heart." The classic illustrations are by Gustave Dore and Harry Clarke.